Book One: Prophecy

The Callembria Chronicles

Book One: Prophecy

By Heather Ann Hall

The Callembria Chronicles

Book One: Prophecy

Copyright © 2024 Heather Ann Hall

All rights reserved.

No part of this book may be reproduced, stored in a retrieval system, or transmitted in any form or by any means—electronic, mechanical, photocopying, recording, or otherwise—without prior written permission from the author.

This is a work of fiction. Names, characters, places, and events are products of the author's imagination or are used fictitiously. Any resemblance to actual persons, living or dead, events, or locales is entirely coincidental.

ISBN: 979-8-9922498-8-0

Cover art by AmbientPixel Designs

Independently Published

Printed in the United States of America

First Edition: December 2024

DEDICATION:

For Mom and Cyndol

ACKNOWLEDGMENTS:

I would like to dedicate this book to my mother, Kathy Cadoux. She has been there since the very start and was always ready and willing to read whatever chapter I came up with next, offering ideas, asking the right questions, and generally just falling into this story with me. Thank you, Mom, from the bottom of my heart. I could not have done this without you!

I also need to dedicate this to my incredible niece, Cyndol Hall, whom I have missed over the years living so far apart. Thank you for letting me use your name in my book. It made me feel closer to you when I couldn't be in real life. And thank you to your brother, Ethan Brendmoen, as well. I hope you both like it!

I would like to thank my husband, Devin Dupuis, who sat patiently by me as I vividly hallucinated on the page while he sat next to me, playing video games or listening to me read aloud to make sure something sounded right. He was never too busy to help me, and that was the very best gift I could ask for! I love you, Favorite!

Thank you to my brother, Brandon Hall, his wife, Gilly, and their son, Cutter. Having you read my book and enjoy it like you did is the coolest possible thing that has come from writing this! I absolutely pictured you reading this to your son like they did in *The Princess Bride*. What an honor.

To my dad, Steve Hall, I love and miss you every day. I wish you could've read this. You would've really loved it. Thank you for always being so supportive of me. Until we meet again.

I would not have the best version of this book if not for the help of my exceptionally talented and amazing friend, Michelle Craddock. Thank you for catching my mistakes and teaching me how to improve. I can never thank you enough. (You should go check out her books! They are wonderful!)

To my best friend, Edna Vicente, thank you for sticking with me all these years, and for not teasing me to my face about all the things I would say about my book that made zero sense, as at the time, they were all still living in obscure connectivity in my head. Also, thank you for reading this!

A huge and heartfelt THANK YOU to all of my beta readers. Thank you for taking the time to immerse yourselves in this book and help me bring this story to life! Your feedback was very appreciated! Athena Dupen, Phil Pinheiro, Adrien Cadoux, and Dustin Hendricks.

And finally, thank you to Matt Derby for getting me a computer when mine died and I didn't have a way to keep writing. Thanks to you, I was able to finish this book!

I love you all! Thank you forever!

Dear Reader,

For almost a decade, I have lived with a magical world inside of my head that no one else could see, hear, feel, or access. On one hand, it was wonderful, having my own world to escape to, where I could take a backseat to my own life and focus on the lives of others. So what if they weren't all human and had no idea that I existed? I knew that *they* existed, and that's all that mattered to me. I spent many years taking notes on these people, places, creatures, and things, and the crazier I felt, the more I knew I had to write this all down to share with you.

So, here it is. My own little world, far, far from home, full of mystery, life, and adventure. I hope you enjoy the ride!

With Love,

Heather

Contents

PROLOGUE: ETHAN'S DISCOVERY 1
CHAPTER ONE: AMY'S JOURNEY 4
CHAPTER TWO: CYNDOL'S PATH 8
CHAPTER THREE: AMY'S ISLAND 16
CHAPTER FOUR: COLT'S FIND 21
CHAPTER FIVE: CYNDOL'S NEW FRIEND 22
CHAPTER SIX: ETHAN'S CAPTIVITY 28
CHAPTER SEVEN: RUSKIN RECEIVES NEWS 31
CHAPTER EIGHT: AMY FINDS A TUB 33
CHAPTER NINE: IBRAXUS AWAKENS 47
CHAPTER TEN: CYNDOL'S CAPTURE 51
CHAPTER ELEVEN: ETHAN'S NIGHTMARE 67
CHAPTER TWELVE: AMY'S QUEST 71
CHAPTER THIRTEEN: MIAWAE'S SURPRISE 84
CHAPTER FOURTEEN: KAVEA'S DISAPPOINTMENT 89
CHAPTER FIFTEEN: CYNDOL'S TOUR OF GALLANOR 92
CHAPTER SIXTEEN: IBRAXUS RETURNS HOME ... 107
CHAPTER SEVENTEEN: RUSKIN REQUIRES DAVINA 115
CHAPTER EIGHTEEN: AMY VENTURES TO THE OUTPOST 120
CHAPTER NINETEEN: CYNDOL HEARS A PROPHECY 143
CHAPTER TWENTY: KAVEA SETS OUT 148

CHAPTER TWENTY-ONE: AMY GETS INFORMATION 153

CHAPTER TWENTY-TWO: COLT'S MISSION......... 163

CHAPTER TWENTY-THREE: IBRAXUS TAKES A DIVE... 167

CHAPTER TWENTY-FOUR: AMY MEETS COLT 171

CHAPTER TWENTY-FIVE: ETHAN'S FINAL SESSION 192

CHAPTER TWENTY-SIX: CYNDOL SETS OFF TO SAVE HER BROTHER... 196

CHAPTER TWENTY-SEVEN: RUSKIN'S REQUIREMENT 209

CHAPTER TWENTY-EIGHT: CYNDOL ENTERS THE SKY PRISON.. 212

CHAPTER TWENTY-NINE: DAVINA'S IDEA.......... 236

CHAPTER THIRTY: AMY'S IMAGINATION 240

CHAPTER THIRTY-ONE: CYNDOL'S DASH TO THE FAE.. 279

CHAPTER THIRTY-TWO: RUSKIN'S ROOM........... 286

CHAPTER THIRTY-THREE: AMY'S HEADACHE ... 290

CHAPTER THIRTY-FOUR: MIAWAE SPEAKS WITH A FRIEND 294

CHAPTER THIRTY-FIVE: ETHAN PROVES TO BE A PROBLEM... 297

CHAPTER THIRTY-SIX: CYNDOL MAKES A FRIEND 300

CHAPTER THIRTY-SEVEN: COLT'S BREAKFAST . 312

CHAPTER THIRTY-EIGHT: MIAWAE'S WARNING 318

CHAPTER THIRTY-NINE: AMY ATTENDS A MEETING 321

CHAPTER FORTY: KIARA'S REQUEST 335

CHAPTER FORTY-ONE: CYNDOL'S TRAINING 343

CHAPTER FORTY-TWO: AMY'S ONSLAUGHT 348

CHAPTER FORTY-THREE: COLT'S MERRY CHASE 352

CHAPTER FORTY-FOUR: CYNDOL'S MESSAGE 361

CHAPTER FORTY-FIVE: RUSKIN RECEIVES AN UPDATE 368

CHAPTER FORTY-SIX: TRIPP'S UNINVITED GUESTS 370

CHAPTER FORTY-SEVEN: DARRIAN'S DISGUISE . 379

CHAPTER FORTY-EIGHT: KIARA'S CONFRONTATION 384

CHAPTER FORTY-NINE: IBRAXUS FINDS A CRY FOR HELP 391

CHAPTER FIFTY: AMY GAINS A NIECE 405

PROLOGUE: ETHAN'S DISCOVERY

One glint.

One single glint from the midday suns would change his life forever, would change everyone's lives forever.

Ethan reached down slowly, heart drumming in his ears. He dug with his fingers in the warm dirt until he was able to free what had caught his eye.

It was beautiful. He had never seen anything like it in all his seventeen years. It was a single golden sun, just a tad smaller than the palm of his hand, with fine blazing yellow spires protruding from its circumference. A hook at the top suggested it belonged on a chain. He was transfixed, unable to breathe. *Why was there only one sun, though?*

Voices off in the woods to his right shook him from his stupor. Ethan jammed the prize into his pocket and dove behind a nearby tree.

"I saw him over there, sir. Right where she said he found it."

A sudden bolt of fear caused Ethan's heart to slam into his ribcage. Were these men looking for his new treasure? Would they take it from him? His breath came in painful gasps, so he covered his mouth with his dirty hands in an attempt to muffle the noise. When several minutes went by without another sound, he crept quietly out of his hiding place to look around. With no sign of movement, he quickly made his way back along the dirt road that brought him here.

Not ten steps in and he was turned roughly around by his shoulder, bringing him face to face with the biggest man he'd ever seen.

"Where is it? She saw you find it! Where is it?" The man gave Ethan a shake and lifted him off the ground by the front of his once-white linen shirt.

Terrified that this behemoth would try to take it from him, Ethan slipped his hand into his deerskin pants pocket to locate the sun while the man continued to shake him. The motion thankfully went unnoticed in the abuse. The guard was either too dumb or too distracted to notice. Either way, surely a win for Ethan. He located his target with sweaty fingers and in one smooth motion flung it swiftly into the nearby ferns, out of sight of King Ruskin's men.

"I— I— I don't know what you're talking about," Ethan said. "Find what?"

"Don't play dumb with me, kid! Empty those pockets before I turn you upside down and shake them out myself!" The massive guardsman hurled him to the ground, locking his meaty hands around Ethan's ankles to prevent him from escaping.

Without thinking, Ethan whipped his fist around and connected with the big man's face, almost shattering his hand. The man stopped, blinked, laughed vigorously, and hoisted Ethan above his head.

"You're welcome to try that again, little boy, but I don't think you'll like the consequences. Now, where is it?"

Ethan said nothing.

"Have it your way, boy."

With one mighty wallop, he knocked Ethan into oblivion.

Book One: Prophecy

CHAPTER ONE: AMY'S JOURNEY

It was a misty October morning in Sebastopol, California. I walked from my apartment to my favorite coffee place earlier than normal. I wanted to get to my crystal shop on Main Street well before my 8:00 a.m. opening to put the final touches on the display window for my latest arrival: A five-foot tall amethyst geode. It was glorious! I'd had other geodes before, but there was something different and exciting about this one. Something about it sang to me, felt familiar in a way that nothing ever had. I had to have it.

Stoked as I was to start the day, I was already exhausted. Not a whole lot of sleep, thanks to that "Kid at Christmas" feeling. That's great when you're young, but the older you get, the more draining it can be. When I finally did get to sleep, I'd been plagued with intense dreams about a place I didn't recognize. It had two suns, tons of forests, waterfalls galore, and even a dragon or two, if memory served correct. I chalked it up to too much TV over the weekend and tried to shrug off the ass-draggery as I approached the door to my shop. I hoped the large vanilla latte I'd just purchased would give me the jump-start I needed to kick the day off with a bang.

I fit the key into the lock and the glimmer from the amethyst in the window caught my eye. I stopped to admire its ethereal lavender facets.

The sudden blaring alarm from the bank across the street startled me so badly that I flattened myself against the window and searched for immediate danger. My latte sloshed over my pristine white blouse before crashing onto the sidewalk below. What I saw next was the scrambling figures of two burly men running with duffel bags from the bank right toward me.

Fear slammed through me with the force of a freight train.

"You said no one would be out here at this hour!" The first man said. "What do we do?"

I watched in horror as the second man thrust his hand inside his bomber jacket, pulled out a gun, and aimed it directly at my chest! He pulled the trigger without a moment's hesitation.

BANG!

I heard the glass behind me shatter as I flew backwards into the amethyst geode, knocking the entire display over and landing with my back in the purple spikes. The bullet firmly lodged in my breast stole the air from my lungs with no remorse. The glass shards sliced at every available inch of skin, the multiple lacerations feeling as though I was being flayed from head to toe— like ripping a hangnail to the quick, but everywhere. My adrenaline spiked so hard that I didn't even register the amethyst as anything more than a landing zone. Hot blood trailed all over me, coating the cuts and sealing in the shards.

In that moment, I felt my life slip away. A soft lavender light emanated from the gemstone and pooled around my body to cocoon me. It was calming amidst the chaos, and I was drawn into this heady mixture of coziness and serenity.

The men's footsteps quickly faded into the distance. I thought I should have heard sirens by now, the sweet sound that confirmed that help was on the way, but I couldn't hear much of anything except a bird chirping in the distance. Or was that my heart, gasping for life? I knew I should be more concerned, but I was forgetting something important. Move? Breathe? I couldn't do either of those things. All I could do was fade...

The light in my eyes dimmed and went out. I felt myself detach from my body, from pain, from fear, from care. Where was I going, Heaven? Perhaps. My spirit rose out of me, steadily rising to the sky until it fused with other lights that were making their way along this same path through the atmosphere. I wasn't scared, just mildly curious. I was vaguely aware of conscious thought as I drifted amongst the stars. I felt as if I was moving with some kind of purpose, so I gave in and surrendered to the journey, wherever it was taking me.

Time ceased to have meaning. I was floating past things I'd only ever seen on screen: Baubles of reds, blues, and oranges appearing like titans in the darkness. Gas clouds with shades so bright they made rainbows seem dim. It shrunk my existence to obscurity, and I was in awe of it all. I was one with the universe. I had joined the stars.

After what seemed like an eternity, I saw a pinprick of light growing larger before me. I had enough time to register that I was seeing a planet, one with two suns and a small moon. And... were those *rings*? It looked similar to Saturn, but with another set going the opposite direction, forming an intersection. The rings were made up of glowing geodes and loose crystals, sporting every color I could think of, and some that I had never seen. Their sizes and shapes varied, like a jar full of sand and pebbles on a much larger scale.

Curious, indeed.

Then my cluster hit a patch of glowing amethyst gemstones and dispersed. I felt my spirit detach from the bunch and descend toward the planet below.

Blurs of color were becoming distinguishable now: A vast, glimmering cerulean ocean, stretches of lush forest covering rugged terrain and, right as I was about to collide with this unknown earth, a small turquoise pool under a waterfall.

With no way to steer myself, my essence plummeted deep below the surface of the pool, and everything went dark.

CHAPTER TWO: CYNDOL'S PATH

Dusk. Cyndol's favorite time of day. That stunning moment in the evening when the double suns set beyond the horizon, casting a dusty mauve glow across the shore of her seaside village. Today, like every day, Cyndol sat along the beach, knees pulled up to her chest, toes tucked into the wet sand as she let the last rays from above exhale around her. She smiled as she felt a light breeze tickle across her face, while seabirds called lazily to each other overhead. Soaking in the last beams of the second sun, Cyndol breathed in deeply, taking in the spicy pineapple scent of the nearby amber and cream colored Callamay flowers, her very favorite. The smell reminded her of her mother's sugary summer cakes and how they would melt in your mouth but stick to your fingers. She listened to the sounds of the day winding down around her as salt water licked at her toes.

"Cyndol!" Her mother's voice broke her out of her reverie. "I've been calling you. It's time for dinner."

"Coming mother." Reluctantly, she dried off her feet with the hem of her long shirt, slipped them into her well-worn leather boots, and started toward her back door, not far from where she'd been sitting. Her stomach may have been rumbling, but her heart was out over the water. She paused in the doorway to take one last longing look at the waves before entering the dining room to join her family.

"Did you finish your chores?" Darrian asked as he loaded up his plate with potato mash.

"Yes, Father," Cyndol replied. She plopped down on a wooden chair and filled a plate of her own. Her mother, Enid, wiped floured hands on her homespun apron and came around to scoop a generous spoonful of brown beans onto Cyndol's plate. Cyndol made a face of disgust but knew better than to argue.

"Have you seen your brother today?" Darrian asked, furrowing his bushy eyebrows. "It seems he skipped out on helping muck out Zachariah's stables."

Enid slopped an oozing pile of beans on Darrian's plate as well. His mouth twisted downward, but he did not object.

Cyndol kept her smirk hidden. "I can't really blame Ethan for not wanting to spend his day shoveling horse manure."

Darrian stopped mid-bite and looked her square in the eye. "There's nothing wrong with hard work." He slammed his elbow down, gesturing at her with his fork, subsequently flinging potato mash across the circular tree-stump table. "When your brother gets home, he's going to have a lot to answer for, mark my words."

A gentle knock at the door saved Cyndol from having to respond. Darrian wiped his mouth with his napkin and got up to see who was calling at this hour. "And clean that up!" he said over his shoulder.

When her father didn't return after a minute, and the quiet stretched on for eternity, Cyndol's unease began to grow. Enid left the table to see what was taking so long. When she didn't come back either, Cyndol felt her tension mounting.

A crash from the front room frightened Cyndol so badly that she bolted toward the sound before she realized she was on her feet. Her mother was now sobbing in a heap on the floor; her father's short but imposing frame was shaking, clutching her older brother's favorite green coat in his fist. The king's emissary, Malcolm, held an official missive in his wizened hands.

Cyndol felt her heart plummet. She wanted to run, to fight, to hide— to something! Anything but just stand there and wait to hear that Ethan would not be coming home again. But she was frozen in place, neither fight nor flight mode responding.

Darrian cleared his throat. "Your brother has been taken. He is being held at the Sky Prison in Padagonya."

Trying to process what her father just said was nearly impossible.

"But… but why? What happened? What did he do? You can't be arrested for skipping a day of work, can you?"

Malcolm shifted his gaunt face from Darrian to Cyndol. "It, ah, it appears he has stolen a precious artifact and refuses to return it or reveal where he is keeping it. The king considers it a serious offense."

When neither of her parents leapt to Ethan's defense, Cyndol felt her temper rise.

"Why would Ethan do something like that? He's never stolen a thing in his life! And how would he have gotten his hands on something that would matter to the king?" Almost as an afterthought, she asked, "What did he supposedly steal, anyway?"

"I am not at liberty to give that information," Malcolm said. "But now King Ruskin is involved, and the artifact is considered something of great importance."

"So, what can we do?" Darrian asked.

"I've been ordered to search the premises. I'm sorry to have to do this to you. You understand."

"Of course. Take all the time you need," Darrian said.

Cyndol couldn't believe her ears! Why weren't they shouting at him? Why weren't they throwing Malcolm and his missive out the front door? Why were they just accepting this accusation against their son? She'd had enough! She swiped her pouch from the hook in the entryway and burst out the door, speeding down the path as fast as her legs would carry her. Her parents' astonished voices faded the farther she got from home.

Faster and faster, she ran, through the trees and up the hill, no clear destination in mind, just anywhere but here. Anywhere that she could sit and think about how to help her brother. *There was no way that he was guilty of this. No way! He doesn't even cheat at cards! Why would he start stealing stuff?*

She rounded up the cliff that hung over her family's bottom-dwelling tree house and stopped right at the edge. She rarely found herself up this way, as she was not exactly thrilled with heights, but, tonight, it seemed more welcoming than her own home did. The village hosted a smattering of both tree dwellings and glass houses that were made from the very sand they occupied. It was a gorgeous place, and this viewpoint was one that usually brought her comfort, when she could get past the idea of being up so high.

She sat on a large boulder and tried to catch her breath. So many thoughts were swirling around in her head, if only she could catch one! She needed to focus, to give herself some direction on what to do next. Out of habit, she pulled a small pocketknife that her father had given her from her side pouch and began whittling a stick she'd picked up, just for something to do with her hands.

After about an hour, she had a pile of sharpened arrows, and she was starting to get cold. Not quite ready to go back home yet, she pulled her fur lined coat tighter against her body and settled into the bottom of the boulder, laying her head against its solid base.

She must have fallen asleep because, when she woke, it was nearing dawn. She wasn't sure what woke her, but a strange chill came over her body that had nothing to do with the early morning temperature.

Cyndol looked at her village from her vantage point on the cliff and saw a small fire spark up in the middle of town. A shrill scream pierced the air and every hair on Cyndol's head stood on end. One by one, she saw rooftop after rooftop start to burn, alighting homes and trees alike, until everyone in the village was outside, screaming, crying, trying to hide. But along with the fires came something much worse: Men.

Men with weapons and authority. Some were on foot, others on horseback, but they all seemed to be searching for something. They were brutal and violent in the process, and Cyndol saw villagers get cut down in the streets. She couldn't make out faces from where she stood, but she knew these were people she had known for her entire life— twelve years' worth of friends and neighbors, possibly even her family— chopped down like vermin, and for what? What was going on?

Her hammering heart skipped a beat as she realized what they were looking for: The missing artifact. It had to be! But why send in these men? Malcolm was already looking for it on behalf of the king.

"Ethan," she whispered, "what have you done?"

Movement to her left caught her attention.

"Well, well, well. What do we have here?" asked a figure dressed in black.

Cyndol tried to bolt back down the pathway, but the stranger caught her by the upper arm and held on tight.

"Ah, ah, ah, not so fast!" he said. Cyndol made a mental note to call him The Repeater and attempted to kick him in the shin. "You're not going anywhere, child. Not until we get some answers."

"We?" she asked.

In answer to her question, two more armed men dressed in black appeared from the tree line to join them. Cyndol bucked and swung every limb that could move until she wrestled free of his grasp.

"What are you doing? Grab her!" The Repeater said to the approaching men.

The way back down the path was blocked, and the only other way was straight off the cliffside into the water. There was no choice. Cyndol knew if these men got a hold of her a second time, she wouldn't stand a chance. She sucked in a deep breath, swallowed her fear, ran toward the edge, and pushed off with her feet, diving headfirst into the ocean.

Time seemed to stand still. Cyndol expected to feel the harsh sting of freezing water, or at least get the wind knocked out of her but, instead, what she felt was... nothing. It was a total lack of temperature and sensation.

She opened her eyes and saw the sparkling waves dancing above her head, the early morning sunlight glittering across the blues and greens around her. It occurred to her that she was in some sort of bubble. *How did that happen? What sort of magick was this?* She had never seen anything like this! She moved her arms as if to swim, but nothing happened. Kicking her legs proved to do nothing either. And though she felt silly even trying it, she blew her breath as if blowing out a candle but, again, nothing. Her bubble was bobbing farther and farther away from the burning village, and she couldn't do a thing to stop it. She just continued to drift out to sea.

It felt like hours had gone by before she began to see anything besides the two suns and water. Her bubble bumped up against this new shoreline and popped, depositing her onto the rocky bank. Cyndol was able to take her first gasp of clean air in who knew how long?

She crawled onto the bank and looked at her surroundings. Nothing looked familiar. It was just a bit of rock and dirt and then trees as far as the eye could see. How far was she from home? Was there even anything left? Though she had been crying a lot of the way here (where was she, exactly?), she began crying anew, thinking again of her parents, her friends. Was she the only one left?

Not knowing what else to do, she locked onto the only idea that made any sense now— Find Ethan.

So, squaring her shoulders and swiping her sleeve across her tear-stained cheeks, that's what she set out to do.

"Hold on, Ethan," she said, "I'm headed your way."

And with that, Cyndol took her first uncertain steps into unknown terrain to rescue her brother from the Sky Prison.

CHAPTER THREE: AMY'S ISLAND

I'm floating.

That was my first conscious thought as I found myself floating along the warmth of swirling wet ripples that caressed my entire body. I felt everything in me stretch to its fullest extent and then some. A tickle of electricity began in the tips of my toes, up my legs and enveloped my lower regions. It continued into my torso, arms, and fingers, all the way up to the top of my head, elongating me as it went. And just when I felt that I was going to explode if I didn't take a breath, I crashed through the surface of the bluest pool I had ever seen.

My soul flared to life as I pulled myself out of the nothingness. My eyes scanned frantically across the top of an aquamarine lagoon, surrounded by bright emerald-green trees. I could feel the gasping of air and the beat of my heart as they both came back to me at the same time.

After a moment of bobbing against the ripples I'd created in the water, I managed to catch my breath. Once that was accomplished, I stopped to listen to my surroundings and get my bearings.

I was able to hear a soft wind, the confident chirping of something off to my right, and the echoing cry of an animal nearby. I tilted my head to see if I could spot it, but saw only a small white tail, like that of a rabbit, dart behind the trunk of a palm tree and disappear. Redwood trees towered above intermittent palms as if to protect them, and spiraling ferns and morning glories carpeted any empty space between them.

This place was beautiful. It was as if I'd fallen into one of the fantasy movies or TV shows I was obsessed with. Everything was just so *vibrant*, as if I'd lived the whole of my life in black and white and was only now seeing color for the first time. The air was crisper, the water more refreshing, even nature itself seemed louder, as if it was breathing.

Swimming to the edge of the pool, I clutched a patch of grass to pull myself out. Something wet and cold slapped against my arm and I flew backward with a scream. It took me a few seconds to realize it was my own hair. My normally shoulder-length brown hair was now jet black and reached down past my navel.

"What the hell…?"

I lifted my arm up to get a look at my hair in better lighting only to realize my arm didn't look the same either. It was tanner, more muscular, with thin wrists and hands that boasted elegance and grace. My normal, stubby, child-like hands were no longer there. I turned around as fast as I could to look at my reflection in the water and saw—

That… wasn't my face.

At least, not the face *I* knew. My green eyes weren't the lavender shown in this reflection, my lashes had never been this thick and long. My frame wasn't nearly this lean and yet, with all these changes, I strangely felt more myself than I had ever been.

A slow smile crept across my face, and I sucked in the first deep breath I'd had since popping up here (wherever *here* was). I felt amazing! Doing an internal self-check I noticed my usual chronic pain was nowhere to be found, and I had more energy than I could ever remember experiencing. There was a tiny tingling sensation that buzzed along my body, waiting for direction.

I had the distinct urge to test out this new me on land, but when I climbed out of the pool and tried to put weight on my feet, I slipped and fell onto the sandy bank.

"What the hell!" I cursed again, spitting sand from my teeth.

I flipped over to assess the damage done to my feet when I noticed that I didn't have any.

Wait—what? *Where are my feet? And are those... fins? Did I die and come back a flipping mermaid?! I can't feel my heart. Am I breathing? Okay... I'm breathing... My heart is pounding, so I know it's still there.*

I gave the... *fins...* a test kick, then another one, just to make sure they were there, and I didn't hallucinate them. My tail (*I have a tail, what the hell is going on?*) was a mix of iridescent greens and teals, not unlike something you'd see on a peacock. Great. So now, not only am I somehow a mermaid, but someone in my past may have loved a zoo animal a bit too much.

I hesitantly inched my way back to the water and stuck my fins in to test-splash-kick and see how that went.

SPLASH!

SPLASH!

KICK!

Hmm... not bad.

SPLASH!

SPLASH!

KICK!

I lowered the rest of my body into the pool and tried to remember the swimming lessons from when I was a kid. It had been a long time since I'd been in any water other than a shower, but I vaguely remembered how to doggie paddle. Thinking I must have well and truly lost my mind, I glided my hands through the surface of the water, allowing myself to float on my stomach. I was all set to start paddling, but my tail decided it had a mind of its own and took off. Without my consent, tail and fins twirled me about the pool as if I were caught in something's clutches which, I suppose, I currently was.

"Help!"

I don't know who I was yelling for or if anyone would know what to do when they found me. *Shut up, Stupid! You are a mermaid! What do you think they'll do to you if anyone finds you like this?* I forced my body to stop thrashing about and calm down.

Finally, I slowed into a more manageable pace so I could stay afloat without fear of drowning. Wait a minute... Could I breathe underwater? I thrust my head under the surface and waited a few seconds before taking that first cautious breath.

I *could* breathe underwater! … for about 4.5 seconds, until my lungs seized up and I choked, coughing so hard that it forced the water back up my throat and ungracefully out my mouth and nose. Very ladylike.

Once again, I pulled myself to shore, gasping for air and struggling to function.

Balls. Now what?

I let out an exasperated sigh and noticed my stomach beginning to rumble. Great. That's just what I needed. Another problem to tackle.

A patch of opalescent mint-green algae clinging to a nearby rock tickled my fins and I jerked my head down, really seeing it for the first time. It was beautiful! And it… it smelled like… cheeseburgers? I stared at that thing for twenty minutes trying to figure out what the hell was going on, how bad could it hurt if I ate that algae, and how bad could it *really* hurt… if I ate that algae?

CHAPTER FOUR: COLT'S FIND

A beautiful young colt was meandering through the woods one sunny afternoon. It was quiet. You could hear the soft sounds of the wind humming through the branches and birds calling from the treetops, his horse hooves stamping the ground. Of course, there were also the buzzing sounds of the flies around his pretty chestnut flank. He was able to whip them away with ease, courtesy of his pitch-black tail.

A flicker of light poked through the patch of ferns he was merrily munching on, and he pondered as he chewed. *What could that be?* he thought. *Ferns aren't in the habit of shining on their own.*

Colt approached the curious fern and, as he got closer, he resumed his rightful shape as a young boy with shaggy black hair and deep brown eyes.

He grasped the golden necklace piece in his hand and peered at it curiously. It looked like one of Callembria's two suns, but he noticed it looked slightly... off... like pieces were missing. Deciding to look into it more later, he haphazardly put it into his worn pocket and returned to colt form, galloping off toward home with his new treasure.

CHAPTER FIVE: CYNDOL'S NEW FRIEND

The suns were waning in the sky and Cyndol knew she only had about an hour or two left before it would be too dark to go on, so she stopped walking to take a look at her surroundings. Nothing but trees, rocks, and more trees. She could see some mountains in the distance, but there was no way she would make it there before dark. With a sinking heart, she knew she would have to build a shelter for the night or risk being exposed to danger. Huffing, she yanked open her hip pouch and pulled out her small knife in case she happened upon any predators. And who knew? If she won the fight, she might even be lucky enough to get dinner out of it.

With a deep sigh and a rumbly tummy, she set off toward the group of trees to her right, nestled close enough together that she could make a functioning shelter.

"What was it Father said to do first?" Cyndol asked herself. She examined the copse of trees closely to make sure she wasn't disturbing any creatures seeking cover. When she found no traces of life (other than a few bugs she never cared to see again), she went about clearing out sticks from her new bedroom area and piled them neatly next to the trees to use for kindling later.

"Big branches, big branches, where are some really big branches?" Cyndol scanned the ground around her. Spotting what looked like an old den of a rather large animal (she hoped it was old, there were no fresh tracks around it, nor any creatures in the flattened area, just stray leaves and duff), she scavenged what was left and made a mental note to keep an eye out for predators.

Pleased with how her structure was coming along, she took a spool of thin rope from her hip pouch and made little ties to connect the branches that weren't lucky enough to fit together when placed along the standing trees.

Wiping the perspiration from her brow, Cyndol stood back to admire her handiwork and assess what still needed to be done. It struck her that, even though she was sweating, she could already feel the goosebumps form along her arms as the suns swiftly made their way across the sky. She wasn't sure her single coat would be enough to keep her warm in this foreign place, but she remembered her father telling her about using leaves and dried grass as insulation. So, she scavenged along the forest floor, collecting as much as she could stuff in her coat or carry in her arms until she was satisfied she'd stand a fighting chance. *Whew! All this work for one night in the woods!*

On her last trip back to her shelter, she spotted a fluffy-looking tree branch, beautiful green needles still springing from its tips, and she decided that it was exactly the finishing touch she needed. Upon lifting it up to take it back though, she saw something small dart out from underneath it and dive directly into her new home!

"Oh!" she shouted. "No! No, no, no, no, no! You can't go in there! That's mine! Shoo!" Without thinking, she bolted in after it, trying to scare it off. Its growl made her hesitate and, in that moment, it occurred to her that small animals bite, too.

Using the fluffy branch as a poking tool, she slowly started to prod the orange ball of fur that had taken up residence in the shallowest corner of her fort. It perked up as if it had been struck by lightning and hissed at her, baring its tiny fangs and back-turned ears.

Cyndol was so surprised to see the tiny fox glaring back at her that she pulled back her branch and laughed.

"Oh! You're just a cute little kit, aren't you? Where's your family, little kit?"

The fox continued to snarl at Cyndol, but it was about as effective as being clawed at by a kitten. Cyndol dropped the branch and gleefully leapt at the little one, grabbing it by the scruff of the neck and pulling it into her arms for a snuggle. Well, the fox was so surprised that it let her.

"Poor little thing, out here all alone. I guess I'm one to talk, being out here all alone myself. I'm Cyndol. Do you have a name? Probably not. I think I'll call you Kit. Do you like that? Kit? A little on the nose, but I think it suits you anyway." Realizing she was rambling on, she stopped and looked the fox square in its eyes. "I might need protection out here, Kit. Think you can help me?"

Cyndol was only half-serious, but she could've sworn she heard soft words in reply. Must have been the wind, because there wasn't anyone else around as far as she could see.

"Because you don't talk, right, Kit?" She giggled at her own foolishness and continued to stroke the fox like they'd been friends forever.

"Well," said Kit softly, "not usually, no."

Cyndol shrieked and dropped him, then flattened herself against the farthest tree in her fort.

Kit landed gracefully on all fours and shot her an irritated look. "That wasn't very nice," he said.

Cyndol could only gape at him. She moved her mouth to speak, but no words came out.

"Now who's the one who can't talk?" Kit said.

Cyndol finally found her voice and took a hesitant step forward. "So... you can talk. *How* can you talk?"

"Because of you, I imagine. I don't just go around conversing with humans, you know."

"But— but— that doesn't make any sense. Why me? Is this all in my head? Am I going crazy?"

"You tell me," Kit said. "I doubt you are crazy, but you could be magick."

She thought about that for a second. Magick? No. She couldn't be. Right? She was 12, she would've known by now if she had any powers, wouldn't she? Though that would explain the bubble she came here in... But only special people got powers, the kind that lived under the Gem Belts or were born into families who had been there for generations, long enough to soak up the magickal energy that fell from the sky. The wealthy and the powerful, not the nobodies who lived on beaches like she and her family do— did.

A sudden pang of grief punched her in the gut, and she crumpled to the ground.

Kit, surprised and unaware of the inner turmoil going on inside of Cyndol, rushed to her side and licked her face. That startled her enough to snap her back to the present, and she pulled him into her chest for a cuddle. It was a bit too hard, though, so he wriggled around until they found a grip that pleased them both.

They sat in silence for a few minutes until Kit ventured a question. "So, what happened that made you so sad?"

Cyndol sniffled back a tear.

"Men. Men happened. They came into my village and burned—" She choked and swallowed. "It's gone. It's all gone. My family... I think they're gone, too."

Kit put a comforting paw on her arm and nuzzled her cheek with his wet nose. She absently scratched him behind the ears as they fell back into silence.

"My family was taken from me, too. I had three brothers and a sister, along with my mother. Some humans came through with packs of dogs and horses and chased us all down. My mother knocked me down a short cliff and saved me from the jaws of a dog just in time. She— wasn't so lucky. Now it's just me."

Cyndol hugged him tighter. "What about your father?"

Kit gave the equivalent of a shrug and said, "I have no idea. Never met him."

"And your siblings?"

"I don't know if they made it, either."

"I'm sorry, Kit."

"I'm sorry, Cyndol."

Just then, Cyndol's stomach gave a churning growl that broke them from their reverie. Kit laughed and leapt back to the ground.

"Come on." He moved to the entryway. "Let's get you something to eat."

Cyndol wiped her face and said, "You know where there's food?"

Kit rolled his eyes in a very human-like gesture. "Well, yes. I do live here, you know. Or at least I did, until you moved my house." He nodded his head toward the large branch.

Cyndol jumped up and immediately tried to give it back. "Here! I don't need it! Really! I'm so sorry!"

Kit rubbed his face on her leg and said, "It's okay. It looks nice in here. Besides, it looks like you've got room for a guest."

"Of course! Please! I could use a friend right now. That is, if you don't mind?"

He nodded again and said, "I suppose that could work. But not until we find you some food. Let's go."

So off they went in search of dinner before it got too dark to see.

CHAPTER SIX: ETHAN'S CAPTIVITY

DRIP.

DRIP.

DRIP.

Ethan awoke to water droplets hitting his forehead. He flinched and tried to brush them off his face, but found his hands and feet were bound to a tabletop.

DRIP.

DRIP.

DRIP.

Ethan struggled against his restraints. No luck.

DRIP.

DRIP.

DRIP.

Ethan screamed for help. No reply.

DRIP.

DRIP.

DRIP.

He wiggled and seethed and screamed some more.

DRIP.

DRIP.

DRIP.

No one came. No one was listening. If they were listening, they didn't care. No. Nobody knew he was locked in a dungeon, freezing cold and dripping wet, in a place that smelled of death and other vile things, in a place where the only sound beside your screaming was that tremendously all-consuming *DRIP, DRIP, DRIP!*

"That's right, Ethan," a shadowed man said. Ethan's pulse spiked as he located the voice in the corner of the dark room. "There is no escape," the man hissed, "save for following my very simple instructions. Do you understand?"

"Who are you?" Ethan asked. "Let me go!" His vigor to fight his way free intensified.

"I will, Ethan, but—you must understand— in order to let you go, first, I will need something from you."

Ethan's fear and annoyance did nothing to deter his need to be a smartass.

"Sorry, man. You're not my type."

The man sighed deeply. "Ethan. Do you feel that water hitting you?"

"Is there water hitting me? I hadn't noticed."

"That trickle, by itself, won't do much damage."

"Obvious."

The man ignored Ethan's curt reply and moved closer to him, just enough to light up those long, billowing robes made of grey spider silk. The sound of dead leaves danced across the stone floor under the train of his robe until he came to a stop by the wall near Ethan's face. Ethan heard a slow squeak emanate from the panel and felt the water pressure increase. This time, the water had a bite to it.

"Ouch! What is that?"

"That, dear boy, is my own secret recipe. You see, it turns ordinary water into a flesh-searing potion. It will slowly erode your skin and your skull until I can access the soft tissue of your brain. From there, I will insert this tentacle finger of mine directly into each grey fold and be able to access the very depths of your memories. Please understand, I don't need the potion to do my work. Believe it or not, the potion hurts less. Now, shall we proceed?"

Fear gripped Ethan in a stranglehold as he realized who was sitting in this room with him: A Mind Traveler. He'd heard about Mind Travelers since he was a young lad. They were extremely rare magickal creatures and were able to access anything they wished in your brain. They could see every memory you ever created and could assume control of your whole body if they remained connected long enough. Some could even do it with a strong enough psychic connection. Ethan stared in shock as this monstrosity came into view. The man smiled, half his face missing, revealing clean white bone where flesh once was.

Ethan screamed.

"Shall I take that as a yes?

CHAPTER SEVEN: RUSKIN RECEIVES NEWS

"Sire!" another idiot bellowed, his squeaky voice reverberating off the castle's stone walls.

King Ruskin massaged his temples for the fifteenth time that day and had no patience left for whatever this was.

"What?" He rolled his eyes from the comfort of his black and blood-red velvet wingback throne.

"I have news!"

"I should hope so, the way you came barging into my courtroom."

"I'm sorry, Your Majesty, but there is news from the—uh…" he looked around the cavernous room, trying to find the right words.

"Well? Spit it *out*, man!" the king said.

The guard flinched but held his ground. "I'm sorry, Your Majesty, but it seems as though the, uh, amethyst has been, um… activated."

"Activated."

"Yes."

"The amethyst."

"Yes."

Ruskin stared at the guard's face, waiting to see if he'd get an explanation from this young dolt.

"Spit it out!"

Just then, another man ran into the room to join the side of the visibly shaking youth.

"Your Majesty!" Silas, the head of his guard, said. He bowed, his long, red beard sweeping the ground. "Firstly, Your Majesty, the boy has been captured and is settling in nicely, currently having his, uh 'chat' with our dear friend."

"It's about time!"

"And, secondly," Silas continued, "what this young lad is trying to say, my liege, is that the Amethyst Stone in the secret lair has lit up. She is here."

CHAPTER EIGHT: AMY FINDS A TUB

I sighed and splashed cold water on my face. It had been two weeks since I'd landed on this island. Yep. That's right. Island. Two long weeks walking the entire island, up and down each stretch of beach, cliff, nook and cranny. Two weeks of missing my home. Two weeks of wondering what the hell happened to me, where am I, is this real, and have I gone and totally lost my mind?

Maybe I'm in a coma, lying peacefully in a hospital bed, drooling on myself while a hot male nurse comes in to sponge me down and— Okay, that last one might have thrilled me, but only for a moment, because *Where the hell are all the people? And where the hell am I?!*

Thankfully, during this time, I learned to switch back and forth between my water legs and my walking legs. Just a bit of mind-over-matter, really. (Okay, fine, so it might have taken a week to figure out, but it's fine, I got it.) I also found out, after being frustratingly naked after each transformation from mermaid to human, that I could include my makeshift clothing of leaves and braided long-grass and have it already on me once I regained human form. Where they went? Well, I hadn't quite figured that one out yet, but I found I didn't much care about the answer. Being able to do it at will was good enough for me!

I'd explored the forest of trees and found enough food to sustain myself, mostly berries, nuts, and clumps of pool algae.

I even built a semi-decent shelter out of sticks and more of the giant fallen leaves. (Look at me putting to use stuff I learned at Camp!)

I spent some time getting used to my new body: Testing out my fins versus legs, of course, but also getting used to my new skin, new hair, new eyes— they were purple! They reminded me of that new amethyst geode I was set to premiere at my store. Man, maybe I really was dreaming?

As much as I was getting used to this beautiful place, I grew lonely and wondered if I'd ever see another person again or, at the very least, catch sight of the elusive animals that keep poking about.

"But, I swear to God," I called out to no one, "if I find a volleyball and go all Tom Hanks out here, I'm really and truly going to call it a day and fling myself into the ocean!" Which would do no damage, as I'm a mermaid.

I let out a deep breath. There was only one spot in this godforsaken paradise that I could not get access to: An old volcano, from what I could surmise. It was the most unforgiving climb in this whole place. I could traverse the island itself with no problem, but this volcano was a different story. Spiky trees along the base with a sheer rock wall all the way up. On one topside, there was a large segment of cliff that looked just like a dragon skull, and I couldn't be sure it wasn't designed that way.

"If there are actual dragons in there, I'm shitting a brick." I paused. "Great. I'm talking to myself. Again."

Part of me wanted to take to the ocean to see what I could find nearby, but not having a clue of where to go or how long it would take made me hesitate. So, for now, I continued to trek up today's cliff of choice and caught a teeny, tiny shimmering at the base of the dragon cliff.

"Now what do you suppose that is?"

I grimaced, realizing this whole talking to myself thing might become a whole... well, *thing*.

I peered closer, hand shielding my eyes from the double sun rays shining through the sky.

It looked like water, impossibly flowing directly out of a solid rock wall. Unless...?

I took off running, speeding towards the bottom of the cliff and stopped where I thought I'd seen the flicker. Grabbing a thick fallen branch nearby, I used it to thwack away towering blades of grass, ferns, and other greenery, sending bits to and fro without a hint of grace.

One last whack and I disconnected the leaves, freeing up a tunnel that was previously obscured at the bottom of the rock. It had a small stream hidden in the underbrush that seemed to lead all the way out to the sea. I eyed the tiny cave tunnel and decided that this called for my mermaid-ness.

I inhaled, then let out a deep, calming breath that allowed me to center my focus.

"Mermaid form, activate!"

My god, I was a nerd. A mermaid nerd. A mer-nerd.

I felt my legs fusing together and my feet becoming ever more fin-like, ready to test the waters. I slipped into the stream and paddled until I was directly at the opening of the tunnel. This water felt different than the rest of the island. Thicker, almost bubbling, and it gave the impression that it was happy. I loved it immediately.

A few more feet in front of me, the tunnel opened up into a cave full of twinkling gemstones in blues, purples, and silvers. Glowing teal and indigo mushrooms, along with fluorescent magenta eggplant mushrooms dotted the rocky floor. Moss and vines adorned the cavern walls, mingling with the gemstones and swaying in the light breeze that filtered through this cavern. It felt like a greeting. Peaceful.

I swam a bit further and the cave closed back into one more short tunnel, then opened up to a hidden paradise.

I could see a waterfall the exact color of amethyst. I'd never seen a purple waterfall before! In fact, it rather matched the shade of my new eyes. (I was beginning to notice a distinctly purple theme going on.) All around it was a wide cylinder of trees, protecting this treasure from all outsiders. Sparks of various bright colors traipsed along the forest floor, leaving trails of vibrancy behind, like low shooting fireworks, or fancy fireflies. It was mesmerizing.

I splashed around, trying to piece together my latest predicament. Okay, I made it to the hidden area. Now what?

Suddenly, I was hit with a massive vision. I saw myself here, in this place, laughing, looking free and happy. It was a montage of life: Picking flowers, feeding animals, dining leisurely, sleeping in a real bed. A real bed? Where was that when you needed it? I'd gotten used to the shoddy sleeping arrangements I'd managed for myself over the last couple weeks of isolation here, but nothing came close to the feeling of sleeping in a real bed! If only this was real, and not some obvious mental breakdown.

Regardless of my sanity, I decided to explore this uncharted territory of my new home and see what I could find. I pulled myself out of the sparkling pool and shook myself free of as much water as I could before trudging off.

My sloshing steps were muffled in this canopy of trees. Maybe I was just being dramatic, but this felt too familiar. Also, it seemed too private to be open to the general public, if there even was one. No, this place… this place was sacred to someone. Why did it feel like it was sacred to *me*?

I braced myself on a nearby trunk to catch my breath and a shock of energy blazed through my hand. Another vision assaulted me, this time showing me a trail that led a short way back from here. The tree I was touching was the marker for the start of the path that led down a walkway to the base of the waterfall.

I let go of the tree and instinctively followed the path. I had to rip a few more fronds and branches out of my way, but I was able to reach my destination: A five-foot-tall stone mushroom statue with vines wrapped around it and a double circle purposefully carved into the front of its thick column.

I peeked around to the right of the mushroom statue (I say statue, but only because I don't think you could, or should, eat this thing) and saw a pathway. An actual, on purpose pathway, with a hand-railing and everything! Well, hand-railing in the sense that tree roots and vines were co-existing on purpose along the inclined pathway to form a structured trail.

With nothing to lose, I followed it. I traversed upward, peering around, keeping an ear out for sound other than water or birds and an eye out for literally anything but trees, rocks, and water. Again nothing. About to give up, I rounded a bend on the other side of the foresty mountain cylinder I found myself in and saw a doorway in the cliffside. *A doorway?* Right in the middle of, well, dirt? I paused and held my breath, heart beating in my chest.

Do it. Open the door.

The sound of rushing blood filled my ears as my hand lightly grasped the clear quartz crystal knob of the ornately carved wooden door. To my surprise, it opened easily. Not even a squeak, just a welcoming air, like I was being caressed by a cloud of memory.

I stared, wide-eyed, at the home I found myself in, for that's what it was: A home, one that had been abandoned long ago... by me. *What?*

I sprang across the cozy, rustic room to rip a painting off the fireplace mantle that looked exactly like me! No, it couldn't be... could it? And who is the guy? His face wasn't clear, probably due to the wear and tear of age. I plunked the artwork back down a little too roughly, just so I could stop looking at it for a second and tried to process this latest shock.

Why is there a painting of me... and some dude... in this abandoned house... all things that I sort of recognize?

A trickle of ownership came over me, and all at once, it clicked: This was my house. I'd lived here before. Before what, though? So many questions! Did I live here alone? Did that guy live here with me? Did I have a family? What happened to me/us? What do I do now?

As I was having yet another mental breakdown, I scanned the house for more detail, hoping something would start to make sense. I saw a kitchen area, complete with a sink, table, two chairs, and some kind of food storage unit. It wasn't a fridge, I could tell you that, but I wasn't sure what this simple box did, as there was nothing in it but dirt and dust. Okay, so, kitchen. Got it. Maybe the first room was some kind of sitting area/living room? I mean, I didn't see too much here besides a carved-out log that resembled the log-cabin-style benches I often saw in Tahoe while on vacation, and there was a small wooden table near the fireplace.

I turned my gaze to the door on the left. A much simpler patterned door with another quartz crystal handle opened to a decent sized bedroom. Aha! I found the bed I was picturing! I suddenly felt every bit of exhaustion I'd been carrying for the last two weeks. Deciding that playing Goldilocks was preferable to standing on my feet for one more minute (and definitely better than sleeping on piles of grass), I brushed off the collection of dust and debris and crawled into the most exquisitely comfortable bed I have ever laid on in my life and passed out.

***

When I awoke after the most restful sleep I've ever had, I yawned, stretched my arms far above my head, and twisted my body enough to hear things *pop*.

"Nice," I said, content to just lay in this cozy bed all day… until I caught wind of myself. Not exactly "Dove fresh". Remembering my long and very sweaty hike, I thought that making my way down to the pool to clean off was an excellent idea.

I exited the room and noticed a small window on the other side of the room that I hadn't seen yesterday. I walked over to it, curious to see what kind of view I would get at the top of a waterfall house.

When I got closer, I saw another door, flush with the wall and almost entirely missable. No discernable handle, so I gave it a cursory shove. The door clicked and slid into a side panel, opening up to a balcony overlooking the entire waterfall. It absolutely took my breath away! While I had grown tired of seeing nothing but trees for the last half-month, seeing them displayed in such a fashion, as if a beautiful accent to this glorious waterfall, well, it was enough to steal anyone's heart!

On the farthest end of the stone balcony was a huge, matching bathtub carved from the same red jasper as the balcony. It had a few levers also carved from jasper, but these were of differing colors: One purple, one yellow, and one Moldavite lever, standing out with its olive-green coloring and leaf-like etchings inside its polished stone. Wow! I'd never had more than a few of those back home in my shop, as they were getting very expensive and I couldn't afford more just yet, having recently purchased that damn amethyst geode. I was stunned to see the Moldavite sitting here so casually in a bathtub.

I couldn't wait any longer. I stripped off my leaf and grass clothing and turned the yellow handle first. When the lever nudged a wooden piping system next to it, a trickle of water was diverted from the waterfall, flowed down the piping system, and began filling the tub with sparkling water. I turned the purple lever and, when I didn't see anything, I stuck my hand in the filling tub and noticed that the temperature was heating with the incoming bubbles.

Now that's something I could get used to!

Deciding to wait to try the third lever, I slipped into the tub and switched off the yellow lever to stop the flow. As soon as my body touched the perfect water, my whole aura collapsed into it. I felt myself relax for the first time since leaving my house that fateful day I got shot.

That still blew my mind! I got shot, then ended up in this isolated paradise. Meh, I'm probably dead. This was Heaven, and I was dead. And right now, I didn't care. I didn't. This was divine.

I languished back against the smooth rock headrest and listened to the birds singing in the nearby trees.

"Someday I'm going to see you, birds!" I shouted at them. "Maybe I'll even have my Picture-Guy build you a giant birdhouse, if you're lucky!"

Laughing at my own idiocy, I stretched my right arm behind my head to get out the last of the morning's kinks and accidentally hit the Moldavite lever.

Suddenly, the tub started draining rapidly, with me still in it! Tilting forward as if to hurry along the contents, the tub bottom opened up and everything was getting swallowed fast! I grasped wetly at smooth jasper, finding no purchase whatsoever, and ended up tumbling helplessly into the void.

What greeted me at the end of that fairly short ride was not what I expected. I thought I would be dumped wherever used water was dumped when one was done with the tub, but instead of sliding down a complex system of plumbing, or even just depositing me into the pool at the bottom of the waterfall, I found myself shrieking as I was shot fully nude through a swirling cloud of colored mist and came to an ungraceful stop in an empty throne room.

What?

I looked behind me, thoroughly confused (and more than a little frightened), and saw that my astounding exit must have been through the throne itself. It had to be, as the only other thing in the direction I had come from was a solid stone wall. I jumped to my feet and approached the ornate chair cautiously, lest it take me on another fun adventure. I poked it lightly, seeing no change whatsoever, so I poked it again, to no avail. Finally, I decided to take my chances. I grabbed and tugged on it, prodding around for a lock or lever, whatever I could find to open the damn thing up.

No dice.

"Fine!" I said to the empty room. "Be a dick!"

I kicked the throne as my echoes circled back to me. I regretted it instantly, remembering now that not only was I stark naked, but shoeless as well. All I needed was for the first person I saw to find me roaming around in the buff.

"Pff," I said, "like it even matters. Who's around to be ashamed for?"

Just to make sure this wasn't one of those secret passageway situations, I groped along the walls, all around the throne as well but, as I suspected, nothing but solid rock.

"Damnit!" I yelled, echoing so loudly that I had to cover my ears. Once the ringing stopped, I sighed and sat on the vacant throne, bare buns meeting cold— *what is this, more jasper? Figures.* It looked like the same stuff the tub was made from.

Realizing that sulking in this quiet castle was getting me nowhere, I made up my mind to do some exploring. Who knows? Maybe I'd find some clothing in this dark Disney fantasy I found myself in.

"Or maybe I'll run into a cache of Orcs and end up running for my life." Where's *Sting* when you need it?

I came across a room whose door was mostly rotted away. I saw the contents inside were much like the rest of the castle: Old, dusty, broken, faded away or eaten by moths. I was losing hope of ever finding anything of value in this lonely place. I took a step to exit and noticed a wardrobe on the far side of the room that looked relatively unscathed.

Walking over to it, I reached for the cabinet door, trying not to get my hopes up.

Inside that wardrobe lay an array of exquisite gowns in a wide range of colors. Jewels and frippery adorned these marvels of medieval-esque fashion, and I itched to try on every single one to see if anything fit. Hell, even if it didn't, I'd still feel better having something to clothe me.

My excitement was brewing, and I started yanking them from their hangers, one by one, each dress getting a turn over my eager head, each one getting pushed away at warp speed in my haste to try on the next. I felt like a pre-teen on a sugar-high at the mall and I was having the time of my life! Each dress fit like it was made just for me!

"Is this like a Traveling Pants situation?" I asked the wardrobe. No response. "Pff," I said. "The wardrobe in Beauty and The Beast would have answered me."

"Beauty and the what, dear?" An eerie elderly woman's voice whispered over my shoulder.

I screamed and jumped four feet in the air. I turned around to see who was behind me and saw nothing there but an empty castle. My heart had now vacated my chest and was firmly taking up residence in my throat, pounding so hard I could hear my blood rushing in my ears and couldn't swallow worth a damn.

"Hell—" I squeaked after a minute. "Hello?"

Maybe it was just more echoing that I heard? Stifling the heebie-jeebies, I stopped clowning around with the clothing and was about to just grab one off the pile I'd made and take my leave when, out of the corner of my eye, I saw one last bit of cloth bundled up in the back of the wardrobe. Fine golden ropes tied this plain beige linen package shut, so all I had to do was pull the string loose and it gave way.

Inside the pack was a pair of small deer-skin trousers, a soft off-white linen long-sleeved shirt, tan leather boots that laced all the way up to the knee with beautiful, fringed cuffs, and a stunning forest green hooded cloak that had a feeling similar to velvet mixed with fleece. It was the most pleasing material I had ever held. I couldn't resist pulling a corner of it to my face and nuzzling it for comfort. I took one last longing look at the pile of pretty princess attire and dressed myself in the bundle pack.

Thinking I should probably bring the packing material and ropes with me on whatever journey I was about to make, I pulled the now empty cloth out of the wardrobe and heard a soft *thunk* hit the ground.

My eyes followed the sound and discovered a ruby about the size of a baseball winking at me from the floor. Upon closer inspection, I could see I was looking at a stunning example of a star ruby: A six-pronged star embedded inside a ruby that shimmered in bursting light all its own. Without hesitation, I snatched it up to put it in my cloak pocket for safekeeping, but when my hand closed around that gemstone, it sizzled in my fist and held me frozen in place.

"Tell it you love it," came that eerie whisper again.

"What?" I asked through gritted teeth.

"Say, 'I love you'. Go on, then," she replied.

"I—I love you," I said, feeling stupid. A jolt slammed through me, and I was knocked flat on my ass, the ruby rolling harmlessly across the floor as I struggled to get my breathing under control.

I heard the lady laughing from somewhere in front of me and, to my surprise, when I looked up to see what I'd thought was nothing but my ever-changing sanity level, I actually saw her. Or, rather, I saw *through* her.

"You're a— a—"

"A ghost, dear. I'm a ghost."

That did it. I passed out.

CHAPTER NINE: IBRAXUS AWAKENS

"I love you..."

"AAAAAHHHHHHH!" came the frozen muffled scream of the fallen lord, Ibraxus, his frozen eyes popping open for the first time in ages.

Known as Brax to his loved ones, he had been missing for centuries after the fight he'd lost to Ruskin. After a fierce battle over the woman they both loved, she had been killed and Ruskin punished Brax for her death. Brax had been so shocked that he didn't see the magick curse that hit him squarely in the chest, putting him into a deep, deep slumber. As continuing punishment, he had been encased in this wall of ice, deep in the caverns of the Snowlands.

"AAAAAAHHHHHHH!" he screamed again. This time, it awoke his guard, a young girl with fiery orange-red curls and puppy dog brown eyes.

She immediately popped up from the crude chair she'd been sitting in and bounced happily up and down, waving at him through the icy walls with a huge smile on her face. Brax had no idea who she was, or where *he* was! And, while he was at it, where in the world was Ifyrus?

"Ifyrus!" Brax tried to shout. He thought it sounded like words, but his throat felt raw, unused, and he couldn't be sure. He tried again, louder this time. "Ifyrus!"

His eyes darted to the girl, still trying to get his attention. He saw her mouth moving, but he couldn't make out any words.

"Hello! Girl! Get me out of here. Hello? Can you hear me? Get me out of here!"

He was fully trapped in this ice cube nightmare and was feeling desperate. He tried one more time for his friend.

"IFYRUS!"

Silence greeted him. He saw the girl had stopped bouncing and was looking concerned now, puzzling out how to help him, if he could read her face correctly.

Suddenly, an unmistakable roar rumbled through the cavern and shook nearby icicles from their wintry perches. The girl's already pale skin turned an alarming shade of alabaster, and she froze in place. Then, the tiniest feathering of cracks slithered their way across the icy walls until they became a cascade of calamity, chunks of ice and snow toppling over and flying to any available open space.

Brax closed his eyes and held his breath as he felt his prison collapse around him. Massive booming sounds echoed off the chamber walls, loud enough to compete with the mightiest of dragon roars, rattling every inch of the cavern. The girl dropped to her knees and held her hands over her ears to protect them, a fierce grimace crossing her small features.

And then… silence. No more rumblings, no more quakes, just silence. He felt a puff of hot air assault his face and it startled him into opening his eyes. There, with a haughty grin on his face, was his obsidian dragon friend,

Ifyrus. Ifyrus nudged Brax softly on his right shoulder, his version of testing that his friend was unharmed.

Brax let out a sigh of relief and pet him on the snout. "I'm okay, my friend. A little chilly, but okay. Thank you for coming to my rescue."

They stayed that way for a few more seconds until Brax realized that he'd forgotten they had an audience. It was her squeak that jolted him back to the present.

"You. Girl. Who are you? And where am I?"

The girl's body shook, Brax thought due to nerves or fear, but then he noticed her eyes; they were not full of terror or panic, but rather, admiration and excitement.

"I am Kavea, and you are on the Island of No Return. You've been frozen in these caverns since before my time, and nobody knows you are here except for me!"

Brax's eyebrows furrowed and he demanded an explanation.

"Well," Kavea continued, "I don't know exactly when it happened. I've just read so many stories about the Long-Lost Lord, that when I found you in this cave a few years ago, I put two and two together. I've been coming to visit you ever since. This is kinda my secret spot, though, maybe not so secret anymore. Someone's bound to have heard that and will come looking."

"How old are you? You look too young to be out on your own."

Kavea brightened even more, as if this line of questioning brought her joy. Stupid girl. Stupid naive girl.

"I'm old enough. Fifteen, to be exact."

Brax clenched his teeth and sighed.

"Where are your parents?"

"They're... well... they're not *here* right now? See, my father travels a lot and, well, my mother, she's, uh... she's not suited for company or travel, or much of anything, really."

Brax grunted.

"I am off to find my way home. You should do the same." And with that, Brax turned on his heel, grabbed Ifyrus by the horn, and leapt confidently onto his back.

"Go *home,* Girl!"

"But—but—!"

Ifyrus peered at her, shoving his pitch-black snout in her face, lightly sniffing, as if trying to figure her out.

"I want to help you!" she said.

Brax let out a mighty guffaw.

"Not today, Girl, but thank you for— uh— watching over me all this time." He turned his attention to Ifyrus and said, "Let us fly!"

Ifyrus nudged a few big ice chunks out of their path, braced his legs and pushed off from the ground with all his might.

"My name isn't *Girl*! It's *Kavea*!" she shouted at the fleeting figures in the sky. Kavea sighed, defeated. "Well, *now* what?"

CHAPTER TEN: CYNDOL'S CAPTURE

Living with a fox for a best friend was shaping up to be quite interesting. For one thing, he always knew where to find food, thanks to his keen senses of smell and eyesight. Another thing, his cuddly coat kept her warm during those chilly nights. And he was quite funny, once he felt comfortable enough to make jokes.

They had been traveling together for the past three days, making their way toward what she hoped was the correct direction of the Sky Prison in Padagonya. She'd heard word of the ghastly conditions of that place. No blankets or cushions or anything that could provide a shred of hope or comfort there. It was unforgiving at the best of times, and she had never heard of anyone leaving that nightmare. But she knew, deep in her heart, they would find a way to free her brother. She didn't know the details that got him locked up there to begin with, but she knew that, whatever it was, he didn't deserve that punishment.

"How much farther?" Kit asked.

"Why?" Cyndol replied. "You got somewhere else to be?"

He did his best foxy eyeroll and chose not to respond.

They walked on in silence for another few minutes before Kit huffed.

"What?" Cyndol stopped and fixed her attention on his back.

"Nothing, just—" Kit stopped walking and turned to face her. "Have you been there before? Do you know how to get there? Or are we just wandering around, hoping to find it?"

"Of course, I know how to get there! It's…" Cyndol couldn't meet his questioning gaze. "You know…" she trailed off vaguely and waved her arm noncommittally toward the waning suns. "That direction."

Kit's eyebrows shot up into his fuzzy ears and he pointed his nose at her. "Aha! I *knew* it! You *don't* know where we're going!"

"Don't be stupid! Of course, I—"

"SHH!" Kit hissed. His gaze darted toward the small cliff to Cyndol's right and they both fell silent, straining their ears to listen for any more sounds.

"What did you—?" Cyndol said but was interrupted by another shushing.

After another minute, she could hear it, too. Drumbeats? Singing? Whatever was going on, it sounded beautiful. Cyndol started toward the cliffside, seeing for the first time the firelight flicking shadows up the cliff face like it had come to life.

"Cyndol!" Kit called from his hiding place in a bush. "Don't be an idiot! Come back!"

But Cyndol was too intrigued, and she wanted a closer look, just real quick. It was a tribe of forest people, gathered around a large bonfire, singing, drumming, dancing! Oh, how she wished she could dance, but she was absolute rubbish at it. Her gaze was transfixed on one woman, pouring out her heart and soul through movements around the blaze. She watched unwavering as this stunning woman swung her long fair braids about her, wild and free, completely lost in music and movement.

Cyndol took one more step forward to try to get a better look and was instantly surrounded by a group of warriors emerging from the surrounding shrubbery. They were yelling and pointing spears and various magickal weapons at her. She tried to bolt but was immediately tackled by a younger woman who'd snuck up on her right. Cyndol hit the ground in a flurry of swinging arms and legs, kicking, punching, and trying to bite anything that got near enough to chomp on. She connected with an arm.

The young woman yelped and clocked Cyndol in the head with her thick wooden staff. Cyndol landed hard on her butt. The woman tied Cyndol up quickly, then pulled her along behind.

"Hey! Stop! Let me go!" Cyndol said.

Kit wanted to help, but knew he couldn't win this fight. He kept to his hiding spot in the bushes and watched helplessly as Cyndol was dragged farther toward the captors' village. He crept along the shrubs, sticking to plants and shadows as best he could.

Cyndol continued to struggle while being dragged past the festivities. The dancing came to an abrupt halt as she passed by. Cyndol turned beet red when she saw the woman who had so fascinated her fix her with a shrewd stare. She wished they'd continue, if only to break the now deafening silence.

Cyndol took note as best she could of her new surroundings: Large, old trees seemed to breathe; the life was so strong within them. Their roots were grown out and entwined with those on opposite banks, making connecting bridges every so often, as their village bisected along a mighty river below. Houses weren't laid out on the ground as hers back home had been. No, these houses were directly inside these giant trees. There must have been some magick that convinced the trees to open up enough of their trunk space to allow for cohabitation. It was fascinating! She knew that magick existed, had even met a few people in her village that knew how to wield it, but she'd never seen it done to this expert level. It *lives* here, had so for ages. She could feel its presence dripping off of every branch they passed. It would make sense, she reasoned, as they lived closer to the Gemstone Belt than anywhere she'd seen before. Even now, in fact, she could see the belt reflecting light from the moon, throwing bits of color here and there amidst the night sky.

After a few minutes, and a gathering crowd behind them, they came to a halt in front of a glorious treehouse that stood out from the rest they'd passed by.

It stood roughly three stories tall, in what had to be the oldest tree stump in the forest. This tree stump was a monument to nature and was a stronghold for all to see. Each level of the stump had something different: The first level was the obvious base and armory, as could be surmised by the weapons adorning the walls. The second level looked like a gathering center, with plenty of brightly colored blankets and canopies draped in elegance and community. The third and final level, she surmised, could be the actual living quarters, where the leaders of this community dwelled. Cyndol saw simple windows with planter boxes in front and drapes of silks behind them. And from the base to the top level were opalescent sets of steppingstones leading up each new flight, with luminescent pink, purple, and blue creeping flower vines to act as guardrails. It was the most breathtaking home Cyndol had ever seen.

One of the warriors broke off from their group, ascended the steps, and entered the domicile. Nothing happened for another minute or two, and Cyndol started to try and break free again, but only half-heartedly, as she truly *was* curious to see who was behind that top door. Her captor gave her a hard shake that threw Cyndol off-balance enough that she stopped what she was doing and sat as still as her nerves would allow.

Finally, a bright white light preceded a figure that stepped through the doorway. A low, gently persuasive voice called out in the twilight, "Bring forth the girl."

Cyndol was hoisted to her feet and brought up the few steps that bordered the treehouse.

"And release her from those bonds at once," the voice added.

Two men instantly freed Cyndol from her mini prison and gestured for her to walk in front of them. She thought it best to comply.

When she got closer, she saw that this new figure belonged to an old woman with skin the color of dark honey glaze. Her face was shaped like a heart, full of life and wisdom. She offered a knowing smile that seemed to live permanently on her stunning face. Her long silver and black hair was braided and wrapped around her head like a crown, and her flowing robes of deep violet billowed around her in the breeze. Cyndol loved her immediately.

Without giving it a second thought, Cyndol dropped to her knee and genuflected to this obvious figure of royalty.

The woman gave a soft laugh in response, glided down the steps, and helped her to her feet.

"Come, child," she said, "you must be exhausted. Sit, rest, have some food. Then you may tell me what brought you to our kingdom."

Cyndol simply nodded and followed the woman up the steps into the second-tier doorway. The door closed behind them, shutting out the curious crowd. Cyndol spared a worried thought to what may have happened to Kit but was ushered to a plush chair by a fire where she was settled in and handed a cup of what smelled like Callamay tea. She looked up at the radiant woman and was rewarded with a wink and a smile.

"You have the air of the sea about you," she said. "Am I correct?"

Cyndol nodded again, cautiously sipping her tea after seeing the woman take a confident gulp herself. It was delicious and helped her find her voice.

"Mmm, that's wonderful! Thank you!"

"You are welcome, little one. My name is Miawae, my husband is Matthias. He is out seeing to the festivities. We rule over this land. You may call me Queen, Your Majesty, Your Highness, or simply Miawae, if you prefer. What shall I call you?"

Cyndol peered into her dark, knowing eyes, searching for any hints of danger, but found none. She let herself sink further into the cushion while clutching her teacup and said, "Me-ahh-way?" She tested the name on her lips. "That's beautiful. I've never heard a name like that before. My name is Cyndol and I'm from a seaside village several days' journey from here. I— um…"

Queen Miawae watched her patiently.

Cyndol let out a long sigh and continued. "I'm traveling to the Sky Prison in Padagonya to try to rescue my brother Ethan, who was wrongly taken from us, and it's up to me to find him! He's all I got left! Our village was raided and burned by a large group of men and I'm afraid we might be the only two survivors. Our parents—"

Cyndol choked on a sob and let her teacup come to a halt on her lap. Queen Miawae flicked her eyes to it, then set her own cup on the small table next to her, placing her soft, wrinkled hands atop Cyndol's.

"There, there. Do not fret." The Queen grimaced and winced, trying to hide whatever dark thoughts just crossed her mind. Her hands were gripping Cyndol's just a bit too tight. "You see," Miawae continued, "I happen to know how to get to this prison."

"You do?" Cyndol asked.

Queen Miawae chuckled and said, "I do. And I might be willing to set you on the correct path, but are you absolutely certain it is the right thing to do?"

Cyndol was taken aback. "Of course it is! He's my brother!" She yanked her hands back. "Who else would help him?"

"I meant no offense, child," Miawae raised her hands in a protective gesture, "I only wanted to make sure it was something you truly wished to do. It is not a safe place, nor a safe road to get there. So, I ask again, is this something you truly have your heart set on?"

At that moment, the door burst open and a girl, not but a few years older than Cyndol herself, flew in Cyndol's face and demanded to know who she was and what she was doing in her grandmother's chair.

The Queen chided her for her rudeness and explained that Cyndol was her guest and not to be attacked or treated unkindly.

The girl huffed and grabbed a pastry from the side table, ripping off a bite and chewing with her mouth open.

Queen Miawae said to Cyndol, "Please excuse my granddaughter's brusqueness. She is still learning to control her temper."

"Hey—!" the girl said but was cut off by her elder.

"Princess Kiara! I would kindly remind you that we do not raise our voices in the company of our guests unless we are under attack, and, unless *you* see an army in my sitting room, I suggest you sit down and allow me to explain this new child and her situation to you so we can all be on the same page."

Kiara bit her tongue but sat stoically while the Queen caught her up on her latest arrival.

"And, who knows?" Miawae continued. "Maybe you'll find you two have a few things in common?"

Kiara ran her eyes over Cyndol, then turned her face away in dismissal. Cyndol made a mental note to not get on her bad side. She also noticed how much she looked like her grandmother and was instantly envious of their shared beauty. Kiara was taller and leaner than the queen, but their features were very similar. Though Miawae's hair was streaked with silver, Kiara's shone like onyx, styled in sleek dreadlocks that were pinned half up and half down with jade clips.

Cyndol let out a sudden yawn and immediately apologized to the queen for her lack of manners.

"It's alright, child. You've earned a good rest. Why don't you stay with us tonight and we can see about setting you off on your path tomorrow?"

Cyndol didn't have room to argue, so she allowed herself to be escorted to a smaller treehouse down the road by Princess Kiara. Kiara insisted, saying she "wanted to make sure she got there okay". Cyndol was pretty sure the princess just wanted to make sure she didn't try to steal anything or cause any more ruckus.

Cyndol glanced back over her shoulder to take one last look at the now resumed festivities and wished she'd been able to stay a bit longer.

"That's not for you," Kiara said, still walking.

"Why not?" Cyndol asked. "What are you all celebrating? It looks enchanting!"

Cyndol could have sworn she heard her growl.

"It is our Day of the Dead. The day each year where we honor those we have lost. You are not invited."

Cyndol sighed and continued onward to her temporary lodgings. When they arrived, Kiara opened the door, did a quick perimeter check, and left without further ado. While she didn't say "Stay" out loud, it was etched on her face with every fiber of her being. So, Cyndol chose to obey, much as she wanted to explore.

The room was just that: A room. Sparse furniture that included a small bed, a small table, and two chairs. The only interesting thing about it was that the furniture was much like the bridges she'd seen coming in: Tree roots that had grown and been molded to shape each piece, as if the tree itself had total control over every bit of it. She made a mental note not to harm the tree in any way, lest it decide to come to life and let her have it by beating her with a "chair".

She sat down on the bed, which was comfortable enough, she supposed, but she was all alone in this strange place, and she missed her family, missed Kit.

Kit!

Cyndol jumped back up and ran to the door, flinging it open and peering outside into the now dark woods. Seeing nothing, she sighed and started to close the door.

"Psst!" a familiar hiss sounded to her right. Cyndol looked around but saw only darkness and the inky silhouette of trees.

"PSST!" she heard again, louder this time. "Down here!"

Cyndol shot her focus to the bushes along her treehouse and saw Kit peeking his snout through the leaves.

"Kit?" Cyndol whispered.

"No, it's the *other* foxy friend you left behind!"

Cyndol scooped him up out of the shrubbery and bolted back inside to hide him, slamming the door shut as fast as she could in case anyone was watching. As he strained against her, she nuzzled him close to her face and covered him in kisses.

"Oh, Kit! I thought I'd lost you!"

"You kind of did," he muffled into her shoulder. "Can you put me down now?"

"Oh, sorry!" Cyndol placed him on the bed with a gentle plop but continued to scratch his head softly. "What happened to you?"

"Well," Kit said, "when you decided it'd be a good idea to take off all of a sudden into wilderness we didn't know, I hid in the bushes nearby. And, yes, I saw what the villagers did to you. Don't you know humans are 'fight first, ask questions later'?"

"But I—"

"They will always find a way to hurt you or profit from you!"

"Hey! I—"

"Of course, I don't mean you *specifically*, you're different. You're kind. Stupid and reckless, but kind."

"Thank you?"

He paused then, and looked her square in the eye, lifting his front right paw to her cheek.

"I mean it, Cyndol, don't do that to me again! I was worried about you! I thought they were going to seriously hurt you! They didn't, did they? I mean, you look okay, but—"

"I'm fine," she said. "I'll probably have a few bruises and scrapes from being kicked and dragged through the dirt, but nothing permanent. I'm okay. These people seem… different. *Good* different, mostly. I don't think the princess likes me very much, though. Maybe she's just mad I spoiled her party? But the queen seems nice."

"There's a queen?"

"Yes! And, Kit, she offered to help us find The Sky Prison!"

"Did she, now?"

"Yes. We leave tomorrow."

"What's the catch?"

"Nothing!" she said. "Well, I think she's going to send somebody with us to show us the way. She said the road can be unsafe."

"Unsafe how, exactly?"

"I'm not sure. Maybe that's why we'll have an escort?"

Kit didn't answer, just gave her a frown and a once-over. "You could use a bath."

Cyndol scoffed at that but had to agree. She blushed when she realized how she must have appeared to the queen.

"You're right."

She looked around the small room as if something would just magickally appear but saw no answers. When she was about to give up and crawl into bed filthy, there came a knock at the door.

Cyndol opened it a crack as Kit darted under the bed. Two village men and one woman were outside her door, the men equipped with a large bath bucket and bathing cloth, the woman with some clothing and bottles of scented things.

The first man said, "The Queen wishes for you to have the luxury of cleaning off tonight's adventure."

Cyndol was astonished at the queen's generosity and let them inside to set up. The men laid down the heavy bucket, already full of warm, sudsy water, and left her alone with the woman.

"Thank you!" Cyndol called to their fading frames. She closed the door and turned to face the other woman. It dawned on Cyndol why she looked familiar: This was the woman she'd seen dancing at the bonfire! She'd so hoped to get a chance to meet her!

"It's *you*!" Cyndol said and bounded over to her.

The woman flinched and she dropped the dress, taking up her sword Cyndol hadn't seen hidden underneath her armful of clothing. With one hand, she grabbed Cyndol by the neck and held her up against the wall, the other hand holding her short sword against Cyndol's heart, baring her teeth at her.

"How do you know me, stranger?" the woman asked.

"I— uh—" Cyndol choked around the woman's grip, "I— saw you dancing... at the fire."

The woman paused and blinked. "You saw me dance?"

Cyndol tried to nod but had no slack to do so. "Yes. That's why I st— stopped— at... your vill—village."

The woman dropped her immediately and Cyndol took a gulp of air.

"Explain."

Cyndol rubbed her throat, coughed, and tried to even out the gasps. When she could speak fairly normally, she continued.

"I already told the queen. I'm trying to find my brother. He's been taken to The Sky Prison in Padagonya. I'm just trying to get there to save him. I only stopped by your village by accident when I saw the bonfire and heard the music. I've never seen anyone dance like you do. I wished I could do that. That's when your people tackled me."

"Child," she started, white-blonde braids swinging around her cream-colored skin, the trinkets she'd decorated in her hair making light tinkling sounds as they moved. "If Padagonya is where you're headed, you'd be better served turning around and going straight home."

"I— um— don't have a home anymore," Cyndol said. This was too much for a girl her age to handle. She just wanted to be left alone to go find her brother. She slid down the wall and puddled onto the floor.

The woman studied this young, pitiful creature in front of her. After a few moments of watching the child weep, she extended her hand to her. Cyndol sniffled and hesitantly took it, righting herself and letting the woman lead her to sit on the bed.

"My name is Evony," she said. "I am War Chief for this land and the right hand of Queen Miawae."

Cyndol felt her eyebrows raise. "War Chief? But you're so… so…" she couldn't find the words.

"So *what*?" asked Evony. "Female? Small? Undeserving?"

"Passionate, maybe? Beautiful, for certain."

Evony paused, her brows drawing together.

"I can't be beautiful and passionate if I'm busy fighting? Is that what you mean?"

"Not at all," Cyndol said. "I just didn't realize that it could all exist in one person. Can you teach *me* how to be like that?"

Evony sat down on the bed next to Cyndol.

"Why?"

"Because I want to be brave and passionate like you! Beauty would be nice, but maybe if I knew how to do all the things you can, I could protect my brother when I rescue him, and we go back home. Or, well, I guess we'll have to start a new home somewhere else, but I know if I knew how to fight, it would make things a whole lot easier, just in case those men ever come after us again."

Evony took a sharp intake of breath and bristled.

"What men?"

Cyndol cast her eyes to the floor. "I'm not entirely sure. There was a great horde of them, and they burned my village and almost got me, too, but I got away."

Evony stood up and made her way to the door.

"Wait, you're leaving?" Cyndol jumped up as well.

"For now. You need to bathe before that water gets cold, and I have some things to discuss with the queen."

Cyndol halted her with one last question.

"So, why did *you* bring me this stuff, if you're the hand of the queen?"

Evony gave a wry smile and said, "Because I needed to know who I'm escorting to Padagonya. See you tomorrow, Wee Warrior."

With that, she closed the door, blocking Cyndol's eager face.

CHAPTER ELEVEN: ETHAN'S NIGHTMARE

Ethan's screams had changed.

No longer were they piercing.

No longer were they rattling.

No.

These were the screams of the dying.

Of the hopeless.

They lived in their own plane of misery and fear.

These were the screams one could no longer hear.

These were the screams of the mind.

Ethan's stomach rumbled half-heartedly in the darkness. He knew he should eat, but the desire for self-preservation was a soft flicker, at best.

How long had he been here, he wondered, chained to this sorry excuse for a bed? This cold, rigid, unforgiving platter he was being served to his captors on? Had it been days? Weeks? Months? Or was it much, much worse? Had he been here forever and only dreamt he had a life outside of these shadowed walls? That was a danger he couldn't bear to consider for long. For if he could convince himself of *that*, well, then he truly was lost.

Just then, he heard a scraping and squeaking from across the room, signaling company. Company here, though, was never a good thing. No, company here meant pain, and lots of it.

"Good morning, Ethan!" said the Mind Traveler. At some point, Ethan was given the name of "Viego" to identify the creature, but he didn't much care. All he could think about was pain. Searing pain. This *thing*, whenever it was near, would make Ethan's soul crumble up into the far reaches of his brain and take cover.

"How are we today, my boy?" Viego leaned over Ethan's prone frame on the rotting cot to examine his captive. "Hmm... I see you are starting to see we mean business here, am I right?"

Ethan's eyes struggled to find his captor's. Heavy lidded and fluttering, he finally managed to meet the probing gaze.

"Mmmgguhh," he said.

"Wonderful!" Viego clapped his hands together and rubbed them vigorously. "Now! Let's see what we can find today, hmm?"

In one swift motion, Viego's finger elongated in an elegant flourish, straight into the over-carved hole in Ethan's forehead. Bypassing skin, skull, and already-seen brain tissue, the creature frolicked amongst the untapped memories and knowledge in the boy's head.

"You know," Viego said, "you could make this much easier on yourself if you just told me where to find the missing artifact. I'd even let you have a good, long break if you'd at least tell me what it was that you recovered for our dear King Ruskin."

Ethan's tired mind billowed and swayed like the waves of the ocean, trying to lock onto any answer that could give him some relief, even temporarily.

"Sun—" Ethan said.

Viego continued his deep dive into Ethan's brain, merrily rooting around, as if enjoying a beautiful piece of music.

"Sun, you say. Which one?"

A cold sweat beaded around his temples, as was his normal physical response by this time.

"Little." His voice cracked over the word.

Viego's mangled maw cracked into a toothy grin. "Brilliant! The little sun. Marvelous. You're doing such a good job, young man! Your good King Ruskin will be much pleased. Now, tell me, dear boy, how did you come upon this? Did you steal it? Did someone hire you? How did it come to be in your possession?"

A tear leaked out of Ethan's right eye and rolled down to his ear, pooling in the pocket of the flimsy cartilage.

"No."

"No?" Viego asked. "No, what?" His tentacle receded just enough that Ethan's thoughts became more tangible.

Ethan tried again. "No. I didn't steal it. I found it. On the side of the road. I promise you! I promise! I never did *anything* to you people! I just saw a shiny thing in the road that I liked. I threw it into the bushes. It's in the bushes!"

"We had our best men comb every inch of that area. There was nothing there."

"It's there! I swear!"

The Mind Traveler tsked and retreated back to the doorway.

"I'm afraid I do not believe you. Rest now. I'll be back in the morning for another round."

Viego left.

Ethan screamed.

CHAPTER TWELVE: AMY'S QUEST

"Owww, my head," I said, rubbing it as I came to.

A snort of derision sounded to my right, and I saw an elderly female's ghost hovering in front of the window, arms folded over her chest, with a look of amused disdain on her face. Still in the castle, then. Not a dream.

"Are you functional?" she asked.

"Am I function—what?"

The ghost lady snorted again, louder this time, making sure I'd catch how much this delighted her.

"Do you have all of your faculties in order?" She peered down at me, still sprawled on the floor, trying to right myself.

I glowered at her, hoping she'd disappear and leave me in the silence I had grown accustomed to.

"Quite alright, thank you." There were no real thanks in my reply.

The woman rolled her eyes at me. "You're fine. Get up."

I did get up. Not to appease her, but so I could more easily get the hell out of there. I dusted myself off and made a big show of checking to make sure I was, *indeed,* fine.

"Everything seems to be in order. Now, who the hell are you? Where the hell am I? And why, also in the hell, am I talking to a ghost? Where are all the people? Am I dead?

Obviously, *you* are, but is everyone else dead, too? Have you seen any animals, or other people? How—"

"Oh, do shut up, girl!" she said. "Have you not the decency to ask one question at a time?"

I inwardly counted to ten and tried again.

"Look, I came here a couple weeks ago, and you are the first... *person*... I've seen. I have no idea how I got here. In fact, the last thing I remember, and you're going to think this is crazy, although, maybe not, since you're probably dead and all yourself—"

The ghost lady sighed and rolled her eyes even harder.

"Right. Sorry. That was rude." Deep breath. "My name is Amy Hart, and I am thoroughly confused. Can you help me? Please," I asked the last through gritted teeth.

The specter's mouth twisted, and she nodded.

"Yes, I can, if you'll shut your mouth long enough for me to do so."

I started to balk at her audacity, but she held up a translucent finger to stop my words before I vomited them at her.

"My name is Dowager Queen Helena, or, as you were getting ready to call me last we met, 'Grandmother Helena'."

"Wait, what—"

"Shush!" she said. "Will you never learn to respect your elders? Impudent child! I have half a mind to leave you here with no help at all!" She started to dissipate, but I reached out as if to physically restrain her and begged her to stay, apologizing until she did.

"As I was saying," she continued, "you were getting ready to call me 'Grandmother'. Last time you were here, centuries ago, mind you, you had just married my grandson, Prince Ibraxus III, or Brax, as you so brashly called him." She gave an unnecessary shudder.

"Brax..." I tested the name on my tongue and little sparks of electric current sizzled throughout my body. "I *married* him?"

Queen Helena nodded. "Indeed, you did, and you were murdered because of it. I always knew you'd be trouble for us, though, admittedly, you didn't deserve that."

"I was murdered? Again? Can everyone please just stop *killing* me? Jesus!"

"Who, dear?"

"Never mind," I said. "That's a much longer conversation than I have time to explain. So, okay, let me get this straight." I pressed my fingers into my temples to massage away the growing ache. "Okay. So, I've been here before, centuries ago, right? Which, ha, laughable, but okay. And I'd just married your grandson. A prince you say? Nice one. And then I was *murdered*! Great! Right so far?"

"That's the simple version, yes, but—"

"Why?"

"Why what, dear?"

"Why all of it! Why any of it? Why do people keep killing me? The hell did I do?"

"Besides ruining our kingdom and beguiling my grandson?"

I halted, blood boiling now in rage.

"That wasn't me! I've never been here before! I don't know you, your grandson, or how any of the weird, wacky, impossible things work here! Like, who the hell has a magic portal in their bathtub? I came out of a *throne* for Chrissakes! Look, I'm just a girl from Sebastopol who misses her home and her shop and her books and her coffee and... just..."

I couldn't take it anymore. I was drained. I sank back to the floor in an undignified heap.

Queen Helena paused in her nastiness to assess the situation. She floated down to "sit" beside me on the floor, which just ended up looking like she was a torso propped on the rotting floorboards. Truly disconcerting.

"You really don't remember," she said. "Unfortunate. That's going to make this much harder."

I tried to be helpful. "Well... I did see a cute little house with a waterfall outside. There was a painting on the wall with what looked like me and a man I couldn't fully make out. Could that have been... uh... Brax? Ibraxus?"

Her eyes locked on mine. "You've been home?"

I felt a jolt zing through me. "So that was my home! I knew it! I felt a strange pull to that place the second I saw it. I was only there for a short time, though, before being shot through that tub like a bat out of hell."

"Bat out of—? Never mind. How did you find yourself there?"

I explained everything that had happened to me, from leaving my house in Sebastopol, to getting shot, to dying, to—

floating through the universe, I guess? Then crashing on this planet and ending up in that very first pool of water that started me on this journey.

"Oh! And I'm a mermaid. Like, what? How am I a mermaid?"

Queen Helena scoffed. "Well, of course you're a mermaid. That's what got us all into this mess!"

I stared at her, mouth agape. "You keep saying this is my fault, but how could that possibly be true?"

Helena huffed a few times and swiped at her misty attire, opening and closing her mouth before deciding on a different tactic.

"Fine. Settle in. I'll explain what I can. Mind you, I don't have all the answers, but I will tell you what I knew before, and what I've managed to pick up over the years."

I arranged myself into a comfortable sitting position and gestured for her to proceed.

"At the dawn of our time, here on Callembria—"

"I'm sorry. Hold on," I said. "Where are we?"

Helena clenched her teeth. "The planet Callembria, dear. You do know your planets, do you not?"

"Well, I know about nine of them, ending with Pluto, and even that one I'm not entirely sure is even still considered a planet."

The myriad of emotional and physical irritation that configured across Helena's face in rapid succession was the most amused I'd been in weeks.

"That'll be a lesson for another day, then. For now, just know you are currently on the planet Callembria, sister planet to one called Earth—"

"That's where I'm from!" I felt like the kid in class that finally knew the right answer.

"Do stop interrupting me, or we'll never get anywhere!"

I shut my mouth and glared at her until she continued.

She made a useless gesture of tucking a sprig of silver curled hair behind her ear and smoothing non-existent wrinkles in her flowy grey dress. "Like I was saying, we are on Callembria, sister planet to Earth. Our planets were separated at birth, so to speak. During that time, a very small rip across the universe kept us connected on a microscopic level. This rip kept our planets tethered to one another and acts as a sort of 'soul recycler,' for lack of a better phrase. When you die on Callembria your soul has a chance to be reborn on Earth, and vice versa."

"Does it do that every time?"

She shook her head. "No. Sometimes a soul can choose to stay, if the pull is strong enough. Some never leave at all. Some never get the choice."

Helena's eyes glassed over, and she went quiet for a moment.

"Did you?" I asked softly.

She shook her head without moving her eyes. I could've almost sworn I'd seen tears there, which seems absurd, a ghost crying.

"I'm sorry," I said. How do you comfort a ghost? "I can't imagine."

"No, you cannot," she agreed, and pulled herself out of her thoughts. "Now, in the story of you: You say you came from Earth, and I believe you, as I haven't seen you in centuries. I haven't seen my grandson either, which means either you were stuck on Earth or stuck here somewhere under a spell, much like I suspect Ibraxus has been."

"A spell? Are there witches here?" I asked. I'd always had an affinity for witch lore.

"Magick here is plentiful but isn't exactly the wonderful thing you seem to think it is. The lucky ones can wield it but like in all things, nothing is as happy and wholesome as you'd like it to be. While there are some beautiful souls on this planet that use their abilities for the greater good, there are plenty who do not, and they take advantage wherever they can."

I started to feel uneasy.

"There are factions, you see. As you've already discovered, you are a mermaid. Your kind is from the sea. Your powers derive from the gemstones that come from the gemstone rings that crisscross this planet. Over time, debris fell from these rings and landed in the oceans. These super powered stones then seeped out their collective energy, creating life in the waters. The mermaids were born.

"Then came the first restless souls. Living in the water was wonderful, for a time, but these souls grew more and more agitated as the years went on. They took to exploring the land. It took many more years for their bodies to form the necessary adjustments for them to be able to develop things like legs, versus fins. I assume by now you've found you can phase your body between the two?"

I nodded, paying very close attention now.

"Good," she said, "I wouldn't know how to teach you that. After these mermaids became land dwellers, they discovered that not only had these gemstones graced their oceans, but they had deposited themselves on the land as well. They found there was another race of land-dwellers long before the mermaids found themselves out of the water, and there were many wars over the centuries for territories.

"That's when the dragons were born. Mermaids and land-dwellers both had the powers to shift forms: Mermaids to humans, and humans to the animals native to these lands. They soaked up all the energy from the gemstones they had available at the time, and, through fire and rage, the dragons were born. This new magick, now infused with angry shifters, created a race that was able to take to the skies and rain fire upon their enemies. The wars continued. Years. Perhaps centuries. Eventually, there were three factions: The mermaids, who generally kept to the seas with occasional land excursions allowed when granted by request. The humanoid shifters, who kept to the land unless they, too, had permission to go elsewhere. And finally, the dragons."

A shiver of excitement ran down my spine.

"The dragons did not have a home in either sea or land, so they had to go somewhere new. But where could they go?"

Queen Helena paused, waiting for me to answer. I blanched, then looked around the room as if one would pop out at me. Helena glanced purposefully at the small window she had first been standing in front of and jerked her head towards it, motioning for me to look outside. I took a deep breath to calm my sudden nerves and approached the glass.

At first, all I could see was a sapphire sky. Dark, resembling night, with a sea of stars blinking their salutations. That's when I realized that the stars were entirely too close to us, and this was not what I thought it was originally.

"Where are we?" I asked.

"Look down," she replied.

Deep breath in.

Deep breath out.

I looked down and saw the world below us, surrounded by crisscrossing gemstone rings, like Saturn got drunk and replicated itself at a 90-degree angle. In a sudden panic, I flung myself to the wall on the far side of the room, somehow scared that I'd find a way to go tumbling through the window I couldn't possibly fit through.

Helena continued. "Welcome to Dragon Moon. With no home to call our own, we took to the skies until we found suitable accommodations. We are still a part of Callembria's atmosphere, so we consider ourselves a part of this planet. But, as you can see, we hover over this planet much like a moon might, just smaller and much, much closer. We founded and colonized it, then built this castle as its royal base."

I let that sink in. "So, you're, like, an actual dragon."

"Well, I was, at one time, able to shift my form into a dragoness, yes, though I was never a full-blooded dragon. I just had a high dragon gene count, so I was able to go back and forth, much like Ibraxus and his father before him. Some dragons decide to stay in their dragon forms permanently, others prefer the human land-dwelling life and forsake the skies for the lands. They either rarely turn because their body no longer knows how, or they can't turn at all because their family line has been too far removed from dragon life. They can get stuck in dragon or human form. Ibraxus's best friend Ifyrus, for example, had his heart broken so badly that he shut himself off from the world and willed his body to stay dragon, so that's what he remains. He chose that life, and so could others, if they wished. It's not entirely uncommon to do so."

I tried to take it all in, but I was starting to get a major headache. This was too much crazy to handle.

"So, where is Brax now?" I asked. "You said something about a spell?"

She gave a blip of a spirit shrug. "Who knows? Every bit of information I've had over the years, I've sent men to go check out. They either come up empty or disappear entirely. Dead, most likely. I imagine Ruskin is keeping him from me on purpose, the wretch."

"I'm sorry, Ruskin?"

Helena looked cross that I didn't know who she meant and launched into a furied explanation.

"Ruskin! *King* Ruskin? King Ruskin, the Usurper? Ruskin the Wretch! The Foul One! The—"

"Yikes! Fine! He's a royal pain in the ass, I get it! But what's he got to do with any of this?"

The Dowager struggled to compose herself enough to say, "He's. Your. Ex. Betrothed. Your *murderer*."

My breath caught, and my heart slammed against my chest.

"Wait, *what*?"

"Yes. You were betrothed to a man who could've given you whatever you needed, and instead, you chose my grandson. While I love my grandson and understand his appeal, your mistakes cost him his life, as well as yours, and Ruskin went mad. He has waged war on this world for centuries, sometimes winning, sometimes losing, but always causing fear and panic. And, yes, I *do* blame you."

I took a breath to argue, but she stopped me with a pointed finger.

"Not a word! I understand this feels new to you, but it's something we've had to live with for far too long, and I can't just dismiss it because you 'don't remember'. However, you can make it up to me, to us, to everyone. You can go find my grandson. With you breaking part one of the spell, he should be free by now, but he isn't here, which means you need to go find him. I cannot leave this place, or I'd do it myself. Bring him home so he can resume his kingly duties, restore our world to its former glory, and bring down Ruskin. Nobody else has ever been able to do it, and I firmly believe that, in a fair fight, Ibraxus would decimate that weasel!"

"But, how—?"

Helena motioned for me to follow her. "This way. This was Ibraxus's room, when he was here. There is a Crannie that goes from his mirrored bed frame to the one on your island. It should spit you out back home and you can swim to the mainland back in your mermaid form. I will give you a map that shows you the outpost where you first met. I can't be sure what he will remember himself, or if he will go there at all, but the two of you spent a lot of time together there before getting assigned to your island, so it's possible he could show up there. Maybe someone there knows where he might be, if he's not."

She floated over to an old map under a thin plate of glass on a table in Brax's room.

"That spot marked with a red X is where the outpost is. Start there. There's a tavern there that he would frequent with Ifyrus that could be a likely place to check out. But be careful! We don't know if Ruskin has spies there, or if he's aware that you've returned. It could be very dangerous, but we have no choice. You must go, and you must act quickly! If he finds you, it could be disastrous all over again."

I swallowed the large lump that had formed in my throat. This was too much.

"How am I supposed to do this?" I asked.

"You use your considerable power! You do everything you possibly can! You don't waste a single opportunity to right the wrongs you did, and you shove off your pity party long enough to fetch my grandson and return the Dragon King to his world! Oh, and one more thing: Hide those damned purple eyes of yours! It's like a bright, shining beacon of 'Here I am!'"

I closed my eyes immediately. I tried to will them back to the green I had when I was on Earth, not knowing if I was even able to do so.

After a minute of harsh squinting, I heard a ghostly sigh above me.

"Put your hands over your eyes. Both of them."

I did as she bade.

"Now, try again."

I took a deep breath, felt warmth from my hands travel towards my eyes, and when I felt everything start to tingle, I whispered, "Green."

"Now, get going. There's not a moment to lose."

And, with that, she promptly shoved me through the looking glass.

CHAPTER THIRTEEN: MIAWAE'S SURPRISE

Queen Miawae of Gallanor was the greatest Seer this planet had seen in centuries. Her predictions ranged from the outcome of wars in neighboring kingdoms (which she would use her Gift to assist where she could), all the way down to simply knowing how long a marriage would last (though she had enough sense to not share this news with any happy newlyweds). Sometimes, however, if she knew there was a problem that was, say, in need of a physical healing, she might slap a few Meya-Meya roots in the traditional floral wedding basket, "For a long and happy life together."

There were many benefits to being a Seer, but there was also a price for knowing these things. It didn't work on a whim most days, so trying to force an answer could prove difficult, if not impossible. Those days were the hardest— the ones where somebody needed an answer, but she couldn't give one. Usually, those would result in death or despair of the asker. Miawae hated those the most, feeling the emotional, and sometimes physical, aspects of every one of those outcomes. She'd tried many times over the years to make it work, to save and spare the lives of her kingdom, but the few times she had been successful, she nearly died. As a result, she'd been bedridden for weeks. Each time took longer to recover, so she was forced to either quit that tactic, or lose herself in the process.

Amongst all her predictions, she'd never once witnessed her own passing. But after piecing together a vision she'd had when she touched Cyndol's hand in her sitting room, she was able to See what was coming. She'd Seen the end.

How to prepare?

A knock sounded at her sitting room door.

"Come!" she said.

"Visitor for you, Majesty. A young Colt, I believe," said her guard, Avery.

Miawae smiled warmly and bid him enter.

Avery ushered a small, shaggy boy about eight or nine years old into the sitting room and sat him down opposite the queen before taking his leave.

Miawae peered at the child on her couch for a full minute before speaking.

"So... Colt, is it?" she asked.

He nodded, eyes on the floor.

"How is your day going? Nice outside?"

Colt nodded again, but this time she saw his eyes peek curiously out from under the mane of mahogany hair hiding his face.

"Would you care for something to eat or drink? We have plenty. Whatever you'd like."

Colt's stomach growled loudly in the quiet chamber.

Miawae chuckled and rang a bell on the side table. Avery reentered the room.

"Yes, Majesty?"

Miawae focused her attention on the boy in front of her and said, "Well? What would you like, Colt?"

Colt fidgeted for a moment before whispering, "Do you have sweets?"

Miawae and Avery shared a grin.

"I know just the thing! Avery, bring the leftover treats from last night's party, would you?"

Avery bowed and left to retrieve the snacks from the festival. When he returned, he placed a large platter on the table between them. It held pitchers of cool water, milk, and a sweet cider that had been brewed from the neighboring apple orchards. There was also a large smattering of some tasty looking treats.

Colt's eyes grew three times their normal size. He hastily grabbed fistfuls of cakes, cookies, and anything else he could reach to stuff in his face. When Miawae laughed, he realized his mistake and sat back sheepishly, dropping the mangled treats back to the platter and wiped his mouth with the sleeve of his dusty, once-white linen shirt.

"Sorry, Your Majesty," he said. "I didn't mean to wreck your food."

"Nonsense!" she said. "Eat as much as you like, dear. It's happy food and *should* be enjoyed with gusto!"

Colt let his body sink back into the sofa, more at ease now than when he first arrived.

"Now, Colt, please tell me what brings you to my home on this fine day."

Colt took a long swallow of cider, wiped his face with his sleeve again, and placed the cup on the table. With his other hand, he slowly reached into his left side trouser pocket and pulled out the golden necklace piece he'd found in the woods. He placed it gingerly on the table next to his cup.

Miawae's intake of breath was controlled, but only due to constant practice. This was not the first time she had seen this piece of jewelry. Though it was, in fact, the first time she had seen it outside of pictures. It was her ancestors that crafted it to begin with. Stories about this necklace had been handed down through the ages to all of her family line, the leaders especially. This necklace was a key, but there were parts missing.

"Where—" she said, then cleared her throat. "Where did you find this?"

Colt shifted in his seat and started playing with his dirty fingernails, the mane of unkempt hair back in his face. He gave a small shrug but offered no words in reply.

Miawae tried again. "Did someone give this to you?"

He shook his head, eyes still on his hands.

"Did you steal it?"

His face shot up in a panic to meet her direct gaze.

"No! I would never steal!"

Miawae laughed. "Finally! A response!"

Colt blushed but smiled back.

"I found it in the woods. It was just sitting there in the shrubs. Nobody was there, and I thought it looked lonely out there all by itself. So, I took it home. I'm sorry if I caused any trouble. My parents said I had to bring it to you right away, that it didn't belong to me." He dipped his head again but kept his eyes on the queen's face. "Am I? In trouble, I mean?"

Miawae shook her head. "No, child, you are not in trouble. Thank you for bringing this to me." She gestured at the necklace fragment. "May I?"

Colt nodded and Miawae lifted the necklace from the table. As soon as it touched her hand, another vision set upon her. She was shown a heartbreaking future in which this little boy would play a part. She sighed heavily and put the necklace back down.

"Colt," she said, "how would you like to do me a favor?"

Colt's eyes lit up as he sensed an adventure was about to begin.

CHAPTER FOURTEEN: KAVEA'S DISAPPOINTMENT

Kavea stood there in the ruined cavern, shivering in both cold and despair. She just couldn't believe it. How could he just fly off like that? After all she's done to look after him for so long, making sure to re-route anyone who got too close and might discover who was hidden here. And there was a dragon here the whole time? She thought they'd either disappeared or gone extinct. To her limited knowledge, there hadn't been a dragon sighting in many years. Last she heard from her father, the humans and land-shifters defeated the dragons and mermaids, sending both parties back to their homes, the mermaids to the sea, and the dragons to the sky.

From her books, she knew there had been a mighty war, and that the dragon lord, Ibraxus, had fallen. Her instinct told her that her frozen mystery man *was* that fallen lord, and it seems she was right! What could this mean for the world now that he and his dragon were back? She fervently wished that he'd taken her with him. What she wouldn't give to be able to fly on the back of a dragon.

"Kavea!" Her guard's voice echoed from the entrance of the demolished cave. "Are you in there? Are you hurt? Kavea! Answer me! Kavea!"

Kavea grimaced. There was no getting out of this just yet. She'd have to come up with a Plan B once she was able to be alone again. She took one last look at the avalanche of awful and yelled back, "In here! I'm alright, and I'm coming out!"

She gingerly stepped around rocks and debris sticking out from the icy clumps. When she got herself back to where her guard, Maxim, was standing, he aimed a furious stare directly at her face so as to be unmissable in his fear and anger. Kavea huffed and walked to his side. He grabbed her roughly around her upper right arm and turned her quickly around, yanking her gruffly beside him back toward home.

"Owww!" she said. "You're hurting me! Stop!"

Maxim didn't even bother to look at her when he said, "Maybe if you'd stop running away every time I take my eyes off you for two seconds, I would trust you to come along at your own pace. But as we seem to keep failing at this simple communication, you're going to be placed under house arrest until your father returns to deal with you directly."

"But—"

"And what did you do to that cavern, huh? You could've seriously gotten yourself killed, which would have certainly gotten *me* killed! Did you think about that, princess? No. Of course not. Why would you think of anyone but yourself? Why would you care about a man who is trying to provide for his family? Why would you care if…"

Kavea tuned him out as he continued his litany of transgressions, opting instead to plan her next escape once she was settled back inside. There was no possible scenario in which she would patiently await the return of her father like her mother had done— staying home as the life drained out of her like a wilting carrot. Her mother was once strong, full of life and color, but slowly became shriveled and weak, checked out of this life. As much as she loved her mother, to Kavea, that was a fate worse than death. She simply couldn't do it. But how to get out of here?

CHAPTER FIFTEEN: CYNDOL'S TOUR OF GALLANOR

A loud clamoring outside of Cyndol's treehouse woke her with a start.

"Eeeeeee!" screeched Kit as Cyndol's covers flung him to the floor.

A knock sounded at the door, and Kit darted under the bed.

"Uh, just a minute!" Cyndol said. She hurriedly threw a blanket around herself, staving off the morning's chill, and jumped up to open the door.

At her doorstep was the woman from last night, Evony. Behind her were two different guardsmen with a wooden trolley on wooden wheels, carrying a small buffet. Cyndol could see steam rising from the teapot and smell fried meats wafting from under the linen cloth atop the plates. Her mouth began to water, and her stomach cried its appreciation.

"Good morning, child. The king and queen send their salutations, as well as some breakfast for you and your—well..." she inclined her head toward the bed, somehow knowing Kit was underneath it.

Cyndol opened her mouth to deny it, but Evony just winked and continued speaking.

"Queen Miawae has asked for you to wait to leave until she can return and speak with you once more. She had to run an errand this morning, but she should be back in a few hours' time, if you're willing to wait and enjoy a tour of the kingdom?"

Cyndol hadn't thought to waste any time, but as she had only seen kindness from Queen Miawae thus far and was grateful for her help and hospitality, she agreed. She cautiously reached for some type of pastry on the buffet board.

"Bobbleberry," Evony said. "My favorite." She gestured for the guardsmen to leave the cart in Cyndol's dinette area and then they took their leave.

Cyndol closed the door and returned to the bed, grabbing more treats from the buffet server.

Kit poked his head out from under the bed.

"Are they gone?"

"Yes," said Cyndol with a wry smile, "but I think you've been discovered."

Kit's fur bristled. "What? How could that be? I was so careful!"

Cyndol hoisted him off the floor and plopped him on the bed beside her.

"If it helps, I don't think it was you that led them to discover your presence. These people, they—" Cyndol struggled to find the right words. "They seem to almost exude... I don't know, magick, maybe? Definitely something going on. But I think the queen truly wants to help. I guess I'll see when she gets back."

She lifted the remaining linen napkins from the serving plates to see what kinds of deliciousness they'd been graced with. Along with the starfish-shaped bobbleberry pastries with mounds of icing drizzled atop, were plates of still-steaming fried meats, spiced eggs, a bowl of wild berries with sugar crystals sparkling along the top, and a teapot of Callamay tea. She was in bliss, especially with the bobbleberry treat, which she decided was similar to huckleberry, but sweeter.

Kit sniffed the whole platter, then dragged a few pieces of meat to the ground. Cyndol scolded him and put his floor-meats on an empty plate, then plunked him back down beside her.

As the pair happily munched on the most extravagant breakfast either of them had ever had, they considered their next steps.

"Evony offered a tour. Should we take it?"

Kit considered that for a moment before saying, with a very full mouth, "Well, does it sound like we have a choice? Like, was it—" he swallowed and did his best imitation of a female voice, "Please do accept our generous offer of help and a tour before we assist you in your endeavors?" Back to his normal voice, he said, "Or was it more—" (back to female voice) "You will take this tour with us, or *else*…" He bared his fangs in a growling fashion.

Cyndol couldn't help but laugh.

"What? What's so funny?"

She managed to quiet her laughter and said, "You're right. I'm sorry. We don't know these people or what they're really about. But I think it's safe to say, if they really wanted to hurt us, they would have done it by now."

Kit didn't seem fully convinced but, as they needed help, he was willing to see where this led.

A little while later, after they had finished eating and making themselves presentable, there was another knock at the door. Cyndol assumed it was alerting them to their tour guide. But as she opened the door, expecting to see Evony, she was instead greeted by Miawae's granddaughter and her beautifully scowling visage.

"Oh!" said Cyndol, partly out of surprise, but also out of fear. This young girl, only a handful of years older than she, had an intensity about her that was definitely larger than her small frame suggested.

Princess Kiara cleared her throat and rolled her eyes, finally landing on Cyndol's gaze. "I'm here on behalf of my grandmother, the queen. I am to show you around our village while we await her return. Do you agree to the tour? Or would you rather wait here with your... friend?"

She turned her grimace on Kit, who stuck his tongue out at her. She looked momentarily surprised, then gave one quick laugh before returning the gesture. Kit gave a soft bark back.

Cyndol found her voice enough to say they would love a tour, so the small group went outside to start their jaunt through the woods.

What Cyndol saw took her breath away. This place looked vastly different in the daylight. While it didn't have the same claustrophobic darkness and dancing fire displays as it did the night before, the daylight revealed a vibrancy of color scattered throughout the forest. Pinpricks of orange, yellow, teal, and mauve bounced joyously in the shrubbery, children trying their best to catch the sparks before they disappeared. And, oh, how these trees seemed to breathe! Every inch of plant life appeared sentient somehow, as if just waiting to start a conversation. Even the animals that hopped, flew, or cruised by them seemed content to exist in this place.

Also, to Cyndol's delight, she saw this community was nestled nicely underneath The Gemstone Belts which, she was sure now, lent them their magickal abilities.

She hadn't felt at ease like this since being home. Kit was enjoying himself as well, by the looks of it. There were several times he took off to chase one critter or another, though never returning with anything that he had caught, much to her relief. She couldn't imagine how her captor (sorry, *tour guide*) would react if Kit ate one of her woodland friends in front of her.

Cyndol didn't mean to think unkind thoughts about Kiara. She just couldn't figure out why she felt such hostility from her.

"So…" Cyndol cleared her throat and attempted to converse with the perturbed princess. "What's it like being royalty?"

Kiara's face hardened even more, if that was possible.

"Peachy." Her pace never slowed.

Cyndol sighed. Why was this so difficult?

"Did I do something to upset you?" she asked.

Kiara came to a sudden stop and got right up in her face.

"Why would I waste my time thinking about you? Don't you think I have other things to worry about?"

Cyndol took a step backward and put her hands up in a show of peace.

"I'm sorry. I didn't mean to assume. It's just that... Well, you're a bit intense, and I'm not used to that. I'm sorry if I offended you."

Kiara's probing eyes bored into Cyndol's as she assessed the younger girl in front of her. When she seemed satisfied by what she saw, she relented and continued walking.

"You interrupted our Celebration of The Dead yesterday."

"I'm so sorry! I didn't mean to—"

"Do not interrupt me."

Cyndol shut her mouth and Kit stuck to her side, on alert to strike if things got ugly.

The princess motioned her towards a nearby bench made up of active tree roots, as most of the structures in the village were. They sat down, Cyndol watching Kiara and Kiara watching the village, not meeting Cyndol's gaze this time.

Taking a deep breath, Kiara said, "It was the anniversary of my parents' death. They lost a battle with King Ruskin and never came home." The evil king's name was spit with malevolence. "It's been seven years now. This was the first year my sister ever missed."

"Sister?"

Kiara nodded. "Davina. She's the elder. She was next in line to rule after my grandparents passed on, as my parents are no longer here to do so. But, when Davina came of age, she got cocky and went to confront Ruskin about killing our parents and somehow fell under his spell instead. She has been with him ever since."

Cyndol gasped. "That's horrible! I'm so sorry!"

Kiara faced her again. "I don't need your pity; I need your allegiance. There are dark forces out there in this world and it will be up to me and my people to put a stop to them. But, in order to do that, I need to know who would be willing to fight for me, for us. You see, I'm now next in line for the throne and I'm doing my best to learn everything I can as fast as possible. I need to know I have allies to help me along the way, as there is no chance I can do this on my own. I need the help of my family, my friends, and my people."

Cyndol was perplexed. "What could you possibly need me for?"

Kiara looked pointedly at Kit. "Talk with foxes much, do you?"

Cyndol's face bunched up in confusion. "Well, I admit, that's been a recent talent. Turns out, they have a lot to say."

Kit gave a foxy chuckle.

"Did you know that it's not normal to be able to do that?" Kiara asked.

Cyndol looked at Kit, but Kit just yawned in reply.

"Can you do it?"

Kiara flinched. "Of *course* not!" she said. "I mean, I can talk *to* them, just never *with* them." She chanced a look at Kit to make sure she couldn't hear him, then shook her head as if to shake away the stupidity of trying. "I could use someone like you. Imagine what we could learn from conversing with animals."

Cyndol chewed on that thought for a moment. She leaned down to Kit's ears and said, "Is there anything we can learn from you?"

Kit stuck his tickly snout close to Cyndol's ear and, after a moment, Cyndol laughed.

"What? What did he say?" Kiara asked.

Cyndol composed herself and said, "He said, 'Please tell the princess I can't wait to chew up her shoes when she's not looking.'"

With an agitated huff, the princess got back up and resumed walking along their original path. "Come!" she said.

So, they did.

As they walked along in silence, each pondered their own problems and tried to decide what the best course of action would be. Kiara made the decision to find out more about her new mysterious friend here. She did not want anything else to take her by surprise.

"My grandmother says you came from one of the sandy coastal regions."

Cyndol nodded and said, "Yes. Cavar. I lived there my whole life. This is my first time away from home."

Kiara was quiet a moment before asking, "How did you manage to escape? My grandmother said you were fleeing from men that were burning your village and trapped you on a cliff, but I didn't get all the details."

Cyndol bit her lip, not answering right away. Instead, she chose to look off into the distance, twisting her fingers and picking at her nails. She watched the villagers go about their daily business, doing laundry, tending their gardens and whatever else they happened to be doing while outside on this lovely day.

"Well…" she replied after a few minutes of silence, "I think it was magick."

Kiara's head swung slowly as she gave her the side-eye. "Oh?"

Cyndol nodded again, feeling more confident without a rebuttal from the other girl.

"Yes. See, I'm not magickal. Never have been, never will be. I know some people were lucky enough to be born with magick, but I've only ever met a few of them in my life, and I'd never really experienced it until that day. Unless, of course, you count talking to Kit."

"Of course," Kiara said. "So, why do you think it was magick, then?"

Cyndol shrugged and said, "How many people do *you* know that can summon a bubble around themselves at will?"

Kiara gave a bark of laughter and said, "Fair enough. The only ones I know that can do that do indeed have magick. But it begs the question, who cast the magick? You say it wasn't you but, if not you, then who? Was there anyone else with you when you went off that cliff?"

Cyndol's face scrunched in thought. "The only people up there besides me were the men who came after me. It was still early in the morning, and everyone else was asleep in their beds, or just starting their day as usual."

Kiara exchanged a pointed look with one of her guardsmen and he wandered off ahead of them, giving them some space. Kit was off chasing pink and purple butterflies that had wandered across their path, so this left the two girls alone on the cliffside, overlooking the beautiful flowing river that cut through the kingdom. Kiara came to an abrupt halt directly in front of Cyndol.

"Hey! What—" Cyndol said, almost crashing into the princess.

"Shh!" Kiara hissed. "I'm going to try something, and I need you to trust me, okay?"

Cyndol tensed and furrowed her brows. "Trust you? How—"

"Shh!" Kiara hissed again. "Trust me! Now," she put her hands on Cyndol's small shoulders and looked her straight in the eyes. "Are you certain that nobody else was with you that morning except for those men?"

Cyndol nodded, anxiety brewing.

Kiara nodded along with her.

And promptly hurled her off the cliff into the swiftly moving waters below.

Cyndol screamed so loud she thought her vocal cords were ripping, and Kit burst out of the nearby brush in time to see her go over the edge. In a rage, he furiously bit Kiara's ankles and tried to take her down.

"Wait, no! Oww! Look!" She pointed to the spot in the river where a giant bubble was bobbing peacefully in the current toward the guard shack along the riverbank.

Kit stopped his gnashing and looked over the side. To his relief, he saw exactly what the princess pointed to: His friend, safe and sound, though cursing up a storm in her own little bubble. He breathed a sigh of relief and turned his livid features on Kiara.

"Oh, don't look at me like that, she's fine! In fact, they're bringing her up now. Go and see."

She pointed to her guards below. They'd caught Cyndol and her bubble as it made its way to them and were loading her into the contraption they used to get to their stations from above, an elevator of sorts. The bubble popped and freed its captive. Cyndol continued her litany of obscenities the entire ride back up.

"...and *another* thing!" she said upon seeing Kiara's smirking face when she exited the platform.

"You are quite alright, I take it?" the princess asked, her voice laced with a smugness that Cyndol couldn't *wait* to smack off of there!

"Quite al— you threw me *in a river*! Of *course* I'm not alright! I'm—"

"Perfectly fine, yes. Tell me again how you don't have any magick." She peered at Cyndol's bone dry clothing. "Hmm. Not even the slightest bit wet." Kiara continued walking along the pathway as if Cyndol's whole world hadn't just imploded.

Cyndol gaped at her as she walked away calmly. Kit sat loyally next to her feet, waiting for a command after sniffing to make sure that she was, in fact, alright.

Cyndol found her footing and went after her.

"Are you saying that... *I* have magick?"

Kiara threw her words over her shoulder. "How many people do you know that can summon a bubble around themselves at will?"

Cyndol stopped walking and lost all ability to stand, landing ungracefully on her rump. Kit immediately tucked his head under her arm.

When Kiara noticed she hadn't gotten a reply, she turned around and saw the Cyndol-Kit heap looking deflated on the forest floor. She gave a massive sigh, steeled her shoulders, and approached the pity-pile.

Cyndol's slackened jaw was locked in place, her misty eyes lacking any hint of their former fire. Kiara was sure her grandmother would be adding extra hours to her etiquette training for this. She composed what she hoped was an empathetic face and quietly sat down next to Cyndol. Kit peeked his head out from under her arm and growled at the princess.

"You're right," Kiara said to Kit, "I absolutely deserve that. It was reckless of me to endanger the life of your— uh... friend? Yes. Your friend. I shouldn't have done that. But to be fair, now we know, don't we?"

Cyndol blinked but said nothing, silent tears pouring down her cheeks.

Kiara grew increasingly uncomfortable with the girl's sudden shift of energy. She shifted her leg out to steady herself and asked, "Were, uh, either of your parents magickal?"

Cyndol shrugged noncommittally.

"Any family members do anything... different?"

Another shrug. "Neighbors—?"

"*NO!*" Cyndol burst at top volume, slamming her eyes shut as if to block out the world.

The force of her scream propelled people, plants, and paraphernalia ten feet in either direction. A new, larger bubble now formed around Cyndol and Kit, who was now clinging desperately by his claws to the belt holding up Cyndol's trousers.

The guardsmen nearby came rushing toward them, weapons poised and ready to take action. Kiara waved them back and ordered them to stand down. They relented, but just barely, hovering close without advancing.

Kiara maintained eye contact with Cyndol now, her body trembling, trying to come to terms with how greatly she underestimated this child. Knowing that what happened next could determine what fate befell the girl, she knew she had to get her calm and make her feel safe again.

"Cyndol," Kiara said, "you have my sincerest apologies. I was out of line. You are safe here, I won't let anyone hurt you, me included. My test was not meant to put you in harm's way, but to answer a question that I believe we now have an answer to, yes? I won't push you further without your permission. You have my word. You are safe. In fact, it's probably time to get back to the village for some food and rest. Perhaps by then my grandmother will be ready to see you. Does that sound good to you?"

Cyndol's eyes began to reclaim their usual alertness, and Kiara could see her take in the magnitude of what she'd done.

"What— what have I—?"

Kiara held her hands up in a deescalating gesture and said, "No, no, it's okay. No one is hurt, everything's fine. You're okay and we're okay, okay?"

Cyndol nodded weakly and allowed her bubble to drop. Kiara took her gently by the arm and led her back the way they came.

Cyndol didn't say much on the return journey. Neither did Kiara. But there seemed to be the start of an understanding between them. Cyndol could see how enormous this woodsy empire was and how many people Kiara had to worry about, and Kiara could see what her grandmother had seen at the start: This girl could be the answer to what they were looking for. That kind of power in someone so young could be harnessed into doing all kinds of great and powerful things. They needed to make sure she did not fall into the wrong hands.

Once they arrived back in the village proper, Cyndol seemed to come back to herself, much to the relief of everyone around her. Kit stayed fixed to her side with no more chasing of interesting creatures.

"Thank you for the tour," Cyndol said quietly to Kiara upon their return.

Kiara gave the girl a small, closed smile and stopped at Miawae's doorstep.

"It was… enlightening." She knocked on the door and took her leave.

"Come!"

Cyndol felt weird just barging on in, but as there was no guard standing there to open the door *for* her, she obliged and twisted the knob.

"Cyndol! Thank you so much for staying to see me again before you departed. I trust you had a pleasant day?" Miawae said.

Cyndol nodded, and when she saw Kit make no move to answer, she gave him a shove with her foot. Kit rolled his eyes and went to sit next to the queen, who gave his head a scratch. He didn't mean to, but Kit purred contentedly.

"Wonderful. Tea?"

CHAPTER SIXTEEN: IBRAXUS RETURNS HOME

The first place Ibraxus and Ifyrus flew was Dragon Moon. The urgency Brax felt at seeing his family was overwhelming. The last time he had seen them was his on Wedding Day, and much had happened since then. He needed them after that horrible, life-altering day.

Brax and Ifyrus braced for landing. When they got closer, Brax noticed the city and its large castle were in shambles. The entire moon, in fact, was hauntingly quiet. His heart began to beat faster.

Normally, you'd see tons of dragons out and about at this hour, along with shifters and other visitors that could manage the climate and high altitude. But, at this moment, there was absolutely no one in sight. Goosebumps dotted his flesh and beads of sweat formed on his temples.

It dawned on Brax that the home he returned to was no longer the rich, thriving epicenter of the Dragondom he once knew. Instead, what he found was a crumbling ancient society covered in dust and disarray.

He cautiously guided Ifyrus to the giant stone doorway that led to his family's castle.

"Mother?" Brax called out as they landed. "Father? Hello? Guards? Anybody?"

He jumped off and approached the door. Nobody was there. He tried his luck at opening it himself and the door gave full purchase, save for the creak as it ground across the floor.

This door was *always* locked and guarded. Now his palms were sweating. Without further hesitation, he bolted through the doorway, leaving Ifyrus to fend for himself.

"Mother? Father? Somebody, *please!*"

He ran down the hallways.

"Father! Mother! Anybody!"

But there was no one there to answer him, no one there to welcome the lord back to his kingdom in the sky, hanging high above Callembria.

Gone. They were all gone.

He ran into the Great Hall. Nothing.

He bolted into the kitchens. No one.

He crashed through door after door, wing after wing.

Nothing.

Nothing.

Alone.

He was utterly and completely alone.

Brax felt the realization seep deep into the marrow of his bones and he was suddenly very heavy. He managed to drag himself to the aging jasper throne and slumped into the grooves his bottom had left there seemingly just a few days ago.

"They're all gone," he whispered.

Ifyrus let out an eerie keening somewhere on the parapets, and Brax knew that the truth had hit him, too. Grief came in fast and furious, clenching its fist around his heart. He felt as if the wind had been knocked from his lungs and taking a full breath was impossible. Molten tears cascaded in salty unison down his face until he felt an all-consuming despair.

"Well, that's no way for royalty to act now, is it?" came the familiar chiding of his beloved, though cantankerous, grandmother.

Brax fairly flew off his chair, startled as he was!

"Grandmother!" He jerked his head around this way and that until he located her ghostly form on the chandelier above him.

"What are you doing way up there?" he cried. "And... are you... *see-through?*"

"I'm dead, you dunce, long ago, and your blubbering isn't going to change that fact! Now, do I have your attention so we can quickly get down to business? Or would you like to continue wailing about like an infant?"

Brax felt his soul shrink at her tone, like he had when he was a boy. He dried his tears and straightened his shoulders.

"My apologies. Please. Explain."

The former Queen Helena floated down from her perch to land silently on the steps by his side.

"Brace yourself, boy, you're in for a doozy."

Brax did as she commanded, getting as comfortable as he could on this dusty old throne, and fixed his gaze on her translucent face.

Helena nodded and began.

"Firstly, I would like to welcome you home, grandson. Your presence has been deeply missed. I don't know what you remember, but I will tell you what *I* do. You have been gone for two hundred years."

Brax let out a guffaw, but Helena scowled back at him.

"You cannot be serious."

"I am, and I'm not done! Why won't anyone let me speak and trust my words? I used to rule this kingdom, you know! I'm not just some poor old woman with no wits about her!"

"Again, my apolo—wait. Who else wouldn't let you speak?"

Helena threw her arms in the air and said, "Amaryah! But that's not the point—"

Brax sprang up from his chair. "What? She was here? When?" He tried to grasp her shoulders, forgetting she was a ghost, and promptly fell forward, bonking his head on the corner of the throne's footstool, earning himself a nice bump in the process.

"Serves you right, you impatient imbecile! Now, pay attention and heed my words! You have missed much while you were away."

Brax rubbed his aching skull and sat down on the steps, grinding his teeth to keep fear and anger in check.

"Now," Helena said, "you've been gone for centuries. Most of the world believes you perished in a fight with Ruskin. Do you recall that day?"

Brax's heart clenched. He nodded, a single tear welling in his eye as he brought back the memory of that fateful day.

"Good! That will save us some time. After the fight, Ruskin took your crown and added it to his own, fusing them together and declaring himself King of Land and Sky. There are others still in power in other regions, but they all fall under his Ultimate Rule. That is, all except those of the Sea. He has been at war with the Merpeople since the death of Amaryah, trying to gain enough power to take over there as well. But their numbers are too great and no land magick can hold up long in the water. As I'm sure you already know, they have their own magick that prevents exactly that. He still holds a grudge against them, and *you* for stealing Amaryah away from him."

"She was never officially his to begin with!"

"Be that as it may," she said, "his Royal Arseness sees it quite differently. When Amaryah was no longer an option, I believe he married the next available sister instead. No one has seen her for a long time either, exacerbating the feud. What few spies I have left have not been able to gather much information."

Brax sat back with a huff. What he thought was just a short amount of time turned out to be more than several human lifetimes. He had to let all of this new information sink in.

"You said Amaryah was here. What did you mean by that? Amaryah died, Grandmother. I saw it happen." He choked back a sob and promised himself a good cry later when his grandmother was no longer in earshot.

"I'm aware," she said. "She came back."

"Came back? How?"

"How should I know?" Helena forcefully threw her arms to the side. "I hadn't seen her since the day you two left and then, *WHOOSH*! Here she comes, naked as a newborn, flying ass over teakettle from that very throne you are currently perched upon! I followed her around the castle for a little bit, trying to decide if it was really her or not, and when I saw that it was, I approached her and told her how to wake you from your spell. And, judging by the fact that you're standing here before me, it worked. You're welcome."

Helena sat back on a tuft of nothing, arms folded over her chest, her mouth pulled in a smug fashion.

"How did you know how to break the curse?" Brax asked.

"I've picked up a thing or two from my spies, never you mind. What matters is that you're here now and you can reclaim your birthright as King of The Dragons and all of Dragon Moon and Sky. See how Ruskin likes *that*!"

"But, Grandmother, if Amaryah came here and broke the curse, where is she now?" Brax's fear began to mount even higher, combining dangerously with hope.

Helena's smirk fell from her face.

"Well, now, I couldn't have known that spell would work as well as it did, and I had no way of knowing if you'd be in your right mind when you came back!"

"Grandmother..." Brax growled in warning.

"She's fine."

"Grandmother!"

Helena twisted her ghostly shawl in her fingers, face hardened in stone.

"I sent her off to find you and bring you home."

Ibraxus leapt up from his throne and got right in her face, eyes blazing.

"When." Not a question. A demand.

"Earlier today," she said.

"Where." Another demand.

"I don't know where she's gotten off to, but I sent her through the Crannie in your bedroom."

Brax let out a sigh, nostrils flaring as he exhaled plumes of smoke. Crannies. He hated having to use them. They were helpful, but he preferred to fly rather than being teleported from place to place. He was a dragon! These Crannies... there was no freedom to them, just rapid immediacy and a dizzying headache that made him nauseous. Amaryah used to love them, being as she couldn't fly and loved the feeling of sliding into oblivion. There were only a few known Crannies in the entire world, though new ones would pop up from time to time. The only ones that concerned him were the two connected to his kingdom. One that ran from Amaryah's bath to his throne (because why would anybody ever check those two very personal places for a portal?) and the one that ran from the mirror in his bed's headboard to the mirror in Amaryah's.

At least he knew where she started. He could trace her from there.

"Thank you, Grandmother, but I believe it's time for me to go hunting."

With that, he called to Ifyrus, packed some provisions, and set out to find his wife.

CHAPTER SEVENTEEN: RUSKIN REQUIRES DAVINA

King Ruskin sat on his throne, chewing his fingernails to the quick. It had been three days since he'd gotten the last report from his personal guardsmen. He trusted them to get done the jobs that required the most effort and they hadn't let him down yet.

However, three days with no information was unacceptable. Ruskin took one last vicious bite of his nail, ripping it halfway down his finger and causing a stream of blood to paint his throne's armrest. He winced only for a moment and wiped the blood away with his servant's robes beside him. The servant knew better than to react.

Ruskin hopped off his cold chair and addressed the lower guards at his throne room doorway.

"You!"

The two men stood at firm attention, ready for orders.

"Yes, Your Majesty!" they said in unison.

"Fetch me my personal guards!"

"Which ones, sir?"

Ruskin slithered up to the man on the left and stuck his face in his face, then said, "How about, *whomever you bloody well come across*!"

The guard, to his credit, only gave the briefest of flinches, but managed to hold his ground and nod.

Book One: Prophecy

"It will be done, Majesty, straight away." The guards bowed to Ruskin and exited the room.

"Oh," Ruskin said to himself, then opened the door to yell at the fading guardsmen, "and fetch me Davina as well!"

The king wandered back to his throne to perch uncomfortably on the clean arm, going over in his head what his next steps should be. He had such a hard time thinking things out by himself. He needed the help of his Mage.

Without his Mage's magick, he was limited by what he could do. She was always taking the time to learn new and terrible spells for him, finding new ways to harness the power of the stones that fell from The Gemstone Belts.

Everyone could harness a little bit of the Belts' magick, *if* they possessed the right stones, but as those were often very small, it could only hold so much power. They would drain out and that would be that. The color would fade, the energy would be used up, and the remaining stone would crumble to dust, useless. Unless you had someone born into these powers, those souls that were lucky enough to pass through The Gemstone Belts on their way to reincarnation, or those born of their bloodline, then those people or creatures could hold magick for far longer and enjoy a much greater lifespan. Those were the ones Ruskin sought out and kept for himself. Those like his Davina.

Davina had come to him about a year back. He'd killed her parents in a war for land some years before and she never quite got over it. They refused to recognize his authority, and it resulted in a bloody war. Davina, a princess and powerful seer with a wealth of magick, came on her own in the dead of night, snuck past his guards, bypassed his magickal security traps, and crept into his bedroom to kill him in his sleep. Such was her fury and despair. But when she went to strike, Ruskin woke and dodged the magickal shard of obsidian aimed straight for his heart! His yelp and following ruckus as the two raced around his room, knocking things over, alerted the guards and they came running. The princess was subdued after a short time and locked in a magick-proof cell. Davina, defeated, alone, and orphaned, succumbed to deep despair. Ruskin found her pitiful and left her to rot. He made the choice not to kill her, though, as one day she could prove to be useful. He decided she would instead be "reprogrammed" by his Mind Traveler, Viego.

After several months of this reprogramming, Ruskin saw her demeanor change. He would often come visit to see the progress they'd made. He saw her powers grow and her mind shift, becoming more and more used to her new surroundings. Ruskin started to take a liking to her, and her to him. A friendship of convenience, then. At least, that's how it started. She would perform small spells or visions for him, he would let her roam the grounds (though always under heavy guard). Sometimes he would even walk with her.

He couldn't remember at what point it became, and he hated this word, *romantic*, but there it was. He didn't love her like she seemed to want, he wasn't sure she really loved him either, he just couldn't be sure. He trusted exactly no one in this life, but he was content to keep this up…for now.

A knock sounded loudly on the throne room door and a head poked in to announce the arrival of Davina.

"Come!" he said.

Davina entered so lightly you'd think she was floating. Her dark hair curled freely about her shoulders and seemed to dance of its own volition. She was wearing the deep plum dress he'd had made for her, and it fit like a glove. Beautiful silks imported from the other side of the kingdom adorned with a swath of purple and pink gemstones of various shades sewn into the skirt and bodice sections. They caught every sparkle of light from the room, illuminating her further. Her dark skin glowed with shimmering gold. She was exemplary.

"You called for me, Your Highness?" she asked.

"I did, indeed," the king replied. "I have need of your services."

"Do you, now?" she asked, running a hand over the fabric to smooth her skirt. "How can I assist you?"

Ruskin leered at her momentarily, but then it was back to business.

"You told me the last time you had a vision that you saw a boy with a necklace piece. Then what?"

Davina's smile wavered. "I told you. I didn't get a clear picture on that one. I was interrupted."

Ruskin nodded. "Of course. That's right. And what did you do after you were interrupted by my latest paper weight?" He gestured to his desk where a fresh skull held a few scrolls down on the wood.

Davina tried to swallow and bring her eyes to meet his, showing her strength. Ruskin admired strength.

"Like I said, I tried to get it back but, you see, being a Seer isn't exact. I can't turn it off and on like one would like. It's a lot like trying to go back into a dream you were having after you've already woken up. Try as I might, I wasn't able to pull the vision back. I don't know what happened after the boy picked up the fragment. I wish I did. I'm sorry."

Ruskin was quiet for a few moments, trying to contain his rage. This was not the answer he was hoping for. Indeed, it was the *same* answer he'd gotten from her since the beginning, and he was done trying.

He granted her a grim smile and thanked her for her honesty and effort.

"Dinner will be in an hour. You will join me," he said.

Davina nodded obediently and Ruskin motioned for his guards to take her away. Once she was out of the room again, Ruskin returned to his throne and sat down to make a new plan, one he could inform Davina of at dinner and see just how far he could push her powers for his own gain.

CHAPTER EIGHTEEN: AMY VENTURES TO THE OUTPOST

I landed on my bed on the island with a soft thump, happy to be back somewhere that felt familiar after being rocketed from place to place. I breathed a deep sigh when the coziness of the bed enveloped me, reminding me how tired I was. I had to fight every instinct I had to not just go to sleep.

"After all," I said to myself, "I have a job to do, apparently. To find my long-lost love, my faceless picture-man. Too bad I don't know what he fully looks like, that would be helpful!" At least Helena gave me a map, so I'd know where to start looking.

I reached into my pocket and pulled out the crude drawing that showed me how to swim from my lonely island to the mainland and begin the search for Ibraxus.

"Map— ha! Doodles and squiggles. Great. Can't wait to see what fresh hell awaits me in a town that looks like I drew it with my feet."

I got up from the bed with a grunt and made my way toward the bedroom door. As I was about to exit, my eye spotted yet another hidden outline on the wall and I couldn't help myself. I had to see what it was.

"I mean, it is mine after all, right?"

I cautiously tapped around the barely visible outline until I felt a soft *click* and the wall panel opened to showcase a closet full of clothing, as well as a small cache of weapons and supplies.

"Now I find this!" *Figures*. I went about gathering things I thought I might need: A few changes of clothing, two very badass looking silver daggers adorned with various gems, a leather belt with a couple different pouches on it (which I promptly put the star ruby in), and some kind of water bottle/flask-looking thing. I gathered the lot and packed up what I could. There were even two spots on the belt that held my pair of daggers. *How handy*. I shoved the clothing and flask into the makeshift bag from Dragon Moon, thankful I'd brought it along.

"I hope this all makes it with me when I hit the water."

I closed the panel and took one last look around. God, I'm gonna miss this place, I just know it. I so badly wanted to just stay here and lock everything away. If any of what the ghost queen told me was true, I was in for quite the adventure, and I wasn't at all sure it would end well. In fact, if any of my movie and TV-watching on Earth has taught me anything, it's that I was in for a world of hurt. What I wouldn't give for some help right about now.

I left the comfort of my new-old home and set back down the trail I'd come up from originally. Giving one last look to the beauty of this sanctuary, I eased back into the waters that had brought me here, tracing my way back to the rest of the island.

I was pleased to find that all of my supplies stayed with me as they were, so I didn't need to fear them disappearing. At least, by magickal standards. I was still a klutz, after all.

When I made it to the beach that faced the open sea, I came out of the water long enough to check the map and set my course for the mainland. With any luck, I'd get there within the next hour or two, as I was very tired already and could use a chance to rest. I couldn't risk doing it here, for fear that Helena would find out and figure a way to haunt me for eternity.

I shuddered at the thought and put the map away.

"Here goes nothing. Bye, Island! I hope I see you soon! Wish me luck!"

I slipped back into the water and headed out.

The sea was filled with what you might expect from Earth's oceans. Obviously, there was water, sea creatures, and coral and rock formations scattered about, but what caught me by surprise was the farther down I looked, the more it looked like cities. They were spread out here and there, but definitely cities of some kind. I felt a pang of wistfulness and a longing to explore, but I knew I had a mission to follow, and until I was able to accomplish my goal, I couldn't veer off-course.

A few brightly colored fish came by to wink curiously at me and scuttled off to parts unknown. Cute little guys. It was nice to finally see signs of life! I wondered what else I'd see on my journeys in this weird new place.

After a while, I came upon a harbor with clear-quartz-bottom boats. Thank God! I was getting so tired I could barely keep my eyes open. I pulled up along the shore, careful to steer clear of any prying eyes, and transformed back to my human self. I shook off whatever water I could, wringing out the bulk of the wetness from my cloak and my bag. Good enough. It looked like it was going to start raining anyway, so I guess I was going to be damp no matter what.

I hid behind a nearby tree and tried to catch my breath and land legs. This swapping back and forth was exhausting! I sure hoped I would get used to this.

Upon first inspection, this harbor appeared to be part of a fishing village, not unlike something you'd see in the Pacific Northwest back on Earth. Lots of boats in the water, people milling about the shoreline, bringing in their catches for the day. Some were on the shore cleaning their fish or packing up their gear to go home. They looked like humans to my eyes, which was somehow both a relief *and* a disappointment. I was kinda looking forward to meeting some new creatures. I mean, if I'm a mermaid, and I already met a ghostly dragon-lady, what else could I expect to see in this world? But, on the other hand, I knew how to deal with humans, so I guess that worked fine for now.

"Alright, Amy," I said, steeling my nerves. "Time to find Ibraxus."

I did a quick scan of the area, trying to see if anything stood out as an outpost where I might have been before. I felt a slight tickle of familiarity, but that might just be because this place could've been somewhere back home on Earth. I don't know what I was expecting, but *normal* somehow seemed stranger than I could have predicted.

"Oi! Miss!" said a raspy male voice from the boat closest to me. Damn. I'd been spotted. So much for being a spy.

I decided to play dumb for as long as I could and see if I was able to learn anything from this guy.

"Who, me?" I pointed at myself, stepping out from behind the tree.

"Yes, you! You see any other yous nearby?"

I looked around then smiled, idiotically. "I suppose not! What do you want?"

The guy chortled and hoisted his catch from his boat to his cart.

"It's not what I want, love, it's what *you* want. It's been my experience that the only ladies I see hidin' behind trees are up to no good. So, I'll ask you again, what do you want?"

This might be harder than I thought. I was never a very good actress.

"I'm looking for... uh... my friend. Yes! My friend. I was told he comes here sometimes."

The look on his suns-touched face showed exactly how much he bought my answer.

"Uh huh. Well, your friend, what's his name? Maybe I can help."

What the hell. "His name is Ibraxus. Brax, for short—"

The man burst into peals of laughter. He put down his things so he could balance himself better, one hand on his boat, the other on his sizable belly, now shaking with mirth. I had no idea what I missed.

"Something funny?" I asked.

The man wiped a tear from his eye and said, "That's a good one, that! Ibraxus. Next, I'm sure you'll be tellin' me that you're his mermaid bride back from the dead and ready to save the world, am I right?" More laughter.

"I fail to see the humor in this," I said. I was too tired and too hungry for this.

The man saw I wasn't laughing with him and sobered up. He locked his weathered gaze on mine, searching for something. He seemed satisfied with his perusal and returned to closing up shop for the day.

"Nah, you're not her, anyway. No purple eyes. Dead giveaway, that."

I sent a mental thank you to Helena for her foresight. I didn't know what kind of attention I'd get if people knew who I really was, and I wasn't interested in finding out.

"So, I take it you haven't seen him, then?"

He paused his work and sighed.

"Look, Miss...?"

"Ariel," I said, laughing silently at my mermaid joke.

"Miss Ariel. Ibraxus was killed two hundred years ago. I'm afraid you are far past too late."

I could see this was going to be a much harder search than I'd thought if this was the first reaction I was getting to his name.

The man softened a bit when he saw me falter. I think he took pity on me.

He sighed again and said, "Miss Ariel, you seem a nice gal, I'm sorry I couldn't help you with your man troubles. It's goin' to rain any minute now and it's gettin' rather chilly out. How 'bout I buy you a nice bowl of chowder at the tavern and see if anyone there can aid in your search?"

My stomach growled loudly in reply, which pulled a smile from his bearded face.

"I'll take that as a yes! Hop in the front of the cart here, and I'll take you over."

Not quite what I expected from my first encounter with a living Callembrian, but at least I'd be getting some food, and some help. I'll call it a partial win.

"What's your name, by the way?" I asked the stranger, climbing into the front seat. (Seat— it was a bench, at best.)

"Moff," he said, and plopped in next to me, taking the reins of his horse. I was glad to see a horse. At least there were some familiar animals here.

"Moff. That's interesting." When he didn't say anything else, I changed tactics. "So, Moff... what do you guys do for fun around here?"

He gave me a side glance that told me "Fun" wasn't part of his vocabulary.

"You're lookin' at it, love," he said.

"What, fishing?"

"You got time for more than work? Good for you. Not all of us are as lucky. Me and the Mrs. spend our days workin' on the water or workin' the fields. Don't got much time for anythin' else, save a pint or two at the tavern."

"What about the outpost?"

"What outpost?" He genuinely looked perplexed.

Now it was *my* turn to furrow my brow. Helena told me that Brax and I met at the outpost in this town. Was I even in the right place? God! This is going to be impossible.

I looked at my surroundings and saw the sparse buildings dotting the pathway through what I could only assume was the town. To call them shacks would be close, as they looked run down and in need of more than a few repairs. Wooden structures similar to houses back on Earth, but the windows looked seamless, as if they were a part of the houses, rather than added in.

"Nice windows on these buildings," I said.

He took the bait. "Yeah, a fella came by some years back and magicked them in as part of a fish trade. Well, that and a room for the night, but mostly the fish."

"Magicked them in?"

He turned his full attention to me then and said, "Boy, you sure aren't from around these parts, are you?"

I shook my head.

"They don't use magick where you're from?"

Another head shake.

"Well, you see, some folks have magick in them, right? The ability to make things happen on the unnatural side. Others can buy it in fragments. The fella that did these windows was part of some far south beach tribe and he specialized in blowin' glass from the sands. He traveled with barrels of it and used his heatin' powers to get everythin' just right. He'd gather heat from the air through his hands and direct it into the piles of sand until it got hot enough to manipulate and then he'd just add it into the holes in the walls! That's why it looks so clean, you see."

"Impressive!" I said. I'd seen professional glass blowers on Earth, but never someone who could do it without the use of proper machinery.

"Ah, here we are. Welcome to Tripp's Tavern!"

"Who's Tripp?"

Moff smiled. "Tripp? Oh, that's not his real name. His real name is... well, I've plum forgotten now, been so long. But he's the owner of the tavern, and a friend when you need him."

I got out of the cart as Moff hitched his horse to the pole out front.

The tavern looked much like the rest of the shacks we'd passed: Wooden, falling apart, with beautifully done windows. The tavern, however, was about twice the size of the rest of them, with a second story that seemed to disappear into the massive tree boughs.

Moff saw me craning my neck and gave a chuckle.

"You won't find a top there, missy. Tripp made a rather profitable trade for a desperate Mage some time ago that added a magickal addition to the attic and now he's got himself a fine dwellin' to escape to when Ruskin's men come by to cause a ruckus."

"King Ruskin's men?"

"Them's the ones. Right lot of mischief-makers, those. They claim they're here to protect the land, but I suspect they're just here to line Ruskin's pockets, the wretch. Been bleedin' us dry for decades, if not longer. Taxes upon taxes, and whatnot."

He saw my eyes widen.

"Oh, but don't worry, love, they haven't been by here in some time, havin' already collected from us a few months back. I don't suspect you'll be meetin' them."

If I've learned anything in my life, it was that words like that lead to trouble. I gave him a forced grin and followed him into the bar.

I got three steps in the doorway and found myself having to dodge a flying chair. It sailed over my head and smashed against the door that had just closed behind us!

"Damn it, Rufus!" yelled the burly barman behind the counter. "That's gettin' added to your tab, you drunken sot!"

"Drunken sot" Rufus swayed back and forth, finger pointing at the man nearest him, and slurred, "So choke on *that*, you coward!" He slumped into the chair next to him and passed out. The man he'd been yelling at saw his opening, grabbed the cup in Rufus's other hand, chugged the remaining contents, and hurried past us out the door.

"Both of you! Rubbish!" the barman said, grabbing the now empty glass and forcefully slamming it into a bin of other dirty glassware. He then hoisted a still unconscious Rufus from the chair and unceremoniously deposited him outside.

He made his way back behind the bar, rubbing his hands on his half apron to get rid of the filth from his patron.

"I see the riffraff are at it early tonight," Moff said.

"If I didn't need the money so desperately, I'd have 'em both banned! Lowlife scum, the pair of 'em." Tripp was scrubbing at glassware with his rag that wasn't much cleaner than the cups he was using it on. He barely hazarded a glance in our direction. "Who's the girl?"

I felt myself bristle for a moment, but Moff held a hand up to stay my tongue.

"This is Ariel. She's lookin' for her friend, Ibraxus."

The barman stopped mid-swipe on the cup and flung all of his attention at my face. I could feel the blush hit my cheeks before I could take my next breath.

"Ibraxus, you say?" His watery-gray eyes dug so deeply into my own that I was sure he'd see the magick sheen of green hiding the purple. "Hmmm. Well," he continued, relaxing slightly, "that's not a name I've heard in a lon' time. Are you talkin' 'bout *the* Ibraxus, or some poor fool named after him?"

"Ummm... the first one?"

"You must be behind on your hist'ry, girl. That one's been dead for centuries."

"So I've been told." I sighed. "Well, what can you tell me about how he died?"

Both men guffawed in unison. I was getting pretty tired of being laughed at today and I could feel my temper start to boil.

"What?" I asked. "What am I missing?"

Moff put a reassuring hand on my shoulder and said, "Ah, girl, don't get upset. We're just not used to someone not knowin' the tale is all. Come, have a seat and some chow and we'll see what we can do to get you caught up." He turned to Tripp and ordered two fish chowders and two mugs of ale.

I unclenched my body and eased into the seat at the corner end of the dingy bar. Moff pulled up next to me and settled his impressive bulk on the small stool as if he'd done it a thousand times before. Tripp clunked two mugs down in front of us, sloshing frothing ale onto the countertop.

"Chowder'll be out in a minute. Be right back," he said, and disappeared behind a tattered red curtain.

Moff grabbed his mug and took a deep draught, wiped the froth from his mustache on his grubby sleeve, and emitted a satisfied burp. I grimaced and tried to hide my discomfort by taking a cautious sip of my own. I was surprised to find the ale was actually quite delicious and went down a lot easier than I expected. Moff grinned when he saw me go back for a second swig.

"Not bad, eh?" he asked.

I nodded in reply.

"Honey ale!"

"It's lovely, thank you. So, what can you tell me about the man I'm searching for?"

He gave me a knowing look and said, "Ah. The man you're lookin' for. Your friend, yes, the one you know so much about already."

I sighed again, realizing I wouldn't be able to get away with lying to this man, not if I expected any help in return. I took one more sip for courage and readied myself to explain.

Tripp came back with the soup bowls just then and plunked them down in front of us. He surprised me by grabbing a stool of his own and joining us at our corner.

"Well, go on, man, help the poor girl! Can't you see she's missin' her man?" Tripp said.

Both men laughed again, and I had to bite my tongue for the second time in as many minutes.

"He's not—" I began, and realized it was useless. "Fine. I don't know him. At least, I don't *think* I know him. I'm told I do, but I can't remember. What can you tell me about him?"

Moff took one more swig of ale and said, "Well, for starters, he's dead. To my knowledge, nobody's even named their kin after him as he died in a bit of disgrace, he did. Killed by Ruskin after he stole Ruskin's bride away. The dragon lord came down from his pretty perch in the sky and kidnapped Ruskin's lady love and forced her into marriage. Ruskin responded in kind by killin' him when he found them hidin' out on some island. Poor Amaryah was killed in the battle by Ibraxus, furth'rin' the rage and despair of the king. Well, he wasn't king back then, but the marriage would've made that happen. As it was, he still ended up marryin' royalty and securin' his title, but he was never the same."

"Wait, you said Ibraxus killed me— *her*—" I corrected quickly, hoping they didn't notice, "not Ruskin?" I took a sip of the delicious soup so they'd keep talking.

"Nah," Tripp said. "Ruskin says the dragon lord changed into his dragon form and tried to chomp him to bits but ended up gettin' her instead. That day, he killed Ibraxus and then hunted down his best friend, Ifyrus, another dragon shifter, to slay alon' with him. Nobody's seen 'em since."

Moff continued, "After that, the dragons tried to have Ibraxus's parents reclaim their rule on Dragon Moon. But they were too old and feeble and distraught over the loss of their son. Plus, they were weary from battle with Ruskin and his armies, because, believe you me, he sent his armies after every dragon he could find. They perished without leavin' an heir behind. Far as we know, that moon is up there, rottin' away. Shame, that. I wouldn't mind havin' a bit of moon to myself for some peace and quiet."

"You and me both, man!" Tripp said.

Well, damn. "Do you guys know where he's buried, by chance? I've sort of been tasked with a mission to find him. You know, make sure he's laid to rest and all of that."

"Who would want to bother with that? All of his family's dead and gone and there ain't nobody left who would give a damn," Tripp said.

I thought quickly. "Some dodgy old lady who thinks he's her grandson. She thinks maybe if she sees his body or bones or whatever that she might be able to find some closure. Poor woman has lost her wits, I'm afraid. But she's offered to pay me handsomely if I'm able to recover his body. So, gentlemen, do you have any helpful advice on how to find his remains so I may be off and leave you to your evening?"

The two men exchanged looks and I saw something pass over Tripp's face.

"Tripp? You got any ideas for me?"

Tripp shifted in his seat.

"Well, Miss Ariel, the truth is, nobody really knows. King Ruskin swore an oath to the kingdom that he was dead and gone and we just had to take his word for it. And seein' as nobody's seen hide nor hair of him since that day, we've come to believe him. But—"

"But what?" I asked.

Moff took over. "But there's an old legend, you see. You've heard of Queen Miawae, yeah?"

I shook my head. These guys must think I'm from another planet. Oh yeah, I was.

Moff sighed but continued. "Queen Miawae, leader of Gallanor a few days' hard ride from here, is a very powerful Seer, you see. She's been around for as lon' as I can remember. Her and her husband, King Matthias, though, if we're bein' real honest, she's the real leader of the lot. He's fine and all, just a bit of a quiet fella.

"Anyway, when she first came into power, lon' before any of us were here, she made her first public appearance under the crown, and with it, a prediction: Ruskin's power would come to an end, thanks to the Dragon King, his Mermaid bride, and their child. Most of the kingdom took it with a grain of salt, seein' as how she was so youn' and new, but they all knew the story of how Ibraxus had killed his wife by accident and Ruskin had killed Ibraxus and Ifyrus in return.

Also, there was never the chance for children, so everyone chalked it up to a misfire of vision and let it go. Over the years, confidence in the Queen grew as every other prediction she made had come to pass, big and small, and hope began anew little by little for the overthrowin' of the man who had been seated in power far past his prime. Ruskin managed to curry the favor of many Mages over the years to extend his life far longer than anyone could have expected, and the havoc it has wreaked on this world grows still."

"At this point, I hope you somehow find him alive!" Tripp said. "High time *somebody* did somethin' to unseat that monster!"

"What has he done that's been so bad?" I was honestly curious.

The men shared another look. This time, I'm pretty sure they were getting even more suspicious of me.

"Have you not been outside, Miss?" Moff asked. "Have you been livin' under a rock somewhere and only now just popped out to say hello to the world?"

"Something like that," I admitted. "More like a very quiet island."

"Ha! Must be nice," Tripp said.

"So? What did he do?" I asked.

"Well, for starters," Tripp said, "he ripped every powerful Mage from every corner of the planet from their families and made them join him so he could rise in power and lifespan. He's gone to war with so many people I honestly don't know how there's anyone left to fight. Those that bow out gracefully and bend to his will are given much lighter outcomes, but the ones who stand and fight?" He shuddered. "Well, let's just say it's best to just give him what he wants."

"And what is it he wants?"

"Power. Fame. Acquiescence. Magick. Eternal life."

"Her."

At the mention of "her", it was *my* turn to shudder.

"The mermaid bride?" I asked.

Both men nodded and took long glugs of their ale. Silence filled the room as the darkness of history settled upon them.

I still had questions.

"So, if this guy Ruskin was so bad, why was the mermaid princess engaged to him in the first place? Why would her family want her to wed such a horrible man?"

"A fair question!" Moff replied. "Alliance, most likely. That's what most of those royal weddin's are all about anyway. Alliances and more power. Ruskin's never been able to access power in the oceans, and I'm sure you've noticed, we've got more water on this planet than we do land. Ruskin's always been keen on tryin' to get down there. Problem is, his magick don't work down there. No one's does, save for the Merpeople, a'course, but they've got their own brand of magick, you ken. Dark, planet-core magick, the likes that we can't get up here. I suppose he thought that by marryin' her, it would open up a whole new world to him and that was just too temptin' an offer to pass up. But she had her heart set on that youn', freshly crowned Dragon King and ran off with him. They wed in secret and when Ibraxus tried to take her back up to the Dragon Moon to rule with him, Ruskin's old Mage tracked them down and Ruskin was able to cut them off before they left. And, well, you know the rest."

That was a lot to digest. I wondered how much of it was true and how much of it was rumor. Also, if this was my history, why isn't any of it ringing a bell?

Just then, thunder boomed overhead and rattled the loose boards of the tavern.

"Damn that weather, anyway!" Tripp got up to shut the door that had blown open. Rain forced its way through the door, soaking the front of his shirt and pants.

"You best get your horse into the stable for the nigh', Moff. I don't think you're goin' anywhere till this storm passes." He closed the door forcefully with his meaty shoulder. "You and the girl can stay with me tonight. Separate rooms, a'course, seein' as how your Mrs. wouldn't like it otherwise. I'll magick her a note explanin' not to expect you home till tomorrow."

"Thanks, Tripp," Moff said.

Both men set about their tasks of seeing to the horse and bringing in the day's catch. When they were finished, Tripp led us past the red curtain, through the small kitchen, and up a set of stairs that led to a hidden inn. "Where the riffraff can sleep it off, when I've a mind to let them," Tripp said with a wink.

We walked down the hallway of this new addition and Tripp nodded toward the first open door on the left.

"That's you, Moff," he said.

Moff said goodnight and entered the tiny room, which boasted only a cot and set of drawers. He smiled with a wave and gently closed the door behind him.

Alone with Tripp, I suddenly got the strangest feeling. We continued a bit farther down the hall.

"And this," he stopped, then said slowly, "is *your* room."

He stared directly into my eyes, and it felt as though he'd blown glitter in them! I flinched and pulled away, blindly swinging just in case he tried to grab me. But he stayed exactly where he was. Didn't move a muscle, just watched my face.

Realizing I was okay, I blinked hard and wiped the tears from my eyes.

"What the hell did you do *that* for?"

Not breaking his gaze, he said, "Look in the mirror, '*Ariel*'," and gestured to the mirror through the open door to the right.

I took a few hesitant steps into the beautifully ornate room, taking in the extreme wealth it must have cost to achieve beauty of this magnitude, especially in a place like this. A stunning four-poster canopy bed with delicately carved wooden posts and deep burgundy drapery scrawled with golden filigree stood against the far wall and it took my breath away. I'd always wanted a bed like that!

He rolled his eyes and said, "For the travelin' royalty, now look at the damn mirror!" He lit a few candles that were placed around the room so I could get a better picture. I braced myself and looked in the polished glass hanging above the waist-high dresser.

"What? What am I looking for? All I see are purple— ah, *dammit*!" I yelled and covered my eyes with my hands.

"Don't worry," he said, "I'm with you, Amaryah. I just had to be sure. You look like you, but I've been wron' before."

"Fine! I'm not Ariel. But who is Amaryah? My name is Amy, which is short for Amethyst."

"Yeah, Amaryah of clan Amethyst, and yes, you would occasionally go by your pet name of Amy."

"Amy Hart," I corrected him.

"Amaryah Amethyst," he said.

"Amy Hart."

"Amaryah. Amethyst."

We stared at one another for a good long minute, the crash of the raging storm the only sounds around us.

Tripp relented first. "Well, whoever you are, you're her!" He stubbornly moved his hands from his hips to cross his arms and glare harder.

"Fine!' I said again. "Now what? You said you're on my side— what exactly do you mean by that?"

It was at that point, Tripp remembered there was another guest in the building, so he hurriedly shut the door behind him. He gestured to the small sofa against one of the walls and I went to join him but, man, was my heart thudding!

"This was your room," he began, sitting down. "Well, yours and Brax's. This tavern has been here much longer than you might suspect. I had it built just over two hundred years ago. I've added some to it over the years, and some's gone to pasture, but I always kept this one up for you two. So in love, you were and battlin' so much offal. T'wasn't right, all that. This tavern here used to be known as 'The Outpost' back then. Pardon me for not sayin' so downstairs, but, as much as I love dear old Moff, he ain't exactly wrapped up in any of this, and I aim to keep it that way."

I nodded my agreement to keep him blissfully unaware.

He continued. "Anyway, I always hoped that you'd come back to us someday, especially after the queen's first vision. I kept expectin' you'd come by with your fella again and things could finally right themselves. But no one's seen hide nor hair of him neither, and I began to wonder if it would ever come to pass. And, well, here you are! Feisty as ever, and obstinate as all get-out, but I'll be damned if I'm not relieved to see you come home."

I was getting such a headache.

"Wait, so, this was our home?"

He shook his head. "No, not officially. This was where you two met. You were both on a mission from your parents to garner goodwill between the two factions and see if terms could be agreed upon to form an alliance. Your father was playin' both sides, see, but not because he was a bad man, err— Mermaid King, he was just pressured by the growin' forces of power and didn't know who to ally with. Did he help the dragons and save them from the tyranny of Ruskin? Or did he allow Ruskin to marry his eldest daughter, Amaryah, in exchange for magick, power, and security? When Ibraxus heard about that, I'm afraid it set him off in a rage and he went after him. They weren't exactly friendly even before you came alon'."

I rubbed my temples.

"Do you happen to have a picture of Ibraxus? I still don't know what he looks like, and I've been tasked by his grandmother to find him."

Tripp looked appalled. "Helena is still *alive*?"

I laughed at the look on his face. Finally! I had some information he didn't!

"Not exactly. I met her ghost. In fact, she's the dodgy old woman I told you about before. First person I've spoken to since I got to this damn planet."

He looked at me gravely. "So, you *have* been over there."

"If by 'over there', you mean Earth, then yes. I was living a great life, too! Had a shop of my own, cute little house. Things were going great until I got shot and died. Now I'm currently losing my mind in *this* fresh hell."

Tripp's face softened and he gently grasped my hands for comfort.

"I know it may seem like a lot right now, but I promise you, this is a good thin'."

I didn't know how to respond, so I just nodded.

He paused a minute, biting his lip, then asked, "What about the child?"

"What child?"

Just then, a loud banging came from down the hallway, followed by a stream of curses.

"Damn Moff and his nightmares!" Tripp excused himself and went to settle his friend back to bed.

I was beyond exhausted at this point and the pull of sleep in that gorgeous bed was strong. I wondered if Tripp would mind if we held off on any more big revelations until morning.

When he came back a few minutes later, assuring me Moff was fast asleep, I asked if I could go to bed.

"A'course, darlin'. Pleasant dreams to you. If you need anythin', my room is back downstairs behind the bar."

"Thank you, Tripp, for everything." I yawned and stretched my aching limbs.

Tripp chuckled and said, "It's sure nice to have you back. I'll see if I can scrounge up somethin' with Brax's likeness on it for you. Shame you don't remember him, but I guess it's to be expected, what with all you've been through. G'night."

"Good night!" I said through another yawn.

He closed the door, and I crawled into that big inviting bed and passed out.

CHAPTER NINETEEN: CYNDOL HEARS A PROPHECY

Cyndol smiled at Queen Miawae and said, "Thank you. Tea sounds lovely."

The matronly monarch went to pour the tea herself and extended a cup to Cyndol. She included various additives on a plate to fix the tea to her liking: Cream, sugar, honey, the works. Cyndol took a little bit of each, not wanting to miss out on luxury when it was offered. When she was through adding a little of each item, she tasted it, sighed deeply in satisfaction, and sat back on one of the comfy couches that adorned the queen's sitting room.

Miawae stirred her tea and implored Cyndol to discuss her trek through the kingdom.

Cyndol blushed a deep crimson, afraid to tell the queen what she'd likely already heard from her guard and granddaughter.

"Well, um... you have a lovely kingdom," she said.

"Yes," Miawae said. "And did you discover anything new? Anything you might have questions about?"

Cyndol reddened further, if that was possible.

"I like your... um... pulley thing. Down at the riverbank. It's very... uh... handy."

Miawae nodded, never taking her gaze from Cyndol's face.

"And?"

Cyndol fidgeted under the weight of that gaze, so knowing, so piercing.

"And," She sighed. "I might have magick in me."

"Yes," Miawae agreed. "I suppose you do. Now, the question is: Do you know how to use it? Do you know where it comes from?"

Cyndol shook her head, looking intensely at a spot on the rug.

The queen was silent for a moment, choosing her words.

"You know, Cyndol," Miawae said, "magick is only given to those that have the power to control it. That must mean that somewhere, deep down, you have a light within you so strong that your soul feels confident enough to activate it for you. It might be scary, my dear, but it is also an honor. I suspect you will live a life of greatness, though maybe not the kind you'd expect. Such is the life of the magickal."

Cyndol didn't know how to respond to that, so she just nodded her head in vague agreement, taking another sip of tea.

"I can help you with that, if you wish?"

Cyndol looked at her face for the first time in several moments.

"You can?"

Miawae looked pleased, almost as eager as Cyndol herself. Her majesty reached for a tome Cyndol hadn't noticed until now, sitting on the table beside her. She set it gently on her lap and opened to the first page.

"Did your mother ever tell you about magick?"

Cyndol readjusted on the couch and shook her head again.

"Do you know the story of Ibraxus and Amaryah?"

"That's my favorite story! Imagine: A dragon king falling in love with a mermaid princess! It's so romantic!"

The queen smiled at her exuberance. "It was, indeed. It was also forbidden, and they met a sad end."

Cyndol's excitement dimmed, and she sat back in her seat, not knowing what to say.

Miawae studied her face for a moment, gauging how much to tell this child.

"Did you hear about the prophecy that followed?"

Cyndol's brows drew together.

"What prophecy?"

Miawae flipped the book she held to the last chapter and began to read:

"When the young queen donned the crown for the very first time at her coronation, a cry came up through her people. Someone had noticed the queen wince and topple as her eyes clouded over in a fine silver storm. The guardsmen hurried to her side to assist her to the throne before she fell. As soon as she was in her seat, a blast of energy shot through her body and knocked the guards into the crowd. Her voice took on an eerie tone, almost melodious, and her body went straight as an arrow. As frightened as her subjects were, they were too scared to move. All eyes were stuck on the queen as she intoned her first royal prophecy:

"'The tyranny of King Ruskin will come to an end, through fire and water and with the help of a child. A child of sea and sky.'

"The people did not know how this could be possible, as the Dragon King and his bride both perished in the fight, leaving no children behind to claim this birthright. In fact, by the time this prophecy came along, King Ruskin had already obliterated every dragon he could find, wiping out any chance of his destruction.

"And so, the kingdom decided that, while it was a pretty thought, it must have been made in error. The rumors of this prediction dwindled over the years until it was all but erased from history."

Miawae gently closed the book and fastened her gaze on the wide-eyed girl, biting her nails on the edge of the cushion. Miawae chuckled and set the book on the small table next to her, giving Kit's ears a scratch as he napped by her side.

"I've never heard that part of the story," Cyndol said.

"Not many have, I'm afraid," her majesty agreed. "It has been many years since anyone has seen this book."

Cyndol nodded noncommittally at first, then a thought struck her. "Wait a minute. How do *you* have this book, then?"

Miawae's face became serious, and she reached out to place her hand on Cyndol's.

"Because, my dear, that prediction was *mine*."

The hair on the back of Cyndol's neck prickled.

"But, if they're dead, then there *must* have been a mistake, right?"

Miawae shook her head slowly from side to side.

"No, dear one. There have been no mistakes in all my years of Seeing. I wish there had been, on more than one occasion, believe me. The cost of Seeing is peace."

Cyndol chewed on that for a moment, taking another sip of tea to calm her racing nerves.

"Why are you telling me this?"

Her majesty got up from the couch to sit down next to Cyndol and looked deep into her eyes.

"Because, my child, I am afraid we need each other."

"How?"

"Well, you need my help to save your brother, and I intend to do that by sending my guard with you to secure his release. What I need from you is to deliver a message to the Ruler of The Fae. Can you do that for me?"

"I think so," Cyndol said, "but what about Ethan?"

"That's the easy part, you see. If what I fear is true, then Ethan will need their healers anyway. They have strong magick that can get him back on his feet. I am sorry to alarm you this way, but Ruskin has a penchant for torturing his guests. Once Ethan is free, getting him to the Fae infirmary will be top priority. Once that is done, I implore you to please deliver my message. So, I ask again, can you do that for me?"

Cyndol was quite shaken at the idea of her older brother being tortured by the king's men, but she nodded fiercely, determined to save the only family she had left.

"Good!" exclaimed Miawae. "You will leave with my guard at first light."

CHAPTER TWENTY: KAVEA SETS OUT

Kavea was determined to go after Ibraxus in case he needed her help. She spent the following day taking inventory of everything she had that was essential for traveling. She had to take a lot of guesses, as she had never been outside the Snow Lands before, but she'd read several books she'd snuck from her father's immense library and was certain she could manage this on her own.

Her father had no knowledge of her taking these guarded tomes. One night, after lessons, she saw her tutor drop his library key, unnoticed, on his way out. With bated breath, she waited until the guards' backs were turned to escort the tutor out, then snatched it up before anyone could spot her. When everyone was asleep, she crept down to the locked library door, inserted the silver and garnet encrusted key and, with trembling hands and shaking breath, opened the door to enlightenment.

She'd discovered books about all sorts of places touting incredible adventures! Why, there was even a beautiful fantasy about a place called "Earth". It was wonderful and sparked enough thirst for an adventure of her own. She snuck a few of these books into her skirts and, once back to her room, hid them in the secret wall cubby she'd fashioned behind her bed. Her tutor "found" the key right where he'd left it the next morning, and no one was the wiser.

Kavea chuckled at the memory and continued packing. She looked wistfully at her Earth book and decided to bring it along. After all, wouldn't she need some form of entertainment on her travels?

She looked shrewdly at what she'd packed in her makeshift reindeer skin rucksack so far: Her Earth book, two knives she'd stolen from the kitchens (one large and one small), several dark bread rolls, dried fish, reindeer jerky, some reindeer cheese, a large bunch of roasted elden roots, and a jug of water, which she figured she could replenish as she went along. She hesitated for just a moment, then threw in the small jar of candied nuts her father had brought back for her on her last birthday. After the food went a few changes of clothing and a thick blanket. She tied the whole thing up with two old leather boot lacings to keep it all intact. Lastly, she utilized her sewing kit to attach two of her leather belts on either side, starting at the bottom of her pack and ending at the top, so that she could wear it on her back during her travels.

She grinned at her rough handiwork and shoved the bulging sack into her wall cubby until nightfall.

Exiting her room, she went in search of her mother, Orelle. These days, Orelle could usually be found sitting in front of the massive fireplace located near the rear of the castle in her lonely wingback chair. When she wasn't staring into the snapping fire, she was writing. Nonsense, mostly, though occasionally there would be fragments that were intelligible.

As most of these pages went right into the flames when they were done, Kavea didn't feel too bad snatching a few here and there. Nobody noticed anyway. It was just a way to feel close to her best friend again. It had been so long since she'd been able to have a full conversation with Orelle that it felt like a way to keep the spark going. The last several years had seen her decline further and further until she was but a lingering husk of a once lively woman, teetering close to catatonic. It broke Kavea's heart.

Sure enough, she found Orelle in her spot near the fire, writing away.

Kavea cleared her throat to announce her arrival without spooking her. When she took no notice, she tried again, a little louder this time. Still no response. She inched closer and put a gentle hand on her mother's writing arm, pausing it in place.

"Mother?" she said.

Orelle stopped writing but took a moment to return to the present. She gingerly lifted her gaze to meet her daughter's concerned eyes.

"Mother, are you alright?"

Orelle blinked a few times and nodded, though Kavea wasn't fully convinced she knew where she was.

"It's late. Would you like help getting to bed?"

Orelle tried to speak but her throat was dry. She pointed to a glass of water that sat on her side table and Kavea retrieved it for her. After taking a few small sips, she tried again.

"No, thank you, dear. I need to finish my letter to the king." She placed her glass back in Kavea's hand and went back to writing.

Kavea sighed and looked down at the paper she was scrawling on. It looked like a collection of random words to her eyes but, if it made her mother happy, she was glad she had that small bit of escape.

"I'm sure he will be very pleased," Kavea said, putting the glass back on the table.

Orelle bobbed her head absently as her quill flew across paper with practiced skill.

"Which king are you writing to?"

A look of irritation crossed her delicate features, and she shook her graying-red curls without looking up from the paper. "The Dragon King, of course! Who else would I be writing to?" Then, directly to Kavea's face, "But, please, don't tell your father! You know how jealous he gets." She returned her attention to her scrawlings.

A moment of silence passed, marred only by the snapping of the flames and the scratching of the quill. Kavea didn't want to leave her mother all alone in this frozen nightmare, but she couldn't take her along, either.

"Perhaps," Kavea said, "if you like, I can make sure this one gets to the king personally, instead of throwing it into the fire this time?"

The frail woman nodded again.

"That's fine, dear, thank you. He'll want it straight away."

Orelle let her take the page and then immediately went to work on another. Kavea slipped the letter into her pocket. More silence passed.

"I'm going to miss you," Kavea whispered.

"What, dear?" Orelle asked.

Kavea bit back threatening tears.

"I said, 'Goodnight, Mother'."

"Oh. Goodnight, dear. Love you."

Kavea leaned over and gave her mother a hug, much longer than normal. "I love you, too." After a moment, Kavea kissed the top of her head and left her alone with her pages.

When everything was dark, and all had gone to bed for the night, Kavea grabbed her sack from its hiding place and slipped out her window to land softly on the snow below.

Righting herself, she searched the clear night sky until she located Dragon Moon. Finding her target, she took a deep breath and began her trek to find His Majesty, Ibraxus.

CHAPTER TWENTY-ONE: AMY GETS INFORMATION

A knock at my door the next morning woke me, along with Tripp's raspy tone.

"Good mornin', Princess," he said, letting himself in. "I brought you some fresh coffee, just how you like it! Well, how you *used* to, anyway. Hope you still take it with cream and dark sugar?"

What the hell is dark *sugar? Is that like* brown *sugar?* It was too early for my brain to work that one out. I peeked at him through one grumpy eyeball and saw him place a tray on the table by the fireplace.

"Lemme get this goin' for you. It's rather chilly this morn." He proceeded to light a fire, and the room took on a warm glow. "There you are!"

My stomach grumbled when the scent of hot meat and coffee reached me. Tripp seemed eager to get me out of bed, so I gave my pillow one last cuddle and lifted my head all the way.

"Thangyoutrip," I slurred from my half-awake face. "'Snice of you."

"Aww, it's no bother. Happy to do it!"

Instead of leaving like I thought he would, he sat down in one of the two chairs by the fire and began to dish up food for himself. I guess we were dining together then.

"Hurry up, now! Before it gets cold!"

I hate morning people.

"I'm coming," I said with a yawn.

I flung the covers off me and was greeted by a nip in the air. Thank God he started that fire, or I'd be right back in those blankets! I shivered and grabbed a cozy throw from the foot of the bed.

"How'd you sleep?" Tripp asked.

I plopped down in the other chair, and he poured me a cup of what was apparently my favorite beverage.

"Best sleep I've had in weeks," I said. "That's quite the bed you've got there."

"I should hope so!" he said through a laugh. "You picked it out!" He munched on a piece of buttered toast with jam as crumbs lodged themselves in his graying beard. I hid my smile.

"Well, what can I say? I've got great taste."

"That you do, li'l lady, that you do."

I reached for some toast of my own, and a side of what I hoped was bacon, and bit down on the hot, salted meat. *Mmmmmm*! Holy hell, that was good! Appetite awoken, I took a bite of jam toast as well and washed it all down with the coffee. All of it was sublime.

"Damn, Tripp! You cook a hell of a breakfast!"

"Why, thank you! I do the best I can. It's always nice to be appreciated, though, 'specially comin' from royalty."

Something struck me, then. This isn't the first time he's mentioned me being royalty. In fact, he's also called me

"Princess", though I thought it was more of a jesting moniker than an actual title.

"Tripp?"

"Yes, Amy?"

I looked into his earnest face and decided now was as good a time as any for answers.

"Why do you keep referring to me as royalty?"

Tripp choked on his toast and had to take a sip of coffee to get his throat back.

"Why do I— do you not know who you are at all, lass? Did it not make sense to you last night?"

I sighed. "No memory, remember?"

Tripp looked sad for a moment, then brightened again.

"Sorry. It's a strange thin' to not know who you are. Like I said last night, your father was the king of the Merpeople. Err, you know you're a mermaid, right? That's not news to you, is it?"

I chuckled. "That one I found out the second I got here, actually."

Tripp looked relieved. "Good! I didn't know how to explain that one if you didn't already know. So, like I was sayin', your father was the king. Well, might *still* be king for all I know. I can't say that I'm all caught up on the goings on in Merworld. But you were his eldest daughter, makin' you, by all rights, a princess. *The* princess, actually, one that is still spoken of in son' and story to this day."

Interesting. I never thought of myself as much of a princess type. Huh.

"Do you know if any of my family...? You know what, never mind. It's been two hundred years, of course no one's still alive." I tried not to let my disappointment show.

"Were you not listenin', love? I said I wasn't sure if he was or not. It's been a while since I've had a chat with the sea folk, but it's not unheard of for lon' lives around here. Just look at Ruskin, for example! He's been wreakin' havoc ever since you left! Who knows who else might still be kickin' around?"

I took another sip of the delightful brew.

"Tripp?"

"Amy?"

"If you were me, and you just woke up in a new place you didn't remember, and you had the choice to find your family or find your long-lost love, which would you choose?"

Tripp sighed heavily. "That's not for me to say, lass. I wish I could answer that one for you but, the truth is, I have no idea how you must be feelin' right now and to have to choose between one's heart and one's roots is somethin' I wouldn't wish on anybody."

"Queen Helena seems to think finding Brax is the *only* way to proceed."

Tripp laughed. "Well, to be fair, Helena always did put her family first, so I can't say as I'm surprised. Terrifyin' woman, that one!" He gave an exaggerated shudder.

Now it was my turn to laugh. "Oh, she is that! That's honestly why I'm trying so hard to find Brax. I'm afraid she'll leave her ghostly post and haunt me until I die all over again!"

"That's enough to strike fear in the hearts of even the bravest men," he said.

I finished the last few bites of my food, swallowed one more blissful sip of coffee, and sat back contentedly in my seat to stare into the fire.

"She claims that I broke the spell that was holding him captive, but I haven't seen him or heard any word that would make me think he even survived in the first place, have you?"

He shook his head. "No, but I have faith in Miawae's predictions. She's yet to steer anyone wron'. In fact, years back, when she and her husband, King Matthias, visited here, she predicted my wife would catch a chill that would lead to her death if she wasn't careful. My poor wife, Emilia, thought it was all hogwash and shrugged it off. A few months later, we were pullin' in the day's catch, and she slipped on some pooled water in the boat and tumbled over the side. Well, we had a good laugh, as we were already pulled up on the bank, and she just wrun' out the water from her clothes and went to dry off. Well, the next day, she had a nasty fever goin' and within three days, she was gone. Forty years together, and it was over like that." He snapped his fingers.

I gasped, utterly heartbroken for him.

"Oh, I raged," he continued. "I yelled at everyone and everythin' in my path. I trekked all the way to the queen's front door, screamin' and hollerin' and demandin' she brin' her back to me. Her guards tried to escort me from the premises, but the queen herself came out to invite me in. I went in, a'course, as I hadn't come all that way for nothin', and she sat me down in her parlor, pleasant and calm as could be. Hard not to be impressed with that level of royalty and civility. She had food and drinks brought in, but I couldn't taste nothin'. I'd had no appetite for days. Kind of her to try, though. When I tearfully asked her to brin' my wife back, and asked her why she killed her in the first place, do you know what she said to me?"

I shook my head, hanging on his every word.

"She asked me if we'd had a good life together. Well, a'course, we did, I said! What kind of question was *that*? And she said it was important to remember all the wonderful years we had. Not so many people were as lucky as we were to have a love like that. Well, to say I was confused at this point is puttin' it mildly. I told her I didn't come here to discuss my relationship; I just wanted her back! The queen looked at me, calm as you please, and asked me if my wife had heeded her warnin'. Well, I can't tell a lie, you see, so I told her no. She reached out and held my hands, my dingy, dirty, callused hands that were shakin' in anger and despair, and the second she touched them, I felt peace. I don't know how else to describe it. She said that Emilia's soul was on its way to another place, one where she would be waitin' for me, but that I shouldn't be in a rush to get there. I had a different purpose in this life, one as a Protector from here on out. I may not have been able to protect my wife, but there were other souls I would need to be here to help. And, this time, I would listen."

I shivered.

"That's why I created The Outpost, you see. I've helped many a soul since those first awful days of despair, and that's thanks to Queen Miawae. And you, a'course, though I wasn't able to save you either, just like I couldn't save my poor Emilia."

I wanted to hug this man.

"I'm so sorry, Tripp. I can't imagine losing a partner like that."

He wiped a tear from his eye with a gnarled finger.

"Well, you sort of did. Or he lost *you*. Either way, nasty business. But," he stood up and made a show of brushing off the crumbs of breakfast, "on the bright side, we're here now, we have a purpose, and I think I know where to send you first."

I stood up, too. "You do?"

"I'm goin' to send you to Miawae, a'course! She'll know what to do."

A bolt of nerves shot through my body.

"You're sending me to the queen?"

He chuckled good naturedly. "I suspect she already knows you're here. No sense in wastin' time. Get dressed, and I'll show you the way."

He cleared the table and went back downstairs to deposit the dishes, leaving me up here to freak out all by myself. *The queen! Holy crap! What would I say? How do I greet a queen?* I know I already met one, but she was a ghost and not necessarily a very nice one. *This* one, however, already felt vastly more important to me and I hadn't even met her yet. I hoped I didn't find a way to screw this up. Though, knowing me, I'd do just that.

Tripp came back a few minutes later, armed with an actual backpack of sorts, looking to be filled with provisions for a journey. I loved this man so much in the short time I'd known him.

"I brought you a few thin's for your trip," he said while blushing. "Nothin' fancy, just food, water, and some extras. I penned a letter to Miawae just in case she doesn't believe you, though, if *I* believe you, I don't see how *she* wouldn't. Oh! I almost forgot!"

He did that damn eye trick on me again and my eyeballs filled with tears.

"OUCH! Damnit, Tripp! Warn me next time you're going to do something like that! That *hurts*!" I rubbed my poor eyes and checked them in the mirror to make sure no purple was visible. I saw in the reflection that he looked properly abashed, and I instantly felt sorry for snapping at him.

"Sorry, Princess," he said.

"No, you're fine. It just smarts, is all," I replied.

"You ready to go?"

I took one last look around the room, trying to burn its beauty in mind, and nodded.

I went to move towards the door, but Tripp blocked me and pointed to the fireplace behind me.

"Nope, not that way. *This* way!" He proceeded to shove the fireplace to the right, revealing a portal hidden behind it.

"Is that...?"

"Your very own Crannie! Leads you straight into the start of Matthias and Miawae's kingdom. I'm afraid I couldn't get you right to their doorstep, on account of it breachin' magickal wards and such, but this is the next best thin'."

"Thank you, Tripp, I mean it. For everything. I sincerely hope I see you again." I hurled my arms around the bulky bartender. He returned the gesture with more tenderness than I would have expected.

"Please be careful. You may be in friendly territory but that doesn't mean you won't have unsavory folk on your path."

I turned to go into the Crannie but remembered I had no idea where I was going.

"Tripp, how do I get there? How will I know where to go?"

He smacked his forehead with his palm and reached into his pocket for a slip of parchment.

"Damn your old noggin, Tripp!" he said. "I plum forgot! Sorry 'bout that. Here, I have a map for you."

I sighed. Another crude map. Yay.

"Thank you, Tripp. This really helps. Be sure to tell Moff I said thank you as well, okay? I don't know that I'd be here if it wasn't for his help."

"I'll be sure to tell him. He'll be sad he didn't get to say goodbye, but he'll be pleased as pie that you cared."

I hugged him once more, then entered the Crannie.

Book One: Prophecy

CHAPTER TWENTY-TWO: COLT'S MISSION

Colt took his mission from the queen very seriously. She'd instructed him to go to the edge of Gallanor's woods and meet up with a woman with dark hair who would need his assistance. He was to help get her safely to the faire a few towns over. Well, to a boy his age, that sounded like the most amazing adventure! Saving a damsel in distress *and* getting to go to a faire? How wonderful! She even paid him to do it! A whole purse full of gems for him to share with his lady fair. He felt very important, and his stride couldn't hide it. He didn't know *how* he was supposed to save her, but Miawae assured him he would know when the time came. He trusted her and would do as he was told.

A trampling in the brush a few yards away caught his attention and he straightened his clothes to look more presentable for his rescue job. But it wasn't a female voice he heard, but a male's. He darted behind a tree and peeked around the corner to see who was approaching.

"So I told her, I says, 'If you didn't want any trouble, then you shouldn't have come a-knocking!'"

Another man laughed at what Colt assumed was supposed to be funny, but to his ears sounded quite dangerous. He decided he could wait for his lady a bit farther down, just to be safe.

Colt took a few hesitant steps backward and slipped on a patch of wet leaves and tumbled into a bush.

"Oi! Who's there?" one of the men called out.

Colt didn't move. The men inched closer. Colt could see the emblem of King Ruskin on their coats: A wolf with bared teeth eating its own tail. Fear ran through him faster now, and he tried to sneak out of the shrubbery to make his escape.

The men spotted him, and one said, "Hey! You, there! What are you doing out here?"

Colt said, "Me? Oh, uh, nothing, sir! Just— ah— passing through! Gotta get home to mum, and all—"

He tried to get up and keep distance from the man questioning him.

The man shouted, "Halt, I say! You shouldn't be out here by yourself, son! Come back here and let us take you home."

His sneer said he knew full well this kid was lying through his crooked teeth.

Colt kept up his quick pace, but he saw that not only had this man not given up his forward progression, but that even more men had fallen in line behind him. Colt knew he was in trouble.

Colt bolted away as quickly as he could, earning a marginal lead over them. When he rounded a bend, he noticed *his* intended target was *also* running alongside him, equally harried and equally confused, fleeing from yet another group of Ruskin's men. He clocked the approaching cliff and saw the woman was about to go off of it!

Heart thudding in his chest, Colt ran faster than he'd ever run before, catching up to the dark-haired woman.

He managed to pull in front of her and said, "A friend sent me to help you! Come with me, now! These men will kill you!"

"Who are *you*?" she asked. "How do I know you're here to help me?"

"Queen Miawae sent me!" he said, hoping that would be enough.

Apparently, that did the trick, and, without a second's further hesitation, she grabbed his proffered hand, and they ran as fast as they could.

The woman's face took on a horrified sheen as she saw they were headed straight for the cliff, and she pulled him to a stop.

"Trust me!" Colt said.

The woman took one look at the quickly advancing men, some with arrows ready to fire. Her terror-filled eyes shone with tears, but she nodded her head and continued their path.

Colt inwardly sighed in relief and quickly transformed into a pegasus: A horse body with wings sprouting from his back at breakneck speed. The woman let out a shrill scream but didn't slow down.

As they approached the cliff face, the first arrow fizzed past her ear. She turned around to see they were almost upon them.

"Jump!" Colt shouted.

With a prayer of hope, she ran off the side of the cliff as another arrow missed her, screaming as she fell towards the canyon floor below.

Colt managed to get under her just in the nick of time! She grabbed onto his long, black mane with white-knuckled frenzy, letting out a *"WHOOMP!"* when she landed on his back.

A third arrow whizzed by, sizzling through the top of her shoulder with just enough force to knock her off. She clung to him with her one good hand, dangling off his side as he flew her farther away from the fray. She couldn't hold her grip, however, and slipped off his side, falling heavy as stone toward the ground below.

Colt pushed harder than he'd ever pushed before, getting underneath her again before she hit the large grouping of rocks they were approaching. If only she could hold on a few more feet until they hit the river! She'd be fine if she hit the water!

She slipped again, pain and exhaustion making her grip all the more precarious, but he managed to keep her on his back until they hit the water.

The woman couldn't hold on any longer and slipped into the current. Colt followed immediately after and caught her cloak with his teeth, pulling her to shore. He was surprised when he saw she no longer had legs, but a mermaid's tail instead! He pulled her farther up the bank and watched as she slowly transformed back into a human. They panted on the sand, trying to catch their breath.

From off in the distance, Colt could have sworn he heard the roar of a dragon. But that was impossible, wasn't it?

CHAPTER TWENTY-THREE: IBRAXUS TAKES A DIVE

Brax searched every place he used to go with Amy. She wasn't home, she was no longer at *his* home, and she hadn't been seen near her ancestral home in the sea either. On a last-ditch effort, he and Ifyrus had stopped by the old Outpost and ran into his old friend Tripp.

Finally! Someone who'd seen her! Brax felt a surge of relief and hope was renewed. Tripp told him he'd just sent her off this morning to Gallanor. At least that was somewhere Brax felt she would be safe.

Tripp suggested that he stay for a pint or two and catch up, but both men knew he'd be too eager to find his wife. Brax thanked him for his help and mounted Ifyrus, ready to fly to Gallanor. (Ifyrus refused to travel by Crannie, insisting he could fly there just as fast.)

As they approached the Gallanorian Woods, Brax heard a commotion on the cliffside below. He steered Ifyrus toward it. What he saw almost stopped his heart— it was Amaryah! And some *childling*. They were running for their lives from Ruskin's men, trying to avoid the arrows being dispatched in their direction!

Brax saw the child fly off the cliff as a pegasus and catch his wife in the air. Brax roared his best battle cry and flew his dragon as fast as he could to the fray! When they got close enough, Ifyrus let out a mighty plume of fire and smoke, igniting half the men on the cliff and melting them in their tracks.

He saw an arrow clip Amaryah and felt his heart stop a second time when she fell off the pegasus and drop to rocks below! Luckily, the child caught her again. Brax could swear he felt eight grey hairs pop out of his skull.

Ifyrus roared as he caught an arrow to his side and the two of them spiraled in the air. Brax lost sight of his wife. They went down hard and crashed into a log dam, smashing it to smithereens and cascading water all around them.

They came to a stop at the segment where the river bend hit and formed the rest of the waterway. He didn't see where Amaryah and the boy had gone, but he knew they were close, and he could track them.

"Ifyrus! Are you alright?" he asked, remembering his friend had been hurt.

The surly dragon lifted his massive body, shaking his head free of tree parts and nodded. He went to get up, but the arrow was still lodged in his side. The dragon moaned and tried to bite the fletching, but he couldn't quite reach it.

Brax told him to brace himself and yanked the offending weapon out as best he could. Ifyrus yelped and blood began to pool.

Brax looked grimly at his friend. "I'm so sorry, Ifyrus, but I'm afraid I can't heal you unless you are human. I know you said you had no interest in ever changing back, but I think in this instance, you might make an exception?"

To say his friend looked furious was an understatement.

"I know, and I hate to ask you to, but I'm afraid this looks rather nasty."

Ifyrus hung his head and keened pitifully at the sandy bank. After a moment, he nodded his giant head and puffed out a bit of smoke before transforming back into a man.

It had been so long since Brax had seen his best friend's face, his *human* face, that he'd almost forgotten what he looked like: Tall and broad shouldered, much like himself, but with shaggy, unkempt dark hair and piercing blue eyes. His chiseled jaw was stubbled with a dusting of beard, and his heart-shaped mouth was currently frowning.

Brax shook off his musings and laid his hands over his friend's wounded abdomen. A soft golden glow emanated from his hands and began to work their magick. The skin started to knit itself back together and his blood ceased flowing. Ifyrus grimaced and grit his teeth through the pain, but it was thankfully over quite quickly. He could breathe normally again.

"Thank you," came a raspy reply. Ifyrus hadn't spoken human words in ages. It must have felt odd for him to do so.

"You're welcome," Brax said. "I'm sorry I had to make you do that. And I'm sorry I have to ask you to stay this way for another day or two, just so I know that it worked and will hold. Remember, it's been a while for me as well. I would hate if it didn't take."

Ifyrus agreed reluctantly and grumbled under his breath.

"We'll rest here a few more minutes, but those men will find their way down here. We'd best be gone when they do. On the bright side, now that we know where Amaryah is, it won't be long till she's back in my arms."

The two men sat on the bank and hatched their plan to save her.

CHAPTER TWENTY-FOUR: AMY MEETS COLT

"Hi!" said the boy who saved my life. "I'm Colt. I've been sent to save you!" He grinned widely at me after transforming back into a little boy.

I had no idea how to process everything that happened, so I decided to just go with it. I could always have a mental breakdown later, right? I gingerly tested my bloody shoulder to see if it was still usable and, finding I could still move it (though it stung like a bastard), I pressed on.

"Hi, Colt," I said, getting up slowly. "I'm Amy. Thank you for saving me. Can you explain?"

He told me how Queen Miawae sent him as her hero and that he was to escort me to a safe town a little ways away from here.

"Queen Miawae, huh?" I asked.

He nodded enthusiastically. How cute. I couldn't wait to meet the woman who seemed to have a hand in more than one pie in this world.

"This way, please!" he said, and, once again, went full horse-mode right in front of me.

I shook off the shock of it and followed behind him at a quick clip, trying to put as much distance between us and the mob on our tail as possible.

After finally having lost Ruskin's men, and feeling safe enough to slow our pace, Colt and I were able to continue onward at a more leisurely jaunt. This came at a great time, as

I was thoroughly exhausted, confused, and starving. It had only been a couple hours since leaving Tripp's, but the adrenaline rush during our escape had sapped me of any energy I had left. Colt was munching on whatever came across our path, so I assumed he was equally famished.

"Hey, Colt?" I asked. He looked up from his mouthful of grass and berries, half-chewed and hanging out the sides of his maw.

I couldn't help but laugh. "I'm sorry, this is too much. Can you change back into a kid real quick? I gotta run stuff past you."

Colt gave a whinny in reply, swallowed his treats and obliged. Watching this transformation was going to take some getting used to. I can wrap my head around myself changing into a mermaid, but a *flying-horse-child*? I thought those only existed in Greek mythology or whatever! If only I could tell my freshman history teacher. It would blow his head clean off his shoulders!

When Colt was a kid again, he cleared his throat and wiped his face with his sleeve, dislodging any stray blades of green.

"Yes?" he asked.

"I don't know if you're as hungry as I am, but do you know of anywhere nearby where we can get some food and rest?"

He pointed towards a meadow up ahead.

"See that meadow? Well, just a little bit past that, and past a few trees, is a village filled with all sorts of stuff today.

This week is the big Food Faire and Fun Fest! I'm sure they'll have *plenty* to eat."

I sighed in relief. "That sounds perfect! But how do we pay for it? I'm still pretty new here— to this area, I mean," I caught myself. I didn't know how much he knew about Earth, and I didn't want to bring it up without talking to his parents first. What if he had no idea? I couldn't just blow his tiny mind with claims of a whole different world. "Do we trade for stuff, or...?"

Colt rolled his eyes and reached into his pocket. He pulled out a soft leather pouch and poured several pieces of various gemstones into his hand.

"We use these to pay for stuff," he said.

I blanched. I couldn't take money from a kid!

"Oh. Well, where can I get some?"

"I have plenty. You can have some of this."

"No! I can't do *that*, that's *yours*!" I said.

He rolled his eyes again. "It's okay! The queen paid me well to help you. We can get whatever you need. This is for both of us."

I made a mental note to thank this mysterious monarch the moment I got the chance.

"Well, bless her *and* her foresight, then! Let's get some grub, shall we?"

Colt looked confused. "Grub? Well, I saw some grubs under the log back there—" he turned, starting to point back the direction we came from.

I laughed and grabbed his arm, interlocking it with my own, and pulled him in the direction of the meadow.

"It means 'food' where I come from. Now, let's go to this faire!"

We traversed the remainder of the path to the village. The closer we got, the more people we saw entering and leaving the area. It seemed this was a big to-do for the region. Families, merchants, humans and creatures, everyone seemed happy to be here today. It reminded me of going to Renaissance Faires back home in California. Everyone dressed like they were in a fantasy production! Wherever I looked I saw bright colored banners and streamers swinging from tree boughs, joining long wreaths of glittering flower vines, making the village pop with color and vibrancy. Food vendors set up wooden kiosks and carts and dispersed them throughout the pathways. In between the kiosks were merchants selling weird and wonderful things: Gadgets, clothing, art, music, even live performances of traveling actors and puppeteers! I was enchanted.

Colt took off towards a booth that touted "Candy's Candied Carrot Cakes" and left me to fend for myself.

"Don't stray too far!" I shouted after him. He threw a hand behind him in reply, and I figured that was the best I would get from the boy that he'd heard me. I turned my attention to the food booths.

"Okay. What to eat, what to eat?" I asked, already stuck with talking out loud to myself.

"I hear the mutton is nice," said a voice behind me.

I jumped five feet in the air. *Why do people insist on scaring the crap out of me in this world?!* I whipped around to face the woman who spoke and tried to calm my racing heart. She chuckled and pointed to the booth offering mutton legs and stew.

"There's also Ruby's over there, if you're looking for something sweet," she continued without meeting my gaze, gesturing with a hot mug of something spicy smelling as she studied the crowd passing by.

I glanced briefly at both stations, my eyes stopping at her second suggestion, "Ruby's Rhubarbs", which just appeared to be ruby-red colored pies made of rhubarb encased in a gem-shaped sugar glass. I could see the appeal. My watering mouth seemed to agree. When it caught the light and actually *sparkled* like a ruby, I decided I was getting one.

I turned back to take in this new person.

"Thank you, uh...?"

She swallowed a mouthful of, I don't know, *tea*? and said, "Ellera. I've got this booth right here, if you're of a mind to hear about lost things?"

"Lost things?"

"You'd be surprised what you're hiding from yourself."

Thoroughly confused now, I peered at the etched clear quartz crystal sign on the bench beside her that stated, in jade calligraphy, "Ellera's Recollections". Hmm, catchy.

I turned my attention back to my new acquaintance. She had long black hair with scattered purple braids that snaked flirtily around her small shoulders, dark eyes that seemed to swallow the light, and a wide and beautiful bow-shaped mouth. She was currently smirking at a poor besotted fool chasing after a clearly uninterested woman. She laughed when the girl smacked his face when he tried to grab her hand. The resulting sound was almost hypnotic.

"Ha! The poor idiot. He should just cut his losses and run." She took another sip from her cup as if in punctuation of her statement.

I shook my head to clear it of her mirth and tried to find my manners.

"Yeah. He should definitely save himself the trouble. Hi, Ellera, was it? I'm Amy," I said, and reached to shake her hand. The second our hands met, her grip seized tight and held me fast, her vision clouding over until all I could see was a raging storm behind her eyes. Electric zings pulsed over them, absolutely transfixing me.

I gasped. "Ellera!" I started to sweat in fear now, as this strange woman would not let go of my hand!

With her eerie gaze fixed on me, she said, "Amaryah, you've returned."

"Oh no, not you, *too*!" I yanked my hand back with all my might and went tumbling backwards into a woman with a baked goods tray.

"*Aaaaahhhh*!" she cried, spilling bread and cakes left and right into the passersby.

"I'm *so* sorry! Here, let me help you." I scrambled to collect her goodies before damage or thieves could get to them but, sadly, not much could be done.

"Well, miss!" the rotund woman pointed at me, "guess you've just bought the lot, haven't you!" Not a question.

"Of course! My apologies. Let me pay for—" I started patting where my old jeans pocket with my cash would have been and I realized my mistake. Oh no! Colt has the money! That's right! I shouted towards the direction I thought he'd gone. "Colt? Colt, I need you! Where are you?"

Colt popped up on my right, scaring the bejesus outta me! Smirking, he handed the woman a few gemstones and she huffed her way back to her kiosk.

"Thank you. Again," I said.

"No problem!" he replied. "Do you need anything else, or can I go check out that booth over there? They have this really amazing dagger rack—"

"Dagger?" I said. "How old are you? You shouldn't be playing with daggers!"

He laughed at my scorn and waved it away with his hand.

"Don't worry! I'm only looking! Besides, I already have one." He grinned and flashed her a silver dagger from inside his coat and took off towards the booth he'd mentioned.

"Kids," Ellera said. "What are you going to do?"

I watched him skip merrily over to the dagger rack and bit my lip.

"He'll be fine, don't worry. Now, how about that reading, Amaryah?"

"Amy, please," I said, hoping this strange woman didn't mean me harm.

"Fine. Amy. Follow me. I have a feeling I was meant to meet you today."

I followed Ellera into her multicolored tent and was reminded instantly of the psychic tents I would frequent at fairs back home. It was comfortable here, familiar, or, at the very least, not totally foreign.

"So, tell me," Ellera said, "what brings you here today?" She sat in the chair farthest from me, across from a small table. Again, this felt very much like a psychic reading.

I sat down in the chair she'd motioned to and rested my tired limbs on the table.

"Well, I've been sent here to find someone who apparently is not only dead, but is also somehow, if you can believe it, my husband."

Ellera's lips quirked at that. "You'd be surprised what doesn't surprise me."

"I don't doubt that," I replied. "I imagine you see and hear all kinds of weird stuff in this line of work."

She nodded and reached for my hands again. I let her, not knowing what else to do. I winced when she tugged my arm a little too hard and my shoulder throbbed, reminding me I'd been shot by an arrow today.

"That looks painful," she pointed out. "You okay?"

"I'm fine. It's just a scratch."

She was quiet for a moment, studying my hands before frowning.

"May I touch your face?" she asked.

"Uhh, is that absolutely necessary?"

"It is if you want a more accurate reading. I can do all the standard stuff like reading your palms or aura but, if you'd like more in-depth answers, I'm afraid I will have to get a bit closer. Now, may I touch your face?"

I clenched my jaw but agreed. Ellera got out of her chair and stood behind me, placing her hands on both sides of my head at the temples.

"Do you see anything?" I asked.

"Shh! I'm trying to concentrate!"

"Sorry," I whispered, blushing a bit.

Another minute went by, her hands warm on my face, getting hotter by the second.

"Ah, aha. I think I've found him."

Surprised, I said, "You've found Ibraxus? Where?"

"You will find him deep within the mountain, far below ash and rock and soot."

"Seriously?"

Ellera laughed. "No. He's right behind you."

"What?" I stood and whipped my head around, immediately bonking it on a wooden support beam. *Ouch*! No real damage, just my pride. No big deal. Ellera had a laugh riot.

"That wasn't very nice," I said, rubbing my forehead.

"No, buuuuut, it was funny. And accurate."

I whipped around again, this time knocking over a teapot from a table that shattered on the ground where I fell. Ellera howled with laughter as I rolled down her steps. I felt myself being hoisted up by big, strong arms.

Ellera managed a, "HA! Told ya," and proceeded to gloat from the doorway I'd just tumbled out of.

"Amaryah! It's *you*!" came the man's deep, silky voice.

He immediately crushed me in a massive bear hug that left me fighting for air. He relaxed his grip only a fraction when he heard my squeak.

"Hey... Man!" I looked to Ellera for help, but she just shrugged a dainty shoulder at me. "Who might you be?"

The gorgeous man's face fell and looked like I'd just kicked his puppy. He let go of me and I fell like a sack of potatoes.

"Oof!"

"Amaryah, do you not recognize your own husband?"

"What? Brax? You're Ibraxus? Ha! Ha ha ha ha ha ha! Nooo... no. No, you're like, hot, like *super* hot! You're like, *Marvel* hot, that's— nooooo, no no no no no no no..." I trailed off like a giggling idiot.

Obviously, Brax was confused. He had a half smile behind a beard of blonde and brown that matched his shoulder length hair, like he was waiting for me to say I was just messing with him or something. He had no idea what I'd been through, nor the fact that I couldn't remember him.

"Your shoulder," Brax said. "Are you hurt?" He reached for my wound, but I shook him off.

"I'm fine," I said, almost certain that was true.

He looked to Ellera for assistance, but she was content to lean on the tent pole of her hut.

"You're telling me we're married," I said, completely off guard. This felt like the most bizarre dream.

Brax cocked his head at me and tried to approach, slowly, hands out as if to grab my hand but worried I might run away.

I jumped back, not quite ready for all of this.

"I— I don't understand. Are you unwell, Amaryah? I can't say I'd be surprised by that, seeing as how I watched you die."

That sobered me. "First of all, Brax— may I call you Brax?"

He nodded, brows furrowed.

"Great. Brax, it seems as though I died and got transported here to this planet of crazy, and I have no idea what the hell I'm even doing here, aside from trying to apparently find *your* also dead ass, so you tell me. *Am I unwell? Am I dead? Am I un dead? Am I a zombie? Or just a mermaid? Or a zombie mermaid? Oooh! That's a new one! What would that be? A zombaid? A mermbie? A mermbie.*"

Ellera finally stepped in, seeing I was spiraling.

"Okay, you two, that's enough. Come with me." She finger-beckoned both of us back into her tent. "Let me show you what you've missed. Free of charge, against my better judgment."

She pulled up an extra chair from the side of her tent and we all sat down at the table. Brax was eyeing me strangely, and I was blushing under the weight of his gaze. Seriously, that man was hot enough to fry an egg. *Am I sweating?*

"Okay, Ibraxus, I take it?" Ellera asked.

"King Ibraxus of Dragon Moon, yes."

Ellera rolled her eyes and grabbed his hand, plunking it roughly on the table.

"Good for you."

"And you are—?"

"Ellera. I'm here to show you your memories. My good friend Amy here was just telling me about her search for you, but it seems as though she's lost her memory and I'm hoping you're just the man to help her find it. Now, shall we?"

She grabbed his other hand and dropped it down brusquely on the other side of the table, then lightly grabbed mine to join with his. I felt the sizzle of electricity humming between us when our hands touched. I yanked my hand back in surprise.

"Steady, now! You don't want to break my concentration!"

I reddened deeper at her tone and put my hands back where they were.

Ellera sat down and splayed her fingers above our interlocked hands, hovering enough to not be touching, but enough to feel the heat in the space between.

"Alright, now, both of you, close your eyes."

"But I—" I said.

"Close your eyes!" she said.

I slammed my eyes shut as fast as I could, and I felt, rather than saw, Brax chuckle at the chiding. I kicked him under the table. He gave me a soft kick in return.

"Children! Can you two stop it? I need to focus!"

We both settled down and I felt my body relax.

Ellera's voice took on an eerie cadence. "Ibraxus, where have you been all these years? I feel cold, but it does not feel like death."

He cleared his throat and said, "I woke up yesterday in an ice cave somewhere in the Snow Lands. I have no memory of getting there. My friend Ifyrus was there with me in his dragon form."

"I'm happy to learn there is still a dragon alive in this world, besides yourself, of course," she said.

I felt Brax tense at her words.

"I visited my home. There was no one left. I... didn't know."

"It must be hard being so alone."

"It is," he said. "And I was cursed before I died. I can no longer take the form of my dragon."

Ellera said, "That must be tough as well."

He chuckled without mirth. "You have no idea. It makes me feel... less than."

I felt sorry for this man. I'd only been a mermaid for a couple weeks and I already couldn't imagine not being able to connect to that part of myself. I gave his hand a reassuring squeeze and was surprised to feel a light squeeze back. I chanced opening one eye to look at him and saw he had done the same.

"CLOSE YOUR EYES!"

I shut my eyes fiercely again and tried to return my attention to the present.

"Now, Amaryah—"

"Amy," I corrected.

"Amy," she said. "I am having a hard time seeing anything from you. I need you to focus on where you were before coming here."

I took a deep breath and focused on my home in Sebastopol. I thought about my cute little one-bedroom home, my crystal shop that I'd spent so much of my time in, and the few friends and family I'd left behind.

"Are you focusing? I can't see anything."

"I'm trying!" I squinted harder, trying to force the images into her head.

Ellera tittered and said, "Are you trying to poop? What's with the face?"

I blushed a deep crimson and thought some very mean things aimed in her direction.

She laughed again and said, "Now *that* I heard! Okay, try again. This time, don't force it, just let it flow naturally. Maybe find a happy memory?"

I thought about it for a moment before deciding on a hike I had taken just before I died. I went out to a nearby state park called Armstrong Woods to wander around the marked trails, connecting to the dense forest around me. I saw a doe and her fawns that had come down from the small mountain for a snack. I sat on a nearby bench and watched them. It was a simple memory, but one that filled me with peace and joy.

"Amy, where were you? I don't know this place."

"Earth. I was on Earth."

"Earth? What, or where, is that?"

Just then, there was a sudden commotion at the doorway and all three of us jumped.

"Brax," said a man, clutching his stomach. He toppled over and landed hard on his knees. Brax caught him before he landed on his face and helped prop him up against the tent lining.

"Ifyrus! What happened? You were fine on that bench I left you on a few minutes ago!" Brax said.

The man lifted his shirt to reveal a gaping wound, oozing blood and ichor on the dusty flooring.

Ellera made a choking noise and said, "Watch the floor! I still have to have customers in here for the next two days!"

Both men shot her a sneer and Ifyrus said, "So sorry to sully your sanctuary, sweetheart, but I seem to be dying, do you mind?"

Thinking quickly, I grabbed the first swath of fabric I could find and handed it to Brax.

"Here! Put pressure on the wound with this!" I pressed my hands over his onto the wound. Ifyrus yelped. "You need to stop the bleeding!"

"Ahhh! My cloak!" Ellera shrieked. "What did you do that for?"

"You have to apply pressure to stop the bleeding!" They all looked at me as if *I* was the strange one here. I threw my hands up in deference and sat back down. "Fine! Let him bleed out. No skin off *my* nose."

Brax huffed and said, "Will everyone just please calm down a minute and let me fix him?"

He placed his hands over the suffering man, and I could swear I saw a bright white light emanating from them to penetrate the bloody hole. But the light started to flicker, and both men were cursing now, so I wasn't quite sure what was supposed to be happening.

"It's—" gasped Ifyrus, "not working. I think— ah! I think they poisoned the arrow."

Ellera let out a long breath and steeled her composure.

"Okay, out of my way. Let me see this thing."

"I beg your pardon?" Brax bristled. "What makes you think *you* can help when my magick is failing to do so?"

"Because," she said, rolling up her sleeves, "I'm not just a traveling mind reader, you dolt. I've learned a thing or two in my time and I might be able to help. So shut up, get out of my way, and let me see if I can keep your friend from expiring on my floor!"

Brax took a breath to give her a piece of his mind, but the man on the floor chuckled through his pain and said, "Imagine that. A Mind Traveler giving the Dragon King the old what-for like a child caught stealing biscuits. I never thought I'd see the day. Almost makes dying worth it."

Ellera paused. "You know what I am?"

"Lucky guess."

"Lucky guess, my foot," she said, and prodded the wound with her finger.

"OW!" Ifyrus yelped. "Be careful, woman!"

"I'm sorry, did you want my help? Because this is me helping. Now, shut up, you big baby." She stuck her finger in the hole even farther and closed her eyes to concentrate.

I was gonna be sick. Forcing my nausea back down, I peeked at the situation unfolding before my squinted eyes. The room was crackling with tiny energy bolts, like static electricity dancing in a darkened room. It was strangely beautiful, and I found it overrode my impulse to puke.

Ellera's hair began to lift up and she tilted her head backwards, then to each side, and back to center again.

"What are you doing to him?" asked Brax.

"Searching," she said in that odd cadence from earlier.

"For what?"

"What kind of poison it is. From what I can tell, it's not one I have an antidote for."

"Well, then, what good are you?" he asked, glaring daggers at her.

"How*ever*," she continued, "I do know someone who can help, but it's a ways away from here. I can place a temporary blocker on the spread of it and close him back up, but like the patch job *you* did on him before, it won't last long. Still, it should get you there in enough time."

"Enough time for what?" Ifyrus asked.

"Enough time to save your life."

"Do it," Brax said.

"You got it, pal."

Ellera began to work her magick, inserting a spell directly into the wound and speaking in a language I didn't recognize. The room was now zinging with sparks of color and my hair lifted with the electric charge. I noticed she'd slipped a gemstone from her pocket and was using it over the hole. I watched as the smoky quartz went from looking brand new to then dust when it was taxed. Ellera let the bits drop to the floor, empty and forgotten.

"Now," she motioned to Brax, wiping her hands together to clear the quartz, "try again."

Brax knelt by his friend and repeated his healing process. This time, it seemed to be working. The skin on the wound pulled closer together, and the man's breathing became less ragged. After a moment, he was breathing normally again.

"There isn't much time on that patch, so you'd better get going," Ellera said.

Ifyrus tried to stand but was very shaky.

"What? Aren't you coming with us?"

"I don't think you'll need my assistance any further," she said.

He walked up to her until their noses were nearly touching. I could hear the intake of her breath.

"But if you don't come with us, you'll miss me terribly," Ifyrus said, winking at her.

"Hardly," she replied, but I could see a flicker of interest behind that nonchalant face.

I piped up. "I'm sorry, where are you sending us?"

"To the Fae Realm. They have the most skilled healers that I know of. If this is the same poison I've seen in years past, they'll be the ones to have the antidote."

"How do we get there?"

The men looked at me with blank faces.

Ellera let out a bark of a laugh. "Are you telling me that none of you, not even the infamous Dragon King, has ever been to the Fae Realm, even once?"

He shook his head abashedly.

Ellera clapped his shoulder. "What an excellent ruler you must have made."

Brax gritted his teeth and Ifyrus laughed, loving how this strange woman was putting his friend on edge. I didn't want to get in the middle of it.

Ellera chewed her lip for a moment and finally said, "Fine. I will take you there."

"Thank you—" Brax started to say but was cut off.

"But! There's a big *but*!"

Ifyrus grinned cheekily. "Not from where I'm standing, Love."

Ellera reddened and said, "I will take you there, *but…* as it will be costing me the rest of my pay here, I will need to be properly compensated for my time."

"You're looking at The King of The Dragons, Love," Ifyrus said. "He can get you whatever you need. So could I, for that matter."

"I will thank you to stop reminding me of whom I am speaking to, sir, I am not a half-wit! As for your advances, you can keep those *well* out of my reach!"

Ifyrus turned to Brax. "I like her. Maybe it won't be that bad being human after all."

Ellera turned to Brax as well. "If the poison doesn't kill him first, I just might!"

I couldn't help it. I laughed.

Ellera fixed her gaze on me and said, "I haven't forgotten about you, but we will have to attend to your memory issues and that odd little bit of Arth nonsense, or Earth, whatever you called it, later. This one is short on time. Come along, everyone, and help me pack this up. We leave in ten minutes."

With that, we got to work as quickly as we could. Ifyrus, admittedly, was not much help in his condition. As the last bit of tent parts made their way into its unusually small bag, I realized Colt still hadn't made it back to us. I informed the group I would be right back.

"Grab me one of those Ruby pies, Love. Dying really works up an appetite!"

"Anyone else need anything before we go? Make it quick if you do," I said.

After collecting Colt and an armful of snacks, we were ready to hit the road.

"I can't *wait* to tell my family I get to meet actual faeries!" said Colt. "They'll never believe me!"

I pulled him aside as we loaded up the horses Ellera rented for us.

"You know, Colt, it's not too late to turn around and go back. Your family must be really worried about you. Besides, you finished your mission. You brought me to the faire in one piece, and I found Ibraxus. The queen will be so pleased with you!"

Colt's face fell. "You... you don't want me to come?"

He gave me those sad, puppy dog eyes and I was toast. Dammit.

"Fine. You can come. But just for a little bit, then you have to get home safely, understand?"

He nodded so hard I thought he'd snap his neck, but his enthusiasm was adorable.

"Alright, everybody," I said. "Who's ready to meet some faeries?"

CHAPTER TWENTY-FIVE: ETHAN'S FINAL SESSION

As a special form of torture, Viego had installed a mirror above the bed Ethan was chained to. *To see your life slipping away,* he'd told him.

Ethan's gaunt face stared back at himself all day, every day, in this living, breathing, never-ending nightmare. The food had stopped coming days ago, and his body was determined to get the much-needed calories from somewhere. It was taking its toll.

Footsteps echoed down the hall, taking their time, as they were wont to do.

A tear slipped down his cheek. Or, it would have, if Ethan wasn't so dehydrated that he could no longer produce tears.

He thought the fear would have subsided by now, that his brain would have shut off and gone into survival mode. But every day was the same, over and over and over again. Except now he was witness to his own slow demise, thanks to that infuriating and humiliating mirror.

He prayed for death. At such a young age, that should have been unthinkable. He didn't truly want to die, of course, but he couldn't endure this non-life for much longer. He wished to be put out of his misery. If he had anything notable to offer Viego, anything, he would give it, but he didn't know what the creature wanted. He gave him every bit of information he had.

The door opened with the same maddening squeal as usual, and Ethan flinched at the sound.

The smell of hot food assaulted his nostrils with such force that it caused him to vomit, but as there was nothing in his system, it came out as dry heaves. His stomach twisted and churned painfully.

Instead of his normal cheery greeting, Viego simply sat down at the table next to the bed and began to eat in silence. He ate the entire meal. He even crunched the bones. When he was finished, Viego licked the last drops of fat from the plate and set it calmly back onto the table. Ethan's growling stomach was deafening.

Viego turned to Ethan and crossed his bony leg over his knobby knee, steepling his fingers to rest his chin on.

He stared.

And stared.

And stared.

Ethan's stomach took a backseat to his thundering heart.

After an eternity, Viego spoke.

"The king grows impatient."

Ethan tried to swallow, but it got stuck and he coughed. If his mirror was to be believed, that cough contained blood. At least it was liquid, and enough to wet his whistle.

"I've told you all I know," he said through cracked lips.

More time elapsed.

Finally, Viego continued.

"The king has instructed me to utilize my deepest digging."

Ethan's heart sped up even faster.

"Deepest? How could you go any—?"

"This is to be our final session, dear boy. I'm afraid this will hurt. But, if it's any consolation, I don't think you will make it through to worry about it."

Viego pushed the right sleeve of his cloak up to his elbow and unleashed the tentacle finger. Aimed above the now rotting hole in Ethan's skull, he plunged in without further ado.

"Interesting... *very* interesting." He hissed as he found something sparkly in the recesses of Ethan's mind. "Power like this in one so young and stupid!"

Ethan's vocal cords ripped, and his soul caught fire. He thought he'd endured pain before, but this? This was life-altering, life-ending pain.

This was it.

This was the end.

But then...

Thump thump! went his heartbeat.

Thump thump! it went again.

Thump thump! and then *BOOM!*

Viego was shot forcefully backward into the unforgiving rock wall! His body collapsed to the floor.

He didn't move.

Ethan's pain disappeared in a flash. In fact, it felt as though he'd taken the first clean breath he'd had in ages. He looked up at his mirror and saw bright shining amethyst eyes looking back at him.

"What have I done?" he asked his equally shocked reflection.

Just then, two guards burst into the room, weapons at the ready and pointed straight at Ethan's heart.

"Lord Viego!" one shouted at the prone body on the floor. "Lord Viego, are you alright?"

The other guard, seeing the prisoner was still chained to the bed, leaned down and assisted the monster to his feet.

Viego shook his head and gathered his wits.

"Quite alright, gentlemen, thank you for coming. Well, now. It appears as though I require an audience with the king. Our young friend here has something to offer him after all."

With that, the men took their leave and locked the door to Ethan's cell, leaving him alone and terrified with his brand-new purple eyes.

CHAPTER TWENTY-SIX: CYNDOL SETS OFF TO SAVE HER BROTHER

Cyndol awoke at dawn, having barely slept, too anxious to be on her way to save her brother. The idea Queen Miawae had left her with, of Ethan being tortured by the king's hand, was too much to bear, so she slept fitfully all night long, tossing and turning and crying out in her sleep. Kit had snuggled into her for comfort, but after being punted to the floor for a third time, he decided to stay there. After all, one can only be kicked so many times.

The knock came promptly at sunrise, and Cyndol eagerly hopped out of bed, ready to be off. She landed directly on Kit's tail, and he yelped in pained surprise.

"Oh, Kit! I'm so sorry! Please forgive me," she said.

Kit grumbled but accepted her apology, giving his tail a cursory lick to make sure he was alright.

Cyndol opened the door to see Evony and the guards.

"Are you ready, Young One?" Evony asked.

Cyndol chose not to be offended by her address and instead beamed a beatific smile.

"I sure am! Let's go save my brother!" She grabbed the pack she'd made up the night before, gathered her foxy friend, and closed the door behind her. "Goodbye, treehouse! You've been great!"

Evony led her over to the cart and horses they'd set up in case Ethan was badly injured.

"Here you go, Little One," Evony said while gesturing at the cart's front seat. "Have a seat up here. Your furball friend can sit with you, if you like, unless he prefers to roam behind us in the dust of the horses?"

Cyndol looked at Kit and they appeared to have a conversation, though only Cyndol's side could be heard.

"What do you say, Kit?... I know, how do you think *I* feel? She called me 'Little One'!... I didn't tell her you liked to roam around in horse-dust! Maybe she's met other foxes that do?... Okay, I'll tell her." She turned to Evony. "He says he will ride up front with me and thank you very much for letting him come."

Kit glared at Cyndol, displeased, she niced up his irritations. Cyndol just kept her smile plastered on her face, hoping nobody would notice his rudeness.

Both Cyndol and Kit clamored up into the front of the cart and settled in. Evony climbed in next to her, taking the reins and clicking her tongue at the team to get them to go. The rest of the guard followed behind them on their own respective horses.

Cyndol was curious about the group she was traveling with. Obviously, she knew Evony, but she hadn't met anyone else yet.

"Evony," she began hesitantly, "I want to thank you for coming with me to rescue my brother."

She raised an eyebrow at her and said, "I'm doing as my queen asked of me. We all are."

"Oh," Cyndol replied. "Well, regardless, thank you. I don't know how to get there on my own and I don't know if I'd know what to do once I got there."

"Good thing you have us, then."

"It sure is!" Cyndol said. "So, what can you tell me about the group? I only know you." She was eager to learn more about her hired heroes.

Evony glanced behind her at their party and went on to introduce her small guard: There were the twins, Fenix and Felix, two dashing looking men with ebony skin and fiery orange eyes that had been fighting for the royal family since they were old enough to handle a sword. They were both proficient in many weapons, both carrying swords, daggers, and bows with a quiver of arrows. They were skilled at making weapons as well. They had some small fire powers due to having a touch of dragon blood and used it to forge beautiful swords. It was a great gift, indeed, to those who were lucky enough to have them craft one for them.

Then there was their cook, a pleasantly plump and shyly smiling woman named Bella. Evony had warned Cyndol not to be deceived by her looks. "This one is also a skilled assassin; she just prefers using her knife skills to feed instead of bleed people.

"That man there," Evony said, gesturing to the man in the back of the wagon with long, partially braided reddish-brown hair, presently going through his bag of medicine and healing stones, "is one of our top healers, Druce. He saved Princess

Davina from nearly losing her foot, once. But that's a long story."

Cyndol tried her best to take it all in.

"So, why do we need so many of us?"

Evony looked at her through side-eye. "Because, Little One, we do not know the state of travel on this path and Ruskin has spies everywhere. It does not hurt to be cautious. From what I understand from the queen, we are to treat you and watch over you like you were her own."

Cyndol didn't know what she did to garner such an honor from Her Majesty, but she needed every bit of help she could get to save her brother. She would just have to shut up and be grateful.

A few hours passed by without much to note. Cyndol and Kit excitedly took in the sights around them while the guard kept a watchful eye on their path.

When the second sun started to set in the sky, Evony halted the group and called for them to make camp.

"We can stay here tonight," she said, "and head back out at first light. Fenix, you set up the tents and the fire. Bella, get started on supper. Felix and I will be doing a perimeter sweep. Druce, stay here with the child and her companion. And if anyone sees or hears anything they don't like, sound the call."

Everyone nodded and proceeded to go about their duties. It was a flurry of motion all at once and it made Cyndol's head spin.

"What are Kit and I to do?" she asked Evony as she readied to go scouting.

She turned back to Cyndol and said, "Stay in the cart."

Cyndol harrumphed as Evony and the guard left to do their jobs. The only one left was Druce, the healer.

"Hi," Cyndol said. "I'm Cyndol. This is Kit."

"I know," he said. "I think the whole village knows by now, if I had to wager."

He gave her a good-natured clap on the shoulder and Cyndol blushed. She wasn't accustomed to being so popular, especially amongst so many strangers. It made her both excited and uncomfortable. Kit just preened like the cocky fox he was and was rewarded by a head-scratch from Druce.

After a time, camp had been set up, Evony and Felix had returned from perimeter checks, and supper was finally ready. Just in time, too, as Cyndol's stomach could be heard from across their temporary encampment. Cyndol caught Bella chuckling at her gurgly tummy, and she blushed once more.

"Oh, don't worry dear," Bella said. "I know the feeling well. Why do you think I'm so quick to cook?" She laughed loudly and gave her protruding belly a good shake. Cyndol couldn't help but crack a smile at her confident bubbliness.

Evony called the adults over to the table they'd set up to hold the food, and she instructed them to place it by the logs that had been set up by the fire. They sat themselves around the blazing pit Fenix had lit to enjoy their meal in comfort.

Cyndol gladly hopped down from the cart, Kit on her heels, and she grabbed plates for them both at the end of the table. On hers, she placed some chunks of venison with gravy, along with carrots, potato mash, steamed greens, and a buttery apple cake. Cyndol had no idea how Bella managed the fresh apple cakes but suspected she had some magick of her own. Kit's plate was piled high with meat, plain potato mash, and bits of carrots. He was loving not having to hunt for his meal, and Cyndol had never tasted meat so tender and mouthwatering. And that apple cake? Cyndol could eat those every day, forever.

The party ate and drank their fill. Though they had a feast on their plates, they all stuck to water as their beverages "to keep a clear head". Cyndol thought that very wise, though she would be drinking water either way. She kept a small flask of it in her pouch and filled it as often as possible. Her parents had always said that water was the most important thing she could keep with her at all times. She took that claim to heart.

When supper had ended and the night settled upon them, the group took turns telling stories around the fire. Everyone had something to say, whether it was long or short, funny or sad, some even sang songs instead of the usual storytelling.

At one point, it occurred to Cyndol that the group was louder than she thought they ought to be. After all, it was getting late and she was afraid they'd attract unwanted attention with the large fire, the smell of food, and the sounds of their merriment. She brought that up with their leader.

Evony gave her a tired half-smile and said, "Child, you're going to have to trust us. We wouldn't be this open with our evening if we could not keep us safe." She pulled a turquoise-wrapped moonstone rod from the leather cord at the top of her shirt, showcasing a stunning necklace that was laced with tiny facets of diamonds. "For protection and safe travels. These gems are the best for casting those types of spells. We are camping under an invisible dome. No one can see us, no one can hear us, but we can see and hear them, should anyone try to approach. I can take down the spell in the morning when we go about our mission."

Cyndol relaxed a bit, trusting that Evony knew what she was doing. Why else would the queen appoint her as her Right Hand and War Chief if she didn't know how to safely get someone somewhere they needed to go and protect them the entire way?

"Who else has a story?" asked Felix.

Kit surprised everyone by jumping into the center of attention and landing next to the fire. He began yipping excitedly and making all kinds of noises, but only Cyndol appeared to understand him.

"Does your friend know we don't speak 'Fox'?" Fenix asked.

The group laughed, though not rudely. Kit seemed crestfallen. Whatever he had to say, he'd had his heart set on it.

"No matter at all," said Druce. "I've got just the thing! Give me but a moment."

Druce left the group to root around in his large bag of supplies. After a minute or two, he let out a victorious yelp and rejoined the group, prize in hand.

"Okay, now, this won't hurt at all, Kit," he said.

Kit's eyes grew wide, and he tried to dart behind Cyndol's legs.

Druce took a few deep breaths and centered his focus. He then brandished the item he'd drawn from his bag: Another rod, similar to the one Evony had, but this one was made of blue topaz, flint, and moonstone in equal measure.

"For communication," he said to Cyndol. Then, to Kit, he pointed the rod, aimed his energy, and said, "Speak!"

"No!" shouted Kit. "And you can't make me!"

Everyone became silent. A slow grin spread over Druce's face, and he slipped the rod back into his pocket, satisfied with his handiwork. He sat back down with the others.

"Kit," said Evony, "I believe you had a story for us?"

"Why? You can't understand me anyway!" he said from behind Cyndol's shins.

"Are you so certain?" she asked.

Both Cyndol's and Kit's eyes grew wide in shock as they realized what had just happened. The group burst into laughter at their faces.

"You can hear him?" Cyndol asked, needing to be sure it was true.

"Yes, Little One, we can hear him talk now. Druce fixed that issue for us. Thank you, Druce."

Druce just bowed his head at her.

"So, Kit? Are you still up for your story?" Evony gestured to the fire.

Kit slowly left the comfort of Cyndol's limbs and crept back to the fire pit, more nervous now than he was before. He gave a little test sentence.

"Just making sure you guys can hear me?" he said.

"We can hear you perfectly," Bella said. "Please. Go on with your story."

The group fell silent again and all eyes were on Kit. He grinned toothily and did the fox equivalent of a throat clearing before starting.

"Have any of you ever heard the Tale of Blood Bear?"

He looked purposefully around the group and saw a bunch of shaking heads.

"Well, then, that means you are lucky! For those that hear of Blood Bear know *fear*!" He cocked his head and gave a sinister smile.

A few soft chuckles were heard. Not in disbelief, but in anticipation.

Kit continued. "Once, long, long ago, there was a mother bear by the name of Breyga. Breyga was very much loved by her fellow animal community and often helped take care of not only her own three cubs, but the cubs and elderly in the area as well. Their land was a peaceful land. No one came to disturb them, and there was food and plenty for all. The animals lived a happy existence.

"Then one day, a shout was heard in the distance. The animals had never heard such a sound before! They paused and held their positions, waiting to see if they heard it again.

Silence. Then...there it was again! This time, there was no mistaking it. There were humans headed their way!

"The animals ran and hid in trees and holes and caves and shrubs, all trying to flee from these strange creatures.

"The voices got louder, and so did the noise they brought with them. The men were on the backs of horses, forcing the poor stallions and mares to bear the weight of them. The free horses whinnied in pity and disgust for those being hit by these men. The men were whipping them, trying to get them to move faster to get out of these woods.

"The men's horses were tired. One fell after stumbling over a rock in the path they were creating and man and beast toppled to the ground. One of the other men dismounted and promptly killed the poor horse right there. They did not hold with lame pack animals.

"It was at that moment, one of Breyga's cubs lost his footing in the tree above them and slipped partway down the bark. His claws caught him before he hit the ground, but it was too late. He had been spotted by the men.

"'Aha!' said one of the men, 'I see we've found our sport for the day!'

"That was all the encouragement they needed. The men gathered their horses underneath the tree that held Breyga and her cubs. Breyga tried to pull them up higher, out of the reach of the humans, sensing only danger emanating from their evil faces, but the tree did not have much more room to supply.

"'Take aim and shoot!' another man shouted at one with a nocked bowstring.

"The man took aim and fired at the bears, landing shot after shot until all the bears were tumbling from the branches and landing on the ground beside them. Breyga was roaring her mightiest roar, swinging her massive paws, claws out, at anyone within reach. The horses under the men were frightened and tried to bolt, but Breyga swiped at them as well.

"Blood, guts, brains and bones went flying this way and that! Breyga tore into those men like a monster, not caring about their screams, not caring about their pain, only wanting to cause *them* pain for daring to come into their forest and attack her family! How dare they!"

Kit paused for dramatic effect. The group sat glued to his every word.

"Finally," he said, "when Breyga saw that no one was moving, she relented her offensive moves and turned to attend to her cubs. But she saw they weren't moving either. In fact, all was still in the woods now. The only sounds were her heaving pants. She realized she was covered in blood and ichor. Her coat was stained by it, and she saw she had a few arrows embedded in her as well.

"Now came her own pain. She brayed her pain and despair into the cloudy sky, and it shook the world around her! The animals that remained peeked their eyes out from their hiding places, taking in the sight. A mother, crying at the loss of her children, slowly stumbling from the weapons in her sides.

"She gave one last mighty roar and fled into the trees, never to return again.

"They say her ghost still roams this world, searching for any human that has the misfortune of crossing her path, so that she might drag them kicking and screaming into the next life as payback for her cubs.

"I see we have quite a few of you humans here." Kit smiled cheekily. "Better sleep with one eye open tonight. I don't know if your magick can keep out Blood Bear and her need for vengeance."

He bared his teeth and gave his best loud growl before launching himself into Fenix's lap, effectively terrifying the poor man!

When everyone realized he was just licking his face and not eating it, they all let out a collective laugh of relief and gave Kit a round of applause.

Kit jumped down from Fenix's lap, doing a little bow before rejoining Cyndol on the log.

"Well told, Kit," Evony said, "and well warned. We will keep our eyes peeled, just in case."

Just then, a clap of thunder overhead startled the travelers, and rain began to pour down upon them.

"Oh no!" Cyndol cried. "We're going to get drenched!"

She scrambled to grab her cloak from her pack and threw it above her and Kit's heads to protect them from the onslaught, but it never came. Cyndol lowered her cloak and looked to Evony to explain.

"It's the spell I put up, remember? It keeps out foul weather, too." She then turned to address the group and said, "This is a good time to call it a night. We will have another long day ahead of us tomorrow, so rest up. We leave just after daybreak."

The group dispersed and Cyndol and Kit climbed back into the cart, choosing to lay on the blankets spread out in the back to look up at the rain cascading over their dome. It was so pretty and peaceful that it lulled them right to sleep.

CHAPTER TWENTY-SEVEN: RUSKIN'S REQUIREMENT

"Your Majesty!" Silas said, rushing into the throne room.

"What?"

"Lord Viego wishes an audience with you, sire. He claims to have made progress with the boy."

Ruskin perked up on his throne and shifted himself to a more commanding position.

"Send him in at once!"

"Yes, Your Majesty!" Silas rushed back to the double doors at the entryway and admitted the Mind Traveler.

"What news of the boy?" the king asked.

Viego bowed so low that his nose seemed to touch the ground. Upon his standing, he tried to hide the simpering smirk on his tarnished face.

Ruskin grimaced and said, "My, you are an ugly thing, aren't you?" He turned to face Davina, who was lounging on the throne beside his. "Don't you find him ugly, my dear?"

She granted one quick glance, and her eyes dismissed him immediately. "Simply repulsive, My King."

Ruskin, pleased with their assessment of one below their station, bade him continue.

"My King," Viego said, in a much humbler manner now, "I was able to make some progress with the boy. While I was unable to find the whereabouts of the artifact, I was successful in finding something that could prove just as important."

Ruskin scowled down at him, the vein in his forehead drumming a death march. "What could possibly be more important than the one thing I commanded of you?!"

Viego shrank back a little. "His eyes are no longer blue, my king. They are purple."

"And you believe this to be of importance?"

"Well, yes," said Viego. "They are the eyes of amethyst, you see."

Ruskin's breath caught in his throat. Could it be? Could this be the child he had been forewarned of all those years ago? Was this boy the instrument of his death? He had to be certain.

"I require his eyes," he said to the creature before him. "I need them both, just to be sure."

"Of course, Your Majesty!" Viego said. "I can do it as soon as you like!"

"Tomorrow, then. You and Davina will see that it is done."

Viego looked suspiciously at the dark Mage beside the king.

"Is that necessary, my Liege?"

Ruskin leaned forward in his chair, his fingers clawing the throne's armrests.

"Do you challenge my orders, Monster?" The king growled low, and his face began to elongate, as did the claws on his hands. Dark mahogany hairs began sprouting through skin, and muscle tissue rippled along his body.

Viego, through all of his faults, was also a coward. He shrank back from the wolf shifter before him and wisely chose to bow instead of fleeing in terror. He apologized profusely and the king stopped his growling, point made.

"You will both attend the removal. Now, begone from my presence. Your cowardliness disgusts me."

Viego bowed one more time, this time including Davina in the gesture, just in case, and exited the throne room.

"Keep an eye on that one, my dear," Ruskin said. "I'm not entirely sure what to make of his race. I've heard tell that they can make you see things that aren't there. I trust you to keep that man's fingers far from me."

"Of course, Majesty. You will have nothing to worry about with that one. I will keep his powers well away from you."

Ruskin grabbed her hand, giving it a kiss of ownership.

"See that you do. Now, let us get ready for dinner. I have quite the appetite tonight."

He assisted her to a standing position, then looped his arm in hers as they set off for the dining hall.

CHAPTER TWENTY-EIGHT: CYNDOL ENTERS THE SKY PRISON

The next morning, Evony awoke the group at dawn by singing a pleasing song. It woke Cyndol with a smile on her face that would normally be absurd at this hour. She was most definitely not a morning person. She nudged Kit softly and he snuffled his nose under his tail to cling to sleep. Cyndol giggled and scratched him behind the ears. She was rewarded by him unfurling himself, belly up and purring. She continued to pet him for another minute until she saw the rest of their group coming out for breakfast.

Cyndol noticed that besides Evony, Bella was also already awake and making food and hot beverages for the crew.

"You know," Cyndol said to Kit, "I think I could get used to life on the road like this."

Kit rolled back onto his stomach and said, "As long as we can get belly pets and hot meats, I'm all in."

Evony approached the cart and asked, "Are you ready for travel, child?"

Cyndol nodded excitedly while Kit said, "Thanks for asking! *I'm* ready, too!"

Evony smirked and addressed Kit directly. "My apologies, Kit. I did not mean to exclude you."

They were both surprised she could still understand Kit after the spell last night.

She saw their shock and said, "Yes, I can still hear you and understand you. Druce's gem wand, as long as it stays within range of you, is not broken, and not undone, will continue to work. To my knowledge, it is only good toward you, as including more energies with it could become too taxing for the spell-bearer."

Cyndol thought about that for a moment. "So, basically, we have to be careful what we say now as long as Druce is nearby?"

Evony laughed. "Now you're catching on! Come. Eat some breakfast. We leave within the hour."

She escorted them to the table to dish up this morning's feast. Cyndol grabbed some warm rolls with butter, a few slices of bacon for both of them, and some bobbleberry pancakes with cinnamon spiced syrup. The adults in the group also grabbed some hot tea that was supposed to keep their energy up. It was going to be a long day.

When breakfast was done, they packed up their gear and set out. Cyndol found she didn't care for the path they found themselves on now. It wasn't like the forest they'd left behind. This forest was darker, and the trees didn't seem to breathe as much as they seemed to *seethe,* writhing in the wind with branches curled into claws. When she asked Evony about it, she explained they were entering into a new kingdom, one that was specifically under King Ruskin's command. There was a great battle here long ago that was filled with such tragedy, loss, and dark magick that it left a stain on the land itself, cursing it forever more. Cyndol shivered and pulled Kit in closer for comfort.

"I'm sure glad we're not out here alone," Kit said. "And I'm glad you're with me."

Cyndol nuzzled him and scratched his head. "So am I, Kit."

After a few hours on this dark road (and seeing several curious creatures poke their faces out from caves, trees, and holes in the ground), there was finally a creature that wanted confrontation.

"Oi!" Bella shouted. "On your left!"

The group armed themselves immediately and turned to face whatever was headed for them on the left side of the path. It looked like a tree, but this monster was alive! Dark, charred looking branches swung this way and that at them, knocking Fenix and Felix off their horses. They landed hard on the ground. The horses spooked and took off back the way we came. The creature faced the group with bright red eyes and a large, evil grin, taking yet another set of swings at them. This time, they were ready!

Felix slashed the branch aimed at him with his sword, hacking it off in one chop, while Fenix used his heat power to set another moving branch on fire. The creature howled a twisting shriek and tried to swipe at itself to put out the fire. That's when Evony and Bella attacked from the rear: Evony with her sword and Bella with her frying pan. Druce stayed back to defend the cart with Cyndol and Kit to keep them safe.

Felix and Fenix charged the creature. Everyone was fighting! Swords, fire, frying pans, magick. Finally, the creature was silent. It lay on the ground, unmoving, defeated.

The terror Cyndol and Kit felt was almost too much to bear.

"Are they alright?" Evony asked Druce.

"Yes!" Druce said as Evony approached them. "A bit shaken up, I suspect, but they'll be fine shortly, I'm sure."

Evony shifted her gaze to the young ones, doing her own scan just to make sure. Seeing they were technically fine, she gave one curt nod and gathered the rest of them.

"This path is full of Ruskin's spies and monsters. I need all of you to look alive and keep watch. Padagonya is not much farther from here. If this creature was any indication of what's hiding out here, we should keep our weapons at the ready."

She was answered by a sea of nodding heads and weapon brandishing.

"Good! Let's move."

After Fenix and Felix retrieved their horses, they resumed their journey on high alert.

Evony was right. They did encounter a few more of those things along the way. Mostly the same, but with everyone fighting and knowing how to defeat them, it took less and less time for each one.

Kit looked at Cyndol. "We never would have made it without them."

Cyndol wholeheartedly agreed. The thought that they almost tried getting here on their own without the aid of these wonderfully brave people made her shudder.

As both of the suns in the sky above made their way past midday, a cluster of clouds moved in, darkening their path. Evony brought them to a halt.

The skies opened up and let a burst of rainfall through, just enough to soak them all. Thinking quickly, Felix cast an air spell around them to shield them from the water. Cyndol saw a yellow jasper and citrine rod in his hands, with a blue calcite triangle near the top of it, almost appearing like an eye.

Kit said, "Well, isn't he handy to have around!"

"We are quickly approaching the Sky Prison," Evony said. "Have any of you ever seen it before? And do you know why it was named 'The Sky Prison'?"

Everyone shook their heads. Nobody had been here before. That is, nobody except for Druce. Druce let out a long breath and said, "Yes."

"Can you explain to them what they are about to see?"

Druce came in closer to the group and, in a tone that made Cyndol's hair stand on end, he said, "The Sky Prison. It is not so high in the sky as one would suspect from the name. It was named thus as they house their prisoners so high off the ground that they might as well be up in the sky." He paused to grimace. "The prisoners are hung by their wrists above a grated floor in their sky rooms. They are punished by having to witness how they will die. They are often starved to death, either on purpose from the jailers, or of their own accord as their will to live fails. Their bodies begin to eat themselves without proper food and, eventually, these poor prisoners that starve to death are able to slip through the handcuffs and right through the grates to the waiting graveyard below.

"There is a small river nearby that many of them fall into, but their bodies are so dead or diseased that they poison the water and everything it touches. Do not drink this water, whatever you do, or you will not be making the return journey with us."

Bella choked on a sob and covered her mouth with her meaty fist.

"This is where my father died," she said. "I've just never seen it. I didn't know…"

Evony directed her horse over to Bella's side. "If this is too much for you, I understand. You may wait back here if you like."

Bella nodded and swiped her sleeve over her eyes to dry them.

"The rest of you," Evony continued, "will join us at the prison. I will go to the front gate and deliver the missive from the queen. Hopefully there will be no resistance but, if there is, we can reconvene and see about a Plan B."

She instructed them to move on to their destination. Cyndol's nerves were on fire. If that's how prisoners were treated in this place, what was being done to Ethan?

A few minutes later, they rounded a bend in the road and saw the prison come into view. Surrounded by an unforgiving dark forest, this massive structure looked as if it almost *could* touch the sky. It was shaped like an impossible upside-down triangle with a squared-off tip, with many different levels every eight feet or so up the sides of it. These levels were the cage prisons Druce had warned them of. Seeing those men hanging up there like that was absolutely heart-breaking. Not a word was heard from any of them. Quite possibly, they were already dead.

"Surely nobody could do something so bad they'd deserve *this*!" Cyndol said.

Evony approached her from the side of the cart. "You'd be surprised, child. Men are capable of much damage. You'd do well to keep that in mind. But know this, we will do everything we can for your brother. This will not be his fate."

Cyndol took a deep breath to find her courage and looked up at the prison once more. Her gaze caught something falling. Too late she realized it was a body. It had slipped through its cuffs and floor grate, and, with a sickening wet *THWACK*, it hit the ground and lay still.

Kit shrieked and jumped into Cyndol's lap, and Cyndol's tears coated the fur now pressed to her face.

Druce pulled another gemstone rod out of his bag (clear quartz with sodalite dots decorating the length of it) and gripped it tightly, saying a few words she couldn't decipher but sounded pleasing to the ear. Both Cyndol and Kit relaxed, and their hammering hearts slowed down. Cyndol threw a look of surprise at Druce, who smiled softly and said, "You're welcome, Little One."

Whatever magick Druce had, he was quite an effective healer, Cyndol thought. She had started to feel consumed by fear and despair until Druce did his spell. She couldn't imagine how it might feel to be jailed here. They had to get Ethan out, quick!

They approached the front gate, water pooling around their horses' hooves as the rain began increasing in volume. Evony left the group a few paces behind her and reached the wooden doors barring her entry. She grabbed a wooden staff from the side of her saddle and banged the large gate with it. A solid whacking sound assaulted their ears and Cyndol was sure someone would have heard that.

It took a few minutes, but a guardsman finally popped his head out the door.

"What do you want?" he asked.

Evony met his eyes and said, "We have orders from King Matthias and Queen Miawae of Gallanor to remove one of your prisoners."

The guard furrowed his massive brows and said, "Only King Ruskin gives orders around here. So unless you have a missive from *him*, I'm afraid you'll have to shove off."

He shut the door in her face. Evony tried again. This time, her knocking had an even stronger echo that would surely ring in that man's ears for a while. He flung the door open this time, shouting, "I said no! So you can take your band of merry men and return to whatever kingdom you crawled out of!"

Evony didn't even flinch. She calmly and confidently unfurled the missive from Queen Miawae and began to read it aloud to him:

"To Whom It May Concern~

"By the orders and proclamations of King Matthias and Queen Miawae of The Nation of Gallanor, you are to secure the immediate release of the young boy Ethan of Cavar, being held without proper rights, without the permission of his family, and without proper trials. He will be remanded to the protection of my guards and to the care of the Queen's Right Hand, Evony of Gallanor. They will deliver him into the custody of Queen Miawae to stand any credible trials thereafter.

"Signed, King Matthias and Queen Miawae of Gallanor."

Evony looked expectantly at the guard, who had the decency to blanche.

"Well?" she asked. "May we come in now?"

The guard swallowed and said, "Look, miss, I don't want any trouble. The thing is, I really and truly cannot let you through these doors without express permission from King Ruskin. He's of a mind to slay first, ask questions later, if you catch my drift? I'm afraid I can't afford to put my life, or my family's lives, at stake for your mission to free the boy."

Evony studied the man for a moment. Then she leaned in close, eyes locked on his and pointed behind her where Cyndol sat cuddling Kit in the cart.

"Do you see that sweet little girl sitting in the wagon?"

The man looked over her shoulder to see the girl with her pet and nodded.

"That little girl is the younger sister of the boy you are holding captive. That boy is the only family that poor child has left. She watched her whole family be killed and you would deny her the chance to say goodbye to her brother? Tell me you wouldn't deprive an innocent child like that."

The man was sweating now, eyes darting back to her, then to Cyndol, then back to Evony again.

"Fine. I will allow her to come in and say goodbye. Truth is, I feel bad for the lad, myself. He hasn't had an easy time of things. And, between you and me, well, with the removal of his eyes scheduled for today, I'm sure having his sister here as the last thing he'll see may bring him some comfort. I'm sorry I couldn't let you take him. Believe me."

Evony *did* believe him. She understood how sometimes a job could get out of hand, but you still had to do it, regardless of personal feelings.

"Thank you, sir. You are very kind. I will let her know."

Evony turned her horse around and rejoined the group.

Druce spoke first. "Well? What did he say? Are they getting Ethan?"

Evony shook her head. "I'm afraid not. Unfortunately, King Ruskin has put his foot down, no matter the request. Only he can free a prisoner. Not even the letter from Matthias and Miawae could convince him otherwise."

Cyndol let a tear escape, and she took a breath to speak. Evony put a hand up to stop her.

"However, he did relent for Cyndol, if you're willing to go in alone. I have a plan."

Cyndol caught a tear on her finger. "Yes! Whatever I can do! Please!"

"Alright. Here's the plan…" Evony explained her idea to the group, and to Cyndol and Kit especially, as this would be their mission. "And Druce? Make sure your magick is at the ready. We don't know what condition he will be in."

"I'll be ready," he said.

Evony escorted Cyndol and Kit to the gate.

"She can have half an hour. After that, he is scheduled for his, uh…" he looked down at Cyndol, "appointment."

"We understand," Evony replied.

"Is the fox absolutely necessary?" the guard asked.

Evony whispered behind her hand, "It helps with her loss. You understand."

The guard thought about it and relented. "Half an hour!" he said, then opened the door enough to allow Cyndol and Kit to enter.

Darkness greeted them first, then a soft hiss as a torch sprang to life in front of them.

"Follow me," the guard said.

Cyndol did as he bade and let Kit walk on his own beside her.

The guard led them through a large, poorly lit lobby area that was filled with several torture devices. Thankfully, they were all currently vacant. Cyndol didn't think she was ready to see that type of agony up close. They traveled down a short hallway which ended with a pulley-system elevator. The guard gestured for them to proceed into it and clambored in next to them, hitting a button on the wall to activate the lift.

Up they went, slowly, painfully slow, so slowly that Cyndol and Kit could hear the alternating moans and screams emanating from each floor they passed.

Cyndol cleared her throat. "So, uh, what floor is he on?"

The guard gave her a half-smile. "Don't like heights?"

She played dumb. "Never been very good with them. How could you tell?"

"My daughter's the same way. Can't stand coming here."

"Might it be the constant screaming of pain that startles people away?" Kit said. Luckily, Druce's charm didn't extend this far, so it just sounded like chirping to anyone who could hear him.

"Cute little thing, ain't he?" he asked, trying to lean down to pet him.

Kit grimaced and let the man's dirty fingers run through his soft copper fur. He had to remind himself not to bite anyone *just* yet. After all, he couldn't mess things up for Cyndol and Ethan. The man finally stopped stroking him when they reached their destination.

"Here we are!" he said, as if giving them a tour of the place. "He's a few doors down that way, Room 1217. I'll just wait here."

So, with the guard waiting in the lift, Cyndol and Kit made their way down the cold, dank hallway toward the cell that held her brother. Cyndol's pulse quickened when she saw another guard placed outside of Ethan's door.

"It's okay, Cyndol," Kit said, "we've got this. Remember Evony's plan. You distract, I'll snag the keys and open the door. Then you can punch him in the face, and I'll bite him until he falls, then you punch him again and knock him out. We'll be out of here in no time!"

Suddenly, the door to room 1217 exploded from its hinges and a wave of amethyst air rammed the guard against the opposite hallway wall! To Cyndol's surprise, it was Ethan who came out of the room, completely dazed, and stepped over the guard on the floor. His eyes were blazing with purple ire and it chilled Cyndol to the bone. *What did they do to him?!*

An alarm split through the air like a whip and forced Cyndol's blood pressure into high gear.

"I can't see!" screamed Ethan as he waved his hands frantically over his eyes. "I can't see!"

Cyndol shouted, "Ethan! Ethan, it's me, Cyndol! I'm here to rescue you! Grab my hand! I know the way out!"

"Cyndol?" Ethan asked. "No, it can't be. You're not really here. You can't be! You're just my imagination playing tricks on me again!" He swiped at the air, attempting to clear the false hope. His eyes sent intermittent bursts of energy singeing through the hallway, burning holes and lines of destruction as he went.

She tried again, and this time was able to grab his left hand in hers. She fastened her fingers around his. "Does this feel imaginary to *you*? Let's get out of here!"

Ethan swayed but let Cyndol guide him up the hallway she'd come from. As they came upon the lift to exit, another guard jumped in their path from a doorway Cyndol hadn't seen.

Kit flung himself into battle mode and sank his fangs into the man's inner thigh. The man screamed and swung his axe, missing Kit by about an inch. Kit held tight and the man swung again, embedding his weapon in the wall. Kit braced his legs on the wall and gave a horrible fast wrenching of his head. A chunk of the man's leg came back with him! Kit launched himself from the wall with his hind legs and landed on all fours, dropping the flesh and growling at the guard, now on the floor, grasping with both hands at his leg. Cyndol took the opportunity and pulled Ethan behind her and over the howling guard. She gave him one swift punch to the face, knocking him out and bringing silence to the room.

They all looked at the front door guardsman, still waiting on the lift, fear prevalent in his eyes at the scene he'd just witnessed.

Ethan's amethyst eyes flourished with new life as he directed his attention to the only guard left on this level.

"I'll be showing you out now," he said wisely.

Cyndol and Kit scrambled back on the platform, dragging Ethan behind them. The guard pushed the button, and they were off toward the bottom again. Halfway down, zings of magick rained down on them like sparks, and a cry of outrage was heard echoing from the floor they had just escaped from.

"Get him back here!" shrieked a woman's voice. "Hurry, you fools!"

Cyndol looked pointedly at the guard. "Will they be waiting for us at the front where we came in?"

"Yes."

"Is there another way out?"

"Yes."

Cyndol was getting annoyed. "Well? How do we get there?"

He held up his ring of keys and said, "I'm the only one with access to the door. You'll need me to open it for you. And, well, after this mess you've gotten us into, I'm sure I'll be swinging in one of these cells by tonight. Unless..."

"Unless what?" she asked him.

"Take me with you? I've got a family," he said.

Cyndol and Kit exchanged a look, and Kit shrugged. "We need him."

"Fine. You can come with us. But only if you help us get out of here!"

He agreed, and he stopped them on the third floor. "There's a small secret door that will lead you outside from here. Follow me."

He led them off the lift and down the leaky hallway, men in various stages of death and decay on either side of them as they ran past. Cyndol's heart broke with every intake of breath.

"Can we not help them?" she asked.

"Not unless you want even more people after you," he said. "You like stirring up trouble?"

"No, sir, just came here for my brother."

They reached the hidden doorway as voices grew louder behind them.

"Hurry!" Cyndol said when the man was taking too long to find the right key.

"I'm trying! It's a little hard with it being so dark in here, and I don't remember which key it is!"

The voices got even louder, the footsteps running closer.

"Come on!" she said.

"Almost got it…" *Click!* The sound of the key grated in the carved rock that served as the door's locking mechanism. "Yes!"

The door panel slid open to the side and tucked itself into the wall. Instead of opening up to the outside, as Cyndol and Kit had expected, it opened up to a tiny room, only big enough to house a hole in the ground.

"What is this?" Cyndol asked.

"Dead drop," replied the guard. "This is where we dump the bodies of those who do not fall through the grates."

"I'm not going through there!" Kit said. "That's disgusting!"

The voices behind them got even closer. They didn't have a choice.

"Go!" said Cyndol, and she shoved both Kit and Ethan in front of her down the chute. Cyndol went next, and the guard followed after that, closing the door behind him before dropping through himself.

Cyndol held her breath as best she could to avoid screaming in both terror and disgust as she slid down this tunnel of yuckery. It was a fairly short ride, only being three levels from the ground floor, but it was the grossest ride of her life.

They landed in a squelch of bone and offal in a puddle of rainwater and decay.

"I'm going to be sick!" Cyndol said.

Kit vomited.

The guard grabbed them both by the backs of their necks and hurled them from the pit to the embankment.

"Climb up!" he said, then repeated the process with Ethan, who was still unable to see clearly.

They scrambled up the embankment of the death ditch and made it back onto solid ground. They could hear the alarms still blaring from inside the prison and, from their position, they could see guards exiting the front gate to search the grounds.

Cyndol spared a worried thought for Evony and the others, fervently hoping they were well hidden and prepared for a fight.

Ethan slipped in a mud puddle and Cyndol hoisted him up to find his footing again. His eyes were still illuminated and casting purple light on everything they touched.

"Ethan!" she said. "Close your eyes! You're going to give us away!"

"But I can't see!" he replied.

"Do you trust me?"

"Yes. Yes, I trust you."

"Good. So, close your eyes and take my hand! I will take you to safety."

Ethan laced his fingers in Cyndol's and allowed himself to be dragged beside her again.

Cyndol went to take a step and saw the prison guards spot them fleeing. One of them took aim with his bow and let loose. Without thinking, Cyndol threw up her hands and flung her protective bubble around all four of them, the arrow plunking off of it to fall harmlessly to the ground.

Cyndol realized too late what she had done. She had just shown the guards that she was a prize worth fighting for. A woman stepped out from their pack and threw all of her attention to Cyndol, smiling like she was her next meal. It chilled Cyndol to the bone. She kept her hands up, trying to hold the bubble as if their lives depended on it, which, as of right now, was absolutely true.

"Davina!" came a shout from the left.

The woman snapped her head toward the newcomer and locked eyes with her old friend, Evony. She smiled once again, even less appealing than before.

"Evony!" Davina said. "I see you've brought us a gift. How kind of you. I will see it gets put to great use in the hands of King Ruskin."

She hurled a bolt of power at Evony and her horse, knocking them both to the ground. Evony's leg got pinned under her steed, who was having trouble finding purchase for its hooves on the wet ground.

Felix came out of the shadows and cast a spell to lift the horse, while Fenix pulled Evony back to the tree line for safety.

During this distraction, Cyndol's guard told them to bolt for the trees.

"Get them!" Davina said to her guards. "Don't let them get away!"

The guards took a few steps towards the fleeing foursome, but that's when Fate stepped in and dropped two fresh corpses from the few floors above them, landing on all of them and smashing them to the ground.

"No!" cried Davina. She hurled another dark blast of power at the children and guard as they made it to the safety of the tree line. She flung blast after blast, running toward them to try to capture them on her own, but it was too late. She could no longer see where they were. Trees caught fire and started to burn the forest around them, but the rain increased, dousing the flames soon after they started. Now it was too hard to see through the smoke and falling water. Without help, Davina couldn't follow. She let loose an ear-shattering cry of anger and disbelief that was heard for miles around.

Cyndol shuddered at the sound as they raced through the trees to where her party was waiting. As they got closer, Kit said, "Wait, don't move! There's someone up there. I can't see who it is."

They paused and hid behind a thick tree trunk, waiting to see who this person or creature was.

"Cyndol? Kit?" came the sweet sound of Bella's voice.

"Bella! Over here!" Cyndol whispered back, hoping she was loud enough for Bella, but not for any unsavory followers.

Bella appeared before them, frying pan at the ready.

"Look out!" she said and swung the pan directly into their guard friend's head, knocking him out cold in one fell *PTONK*! He fell like a log onto the soaked ground and didn't move.

"Bella, no! He's our friend! He helped us escape!" Cyndol rushed to his side, feeling for a pulse. She was relieved to find he wasn't dead. "Here, help me get him up."

Bella bent down to help lift him up and propped him between the two of them. The man was heavy, but Bella was stronger than she looked. They were able to carry him back to their waiting cart several feet away.

As they got closer, the rest of their party jumped in to assist, and they had both Ethan and the unconscious guard in the cart in a matter of seconds. Cyndol and Kit jumped into their seats right after that, and Evony whipped them into a frenzy of flight.

More arrows began to whiz past them as they hurried from the prison, shouts fading in the distance as they gathered more ground. Fenix and Felix returned volleys as they could, but there was no way to tell if any shots had landed as they were going too fast.

They didn't slow down for at least an hour. Cyndol had lost track of exactly how much time they'd been fleeing but, finally, they came to a stop.

"Why are we stopping?" Cyndol asked. "Is everything okay?"

Evony said, "Yes, Little One, I believe we have lost them for now. But we will keep our eyes open for trouble, should it come back to find us before we reach the Fae Realm."

A grunt startled them both, until Cyndol realized their new friend had awoken.

"Where… where am I?" he asked, rubbing his bruising head.

Cyndol left her seat to join him in the back of the cart. "Are you alright?"

"I— I think so," he said, wincing at the pain in his head. "What happened?"

Bella had the grace to blush.

"I hit you with a frying pan. Sorry."

"Why'd you do that?"

"Oh, I'm sorry! I didn't realize I was supposed to know you were helping them!" she replied.

"Why *did* you help them, stranger?" Evony asked.

The guard sighed. "The young girl here reminded me of my daughter, and I felt her pain for her family. I also couldn't stomach the thought of this poor boy's eyes being removed. Not right. I don't care what color they are! You don't just go about removing peoples' eyes."

Evony turned her attention to Ethan, whose eyes were still closed. She lifted her eyebrow in curiosity.

"Ethan," she said, "my name is Evony. I am the Right Hand of Queen Miawae. I'm sorry for what you've had to endure, but may I see your eyes, please?"

Ethan shook his head, throwing his matted hair out of his face and revealing the hole Viego had left there. The group recoiled in horror at the boy's wound.

"Ethan!" Cyndol began to cry. "What did they do to you?" She threw her arms around him and hugged him tightly, letting her tears wash over him, mingling with the grime and mud from the pit.

"I'm alright, sister," he said. "It was unpleasant, of course, but you saved me. I can never thank you enough."

"What about me? Am I chopped liver?" half-joked the guard. "If it wasn't for me, you'd all be dead!"

Evony studied this new addition to their group. "You may be right, sir. What is your name so I may thank you properly?"

The man grinned and sat up, extending his filthy right hand to her in introduction. "My name is Richard, Lady Evony. Pleased to make your acquaintance."

"Thank you, Richard, for your bravery in the face of evil. I'm afraid we will be unable to take you much farther as we are not through with our mission just yet and, where we are going, you cannot come with us. But we are much in your debt for helping our friends here and I wish to reward you for your trouble. Druce?"

Druce directed his horse over to join them and he reached into his bag, revealing a small leather purse tied with soft leather straps. He opened it up for Richard and revealed a handful of various gemstones. Richard's eyes grew large, and he took the bag slowly, as if waiting for this to be a trick.

"Thank you, Lady!" he said. "I can get my family to safety with this!"

"See that you do," she said. "I'm afraid this won't be the last you hear from Davina and King Ruskin. Neither are ones to let slights like this go. Do you feel well enough to leave us now, or do you require assistance from our healer?"

Richard gave his head a few cursory pokes to make sure he was okay.

"I have a bit of a headache, I'm sure you can understand—"

Druce put his hand in his bag to clutch a rod Cyndol couldn't see and put his free hand on the man's head, mumbling more words she didn't recognize. Richard's face relaxed fully and even had a ghost of a smile.

"It is done," Druce said.

"Good," said Evony. "Well, then, Richard, we thank you again for your acts of heroism and friendship and wish you well in the coming days. If you are in need of shelter, hie yourself to Gallanor. Ask for an audience with the king and queen and tell them your tale. Tell them Evony said to make sure you get a hero's welcome. And, so they believe you, give them this."

She pulled a tiny shell from her pocket with an etching on it.

"It was my mother's. Please do not lose that. I would like it back someday."

"Yes, my lady." Richard bowed his head and climbed out of the cart. "I will do that. Thank you. And best of luck to you all, especially you children. I do not envy the chase you will have with King Ruskin and Davina after you. My advice? Hide your powers, if you can. Ruskin has been on the lookout for his downfall since the Prophecy, and I'm certain he will consider you both a great threat."

He waved his goodbyes and disappeared into the swath of dark forest.

"We are not far from the Fae Realm now," Evony said. "We will continue onward for perhaps another half an hour, and we can stop when we get to the sanctuary."

With that, they pressed on into the cold, wet night sky, Felix's dome offering shelter from the storm.

CHAPTER TWENTY-NINE: DAVINA'S IDEA

"What do you mean, 'The boy is gone'?!"

Davina winced at Ruskin's tone but held her ground. She lifted her chin higher and said, "When Lord Viego and I went to perform the eye removal, we found his floor was in absolute chaos. They'd attacked the guards and stolen the boy, fleeing through the Dead Drop chute. We believe they had help from one of our guardsmen at the front gate. Whether he was in on it the whole time or forced into it, we can't be sure. Either way, he is nowhere to be found."

Ruskin's claws etched new markings on his throne armrests. "Send someone to dispatch him and his family. His lodgings can be awarded to anyone who can give me the full explanation of what transpired."

"Of course, Your Majesty," she said. "It will be do—"

"And who are '*they*'?"

"I beg your pardon, Your Grace?"

"You said 'they' attacked, but who is 'they'? I thought my men took care of everyone in his village? Who else even knows he was there?"

Davina swallowed hard and said, "Evony, my grandmother's Right Hand. I'm afraid I do not know the details on how she and her fellow guards came to know that information, nor how they knew of the boy in the first place. I lost all contact with them when I came to you."

"How unfortunate. I wish you could have been of better assistance in this matter. Remind me, why do I keep you around?"

Davina felt tears threatening and she attempted to deflect the situation. "There was also a girl, a young one, who had power."

"Power?" Ruskin tilted forward. "What kind of power?"

Davina inched closer. "She was able to form a protection bubble, one big enough to encase four bodies."

"What type of stones was she using for such a feat?"

Davina leaned in for the blow. "She didn't."

"Really? Are you quite sure? There wasn't one hidden on her person somewhere out of sight? How do you know it was her and not one of the others that cast the bubble?"

Davina didn't have a good answer for that, being too far away to see any great detail. "I... I'm not sure..."

She felt her upper hand fading. Ruskin sat back on his throne, so she threw in one final tactic.

"Also, I know I was unable to provide you with enough clarity on the boy from my first vision. However, now that he is in the clutches of my grandmother's Right Hand, it's possible that Queen Miawae knows quite a bit about our young friend. After all, it was she who delivered your prophecy, and now she has the boy with the same eyes as *Her*."

Ruskin was quiet for a moment, scratching his post and pondering everything Davina had just said. Davina was terrified that he wouldn't take the bait and end up taking out his wrath on her instead. She'd seen what had become of his last Mages and it never ended well for them. She intended to stay on his good side for as long as possible.

"It appears it might be time to return to your home to see if they have our golden boy."

Davina's jaw dropped slightly. "You would let me go back? To my—?"

He continued speaking over her. "See what you can find out. See if they have him and won't give him back or, if they know more than they are letting on, such as this boy is the route to my destruction, perhaps it might be time for a visit from *me*, time for war."

"And you'd be okay with letting me go do that instead of someone else? I would've thought you'd send someone like Ikah. She would not only love a chance to do some damage for you but could probably make it farther with them than I could, in my present standing with them, you see."

"Are you so determined to lose your standing with *me*?" he asked, then paused. "Or maybe you're afraid that you've made a grave mistake in coming to me in the first place? You wish to be back with your loved ones, is it that? Maybe you're afraid that if you go back there, you won't want to return here? Is that it? Is that why you let them take the boy? Do you wish to see me *dead*?"

The room was shaking with his fury, his wolf side kicking in and his teeth gnashing, itching for an excuse to rip her to shreds for even considering such a thing.

"No! Of course not, Your Majesty, Your Grace, Great King of All!" Davina flung herself to her hands and knees. "Please, I will do whatever you ask of me! I'm sorry. I did not mean to imply I wanted to return there. I wish to stay here with you, I swear!"

The Wolf King snarled and snapped his protruding jaw at her. When he saw Davina was property cowed, he allowed himself to calm once more.

"Perhaps you are right," he said, fixing his human features once more. "Perhaps I should send Ikah. She does have a certain penchant for discovering truths."

He clapped his hands together and yelled for Silas.

"Yes, Your Grace?" Silas asked, standing at attention.

"Bring me Ikah! I have a mission for her."

CHAPTER THIRTY: AMY'S IMAGINATION

The road to the Fae Realm was beautiful. Everything seemed to sparkle or glow, as if this swath of nature was somehow happier than the rest of the planet. Strange thought to have, but I didn't know how else to describe it. Stunning trees that reminded me of the redwood forests of California mixed with an abundance of waterfalls, each with its own shining rainbow. It delighted me to see so much beauty in this world. My mermaid tail was just itching to explore all of them. I promised myself a swim as soon as I was able.

Brax pulled his horse up next to mine and set his pace to equal my own.

"So," he said, "is any of this familiar to you?"

I humored him by looking around for another minute, but my mouth twisted into a half smile/half grimace, and I shook my head no.

"I'm sorry. I wish it did, truly. This place is amazing! But the only memories I have are of the place I came from."

"You came from *here*!" A plume of smoke huffed from his nostrils and ruffled his scruff.

"Did you just— did you—? Did you just *puff* at me?"

"I'm a dragon, remember? At least, I was."

"You did say that," I said. "This world is so weird."

He frowned at me. "You really don't remember a thing."

I shook my head again and looked away. I couldn't meet his sad eyes right now.

"I'm sorry I can't be more helpful," I said. "I'll do my best to do what I can, but you have to understand, this is all new for me. I mean, try to see it from my perspective. Imagine you died and woke up on another planet, totally unfamiliar to you, and everyone you met insisted you've been there before, that you were someone special. Who, by the way, went by a totally different name—"

"Mostly the same name—"

"—and had all of these abilities you'd never even dreamed of. Wouldn't that feel strange to you? What would you do if you were in this situation?"

His shoulders drooped and his head hung on his chest.

"I couldn't imagine," he said. "You're right. Just because *we* know you, does not mean that *you* know you, or us, or all of this." He gestured vaguely around the landscape. "I'll do better to keep my patience, and I will do what I can to help you as well. What can I do to start?"

I thought about that for a minute. "Well, I suppose you could tell me a bit about yourself, how we met and fell in love, and what Ruskin has to do with this."

He chuckled and said, "That I can do."

The next half an hour was the most entertaining block of time I've spent since landing here. Brax told me that I was the eldest daughter of the MerKing, Volmar. When he said the name, my brain pinged, as if it recognized the name, but couldn't recall much more than that. He said that King Volmar and King Ibraxus II both pledged their eldest children to stand guard over the Ancient Stone (as *they* both had in their youth) and make sure nobody tried to access it and its powers. I came to find out he was referring to the mushroom shaped statue I found near my house back on my island. This Ancient Stone was the only way to access the cores of Callembria and was only to be used in the case of planetary emergency. Since it stood over the only access to the planet's core (that was located in the Mer Kingdom) and reached the limits of our atmosphere (closest to the Dragon Moon) guard duty fell to the houses of the royals from each faction. At one time, the humans and their respective magickal offshoots (Shifters, Mages, etc.) also kept a guard on duty, but they proved too unreliable and untrustworthy, as there had been more than one occasion of attempted forced access. Fortunately, each attempt was foiled and there had been no emergencies that called for the need of its power. This allowed the guards to enjoy their time alone on the island until they took command of their respective kingdoms and new guards would be selected. (If there were no heirs of age at the time, a proxy was chosen from the most trusted guards in their kingdom.)

"So we were on constant guard duty?" I asked him.

"Yes, however, we didn't have to stand literally right next to the stone at all times. We had an alarm system that automatically alerted us if another's presence was noted on the island. It consisted of three large amethysts that, once lit up, we were called to swift action. The magick imbued in the island allowed for a protective shield to come up and encompass the entire stone. If whoever came in contact with the stone did not have the key, the island would start to sink below the water line, drowning any trespassers."

"That's brutal!" I said. "Well, if the island already has its own security system, what were we needed for?"

"First line defense. If the island goes under, there's no telling how long it would take to get it back, if ever. It's never been done before, to my knowledge. I know I've been gone a long while myself, but if you've been there and everything is still fine, nothing has happened since we left. Were there any guards?"

"Not that I ever saw and, believe me, I looked for weeks. I guess it's just been a very lucky island."

Brax chewed on his lip. "Hmm. Perhaps."

He went on to tell me about our first meeting at Tripp's Tavern (back then it was called The Outpost) before claiming guardianship of the island. It was also the same day we met Tripp.

"Aww, Tripp!" I chuckled. "That guy is something."

Brax laughed as well. "You can say that again. I was saddened that I couldn't stay to have a pint with him earlier."

"You saw him?"

He nodded. "I did. He sends his regards. He also told me about that spell over your eyes. Handy trick, that. You know, I think he's always thought of you as the daughter he never had."

"Yeah?"

"Oh, absolutely! He doted on you like crazy! I would've suspected he was in love with you except the one time I joked about it, I received a sock to the eye!"

I couldn't help it, I cackled so hard I nearly fell off my horse.

"Wait, Tripp *punched* you?"

Brax's amusement was laced with sentimentality. "He did. And I deserved it, too. I was being a jealous fool, and he only ever wanted what was best for you."

"Huh," I said, smiling at the thought of my unofficial protector taking on this glorious man. "I would've liked to have seen that."

"Technically, you did."

"What?" I startled the horses into a trot. "I was there for that? Dammit! I've never wanted my old memories back more than I do right now!"

"Whoa, there!" Brax called to the horses, getting them to resume their previous pacing. He turned his attention back to me. "Don't worry, my love. We'll get you there, I promise. No matter what it takes, you'll remember."

I gave him a thin-lipped smile in return. "And if I don't?"

A spark ignited behind his whiskey-colored eyes. "Then I'll have to win your heart all over again."

"You're welcome to try," I said.

The spark in his eyes grew into a flame and I could see his desire as clear as day. My blush rose to accompany his fire, and I felt the first pulls of something more.

Just then, a *CRACK!* was heard in the distance. It spooked the horses, but Brax was able to steady them.

"The hell was that?" I asked the group.

Ifyrus growled. "Ruskin's men."

"Hell?" questioned Colt.

"Never mind," I tossed over my shoulder.

"I recognize that cracking sound," Brax stated in a tone that raised the hair on my neck. "That's the sound of Daegan's whip. Let's just say, we've met before."

"He *whipped* you?"

"Spikes and all. You've seen the markings he left though, it just occurred to me, you wouldn't remember. It's better that way." He addressed the group now. "We'd better make haste! I have no intention of meeting the wrong side of that whip again."

Ellera pulled up next to us, Ifyrus and Colt right behind her.

"It's not much farther, now," she said. "Follow me!"

We plunged into action behind her, crashing through forest and brush, putting as much distance between us and Ruskin's men as possible. We wouldn't stand much of a chance with an injured dragon and a child in our care, not to mention an inexperienced mermaid, a no-longer-a-*dragon* dragon, and, well, whatever the hell Ellera was, but I had no doubt she'd at least put up a fight.

"Over here!" an angelic voice called to our right. "Quickly, before they see you!"

A comely, chestnut-haired woman slipped from behind the trees and came forward, motioning us over while frantically glancing into the forest behind us. Her forest green and gold etched longbow was nocked and at the ready, a fully stocked quiver on her back, bouncing with each step.

Ellera burst to the front of our pack and said, "Latreya! I've never been so happy to see you! We seek your help! Our friend was poisoned by an arrow. I think it's the same concoction they used on the dragons in the Great War."

"I see," she said, quickly assessing the ailing Ifyrus. "Please, follow me. I will get you to safety."

We followed this woman off the path and through a patch of ever-darkening forest. Our horses kicked as hard as they could to get through the dense shrubbery.

"Is there not an easier path for the horses to get through?" I asked.

"My apologies," Latreya said. "The intention was not to let anyone through at all, lest they discover how to get to the Fae Realm."

"I see," I replied. "Sorry, Horse, you're just going to have to keep going." I patted my horse's head. "You've got this!" I felt him immediately stand up a little taller, as if he understood me and was trying to give it his all.

"He likes you," Latreya said.

The horse whinnied in response, and I just patted his head even more.

"The feeling is mutual. I think this is my first time on a horse since... well, probably since I was a little girl. Almost like riding a bike, you know?"

I realized what I just said and felt like an idiot. Of course she wouldn't know what a bike was! At least, I hadn't seen anything here that would qualify as one.

"I'm sorry, I'm afraid I don't know what you are saying," she gave an awkward half-laugh and looked behind us once more to check for signs of close pursuit.

I pulled my stupid foot from my stupid mouth and told her, stupidly, not to worry about it. Man, this whole "not connecting with people over everyday stuff" thing is exhausting. I never know if someone is going to understand me or think I'm nuts. Now that I mention it, the jury is still out on that.

"Here we are," Latreya said as loudly as she dared. Everyone gathered around and she motioned us towards a small, perpendicular river ahead. The place she was specifically pointing to was a thick, fallen tree with its roots sticking out towards the water, allowing for a small space to exist between the right side of the tree and the bank of the small river.

Blending into their environment, two guards shifted as they saw Latreya coming with guests. They took a ready stance to defend their doorway.

"Finn, Dodger, stand down," Latreya said. "They are friends seeking help and we've got Ruskin's men on our tail.

Let us pass, quickly! I will bring them straight to our healers and make sure that Sovereign Sai is notified."

They saw the injured man in need of help and nodded their consent to enter. We plunged through the shallow stream with our brave steeds and arrived without a hitch on the opposite bank.

"Finn, can you take care of the horses, please?" Latreya asked.

We instantly dismounted and grabbed whatever we could carry. Finn, the burly brunette lad, took the horses with great care. He handed a few of the reins to Dodger, a striking blond with a wiry frame, who looked just as intimidating as his cohort. I saw them pull out a few gemstones and recite words over them, directing the spell's energy over our equine bunch. It shrunk the horses before my very eyes, so small they could fit in the palms of their hands!

Ellera said to me, "Get ready, kid, because you're next!"

"*What?*" Before I could get confirmation on what exactly she meant, I was hit with a spell from the Fae guards and saw my world diminish rapidly. It was dizzying, to say the least. Bright lights, cacophonous sounds, and a whoosh of air all vying for the same space around me. I was going to black out.

"Amaryah— I mean, Amy, are you alright?" came Brax's voice above me.

I realized then that my eyes were clenched shut and that loud noise I'd heard was actually *me* screaming. I was on the ground, head to my knees, keeping my body as tight a ball as I could make it. Charming impression I made.

I cracked one eye open as Ifyrus let out a chortle, followed directly by a cough, the mirthful action causing him too much pressure on his wound. *Good. Serves you right for laughing.*

Brax laid a comforting hand on my shoulder, easing my nerves.

"Better?" he asked.

I sat up and opened both my eyes now, letting my body relax into a more comfortable sitting position. Taking a few deep breaths, I nodded.

"Good. Shall we continue? We have a dragon to fix."

Latreya stepped forward. "My apologies, Lady. I did not think to warn you the toll it can take on changing one's size. Unfortunately, there is no getting around that if you want to access the Fae Realm. You will see. Follow me."

It was then that I realized we had *all* been resized, and I took some assurance in that. Still, it would've been nice to know that that was the plan.

"You can't just go all 'Honey, I Shrunk the Kids' without permission," I mumbled, wiping the excess dirt from my rump.

We gathered ourselves and followed our new leader into the space under the fallen tree which, turns out, was another Crannie. Yay. My favorite.

I braced myself for the odd feeling of zipping from one realm to another at dizzying speeds, but this one was much smoother and shorter than the ones I'd been through thus far. I barely noticed a thing this time. Maybe I was getting better at this? Or maybe it was just anticlimactic after losing most of my body's mass in .07 seconds?

I heard a tongue-clicking noise and saw that our horses were being escorted to the stables by another young Fae.

"Micah!" Latreya called to him. "Make sure they are fed, watered, and rested. But keep them close, they may need to leave at a moment's notice."

Micah promised he would see to their care personally, and off he went with our steeds.

I walked alongside Ellera in hopes she would be able to give me some info on this place.

"So," I said, "anything else nuts I should expect from here?"

"I've only been here once so I can't promise you there aren't more strange things to come. There is the crossing of the pond coming up, though. You'll want to pay close attention to Latreya when she gives instructions on that."

"Pond crossing. Got it," I said. "So, if you don't know about anything crazy, how about something interesting? Is there a King and Queen? If so, do you think we'll get to meet them?"

"You know," she said, "you can direct your questions to Latreya. She's very nice, and way more knowledgeable than I am."

I sighed. Suddenly nervous, I quickened my pace to meet up with Latreya at the front, falling into step beside her.

"So, Latreya," I began, slightly out of breath. "Got a few questions before we get where we're going. What can I expect when we arrive? I'm afraid I know nothing about this place. Does your realm have a king and queen? If so, will we get to meet them? Do I bow or curtsy? I've been so confused ever since I was kil— uh, ever since I left my last place."

I looked back at Ellera, who was hiding a smug smirk, and she winked at me in encouragement, I think? Hard to tell. I found I liked her a lot, but she was very hard to read. I raised my eyebrows at her, and she rolled her eyes right back. She made a 'go on' sweeping gesture with both hands at me, so I turned around and pressed on.

"Really, anything would be helpful."

Latreya's energy went immediately from guard duty to tour guide, and it caused her whole face to light up— literally! Her matronly face took on a youthful glow that was easier to see now that the second sun had almost set.

"I would be happy to help!" She tucked a loose lock of hair behind her slightly pointed ear. "First of all, we are on our way to the entrance of the kingdom and, when we get there, I will show you the correct path to take so you don't fall astray. Secondly, we do have royalty here, as is tradition, but there is not always a king and a queen. Sometimes we only have one or the other, sometimes we have a ruler who is both. Currently, our kingdom is ruled by Sovereign Sai, who falls into that last category. You can address our sovereign as such, or by Your Majesty, Your Highness, Your Grace, or they and them."

I breathed a sigh of relief. Thank God! Something that made sense to me in this crazy place.

"How cool! I wouldn't have expected that here. I had a friend back home who identified as they/them, though it was fairly new to the people of my land. They had a rough time of it. It got better but it was still a work in progress. I'm thrilled you all seem open to that. I wish more people were."

She smiled beatifically at me and said, "You have a good heart. That will serve you well in this life, and the next."

Her knowing expression told me she was well aware of other worlds, and I felt myself relax even more. It was nice being around people who wouldn't think I was crazy for claiming I was an alien here. I know the opposite wouldn't be true back on Earth. If I was back home and told someone I was from Callembria, I'd be drowning in medication.

As we walked the short distance to our destination, I took stock of my surroundings in this new realm. It was very similar to the realm we'd just left behind, both being forests and all, but this new territory seemed far too ethereal to exist. Being here gave me the feeling that I was being enveloped with love and acceptance of my entire being. The sigh of relief that escaped me was more beautiful than any paradise back home. This place *felt* like love and light.

"Here we are," Latreya said.

We rounded the bend and the kingdom's entrance came into view.

There was a *massive* oak-like tree in the middle of a large lake. The water was broad enough that this tree existed as an island. Its branches stretched high and far, its boughs cascading down into a weeping willow romanticism. Burning gold lights decorated its entirety, lighting the way for us now that the suns had set, and darkness had descended on the land.

"From here, you'll all need to follow my footsteps exactly!" Latreya said. She came to a full stop at the edge of the water closest to us. "There is a certain pattern of steps one must use while trying to cross. These are the enchanted crystal quartz steps that you will see me walk on. Do not stray from my path, do you understand? They are not in a continuous line, so watch your step! Also, in order to be allowed into the Fae Kingdom, you must not wish harm to anyone here. The magick instilled here is alive and can sense ill-intent within seconds of breach. It does not hesitate to react."

When she didn't elaborate on what she meant by "react", I found her eyes. She left it unsaid, but her face told me it wasn't pretty.

"Got it," I said.

Latreya continued. "Alright. Remember: No ill-intent and stick to my steps exactly! Let's go."

She turned her back on us and walked confidently onto the water. The others fell in step behind her. Colt was first in his eagerness, then Ellera, helping to hold up Ifyrus, who was getting progressively shakier on his feet. Next was Brax, making sure Ifyrus was sandwiched between himself and Ellera in case he needed assistance, and, finally, myself.

I was suddenly terrified to cross this pond. The nighttime woods around us did my anxious brain no favors at all, even *with* the lights to lead our way. While I didn't wish anyone here any harm, I couldn't help but let my movie-warped brain run away with me. I thought about the old slasher flicks I'd watch with my friends in high school where the kids would go to summer camp and get killed in a lake, or literally any movie about crocodiles, alligators, or sharks. Aw, damnit, are there *sharks* in this water?!

"Amy?" Brax whispered so as not to alert the rest of the group there was anything to worry about. "Are you alright? You seem a little pale."

I stopped scanning the calm waters to meet his questioning gaze. I dazzled him with my best smile, but his brows furrowed in skepticism. He said nothing, just pressed on along the quartz path.

My eyes darted back to the water and a feeling of dread came over me. "Okay, Amy," I said under my breath. "Stop being an idiot and watch where you're going."

I took a deep breath and noticed a ripple form across the water. I froze on the step and glued my eyes to the small current.

"Guys?" I addressed the group, my tongue suddenly dry like an old leather belt. Nobody heard me. I tried a little louder as a second ripple joined the first. "Guys?"

Brax turned around first. "What is it?"

I pointed to the moving water. There was a soft splashing sound I hadn't heard before. Brax shifted his entire focus to the movement and gave a soft whistle to Ifyrus. This caught not only *his* attention, but that of the others as well. We paused, waiting for something to happen.

"Amy," Latreya said, "we have about a quarter of the way left. Are you alright? Do you need help?"

I tried to swallow past the lump forming in my throat. I croaked, "There's something in the water." Now my hands were shaking.

"No," she replied, "there isn't. What are you thinking about right now?"

How the hell could I explain horror movies to the people of this planet? Their brains would explode!

"Um," I stalled dumbly. *Do they even have sharks and gators here?* I took my chances. "Really big... um... water animals? Like, a shark, maybe?"

As if on cue, a steel grey shark fin pierced the top of the water and slowly made its way to us.

"What is that?" Colt pointed. "It's headed right for you, Amy! Watch out!"

A shock of adrenaline coursed through my body, and, in a panic, I launched myself off of the crystal step to flee the beast. I stepped on a different stone of solid jade and my footing slipped. I felt myself plummet backwards toward the surface and it was as if all of time stopped. I couldn't breathe, I couldn't stop, my arms grasped desperately at the air around me. I was trapped in this moment, forever falling into the swirling black lake with the real-life Jaws. But just as I made contact with the water, Brax's strong arm shot out and grabbed me by my cloak. He wrapped his fist tight and strong in the fabric, catching me right as the shark came up to invite me into its razorblade maw. It snapped its jaw shut, catching the hem of my pants as Brax pulled me back to the safety of his arms and the crystal step, leaving the monster with only a scrap of trousers for its troubles.

"Hurry!" Latreya shouted. "We are almost there! Just a few more steps!"

Everyone jumped into action, running across the curving stones as quickly as we dared.

In addition to the shark, there were now alligators, crocodiles, and other creepy creatures all zooming at us from various parts of the large pond. The waters were now violently thrashing, and it was next to impossible to see the quartz! My feet kept slipping off the stones, but Brax held my hand firmly and would not let me go.

"Latreya!" called a Fae woman on the shore we were rushing to. "Duck and cover!"

Latreya repeated the order to the rest of us and we stopped where we were to duck down. She released a massive jolt of purple tinged energy, and it cocooned us like a warm blanket. The Fae woman on the bank did the same, but hers was even bigger and tinged with shades of orange, yellow, and red. Her flaming magick hit everything in the water except for us, hiding protected under Latreya's canopy. Every creature was instantly incinerated. The woman pulled her magick back over and fell to her knees on the shoreline.

Latreya pulled back her magick as well and the waters eased enough to see the correct stones. We made our way quickly to the shore where we fully collapsed, panting and terrified. I noticed we were all scanning the water to make sure those creatures were gone. There was nothing left but lingering wisps of smoke on the water top.

Latreya focused her irritated gaze on my face and said, "No ill intent, even to yourself!"

Her comment stung, but I knew she was right. This was somehow my fault. I *thought* these creatures into being and they came after me! I don't know how I did it, but I did it. Damn it.

"Way to make an entrance!" the Fae woman said. She got back to her feet, brushing dirt from her skirts.

"You'll have this one to thank for that, Colonna," Latreya told her, ratting me out. I blushed. "They've come for aid. They have an injured dragon that needs tending to."

"A dragon?" Colonna asked. "I thought they were extinct?"

"Apparently not, Love," Ifyrus said. "But if we stand here much longer, that might end up being true." He held his left side tightly with his right hand and grimaced.

"Of course, my apologies!" Colonna said quickly, dark curls bouncing around her heart-shaped face. "I will take you to our healers right away. Come!"

The small, strong woman grabbed one side of Ifyrus and Ellera grabbed the other, making quick but careful steps to the entrance of the tree. The rest of us gathered close behind.

"You know," Ifyrus said between gasps, "a dragon could get used to being fawned over like this."

"Don't get *too* used to it," Ellera said. "I'm not always going to be here to help you, you know. You're just having a *really* lucky day."

Ifyrus giggled, getting progressively loopier in his poisoning, and said, "Did you hear that, Brax? She thinks she can be rid of me that easily!"

Ellera tightened her grip just a bit too hard, eliciting a yelp from the roguish drake.

"I think she likes me, mate."

The ladies escorted him up the steps to the entryway.

Brax placed a steadying hand on my shoulder, then to my back, then he simply just held my hand. Anything that could physically reassure him I was okay. Man, he must really love me to be this concerned. I still had a hard time wrapping my head around it.

"Are you sure you're alright?" Brax asked me.

"Yes! I'm fine! I feel like an idiot, but otherwise okay."

He puffed out a plume of nostril smoke and let the topic drop.

As we approached the double doorway on this tree that felt like a fortress, I saw another pair of guard Faeries perched on opposite sides of it, each on their own thick branch above the entrance.

"Draymon," Colonna said, "open those doors at once! We need to save this dragon! Quickly!"

"Yes, Lady!" Draymon and his cohort immediately jumped down and pulled both doors open to let them enter. "Wait, did you say *'dragon'*?"

Colonna brushed past them, pulling poor Ifyrus behind her like she was racing a toddler to the bathroom. "Quickly! Before he expires on the floor!"

As if on cue, Ifyrus vomited a pile of black goo onto the pristinely clean pearl-colored floor of the entryway.

"Not the floors!" Colonna said. She picked up the pace even faster, practically dragging him now in her haste.

The floor (sans vomit) was indeed gorgeous. There was a stunning spiral pattern that encompassed the whole of the room. A myriad of gemstones and flower vines cascaded down the tree bark walls, and the twinkling starry-sky ceiling seemed to go on indefinitely. I was transfixed.

"Once we leave this main hallway," Colonna said, "we will get our powers of flight back and we can get you to the healer's hut faster. Sorry about the protection spell out there. Believe me, it's for everyone's good."

We came to a twin set of doors from the entrance that exited to the kingdom proper. A wave of perfume washed over me like a cloud of fresh flowers. It was both calming and lovely. I also noticed that even though it was nighttime, the land before me sang with brightly colored twinkling lights and an abundance of laughter. *Was there a party going on?*

Without warning, both Colonna and Latreya sprouted stunning butterfly wings and gathered Ifyrus's pitiful frame between them. Taking off in the air and flying him to the healer's hut, they left us to fend for ourselves.

We all turned to face Ellera.

"What? Why are you all looking at me? I've only been here once. I don't know what we're supposed to do now." She crossed her arms over her chest.

"I might be able to be of some service, then," came a warbling male voice to my left. I looked to see who was speaking but, to my surprise, I found only air.

"Down here," he added with a tinge of amusement.

I looked down and was surprised to see a rather rotund and *very* short Fae. He had a chest-length white beard and shining bald pate and was currently smiling up at me.

"Oh!" I said. "I'm sorry! I didn't see you there!"

He chuckled and replied, "That's quite alright, dear, happens all the time. I am Andre, and I'm here to be your guide. Welcome to the Fae Realm. Please, follow me!"

With a flourishing gesture that swept our entire view, he assumed quite confidently that we would all follow him down the steps he was descending.

Not having much choice in the matter, we fell in line behind him and made our way to the beautiful gardens in front of us.

This had to be a dream. I suddenly felt like I was in the middle of every fairytale I had ever heard, and I was the lucky princess that got to stroll about the marvelous castle grounds.

Since arriving on this planet, I have seen all sorts of beautiful sights and incredible things, but nothing quite prepared me for the Fae Realm. I'd never seen such a kaleidoscope of colors in my life all in one place, especially those that existed so harmoniously and lived in such great balance with each other. The vibrancy came from a mix of polished gemstones and incredible flower displays, all showcasing a myriad of botanical brilliance. Why didn't I think about adding plants to my window displays? What a stunning compliment to each other!

"Is there some kind of event going on Andre?" I asked our new tour guide.

He smiled in response and continued onward. We followed him toward the fray.

Enchanting music floated along the lined tree pathway in front of us and the sounds of merriment filled the lulls between the notes. It was the most enticing sound and I wanted to drown in it.

We came to a large structure the size of a small hill surrounded by trees. Long, twisting, vibrant jade vines dripped down from the top of it like a curtain of mystery over the shadowed half-oval opening leading into the party.

As we approached it, Andre gestured for us to push through the vines and enter. Brax decided it would be safer if *he* went first. Ellera scoffed and said that *she* should be the one to go first, seeing as she was the one who brought us here to begin with. While they argued about who was best suited to go first, I turned to Colt, put my finger to my lips, took his small hand in mine, and pulled him through the vines.

"Hey!" Brax and Ellera shouted in unison. But it was too late— we were in.

Colt gripped my fingers tightly in his as we took in our new surroundings. Right away, I noticed the ceiling: In a spiral pattern that encompassed the whole of it was a grouping of pink and violet-hued flowers hanging upside down. There was just enough space in between each spiral to see the golden twinkle illumination layered even higher. A fine sheen of mist leant a snaking glow to the plants and vines above us, so the entire ceiling felt alive! The foliage continued downward to drape along the walls that were spelled to look like rock and running water. It gave the illusion that we were enveloped in a cave under a waterfall, and it filled me with peace. The floor, however, was not made of rock, but consisted of the softest grass I had ever set foot upon, making me wish I could frolic through barefoot. I wondered if they'd mind if I took my shoes off.

"Sugar Shard?" a Fae server offered. He held out a flintstone platter, showcasing shaped sugar art that looked like dewy blades of spring grasses. Pale seafoam green, about the size and length of a letter opener, with tiny clear juice baubles dispersed over each. They reminded me of Boba tea pearls. I couldn't resist; I had to try one.

I thanked the young Fae, and Colt and I each took one from the plate, a small white linen napkin underneath. Exchanging a look of excitement, we bit into our Sugar Shards at the same time. The crunch hit my mouth first: A sharp, lime taste with a texture that snapped like rock candy. The baubles burst next, flooding my mouth with a sweet coconut flavor that transported me back to my trip to Hawaii. It was the most delicious treat I had ever tasted, and I was already mourning the loss of more as the server left with the rest. By the look on Colt's face, he felt the same.

"There you are!" Brax said. "Why did you take off like that?"

I flushed at his tone. "Calm down! We went ahead because you guys wouldn't stop arguing and somebody had to do it, so here we are! Besides," I continued with a wink at my little buddy, "Colt and I are becoming pros at this festival thing."

Colt beamed at me and bobbed his head in the affirmative at Brax.

Ellera made her way over to us, her wide eyes admiring the decorations.

"You know this is a wedding, right?" she asked me. "We are intruding on someone's wedding party here."

"And?" I countered, taking another bite of the shard. "We were invited here by that Andre guy, remember? Lighten up! Grab a shard! They're amazing!" I continued crunching mine loudly, squeaking happily when I bit into a granule of salt. God, this was insane. I *love* Faerie food!

Ellera spotted a shard server on the other side of the room, and took off to try the tasty treat, leaving Brax shifting uncomfortably at my shoulder.

I raised my eyebrow at him and said, "I take it you're not much for parties."

He blinked as if I had just woken him.

"What? No." He shook his head. "Well, I don't mind them, I'm just worried about Ifyrus. He's like a brother to me, you know? I hope they're treating him well." His eyes scanned the room as if he could find the answer here.

I laid a comforting hand on *his* arm this time. "I'm sure they're doing everything they can. I don't think they'd make such a fuss about getting him to the healers that fast if they weren't going to give it everything they've got."

Brax grunted noncommittally and continued his anxious perusal. I sighed and snagged another tasty morsel from a passing server, popping it in my mouth without thinking.

"Amy! Wait! Those are—!" Colt tried to stop me from swallowing, but it was too late. "Faerie Mushrooms." He pulled a face that made me worried about whatever it was I just put in my mouth.

"I like mushrooms," I said.

"But you're a—" he lowered his voice, "mermaid. Mermaids can't eat Faerie Mushrooms."

This caught Brax's attention, and he immediately panicked, shoving his dirty fingers down my throat to retrieve the offending hors d'oeuvre.

"Wha— are you do—?!" I tried to say while clawing at his strong hands.

"Hold still!" he said, going farther down my esophagus.

Tears rolling down my face in earnest and gag reflex working overtime, I felt like I was exploding from the chest up and my own panic hit top tier.

"Hurry up!" Colt said.

A small crowd had started to form as we made a ruckus of their celebration. I ended up kicking a chair in my haste to get away from the assault. It knocked a poor Fae couple over, and they landed in the small stream that bordered the inner perimeter of the spelled enclosure. The music came to an abrupt halt. Now all eyes were on us as we jerked dramatically back and forth, knocking even *more* chairs over. I was pretty sure I was about to die or lose consciousness.

"*Enough!*" thundered a powerful voice from the front of the room.

Brax growled an expletive, but relented and let me go. I fell in a heap where I stood and gasped for air, clutching and rubbing my poor face and throat. I choked and retched but nothing came up except a disgusting wad of spittle.

"What is the meaning of this?" the commanding voice continued.

I looked up at this new Fae and saw a beauty I couldn't properly fathom. A light shined so brightly from this person that I couldn't make out much detail, but that could have been from my brain trying to shut all of this down, so I wasn't exactly a reliable describer at the moment.

Brax huffed and said, "My apologies, Your Grace. She... well... she's allergic to mushrooms. I was trying to help."

"Allergic?" the Fae repeated. "To mushrooms?"

This was absurd. *I love mushrooms! I have no idea what's going on right now.*

Brax shot a look at me but replied to them, "More of an adverse reaction, really."

"How so?"

"You're about to find out."

At that moment, I felt my feet sweep straight up into the air and take the rest of me with them!

"Grab her!" Brax yelled.

"I've got her!" Colt said. Quick as a whip, he went into pegasus mode and confidently thrust his wings out while kicking off from the ground. As I whimpered pitifully, upside down in the air, he shot up and grabbed me by my ruined pant leg with his squared off chompers, pulling me back to the safety of the ground. The crowd erupted in cheers for the impromptu rescue show and, once Brax had me back in the prison of his arms, Colt took a few cocky trots that ended with a flourishing bow. This kid. Apparently, his fate is to just continue to rescue me and my increasingly useless self.

"Thank you, Colt," I said, patting his head. "Remind me to tell Queen Miawae that you were severely underpaid."

He strutted a bit more, collecting pets and snacks as a reward for being a hero, then transformed back into human form with one final bow.

The reigning ruler descended from the dais they were on and approached us, parting the guests like water on either side of them.

They came right up to Brax and I and said, "That was quite the commotion. Are you alright now?"

I nodded and said, "I think so, Your Highness?"

"She should see the healer, if it wouldn't be too much trouble, Your Majesty," Brax requested, calmer than I would've given him credit for. His grip around me hadn't loosened since I came back down to the ground, and in this moment, I was grateful for that.

Sovereign Sai nodded once and motioned to Andre, who was peeking up at us from behind a fallen chair, looking chagrined. He gulped visibly and came at his master's request.

"Apologies, Sovereign Sai. I thought it would be nice for our guests to get to see what life was like here, but I had no idea that she could not tolerate our food."

Sai placed their hand atop Andre's shining head and said softly, "It is alright, my friend. However, it does seem that a trip to the healer's hut might be in order. Please escort them there at once."

He bowed almost all the way to the ground and said, "Of course, Your Grace, right away!" Then, facing us, "Come! Let us be off to the healer's hut!"

Ellera popped back up then and said, "I was gone for five minutes! What did you *do*?"

"Ate something she shouldn't have," Brax grunted. "Follow us."

With that, the four of us followed the Fae as we exited the party and made our way to the healer's hut.

Fortunately, the healer's hut was not too far away. It took us about seven minutes to walk there from the wedding party, and I got a glimpse of more of the Fae Kingdom. Even though it was nighttime, I could still see the beauty of this land shining through the dark. Everywhere I looked there were gemstones and plant life, often sharing the same space as each other, even being used as buildings and living quarters for the

Fae. The cutest house I saw was built to look like a rather large mushroom that had been hollowed out for the purpose of homesteading, and it reminded me of a bigger version of the mushroom statue back on my island.

I tapped my head against Brax's shoulder to get his attention (as he still had me fully trapped in his arms so I wouldn't fly away again) and asked, "Does that mushroom house look familiar to you?"

He spared a glance in the direction my head was bobbing and said, "You mean, the one that our statue back home was modeled after?"

So I *wasn't* crazy! It looked just like it, only bigger!

"Yes. Wait, what? Our statue was modeled after this house?"

"The Fae were the ones that crafted that statue. At the time, the Fae were completely neutral to any and all rulers, still are to my knowledge, so they crafted the podium based on what was sacred to them. This is the oldest standing home in the Fae kingdom. I've heard tales of it, but I have never seen it until now. That was the first home of the first ruler. It was considered a great honor to replicate it for our purposes."

"How interesting," I replied, not knowing what else to say. Luckily, I didn't have to elaborate, as we had arrived at the healer's hut.

"Ah! Here we are!" Andre called and strolled jauntily up the small flight of steps to the hut.

"Hut" was an understatement for what this building was: A huge, three storied wooden building that looked like an enchanting rustic lodge, made from what appeared to be living trees. It was covered in snaking vines of morning glories in shades of scarlet, violet, and indigo. A fountain out front burbled happily from a trifecta of stone sprites playing in the water, and several bubbles drifted peacefully from it toward the sky above. Just laying my eyes on it brought me a sense of calm and well-being and I couldn't wait to get inside.

As we got closer to the door, an elderly Fae woman came out and greeted us with an easy smile.

"Welcome to the Healer's Hut," she said. "I received a message from Sovereign Sai to expect you. Please, come in." Braided grey hair, piled loosely on the top of her head, wobbled at us as she nodded in our direction. The braids threatened to fall with each tilt of her head, but they held their place all the same. She gave me a wink as she noticed I was staring, and I blushed at being caught.

"Magick, my dear," she said. "Comes in handy at my age."

I gave a soft laugh in response, and we followed her into the hut.

I felt like I had entered a fancy spa back home. The walls were teeming with flowers and vines with relaxing music floating in the air. There were several mini waterfalls interspersed throughout this too-large lobby that I'm sure were there by magick. The whole place was lightly misted so as to keep the air from being too dry. It had a refreshing smell as well, a cross between the ocean and a misty morning in a forest. Of course, there were also more gemstones all about the area, ranging in sizes, colors, and shapes. I wanted to touch them all and then take a nap in the flower beds. The word "cozy" inadequately expressed how this place made me feel.

"Do you like it?" the woman asked me.

I exhaled the breath I didn't realize I was holding, and said, "I could happily live here. It's breathtaking!"

She grinned and said, "Thank you. We do our best here to make sure everyone leaves feeling better than when they came in. My name is Belinda, and I am here to help. So what brings you in today, other than seeking your dragon friend?"

Brax stepped in to answer for me. "Amy ate one of the Fae mushrooms and I'm afraid she cannot tolerate them."

Belinda's eyebrows drew together in concern. "Cannot tolerate them, you say? What happens when she eats them?"

Brax peered around to make sure Belinda was the only one listening. "Can you keep a secret?"

"I can."

"Good. Then please keep this one. Amy here is actually a mermaid. Mermaids cannot tolerate Fae mushrooms, as I'm sure you know. It can take away their ability to change into mermaid form, as well as cause them to lose their grip on gravity. There is something in the chemistry of it all that just does not work. Now, hopefully, nobody at the wedding party knows of that reaction, as we don't want to advertise that Amy is a mermaid. We are hiding from Ruskin and his men, and I don't want anyone to know where we are."

Belinda nodded once in affirmation. "I understand. Please. This way."

She gestured toward a door to our right, and we followed her inside. Once in the similarly decorated room, we saw another healer setting up what looked like a massage table. Nice! I could use a massage! It had been too long.

"Dom," Belinda started, "this is Amy, and she needs your assistance with a delicate matter. Please keep this information under wraps. She is a mermaid that has eaten one of our mushrooms and is having an adverse reaction. Please give her an antidote for the mushroom and we will see if we can keep her fins on the floor." She smiled at her good-natured quip. I couldn't help but do the same.

Dom gave a slight bow. "I will see that she gets the help she needs."

"Thank you, my dear," Belinda said, then turned to me. "This is Dom. They will take excellent care of you. Trust me, you are in the greatest of hands."

Before Belinda could take her leave of us, Ellera asked, "If everything is being handled here, can I go check in on our friend Ifyrus?"

"Certainly, dear. Follow me."

The two of them left to attend the dragon, leaving me with the others.

Dom had me lay as flat on my back as I could on the table, with Brax holding me down as firmly as he was able without crushing me. Colt sat on a nearby chair, kicking his feet while waiting for the adults to be done so we could get back to adventuring.

Once Dom was assured I was as settled as I could be, they gathered a plethora of ingredients to concoct a potion for me to ingest. They appeared to know what they were doing, so I laid there, waiting patiently, letting my eyes take in all the beautiful details of my current surroundings. If I ever made it back to Earth, I was absolutely copying their decor.

"Here we are," Dom said, blond and blue dreadlocks swinging about their head. "One mushroom antidote." They presented me with a vial of a greenish-yellow potion that was bubbling and fizzing. I wasn't convinced it was something I wanted to swallow, and I'm sure the look on my face said as much. "It's alright, my lady. I promise it will help you. You're not my first mermaid, it's just been a while since I've treated one. I also promise to keep your secret. I know there are those who cannot be trusted in this world but, as a healer, I am sworn to help you. So, please, drink up."

Brax's nostrils flared in agitation when he saw I hadn't reached for it, so he took the vial from Dom and shoved it in my face. Moving his hand freed one of my legs, and I felt it immediately drift back up to the sky. It was then I saw I really had no choice at this point but to trust the Fae and take the potion. With a grunt and a gulp, it was done. The weightless reaction I'd felt was slipping away, and I had the strangest sensation that I was sliding into a warm bath.

"Am I...? Am I wet?" I asked.

Dom chuckled and said, "That would be the warming effect. My apologies. It is only temporary, a minute at most, and then you should be fine. It just shows that it's working, which is a good thing! Once that finishes kicking in, and your gravity is stable, I will do a light massage to make sure that the potion seeps into every section of your body. You will be fully functional in no time."

By the look on Brax's face, he was not thrilled with the idea of another person with their hands on me, but he was also smart enough not to argue.

Dom politely sent Brax and Colt back out to the main lobby for refreshments once they saw I was no longer floating and in need of Brax's strength. Dom told me they were going to step out for a moment while I got undressed, and to slip under the sheets, face down on the table.

After a minute or so, Dom returned and set to work on my massage. It was the most exquisite massage I'd ever had! I used to get them all the time back on Earth, as I lived close to a massage school and took advantage of the low prices. I also had a friend who was once a teacher there, and he was the most skilled massage therapist I'd ever had the pleasure of knowing. But this? This was a new level of skill I had never experienced before. Dom used a potent mix of oil, herbs, and gemstones to enhance the healing, as well as a form of reiki that was more powerful than anything I'd encountered. I felt every inch of my body sink into this healing session and all of my chakras snapped into alignment like an army platoon getting orders from their sergeant. Every bit of fear and stress I'd collected since my arrival here melted from me like candle wax, and my entire being felt as if it was being reformed.

"How's everything feeling?" Dom asked.

"Mmmphh mmph hmnn," I replied, face still smashed languidly in the face cradle.

They chuckled and said, "Good! Now, in just a moment, I am going to release you and, when I do, I want you to take a deep breath over four counts, hold it for four, then release it over eight to clear it, okay?"

"Mmm hmm." I didn't want this to end. It was too heavenly.

"Alright. Three... two... one... breathe in... hold it... and breathe out," Dom instructed, giving my body one final sweep with their warm hands, bringing my healing to a close. They collected the crystals and wiped me down with a soft towel while my brain fought against the idea of getting up in a second.

"Take your time getting up, you've been through the wringer."

I heard them open the door and exit so I could put my clothes back on, but I had no desire to ever move again. I just wanted to stay here for an eternity. But I knew I had people waiting for me outside of this room, and I had to get up and rejoin them.

Prying myself from that table felt akin to pulling apart frozen chicken breasts, but I somehow managed it. I fumbled with my clothes until everything felt close to presentable, then stumbled out the door.

Brax didn't let me get two feet before clutching me to his chest and squishing my face against his pecs.

"Thank goodness!" he said. "I was so worried about you!"

"I'm fine," I tried to say into his rather large muscles, "though you're making it hard to breathe."

He let me go a fraction of an inch.

"Oh! Sorry."

Able to breathe a bit better, I asked, "How's Ifyrus?"

Brax's grip relented and I lightly pushed myself away from him to show I was able to stand on my own again.

"He had a few close calls, but things seem to be under control at the moment. They administered a potion that would counter the poison in his system, as well as a few other precautionary methods, just in case. Turns out, dragons are intolerant of malachite and blue lace agate. They are ground up and combined to make a glorious kind of nightmare for us. Apparently, it was once used in conjunction with oils and poured onto every bit of weaponry Ruskin's men had. They used it to kill off my kind. Ifyrus happened to take an arrow that was dripping with the same torment." He sighed. "If we'd gotten here any later, he would not have made it."

"I'm so sorry, Brax. How awful! I'm so grateful we got here when we did." My god, that sounded too close for comfort. "Can we go see him?"

Brax scrubbed his face with his hands as if he could erase the terror he was holding onto, then nodded. "He's up there."

He pointed to a winding staircase that spiraled up the wall, ending at a set of rose gold doors at the top. I shot him a questioning face.

"For special cases," he answered.

"Ah," I said.

We made our way up the stairs, Colt at our heels, and pushed through the ornate blown glass doors, entering the special circumstances wing. If I thought *my* room had been beautiful, this large open space was stunning. I felt like I was somehow both up in the sky and under the sea at the same time. A light blue haze enveloped the entirety of the building, but was not so thick that you couldn't see through it. Sparks appeared throughout the air as well, giving the impression there were lightning bugs in here. I didn't know their purpose in this place, but it was very pleasing to see. The walls were a cylinder of thin sheets of running water, keeping the air moist and breathable.

There were several patients here from what I could see. There were no curtains or walls between the patients, but there were blurs around each one to ensure some modicum of privacy. There were people both above us and below, but the only walkways were along the perimeter itself. The Fae used their wings to fly back and forth to each patient as needed, leaving the walkways for visitors and patients who lacked wings of their own. Each "room" had a floor big enough to support one bed and two visitor chairs.

I had no idea where to start. Luckily, Brax had come up with Belinda while I was getting my healing done and knew precisely where to go. So did Colt, I assumed, as he rushed past me to Ifyrus's bed.

We found Ellera seated next to Ifyrus's bedside, hands picking nervously at themselves in her lap, her lip bitten down just a bit too much. Ifyrus was resting peacefully. When she saw us approach, she jumped up and flung her arms around me.

"You're okay!" she said. "I'm so glad! How are you feeling? You okay now? No more mushroom poisoning?"

I laughed and returned the hug. "Yes, I'm fine, thank you. Much better now. And it wasn't poisoning, just an apparent intolerance of Fae 'shrooms. I should've known better. Plenty of fairytale— err, I mean, plenty of kids' stories growing up told me to watch out for that. It was a rookie mistake, and one I won't make again," I said, grimacing at my blunder. "How's our dragon?"

Ellera let out a big breath and raked Ifyrus with concerned eyes.

"Not going to lie, that was terrifying. While you were in getting fixed up, he vomited up more black goo and wouldn't stop bleeding from his wound or his face holes, so that was a real treat to witness. He stopped breathing a few times, and a group of Fae came to the rescue. Luckily, they made it in time but, wow, was that close."

I shuddered and clasped her hands in mine. "Thank you for staying with him. I know that could not have been easy," I said, then added with a coy smile because I couldn't help myself. "Especially since, you know, he's an awful brute and all."

Ellera flinched. "Well, he's not *that* bad. I mean, sure, he can be annoying, and irritating, and obnoxiously full of himself, but... I don't know... I think he's kinda growing on me."

I knew it! I had a good internal laugh.

"Oh, do keep going," Ifyrus croaked. "I love how you flatter me so."

"Ifyrus!" she shouted, leaping to his side and fighting with Brax over the chair closest to him.

Colt chuckled. "I wonder if they'll let me be the ring bearer at their wedding?"

He waggled his eyebrows, and I burst out laughing.

"Shhh!" came the admonishment of a passing Fae. "This is a house of healing! Please, keep your voices down!"

"Sorry!" I waved as she flew away in a huff.

I turned back to Colt, but he was already off exploring again. Just as well. Poor kid must be bored to tears in a place like this, no kids his age to play with or things for him to do. Not for the first time, I wondered what his parents must be thinking. We'd been traveling for several days now, and I had yet to see him make any sort of contact with them. Wouldn't they be out of their minds with worry? Or was Queen Miawae able to quell their concerns? Either way, I knew we had to get back on the road as soon as we were able.

CHAPTER THIRTY-ONE: CYNDOL'S DASH TO THE FAE

The gang made their way through the frightening forest, every minute closer to the Fae Realm. Luckily, it had stopped raining, and the protective barrier was taken down so that Felix could rest. They *all* deserved rest after what they had been through!

Cyndol was worried about Ethan. He hadn't said much since getting in the cart. She thought he might be in some kind of shock, which worried her even more.

"Ethan?"

He didn't respond, just stared off into the distance, eyes unfocused and haunted.

Cyndol couldn't help but picture the atrocities he might have endured in that prison. It was bad enough she knew the usual process of how the prisoners ended their stay there. Thinking of what could've become of her brother in that castle of corpses shattered her heart.

Cyndol clasped Ethan's hand in her own and gave it a little squeeze. "How're you feeling?"

Ethan gave a gentle squeeze back when *normally* he would've crushed it while laughing about what a weakling she was. That alone was enough to tell her just how bad this situation was.

"Mother? Father?" he asked with a shred of hope. Cyndol's heart broke all over again. She could feel the dam she'd put up around her feelings threaten to collapse.

"Um," she started, biding her time to find the right words. She took a deep breath and let it all the way out before speaking again. "The day after you were taken, there was a, uh... a small army that raided our village."

Ethan jerked his head to face her, momentarily forgetting his eyes. He opened them to focus on her face to gauge if this was a sick joke but, when his lids lifted, bolts of purple energy came shooting out of them, singeing off a lock of her hair.

"Ethan!" Cyndol screamed, ducking and trying to get away from the violet beams.

Ethan slammed his eyes shut again, apologizing quickly. The horses startled a bit, but Evony managed to calm them down.

"Everything alright back there?" she called over her shoulder, eyes remaining firmly on the dark road before them.

Druce laid his hands on Ethan's shoulders, holding him firmly in place, and said, "It's alright, Ethan! Just, please, keep your eyes closed until we can figure out a solution."

Ethan grunted in frustration. "I'm sorry! I forgot. It won't happen again."

His promise seemed to satisfy Druce and Evony for now, so they settled back in to continue their course.

Ethan turned his attention back to his sister and lowered his voice again.

"I'm sorry, Cyndol," he said. "Please, tell me what happened."

Cyndol shifted to his side and grabbed his hand again. This time, neither of them wanted to let go, needing that closeness.

Cyndol took a deep breath and explained to him everything she'd gone through since he left. From the emissary that arrived to explain his imprisonment, to the army that burned down the village, even the new powers she'd seemed to have acquired from nowhere. She told him of Queen Miawae and the kindness she'd seen from the people of Gallanor, and how that had led to her coming to save him.

In turn, Ethan explained about finding a beautiful piece of jewelry on the side of the road that started this whole mess in the first place. He left out the most gruesome details from his suffering at the hands of Viego, but he did mention how he'd thought he was all alone. He didn't know Cyndol was out there looking for him, but he had been told at some point that their village had burned, and no one made it out alive. He'd hoped that was just the torture speaking and didn't bear any truth. It devastated him to find out it was not a lie. Then, there was the problem with his eyes. He couldn't quite understand or wrap his head around it. Cyndol promised they would get to the bottom of all of this once they got to the safety of the Fae Realm. She assured him she'd heard talk of their great healers, and that Druce would do what he could until they arrived.

"That's right," Druce said, confirming to Cyndol that every word they'd spoken had been heard. "In fact, let me take a look at that hole in your head, see if I can get some magickal stitches in there for you."

Ethan begrudgingly lifted his matted hair from his unwashed forehead and grimaced, feeling overwhelmingly ashamed of his wound. It wasn't so much that it hurt (it did), but he felt violated, vulnerable, and wide open for the world to see.

Druce poked around gingerly, whispering a few words here and there, cleaning it as best he could. He pulled a spool of opalescent thread from his satchel of goodies, along with a clean white bone needle, and began stitching Ethan's head.

"Ow!" he yelped, squinting his eyes shut even harder. "Careful!"

"My apologies," said Druce. "I will try to be as gentle as I can."

He continued his task for a few minutes while Ethan gasped and groaned. When Druce was done, he smiled at his handiwork, proud of the clean job he had done with the stitches. But just when all seemed to be well, the wound began to dissolve the stitches and pulled them back into Ethan's open tissue.

"What the—?" Druce said.

"What?" Ethan asked, panic rising. "What happened?"

Cyndol got right up next to it, trying to figure out where the thread went, but there was no trace of it now. It had been completely absorbed!

"Well," Druce said, looking thoroughly confused, "I don't think the stitches will work in this case. That wound has some powerful magick even I can't seem to touch. I'm afraid you're going to have to wait for the expertise of the Fae."

"Luckily," Evony said, "you won't have to wait much longer." She pointed to a river up ahead with two men standing outside a tree along the bank. "We are here!"

Everyone but Ethan clamored to get a better look. None of the group had ever been here before except for Evony, at the request of Queen Miawae.

"Finn! Dodger!" Evony hailed the guards. "Do you remember me? I am Evony—"

Finn stepped forward with a grin and said, "Right Hand of Queen Miawae, yes. You're hard to forget."

Evony hid it well, but Cyndol could see she was pleased he remembered her.

"We seek the help of your healers. We rescued this young lad from the Sky Prison at the behest of the King and Queen of Gallanor. I'm afraid Ruskin's men roughed him up before we could get there. He needs help, quite a bit of it from what we can tell. May we enter?"

Dodger stepped forward with an odd look on his face. "Been a busy day, wouldn't you say so, Finn?"

"It certainly has been exciting," Finn agreed. "Normally, Latreya would be here to approve or deny entry, but she had to escort a group that was *also* in need of our healers."

Evony dismounted her horse and approached Finn and Dodger with the missive from Matthias and Miawae.

"Here's the proof that I had their blessing to retrieve the child. He was just in poorer condition than expected. Please. Look at the kid. He needs help. We tried with our healer, but I'm afraid it's beyond our magick. We need Fae magick, or we might lose him."

A clamoring in the woods behind made them fall silent, all eyes scanning the trees and surrounding area for its cause.

Evony continued. "When we left, things got a bit messy. The guards at the prison did not see the validity of Gallanor's claim to the child so we had to improvise his extraction. I'm afraid we might have some unwanted guests on our tail. You have my apologies. We did our best to lose them on the way here and thought we'd managed. I hope for everyone's sake that that's just an animal out there and not anyone from Ruskin's party."

Finn and Dodger exchanged a look; they both knew what they had to do. Dodger peered at Ethan in his pitiful current state and nodded.

"You may enter. But keep that missive with you at all times! I don't want to be responsible for you if you lose it, got it?"

Evony smiled graciously and bowed to them both. "Thank you. We will be on our best behavior."

"See that you are." Finn winked and waved a crystal rod in their direction.

Cyndol and the others felt a blast of magick and saw the world disappear as they shrank to the size of the Fae.

Once shrunk, Cyndol witnessed the remaining Fae guards shrink themselves as well. They cast a spell over the entrance to the Fae Realm and sealed it off. She assumed this was done to hide access to the potential intruders that followed them here. That gave her a modicum of comfort that she needed right now.

Finn came over to them, a worried look on his face. "Alright. Let's get you to the healers."

CHAPTER THIRTY-TWO: RUSKIN'S ROOM

Ruskin was pacing. Again. He did this when he was agitated and, lately, it seemed he was always pacing. He'd just received word from his trusted lieutenant, Daegan, that they'd tracked the targets to the Fae Realm, though they were unable to access the entrance, nor even find it. A spell had been put into place that cut off all forms of tracking, and they were unable to break through it. One minute, they had them in their sights and were ready to attack, the next minute, everything was gone in the blink of an eye. Even the river in front of them seemed to have disappeared.

Upon receiving that news, Ruskin flew into a fit of rage, smashing everything in sight, until he was surrounded by rubble and dust in his chambers. The only things untouched were his thrones.

"How could they have gotten away?!" he'd shouted at his guards.

Ruskin shifted into his wolf form and ripped the throats out of the guards closest to him before calming back down and sending for a fresh batch.

Silas, who'd managed to avoid the attack, brought in a new pack of guards, claiming these men were better suited to protect the king and his interests anyway. Ruskin took one look at the group and gave his loudest, most aggressive snarl. He was pleased to see that not one of them flinched. He nodded his head in approval, and Silas let out the breath he had been holding.

"They will do, for now," Ruskin said. "And Silas?"

Silas stood up taller. "Yes, Your Majesty?"

"See to it that Daegan and his men keep trying. I will not lose."

"Yes, Your Majesty. I will see to it myself."

"Good."

Silas bowed and took his leave. Ruskin glared at the crop of new guards and barked, "Clean up this mess!"

The men snapped to and began to clear the debris.

While the men were cleaning, Ruskin left his throne room to go deeper into his fortress. He made sure that no one was following him and slipped to the small hidden room he kept at the far corner of the castle. Only he and Silas knew of its existence, and that was because Silas had been the only guard Ruskin trusted with his life. There was the young guard that had alerted him recently that the amethyst he kept here had awoken, but he'd been among the pack of guards he'd killed in his rage this morning, so he didn't have to worry about him any longer. *He shouldn't have been back here in the first place.*

Using the wrought iron key from the chain on his neck, Ruskin opened the door to his secret room. The thick wooden door swung open on creaky hinges, just as Ruskin liked it. The sound reminded him of scraping claws, and it pleased his inner monster.

This room boasted nothing but stands for his trophies, or, rather, stands for his *eventual* trophies. These were the ones left unfinished. His victories were displayed proudly in the main hall for all to see, to instill fear. These were the ones that plagued him still, so he hid them out of shame and anger.

On the far side of this oval-shaped room sat a large amethyst geode. This geode had sat dormant for centuries, ever since Amaryah left this world. It used to have a twin, which was highly irregular, but it disappeared when she did, and the power this one used to have went out like a light. Ruskin kept it here in the hopes that she would one day return, and he could start all over again. With Ibraxus out of the way, he would have another chance with her. For all his anger and foulness, he found he still cared for her, even after all this time. When he was told the geode had lit back up, it ignited the small flame in his heart that he'd locked away upon her death. The wife he had now, Orelle, meant nothing to him, and was just a means to achieve an heir. However, she was unable to bear him a son, no matter how much they tried, nor how much magick was used to conceive one. He gave up on her and left her to rot in his old castle in the Snow Lands.

He did wonder about his daughter, though. Kavea was not what he pictured an heir to be, nor what he so desperately wanted, but he did hold a soft spot for her, nonetheless. He'd gotten word that she'd run away, and he wondered if she was coming to find him. *Good. Let her.* If she could find him, perhaps she would be willing to join his side, now that she is no longer so young?

Ruskin's musings were interrupted when his eyes landed on what he came in to admire: The suns necklace. It was still missing the smaller piece that locked it all together, but he knew it was only a matter of time until he got his hands on it. He had been so close until that wretched boy got in the way! Where did he put it?!

In his frustration, Ruskin's claws came out and he raked them forcefully across the geode, causing sparks to fly off in all different directions.

"Where are you?!" he screamed into the purple spikes. "Where? Are? *YOU*?!"

CHAPTER THIRTY-THREE: AMY'S HEADACHE

A sound like nails on a chalkboard echoed in my skull. *"Where? Are? YOU?!"* I stumbled and covered my ears.

"Oww!" I shouted, alarming everyone in the healer's hut around me.

Brax rushed to my side and cradled me in his arms. "What's wrong?"

"Did you not hear that?" I asked.

He gave me a strange look. "Hear what?"

I looked around the hut and saw everyone in the room turn to me with concern.

I shook my head as if I could rid it of the noise. "Huh. Must just be a headache."

Ellera came over and peeled Brax's hands from my shoulders. She flung them into his lap and gave him a pointed look. "Do you mind?"

Brax huffed but let Ellera take over. He shuffled to Ifyrus's bedside to check on the napping dragon-man, but kept one eye on us, just in case.

Ellera gave me her attention, eyes locked on mine as if searching for something.

"Now, then," she began. "Tell me what you heard."

Well now I just felt silly. I must have imagined it, or maybe it was a side effect of the healing I just had? Some random bits of energy that didn't settle or something. Maybe it was just plain ol' ringing in the ears?

"I'm fine," I said. "It was just a scratching noise. Probably nothing."

Ellera's gaze never left mine and, in fact, I noticed that her eyes started to cloud over, like they had back in her tent at the faire.

"Ellera, what are you doing?"

"Shut up. I'm looking." Her hands came up to both of my temples and latched on. I felt as if I were frozen on her fingers, unable to move or look away. It was paralyzing, and I was suddenly scared of my new friend.

"Ellera!" Brax shouted. He tried to pull her off me, but she sent him a jolt that flung him backwards into the corner of the bed.

"Stay down!" she said. "I'm almost done! This is important!"

A crowd of Fae healers began lining up around our platform to assist as needed, but Ellera blocked their access as well. *How much magick did this woman possess?* I felt as if my brain were being swam through at high speeds.

"Ellera..." I croaked, "stop... please..."

A sound like a door latch clicking into place snapped inside my head and our connection was broken. Ellera dropped her hands and gasped a few breaths. Brax got up from the floor and pulled me away from Ellera's reach.

"What was that?" he demanded.

I was shaking all over and also wanted some answers.

Ellera caught her breath and said, "Ruskin. He knows you've returned. He is looking for you, Amy, and a boy with a necklace."

"What?" I shrieked, earning another shushing from the healers. "Sorry!" I faced Ellera and lowered my voice. "What? Why? What does he want with me? And how would he know about me anyway?"

Brax's face showcased a storm of emotions. A vein in his forehead was throbbing and I could tell he was grinding his teeth. "Answer her."

Ellera sighed. "I saw a large geode, one made of amethyst. It lies in Ruskin's lair, and I caught a glimpse of him raging into it."

My skin prickled. "Was it..." I gestured with my hand at about the five-foot mark, "about yay big?"

She nodded. I gulped.

"That sounds like the one I just put in my shop. The one I died in."

"There were two of them here, once upon a time," Brax said in a low tone. "They were a symbol of your family's power and bloodline. Your father, King Volmar, gifted them to us on our wedding day, via Tripp. Volmar wasn't happy about us, but Tripp mentioned how important it was for you to stay connected to your power and your family. True amethyst power is hard to come by, but it ran so easily in your bloodline, and was coveted by many, Ruskin included. If the geode is with Ruskin, you can believe he stole them after your death."

"But if he stole them from here, how did one end up in my shop?"

"Now *that* is an excellent question, love," came Ifyrus's voice from the bed, scaring the crap out of me.

"Jesus! How long have you been awake?" I gasped.

He chuckled. "My name isn't Jesus. And who said I was sleeping? What was that other part about the boy and the necklace? Is Ruskin into jewelry now?"

Ellera graced him with one soft laugh. "Yes, he's into all sorts of fashionable pieces. As for the boy with the necklace, I don't know much about it, just that he has a part of a golden suns necklace and is looking for the missing piece. The boy had it last."

"What boy?" I asked.

We were interrupted by a group of people entering the healer's hut below us.

"Quickly, now! Be careful!" said a Fae healer. "And watch his head!"

We all watched with rapt attention as the newcomers settled in around their friend in need. Before the magickal privacy screen went up, we caught a glimpse of the face of the one they were putting in the bed.

Ellera laughed fully this time. "That one."

CHAPTER THIRTY-FOUR: MIAWAE SPEAKS WITH A FRIEND

A soft tapping at the dining room door interrupted the royals' dinner.

"Enter!" Miawae said.

Avery came in, looking quite surprised. "Your Majesty, you have a communication from Sovereign Sai of the Fae Realm."

Miawae smiled in relief, grabbing her napkin to wipe her face.

"Finally!" she said, getting up from the live oak table the family typically dined at. "I will return soon, my love. Enjoy your dinner." Miawae kissed Matthias's forehead and left the room.

"I have it set up for you in your sitting room, Majesty," Avery said.

"Thank you, dear," she answered. "That will be all."

Miawae sat down on her sofa and reached for the glowing clear crystal quartz ball perched on the sitting table.

"Good evening, Sovereign Sai. To what do I owe the pleasure of your call?" She clasped both her hands under the ball so that she might hold it closer to her face.

Sovereign Sai smiled in return, truly happy to see their dear friend's face again. "We know it has been long since our last conversation, and for that you have our apologies."

"There's no need to worry, I completely understand. Running a kingdom is exhausting on the best of days," Miawae said.

"It certainly is. The reason for the call this evening is that we have had quite the night so far in the Fae Realm. We currently have in our healer's hut a few strangers that claim to be of your employ. Are you aware of these people?"

Miawae chuckled and asked if they had some dragons, kids, and a fox in tow of a rather commanding woman with a small, but formidable army. Sai's nodding giggles confirmed Miawae's suspicion, as well as added to her mirth. Sai's laughter was seldom given and always delightful to witness.

"That's all the confirmation necessary. Thank you. We didn't know *what* to make of the situation, but we've done the best we could. Might you shed some light on the subject?"

The friends spent the next twenty minutes sharing information, catching up on each other's lives, and kingdom happenings. Miawae was having such fun reminiscing with her dear friend that she lost track of time.

A knock at the door sounded, and Matthias peeked his head through to see what was going on.

"I just wanted to make sure everything was alright," Matthias said, seeing his wife glowing. "I was about to start dessert without you." He gave her a wink to show he was only half serious.

Miawae's eyes grew large, and she threw a small pillow at him. "Don't you *dare* eat that without me! You know Harvest Cakes are my favorite!"

Matthias laughed and bowed as gracefully as he could at his age. "I wouldn't dream of it, my love."

"I'll be right there. Go make sure it's ready on the table when I get there!"

Matthias waved to Sai, then blew a kiss to his wife before slipping back down the hall to the dining room.

Sai smiled longingly at Miawae and said, "What we wouldn't give for a love as strong as yours. We have had many loves in this life, but none so unbreakable as yours. It's truly a thing to be marveled at."

"Thank you, my friend. Your words mean the world to me. And, on that note, I am going to go stuff my face full of cake before my husband beats me to it! Thank you for the call! We shouldn't wait so long until the next one. Please, take care of my brood. They have quite the parts to play in our near future. Goodnight, dear friend."

"You have our word," Sai promised. "We will do all we can to assist. Goodnight to you, dear friend."

Connection ended, Miawae settled the orb back in its holder and went to rejoin her husband for her favorite treat: Harvest cake.

CHAPTER THIRTY-FIVE: ETHAN PROVES TO BE A PROBLEM

"Hold still, please, this will just take a moment," said a confident voice above him.

The first few minutes of being here had been chaotic, but luckily there had been someone here who knew how to magick his eyes back to rights. That helped dispel a lot of fear both he and his group had been feeling. If only that were the singular issue going on here.

Ethan knew that *logically* he was in a safe place and in the care of the Fae (which was exciting), but being back on a bed and being tended to was giving rise to his panic from Padagonya. Every new person gave him a fresh chill, every hand nearing his face made his skin crawl as he waited for those fingers to extend and invade. The only true comfort he had was knowing his sister was by his side. She refused every attempt to remove her from his room, stating steadfastly that she was going nowhere without him. Kit had plunked his furry butt down as well and seemed to be content with the long haul.

The Fae woman dabbed at his head wound with a soft stick covered in some type of goo. It smelled of fresh ground herbs and lilac, not too heinous for medicine, but it was most definitely pungent. Cyndol was doing her best to breathe only through her mouth, while Kit buried his twitching nose under his tail. Ethan didn't mind the smell so much. Anything was better than where he'd been. All he could smell in that cell was fear, rust, sweat, and offal.

The healer finished her dabbing and was about to attempt stitches, but Druce gently stayed her hand.

"I'm afraid we already tried that," he said.

"Oh?" she asked. "And what happened to them? Did he rip them out?"

"No, ma'am," Ethan replied, and unfocused his eyes so he could stare at the nothing in front of him. "I absorbed them. Quite quickly, actually. And it was more painful than I'd like, so, if it's all the same to you, I believe I will decline a second round."

The healer looked straight at him with an expressionless face. Ethan refocused his gaze on her but couldn't tell what was going on behind that stoney facade. Finally, after a minute of the most awkward staring contest he'd ever been a part of, she harrumphed and left the bedside, citing she would be back shortly.

Ethan sighed and Druce said, "Don't worry, lad. We'll make sure you get fixed up as quickly as possible. I'm sure they just don't get a lot of cases like yours here. Maybe running to fetch more healers is not necessarily a bad thing. In fact, sometimes the more eyes on a problem, the better."

Ethan nodded but said nothing. What was there to say?

His musings were interrupted by the light snoring of his kid sister and her fox pet. He was glad she had not only survived but had found company and friendship along the way. He was still having trouble wrapping his head around her newfound powers, though. He angrily wondered why their parents had never told them they had magick. Now he'd never get to ask.

The wound on his forehead began to itch.

CHAPTER THIRTY-SIX: CYNDOL MAKES A FRIEND

Cyndol awoke to find that most everyone around her had fallen asleep. She guessed it was late into the night by the low sounds and the darker tones of what lights were still on.

She got up quietly, not wishing to disturb anyone, but needing to find somewhere to relieve herself. She slipped out the magicked privacy screen and began wandering down the hallway, searching for anything that resembled a washroom. Nothing seemed to jump out at her.

She was passing by an open door to a full room with actual walls when she heard some whispered voices coming from it, low and panicked.

"What should we do with the boy?" one of them asked.

Cyndol flattened herself along the wall, needing to hear what they were talking about. Were they discussing her brother? It didn't sound positive so far.

Another one gave a deep sigh after a long pause and replied, "I wish I knew, Marguerette, I wish I knew. I've seen some strange things in my day, but this is something different. We may need Sovereign Sai's direct assessment on this one."

Another pause, then, "My father used to tell me about creatures called Mind Travelers. They were rumored to be nearly extinct. I haven't heard of one in ages."

A third voice joined the others. "Do you think it's one of them?"

The Fae said, "For that poor boy's sake, I hope it wasn't. Nasty creatures, those."

There was a murmur of agreement from the small group. No one spoke for a moment, then a chair squeaked across the floor. "I'm going to go fetch Sai."

Cyndol realized she was about to get caught and tried to throw up her bubble, as if it might shield her from someone's sight. However, when she thrust her hands out to throw the bubble around herself, she ended up encasing the exiting Fae instead!

The poor woman floundered in the bubble and tripped, falling to her hands and knees, but stayed inside the orb. In her panic, she made enough noise that the others came out to see what all the fuss was about and saw Cyndol desperately trying to make it go away.

"I'm so sorry!" Cyndol said.

The healers pooled their powers together and managed to pop the bubble, freeing their friend. The ruffled woman crawled out quickly and clambered to get behind her co-healers. Cyndol's apologies and attempts to fix it were met with astounded faces and elevated worry.

"Go call Sai, now!" one of the women instructed the freed lady.

The lady did as she was bidden and left in a hurry, looking over her shoulder at Cyndol in fear.

"What was that, young one?" asked the woman in charge.

Cyndol felt tears threatening her eyes. "I... I, uh... I was just... just trying to find the uh... washroom," she finished lamely.

"What was that magick that you did to Marguerette?" she asked.

Pinpricks of hot liquid stung Cyndol's eyes but she refused to let them fall.

"I was just trying to find the toilet. I didn't know I was going to see anybody. I was just surprised. I tried to put the bubble over myself. I didn't mean to hurt anyone."

The Fae raised a skeptical brow at her explanation but relented at Cyndol's earnest response.

"Do you have magick, child?"

Cyndol nodded miserably. "It is seeming more and more likely, yes."

The woman studied her for a moment, until Cyndol was squirming under her gaze.

"Very well. I will bring this up with Sai when they arrive and see what the next course of action is. I believe that you did not intend to cause harm, but, young lady, you had better be careful eavesdropping on conversations not meant for your ears."

"But I—"

"Furthermore," she continued, "if that is un*trained* magick you contain, we had best set you up with a tutor, sooner rather than later, if we wish to avoid any future *washroom runs*."

Cyndol hung her head in embarrassment. Why did she have to pee *right now*? Why couldn't her stupid body have just waited a little longer? Now she felt like she was in trouble. *And* she still had to pee! She crossed her legs in the attempt to keep her needs at bay.

"Take her to the washroom before we have a situation," the woman said to the Fae still at her side, "then take her straight back to her brother's station. I'm sure we will have some things to follow up on."

With that, Cyndol was escorted to the short-lived relief of the washroom, followed by the impending stress of the punishment she was sure to follow once back in Ethan's room.

When she returned, she saw a young boy with dark, shaggy hair sitting in her chair, petting her fox. Kit seemed perfectly content, but Cyndol was annoyed.

"Hey," she said. "Who are you?"

The boy looked up at her with a big grin on his face and, without stopping his fox-scratching, extended his free hand to her and said, "Hi! I'm Colt! I like your pet."

Cyndol laughed. "He's not exactly a pet. He's more a friend than anything."

"Oh," he replied, "that's great! Do you know if he's a shifter?"

Cyndol was taken aback by his question. "No, I don't think he's a shifter."

"Have you asked him?"

"No. Why? Should I?" Cyndol was very confused by this boy. Probably someone's bored kid that is wandering around while they're here getting healed.

"I've found it doesn't hurt to ask. You know, I'm a shifter," he said.

"Really?" Cyndol asked, interest perking up now that he was giving her some information. "I don't know that I've ever met a shifter before. What do you shift into?"

Colt grinned. "I shift into a horse, and I have wings, which technically makes me a pegasus, but I can choose either one. It's pretty awesome!"

"Well, then, I guess the name 'Colt' is fitting."

He nodded, then asked, "What's this guy's name?"

"Kit."

"Fitting," he said.

The two children looked at each other and giggled.

"I'm Cyndol," she said. She pointed to the bed with her sleeping brother. "That's Ethan, my brother. He got hurt by one of Ruskin's guys and we're hoping that he can get fixed up here. What about you? What brings you here in the middle of the night?"

Colt pulled Kit into his lap and Cyndol took the vacated seat. Kit stood up and turned around a few times before settling back down and curling his nose into Colt's armpit, promptly falling back to sleep.

"I'm on a mission from the Queen," Colt said.

That got her attention for sure!

"Which queen?"

"Queen Miawae of Gallanor, the most amazing queen that ever was!"

Cyndol could feel her heart beat faster.

"I know Queen Miawae! She's the one who helped me get my brother back! The other people that I came here with are Gallanorians. What was your mission for her, if you don't mind my asking?"

Colt seemed to consider his answer before saying, "Well, I was supposed to save a woman from Ruskin's men, and I did that. But then the people we met up with right after that were in need of help, so here we are. Turns out, the woman I saved was the wife of the man's best friend who is here getting healed. I know, I know, it's complicated, but we had to help. I'm becoming something of a hero around here."

"Hmm," Cyndol humphed noncommittally. "Humble, too."

"What's that?"

Cyndol chuckled. "Never mind. Good job saving people, kid."

Colt beamed and snuggled Kit to his chest.

"I wish I could take him home with me," Colt said. "I don't have any pets."

Cyndol had an idea. "Colt, would you like to talk to Kit? I mean, *really* talk to Kit, and be able to hear him, too?"

Colt's eyes grew as big as dinner plates, and he nodded so hard she thought his head was going to fly off!

"Okay, okay!" She laughed, hands up *just* in case. "Give me one minute. I need to go grab something."

Cyndol snuck quickly and quietly over to where Druce was asleep on the floor, his bag next to him. When her fingers located the object she was looking for, she triumphantly directed it towards Kit and told him to say something.

"What would you like me to say, Cyndol?" Kit asked, twitching his tail.

Colt's eyes grew as big as Dragon Moon, and he held Kit out in front of him with an excited thrust.

"Careful!" Kit said.

"Do it again!" Colt said.

"Cyndol, is this kid okay?"

A voice interrupted them as it came past their entryway.

"*There* you are!" a beautiful woman with black and purple braids said. "I've been looking all over for you!"

"Ellera! These are my new friends, Cyndol and Kit!"

Ellera spared a quick glance at the boy sleeping in the bed before turning to address Colt's new friends.

"Hello, Cyndol."

"Don't forget about Kit!" Colt said.

Ellera frowned but turned to face the unconscious Ethan. "Sorry. Hello, Kit."

Both Cyndol and Colt giggled like the children they were, earning a single eye-opening from Druce before he saw there was no cause for alarm and rolled over to go back to sleep.

"No, silly! That's Ethan, Cyndol's brother. *This* is Kit!" Colt held Kit up to Ellera's face.

Ellera took a few steps backward and put a hand up to stop the furry invasion. "I'm sorry, what?"

Kit puffed out the breath he'd taken and said, "Apologies, my lady. He's just excited I can talk."

Ellera took another step back and put a hand to her chest.

"You're one of the talking animals, then? Are you a shifter? Are you spelled? What... *are* you?"

"Pfff, rude! What are *you*?" Kit retorted.

Ellera blanched. "I'm sorry, I've never met a talking animal before that wasn't a shifter. I was just curious. I meant no offense."

"As it happens, it *is* a spell. However, it's limited, and contained to that crystal wand Cyndol is holding, though she is the only one it's unnecessary for. She and I talk all the time without it. But, if you were too far from that wand, or I was, it wouldn't work anymore."

"Fascinating," she said. "I'm Ellera, and I'm, well, a friend from the faire back in Meadowtown. I'm sure young Colt here can catch you up on specifics. What happened to your brother? Is that a hole in his—" Ellera gasped and recoiled as if someone had slapped her. "Tell me what happened. Right now."

Cyndol suddenly felt very uneasy. Why did this woman react like that? Is it as simple as just being horrified by torture? Or was there something she was missing?

"Um," Cyndol said, "he was tortured in a prison."

"What did he—"

"He didn't do anything!" Cyndol yelled a bit too loudly. It woke Druce again, but he stayed where he was when he saw static electricity dancing along Cyndol's hands, at the ready if needed. Cyndol was suddenly grateful he was there. The others were staying in guest rooms on the first floor and were taking turns watching over Ethan. Cyndol was glad to not be alone with this woman right now.

Ellera's hands came up in a placating gesture. "I meant no offense, child. There's no need for a magick fight, so you can put that away." She motioned at the zinging hands clenching and unclenching at Cyndol's sides.

Kit's shocked expression would've been funny if the situation weren't so tense. "Whoa, Cyndol! When did you get lightning powers?"

Cyndol's intense expression turned to focus on her hands as she brought them crackling up to her face to examine them.

"When did I...?" Cyndol asked out loud to herself. "No, no! I don't want it!" She tried to brush the buzzing magick strands off her hands to rid herself of it, but it just succeeded in sending sparks everywhere.

Druce saw he was needed and deftly shot his hand into his bag without looking. He produced a pair of enchanted cuffs and expertly snapped them on Cyndol's wrists to cut off the power supply before someone got hurt. It mostly worked, though there was a slight bit of static still licking the offending bracelets.

The nurses came in to see what all the ruckus was about and were startled to see the new situation.

"Get these off of me!" Cyndol shouted, scared and furious in equal measure.

Druce tried to calm her by saying, "Don't worry, Cyndol, I promise they won't be on for long. I just didn't want to cause any damage to this establishment or the people and creatures within it. I'm afraid your lightning magick could very easily get out of control. Once you are calm again, I can take them off and we can have a discussion, but, for now, I need you to focus on your breathing, okay?"

"My *breathing*?" she repeated, outrage and disbelief taking up her thoughts in equal measure. "How can I breathe when I'm shooting lightning out of my hands? *How can I shoot lightning out of my hands*?!" she screamed while shaking her fists.

The healers bustled about, trying to get her seated and quiet, but were having a hard time accomplishing either of those things, until...

"Cyndol?" came Ethan's voice from the bed. "What are you doing?"

The intensity in the room seemed to drop to a whisper as Cyndol deflated and sat in a chair. Everyone in the room breathed a collective sigh of relief.

"I— I—" Cyndol stammered. "I don't... I don't know."

Druce's eyes never left her. "Are you okay, Cyndol? If you think you're okay now, I can remove the cuffs."

Cyndol was quiet for a moment, watching Ethan for his response, seeing only fear and confusion.

Cyndol said, "No. Leave them. For now. I don't want to hurt anybody."

"As you wish," Druce replied, backing off, and retrieving his things on the floor. "I'm going to step out for a few minutes to let you two talk, but I'll be right outside if you need me for anything. I mean that." He clicked his tongue at Kit and said, "C'mon, Kit, let's give them some time."

"You don't have to beckon me like a common pet, you know. Just a simple 'Follow me' will do," Kit said.

Druce smiled. "I'll keep that in mind. Follow me."

With a wink to reassure them they weren't in trouble, he left with the nurses, the fox, and the newly suspicious Ellera.

It was suddenly very quiet here. Cyndol sat in her chair, fidgeting with her hands and finding the cuffs were getting in her way. She puffed out an irritated breath and looked up to see that her brother was simply watching her with no expression on his face.

Finally, Ethan asked, "Are you okay?"

Tears welled up in her eyes, but she stubbornly refused to let them fall. Her brother had seen her cry hundreds of times, and he was likely responsible for many of those. But this time felt different. She felt like she had to be strong now, for him, for herself, for what was left of their family. She gave a slow blink to clear away the waterworks and steeled herself to respond.

"Yes. I'm fine. Please don't worry about me, I was just surprised by these new powers. Just focus on getting better, okay? I'm fine. I promise," she lied.

But Ethan lied just as easily, and for similar reasons. He was the big brother, after all, and technically the man of the house with his father gone, if they even had a house to go back to. A shock of anguish shot through his skull and ricocheted around until it found an outlet in his words.

"Don't worry about *me*. I'll be just fine. Nothing some good old Fae magick can't fix, right? Nothing to it." He flexed his young bicep muscle comically, and made an exaggerated 'manly' face until Cyndol gave a soft chuckle.

"See? I'm just fine," he repeated.

She almost believed him.

CHAPTER THIRTY-SEVEN: COLT'S BREAKFAST

"Last night was so fun!" Colt said the next morning. "I made new friends *and* talked to a fox! His name is Kit. He talks back, by the way. And he's *much* smarter than you'd think a fox would be!"

Amy laughed at the child's exuberance as she brushed her knotted hair using a fine-tooth comb. "I was always under the impression foxes were very cunning and clever."

Colt blushed and backtracked a bit, twirling his fingers. "Well, I guess that's true. I've just only ever seen them scurrying about the forest when I'm out for a run, and they never bothered to stop for a chat before." He shrugged as if that was that.

Amy put down the brush and ruffled his unkempt hair with one hand, grabbing her boots with the other. "I can't wait to meet them, then, especially after Ellera said the boy was the same one from her vision."

Colt seemed less excited about that. "He seems okay," he said, "but I dunno. I didn't talk to him that much, on account of him being in bed resting most of the time. I don't like his head wound."

Amy finished putting her boots on and gave him her full attention. "What do you mean? Like, you think it's disgusting and icky and gross? Like, *that* sort of dislike? Because that's okay, you know, to think that sort of stuff is gross. It *can* be, but they're taking really good care of him here. I know he'll be just fine. Nothing to worry about."

Colt shrugged again. This time, though, it came across slower, more deliberate.

"Colt," Amy asked, "are you keeping something from me? Did something weird happen? You can tell me."

Colt was really uncomfortable now. He wanted to explain, he just didn't have the right words for it. "It— well… it felt… *angry*. Dark, even, like it wanted to fight."

Amy's intense green eyes bore a hole through his own, trying to decipher his meaning. She tried again. "How so?"

"Kinda like something wanted to crawl out of it, maybe?" Colt was looking for an escape route now. He didn't like talking about this.

"Like what?"

"I dunno, a spider, maybe?"

Colt saw Amy shudder and grimace. Her face made him chuckle and Amy brightened at his amusement. She did it again, but even more exaggerated this time for comedic effect. Pretty soon, they were both giggling, and the darkness from a minute ago dissipated as quickly as it had come.

"You ready?" Brax poked his head into the room. "They're about to start."

The Fae had been very kind to them. Aside from helping them escape Ruskin's men and provide healing services, they let them stay in their guest rooms at the healer's hut. Sovereign Sai had even invited them all to a lavish breakfast. The wedding ceremony from last night was continuing its festivities, and the newcomers were to be seated with the Sovereign at a place of honor, being friends of Queen Miawae's. Ethan and Ifyrus were still in their beds healing, so they wouldn't be joining them today. Druce volunteered to stay behind in case he was needed. Cyndol refused to leave Ethan's side, and Kit refused to leave Cyndol's, so they stayed behind as well. The rest of them were getting ready to join the Fae in the breakfast tent.

When everyone arrived, they found they were back at the same tent as last night, but the scenery had changed. What once was a flowery cave of magick and wonder, was now a beautiful garden party "hidden" by trees, vines, and various shrubbery. They all went through the gate that led into the garden party and found the inside was now a large blown glass structure that Amy had called a "greenhouse", whatever *that* was. Colt was getting used to her saying weird things that no one understood. She must come from somewhere far away from here.

Their group was ushered to a table hidden behind a large butterfly bush set next to the bride and groom's table. Sovereign Sai was already seated when they arrived. They smiled at the group with a beaming glow that showcased the whitest teeth Colt had ever seen. Sai emitted such a powerful brightness that it almost hurt to look at them. Colt had never been so impressed.

"Please, come sit!" Sai beckoned to the group. "We are so thrilled you decided to join in our festivities. There are plenty of seats for all of you."

The newcomers each grabbed a chair and sat, taking in the merriment around them.

On the large round table, there sat a plethora of tasty treats. There were platters of spiced scrambled eggs, sausage links, fragrant meats, with bowls of brilliantly colored mushrooms that rivaled the brightness of a rainbow. Another platter held beautifully crafted crêpes filled with blackberry clotted cream, blueberry compote, and a drizzling of caramel syrup. The tops of the crêpes housed sugar-dusted blackberries and blueberries, with fresh mint leaves and tiny lavender flowers as garnish. Colt's mouth began to water immediately.

"Dreadfully sorry to hear about your friends," Sai said. "Our healers will do everything they can to get them back on their feet as soon as possible."

"They already did a lot to help *me*," Amy replied. "Fixed me up good as new! They even took the time to patch up an arrow wound I had on my arm. You have some pretty amazing people here, Your Majesty."

Sai bowed their head in thanks and addressed the table once more. "We are pleased to hear it! So our friend Miawae tells us you are on separate missions, is that correct?"

Evony spoke then. "Yes, Majesty. My queen had me and my party escort young Cyndol here to retrieve her brother from the Sky Prison. Ruskin was holding him there without warrant. It— didn't go exactly as planned. They did quite a number on him, I'm afraid. We're going to need all the help we can get with him, poor child."

Sai nodded their head in understanding. "And what about you?" This was aimed at Ibraxus. "What brings you to our realm?"

Brax cleared his throat roughly, not expecting to be put on the spot. "Well," he said, once he found his voice, "my friend Ifyrus and I were on a mission to find my wife, Amaryah. Sorry. *Amy*. When we did come across her, we found out that young Colt here had been the one that saved her life before we could get to her." He turned to Colt and said, "You know, lad, I don't think I properly thanked you for what you did for her. From the bottom of my heart, you have my eternal gratitude. If there's ever anything that I can do to repay you, please ask." He gave Colt a wink and shoveled some sausage in his mouth.

Colt's elated smile almost shattered his adolescent face, and the group chuckled, offering their thanks to Colt as well. Amy ruffled his hair again.

Their majesty cocked a curious eyebrow and invited Colt to tell them the story of this daring rescue, which he was all too eager to do.

When he finished regaling them with his heroic tale of bad guys and mid-air shapeshifting, Sovereign Sai dabbed their mouth with their napkin and came to a decision.

"Would you mind terribly joining us this afternoon for a private meeting in the throne room? There's something Queen Miawae wanted to do to help, so she asked for our assistance. After hearing your tales, we are inclined to help you, but away from prying eyes and ears, just in case. King

Ruskin has spies everywhere, and while we'd like to say it doesn't happen here, we cannot promise you that."

"Something to help, huh? That sounds delightfully vague," Ellera said. "I'm in."

When the others voiced their agreements, Sai stood up and excused themself, saying they would meet them all soon.

Colt was close to bursting! What a fun adventure he'd been on so far! He'd become a hero by saving someone from the evil clutches of Ruskin's army, he'd made a bunch of new friends (including a talking fox!), and he'd gotten to dine with the Faeries! He had no idea what was coming next, but he couldn't wait to find out what Sovereign Sai had planned for them!

CHAPTER THIRTY-EIGHT: MIAWAE'S WARNING

"A young woman entered the village today," Miawae told her husband.

"Oh?" Matthias set down his cup of tea on the small log table to his left.

"Yes," she said. "While I didn't get a vision, I did catch the strangest feeling from her. Something's not quite right, Matthias. I think it best we keep an eye on that one. She has the aura of Ruskin about her."

Matthias gave a soft chuckle in response. "And what makes you say that, my dear?"

Miawae realized that her point might be better made if she just showed him. She left the doorway she was standing in to join him on the floral sofa. Grabbing his left hand in hers and touching her right middle finger pad to his forehead, she opened his third eye and shared her memory with him.

The woman glided down the main village pathway, full of confidence that her feet would keep track of her snaking panther body. Her obsidian eyes oscillated back and forth, scanning everything she could take in before sliding her gaze to the next building or landmark she passed, as if committing everything to memory. People were also scanned in this perusal, and each creature that her eyes touched seemed to shudder. Her movements were quick, but that did nothing to move the short pitch-black curls that were plastered in place to her skull.

Miawae didn't like the looks of this woman one bit. When the woman passed by Miawae, she inclined her head just a whisper to acknowledge she knew exactly whom she was in the presence of. She gave her a mocking wink and a hint of a smile before she continued on her way. She didn't even change her speed. The confidence she exuded would have been envious if it wasn't accompanied by the trailing wisp of an onyx aura.

"Who is that, Grandmother?" asked Kiara.

"I'm not sure, child," she said. "But beware. I feel she might not mean well."

Miawae turned to see Avery approaching them.

"Majesty," he began, "there was a rumor from the direction she came in from that her name is Ikah. She's one of Ruskin's top generals, his elite. It might behoove you to invite her for supper to see what brings her here."

"Marvelous thought," Miawae agreed. "See to it that she gets the invitation."

Before Avery could leave to deliver it, Ikah turned around in the stretch of street she'd put between them and haughtily shouted for all to hear, "I accept!" then continued to walk away.

Kiara's concerned eyes met her grandmother's. "What do we do now?"

Miawae let out a long breath and said, "We prepare for dinner."

Miawae let go of her husband's head as they both sank deep into the couch.

"I see," Matthias said, puffing out a long breath of his own. "This might be a problem."

Miawae nodded absently, her mind running a thousand scenarios in her head at once, trying to find which one seemed the best course. Finally, she reigned in her thoughts and concerns, slapped her hands on her thighs, and stood up, offering her hand to her king.

"Shall we ready for our guest, dear?"

Matthias's worry lines deepened, but he allowed her to pull him to his feet. "I suppose we must."

The two left the sitting room to set up for their evening meal, ready to meet Gallanor's latest threat.

CHAPTER THIRTY-NINE: AMY ATTENDS A MEETING

I couldn't believe how beautiful the Fae Realm was. Literally everything I've seen has taken my breath away. (Okay, maybe not *literally*, but you know what I mean.) You'd think that, at some point, my brain would get used to it and I'd just start to accept things as normal, but nope. Still breathtaking.

We'd finished our lavish breakfast of mixed berry cream crêpes and brightly colored mushrooms (for the others, I just watched in mushroom-envy), then drank our fill of some exquisite apple liquor that reminded me of my stepdad's apple brandy back on Earth. Man, that stuff used to pack a punch! I wonder if they'd let me keep a bottle or two. Probably too late to ask— we were already on our way to the throne room that Their Majesty had invited us to.

I turned my attention to Brax, who smiled shyly at me from under a lock of golden-tipped hair. Lightly reaching for my small hand, he held his large one out for a moment, hanging in the air as an unspoken question. The desire to take it wrapped around me like a warm blanket, and I gladly accepted. I felt a sizzle of energy dance across my palm as his fingers interlaced with mine. We both heaved a sigh of relief. It surprised me, feeling this easy and comfortable with him. Was I remembering him? Or was this just really nice? He *is* super easy on the eyes, after all. Maybe it's just that undeniable attraction factor, like that crush you get when you see a superhero on the big screen? Beautiful. Massively stunning! But even more than that, he had this electric energy that seemed to lap at me like ocean waves, and I wasn't sure I was interested anymore in denying myself these pleasures.

I felt a sudden drowsy coziness come over me and, before I knew it, I was tapping my thumb lightly on his hand, and he was doing the same back to me. It felt like a code, one that was just for us. There was definitely a specific rhythm to it.

We both stopped tapping and looked at each other with mirrored expressions of surprise.

"You remember that?" he asked.

"Remember what, exactly?" I asked.

"*Thump thump thump thump! Thump thump thump thump!* We thumped our fingers like this on each other when we were happy. It represented when we would thump our tails on the ground—"

"Like we saw the dogs do when *they* were happy, and with us, it meant—"

And at the same time we both said, "I love you."

Silence followed, but no words were needed. We smiled at each other, tears forming in our eyes. We gripped our hands a little tighter. *Thump thump thump thump. Thump thump thump thump.*

We stopped walking when we got to Sai's quarters. While most royalty would have a massive castle or mansion, I assumed, Sai kept their abode closer to the structures of their land. While still bigger than most of the other homes here, it wasn't by a tremendous amount. It was a modest mushroom covered treehouse castle nestled within a rather large tree root cluster, giving the appearance of suspending the castle over the creek that passed underneath the exposed roots. Up the roots was a walking path that brought you to the castle's front gate. Layers of moss carpeted the pathway and felt soothing under my tired feet.

    Inside the castle reminded me of being in a log cabin. The walls were dark wood, but polished and rounded off, as if we truly were in the center of these massive roots. Sai kept with the gem and flower theme of the land, and I wanted to move in.

    We entered the throne room where a table and chairs had been set up for our meeting with the sovereign. Sai emerged from behind their throne, wearing a stunning cape of peacock blue over shimmering emerald-green silks that extended to their bare feet. Once Sai was seated on their throne, the rest of us took whichever seat was available, though Brax made sure to get a seat directly next to me. I didn't mind at all, and gave his hand one last *thump thump thump thump* before placing my hands on the table, waiting for everyone to be seated.

    I was surprised to see that my group was not the only one invited. There were also several people from the other party from last night, excluding the boy who was getting care, as Ifyrus was also still doing.

    When everyone was seated, Sai began.

"Thank you all for coming. Queen Miawae has informed us of what is happening and has asked that we gift you a few things that will be helpful moving forward. As we're sure you all know, King Ruskin's thirst for power has far extended past what anyone is comfortable with, and he is destroying our world. Thanks to him, we have no more dragons, save for the returned Ibraxus and Ifyrus. We have only limited magick now, with the Gemstone Belts not dropping as much to us since the dragons have not been around to facilitate that task. Ruskin has plans to make life even worse for us all, and Miawae has seen that each of you will play a part in stopping that madman. Because of this, she has asked that we use some of the magick we still possess to assist you." They stood up and motioned to Colt first.

Colt's eyes grew wide as he jumped out of his seat and rushed proudly to join Sai. I tried to stifle my giggle, but Brax joined in with me.

"Cute kid," he whispered.

"He's kind of the best," I agreed. "My own personal hero."

"For your mission to find and assist Amy so that she reached the safety of King Ibraxus, the queen has asked that we reward your efforts with a special gift. Would you mind shifting into your pegasus form for us, please?"

His look of surprise mirrored my own, but he did it without hesitation. Even though I'd seen him do it a few times now, it still felt like it was a magic trick. Once he was in pegasus form, Sai continued.

"This," they said, brandishing a golden horn, "belonged to a dear friend as well, many long years ago. The old King of The Unicorns, Ahmonrah, instructed us before his death to ensure the passing of his horn only goes to one who could bear its weight in courage. After your harrowing flight, escaping King Ruskin's men and saving Amy, especially at such a tender age, well, we believe you have earned that right. We expect many great things from you, young Sir Colt. Wear it well."

Sai placed the horn over Colt's forehead, and we marveled at the magickal union between horn and head. It was definitely a sight to behold! Sparks of diamond, amber, and gold shot out like happy little fireworks as the horn's tendrils made contact with Colt's head. I felt a moment of panic at this magickal fusion happening before my eyes and away from the knowledge of his parents, who must be worried sick about their little boy! But Brax laid our combined hands on my leg, and he gave an affirming squeeze.

"It's alright, my love. I can feel your worry for the boy, but he will be just fine. This is a gift he is receiving, and one not lightly bestowed. This is an honor."

"But what about his parents?" I whispered. Luckily, no one was paying attention to me, and all eyes and ears were tuned to what was happening with the boy.

"I'm sure his parents will be thrilled for their son. I would be, were he our child. Trust me, this is a good thing. You need not worry."

I did my best to push the worry to the back of my mind and concentrate on what was going on before me.

The horn gifting finished, and we all took part in admiring Colt's new look. He took a few cursory stomps around the throne room, swinging it about and jabbing the air with it, before happily clomping back and forth in what could only be described as a prancing fashion. There were cheers and applause from the group around the table.

Sai told Colt he should shift back now and rejoin the others in his seat so that they may proceed with the rest of the meeting, but that they would make sure he got in plenty of practice time with it later. Colt did as he was bid, looking equal parts elated and dejected once he was a human again. Poor kid. That's like giving a kid a Christmas gift, letting him open it, then telling him he has to put it away and watch as everyone else gets to play with their stuff for a bit. I giggled some more and ruffled his shaggy hair when he came back to his seat.

"Cyndol," Sai said. "You will be next, please."

The little girl with the two wheat-colored braids stood up awkwardly, not realizing she would have to go up.

"Me?" she asked. "Are you sure?"

Sai laughed and it sounded like the tinkling of windchimes. "Yes, girl. You also faced and escaped Ruskin's men. Not only did you manage that, but you were able to withstand the destruction of your old life and take on the task of finding and saving your brother. That, dear, shows exemplary courage and determination! That is a thing to be revered."

Cyndol did a small and embarrassed shrug but joined Sai.

Sai smiled contentedly and stated, "While we do not have a spare unicorn horn to affix to your head like Colt, we do have a few folks here that are trained in many different areas of magick. You will receive training on your newfound powers before you leave so that you may retain control of your gifts. We sense a very strong future for you, child, and we'd like to be helpful in getting you there."

Cyndol blushed a charming shade of crimson and muttered a polite "Thank you, Majesty" before returning to her seat.

There was something so very familiar about this girl. I didn't recognize her from my life on Earth, and nobody had mentioned my meeting her before coming here, so I don't know why it was bothering me so much. Oh, well. Maybe she just had one of those faces...

"Everything alright?" Brax asked. "You have a peculiar look on your face."

I shook my head. "What? Oh, yes. I'm fine. Just lost in thought."

"About what?"

"Oh, it's silly."

"I don't mind silly."

I gave up. "Does that little girl look familiar to you? Cyndol? I've been trying to figure out where I know her from and it's driving me crazy!"

Brax focused in on her as best he could. "Hmm. Now that you mention it, there *is* a certain familiarity there, but I'm afraid I can't place it either."

With nothing more to add, I returned my attention to where Sai was talking to Kit.

Kit followed his summons and sat dutifully at the sovereign's feet.

"For *your* acts of bravery and rescue, dear Kit, a couple different gifts should suffice. Firstly, as your companions have had the pleasure of being able to speak with you via crystal wand magick, and have thoroughly enjoyed your company, we give you the gift of True Voice. Now you will be able to communicate with all around you. May your voice be ever heard."

Kit gasped in excitement. Sai chuckled and waved a complicated pattern in the air with their hands above Kit's head. I couldn't quite make out the words, but it sounded melodic in tempo.

When they stopped, Kit asked, "Was that it? Did it work?"

The group erupted in gleeful applause.

"I'll take that as a yes!" he said.

Sai nodded. "Indeed it has, young fox." Their facade slipped into a slightly more somber expression. "Now, as for the second gift, we were made aware that you tragically lost your family not long ago, is that correct?"

Kit's face fell and he nodded silently. A murmur whispered through the crowd.

"You have our sincere condolences, as do all of you that have loved ones lost behind you. And, Kit, as you are the only one left in your pack, we'd like to give you the power to call upon another in times when a friend could come in handy. Someone that could share in ways of the fox. All you need to do is find any reflective surface and you may call your reflection out to help. Let me show you." Sai pulled out a small gemstone hand mirror and held it up in front of Kit's face. "Look straight into the mirror, Kit, and see the fox before you. Now, either out loud or to yourself, you may invite him over."

"Just... invite him over?" asked Kit.

The group tittered lightly at his sweet confusion.

"Yes, just invite him over." Sai smiled and waited patiently for Kit to try.

He squared up his furry shoulders, pointed his nose at his reflection, and decreed, "I invite you over!"

With that, an orange and cream-colored swirl emerged from the glass like a cloud of cotton candy, forming quickly on the castle floor as the perfect clone of Kit. We cheered loudly. It was adorable, watching as Kit and Kit Two sniffed each other slowly, getting to know one another to the delight of us all. Laughter erupted when they began to play-tackle each other and accidentally rolled into Sai's throne. Both instantly hopped back up like nothing happened.

"To undo the command, simply tell him to go home."

Kit looked suddenly undecided, as if he didn't want to give up his new friend.

Sai placed a reassuring hand on Kit's head and said they would let him pick out any small mirror in their kingdom to keep with him always. That way, no matter what happens, he will never feel alone again.

It was quite touching, actually. They seemed so kind and genuine. I wished more people could be like this.

"And now, Amy. Will you please join us?" the sovereign beckoned.

Now it was *my* turn to blush! But I did as was asked of me and approached Sovereign Sai.

"Amy, we have learned that you are not new to our world, but rather are one of the Returned. We all are at some point, but not many of us get to experience the full spectrum of that journey without the inevitable rebirth. We understand how confusing that must make things, and you have our sincerest apologies. To not have the full range of one's own faculties must be daunting, so our aim is to try to help you with that as best we can. In that vein, we are joining the efforts made to restore your memory to its fullest capacity by enlisting the help of our most skilled healer, Hælgah. This will be in addition to your friend Ellera, whom we have come to find out also has skill in this area and has been able to make a bit of progress. Queen Miawae has informed us that you are a vital soul in this world, and that every effort must be made to make you whole."

I truly didn't know what to say to that. Yes, I felt weird as hell here, and *also* yes, I would love to know what my brain is hiding from me, but it felt strange to be discussing this in front of so many strangers. And "The Returned"? *Is that really a thing? Has this happened before?*

"Thank you, Majesty," I said with sincerity. I also gave a little bow, as I was suddenly nervous, not knowing what to do with my body while all eyes were on me.

I think Sai caught my awkwardness, because they winked and saved me with the announcement of the final gift.

"And last, but not least, Ibraxus, King of The Dragons. Please join us."

Brax huffed out a long breath and went to Sai.

"We did not have the pleasure of your kingship in our lifetime, not having been born to this world yet while you ruled, but we have heard many great things about you and your family, and you have the respect of the Fae behind you. Your throne remains open, as none after you were able to hold it with the wrath of King Ruskin and his ever long reign. We ask that you consider sitting upon the throne and ruling as you once did before it was stolen from you."

Brax gritted his teeth and said, "I mean no disrespect, but to whom would I rule, Majesty? From what I've seen, my kin are dead and gone, save for myself and Ifyrus. Besides, my dragon power was stolen from me as well, long ago by Ruskin himself with the help of his Mage. How could I take the kingdom back now?"

Sai simply smiled and snapped their fingers once. Ifyrus bounded into the throne room to join them, looking right as rain and back to his rakish self. In his arms was an egg. Not just any egg, but a rather large one with shimmering scales of blues and greens in every shade cascading down from the top like a waterfall. Ifyrus presented it to him like he was offering riches to royalty, which, in fact, he was. He even got down on one knee and held it up for Brax to take.

Brax's eyes consumed his whole face, which now lay slack jawed as he took in the meaning of this gift.

"Does this mean...?" Brax started to ask.

"Yes," Sai said. "She is the start of your return, dear Ibraxus. The start of many new dragons, according to the recent prophecy from Queen Miawae. There will be a new beginning for you all, and with you as their leader, we expect many great things for our future."

Brax's breath caught in his throat. "But what about my—" he choked and couldn't finish his question.

Sai put a reassuring hand on his shoulder, and said, "That is our final gift to you, Majesty. May they never leave you again." Their other hand came up so that now both of Sai's hands were on Brax's shoulders. Sai closed their eyes, and a low hum filled the room. It grew louder and was now audible to all. Everyone held their breaths, waiting to see what was happening in front of us. No one spoke, all eyes glued to the pair of leaders.

Warmth, not unlike a roaring fire on a winter day, washed over all of us and we breathed a collective sigh of comfort.

After a moment, Sai lifted their hands and, in doing so, left two small nubs where they had been resting growing right out of the back of Brax's black tunic!

"What—?" he began, but was cut off when full black dragon wings shot ferociously out of the nubs, already twice as long as he was tall! I ducked, along with Sai and Ifyrus, just barely getting out of the way of these massive things!

Brax was so overcome that he stood there, stupidly, while his wings danced around him of their own accord.

"What is a dragon king without his wings?" Sai asked in good humor. "Nobody shall ever strip them from you again, you have our word. Go ahead, take them for a test spin!"

Needing no further convincing, Brax followed Ifyrus out the side door that opened to a large open garden. He quickly finished transforming into full dragon mode and took to the sky, obviously born to it. Ifyrus, in his own glee and restored health, followed suit. Wisely, before taking off, the dragon egg had been placed gently in the caring arms of Ellera, who was now staring in fascination at the pair of dragons putting on a show in the air above us while she softly, yet confidently, clutched the last known dragon egg in existence.

In our excitement, we had all followed them outside to watch the King of the Sky. It was a sight to behold. After a few minutes, the dragons came back down to rejoin the group and we reconvened in the throne room, crackles of excitement now palpable all around us. Ifyrus practically bounced to the empty seat next to Ellera and the egg, and Brax scooped me up in his masculine arms, spun me in a circle, and plopped us back in our seats as well. He smelled of sweat and sunshine and breezy summer days. It was intoxicating.

Catching my approving expression, Brax returned a hungry look of his own, and I could feel a shift in him immediately. Being only half of yourself is a lonely way to live, and I couldn't contain my gratitude towards Sai and the remarkable gift they bestowed him. It also gave me renewed hope that their healer Hælgah and Ellera might be able to help restore my own sense of missing self. A single tear slipped down my cheek and Brax caught it with his index finger.

"Do not weep, my love. This is a good day."

"I couldn't agree more," I said.

Sai brought the attention back to themself.

"Thank you all for all that you have been doing to help, and for what you will continue to do. We may not fully understand yet the impact you all will have on our future, but we do know it will be the start of a very bright future indeed!"

I turned to Brax and said, "I'm sorry, what are we supposed to do?"

CHAPTER FORTY: KIARA'S REQUEST

Ikah had been here for a few days now. Each one of those days, Princess Kiara had sent guards to follow her around town to figure out what she was doing here and whether or not she meant any harm. Her spying had not churned out any decent results so far. All she'd managed to find out was that Ikah had rented one of their most lavish guest treehouses and walked all over the village each day, not saying much to people other than to ask what life was like living in Gallanor. She did it in such a sinister way, though, that it left everyone feeling on edge. She reeked of inky blackness and gleeful damage.

"Just give me *one* excuse, Creeper, *just* one," Kiara said through gritted teeth. Her grandparents didn't condone violence unless absolutely as a last resort, but Kiara knew that sometimes violence was the only language people spoke. She balled her fists and flared her nostrils.

"What has you so upset, darling?" Miawae asked. She sipped her afternoon tea and waited patiently for a response.

Kiara realized she'd been drifting off, barely touching her food and drink. She glanced at her untouched cup and brought her eyes to meet her grandmother's.

"I do *not* trust that woman."

Matthias cleared his throat from his position at the head of the table and set the letter he'd been reading on the top of the daily pile.

"Be that as it may, she remains our guest until it can be proven that she is causing trouble."

"But—"

"No buts!" he continued. "Last I checked, I am still king! I promise you, my dear, if I feel that her presence is cause for alarm, I will take action. You have my word."

Kiara ground her teeth harder, but wisely said nothing. Miawae continued to sip her tea and Matthias went back to his reading, but Kiara was hatching a plan.

"May I be excused, please?" she asked with forced propriety.

Her grandparents exchanged a look, and Matthias nodded his approval. Kiara scooted her chair back with a squeak but was stopped by Miawae.

"Just a moment, dear."

Kiara sucked in a breath and held it, waiting to unleash an argument if one presented itself.

"You hardly ate at all," she said softly. "At least take something with you for later."

Kiara blinked, surprised her grandmother wasn't trying to keep her here, and grabbed the easiest thing she could pocket: A golden apple.

"On your way, now." Miawae winked at her and returned to her tea.

Kiara had the strangest feeling her grandmother knew exactly what she planned to do. Curious.

She left the dining area and made a beeline for her quarters: A stunning room of rich purple and gold silks strung in patterns along the walls that gave the impression of movement, even without wind. She ignored her four-poster bed hanging down from the ceiling, and instead chose to sit at her wooden desk in the corner under the window to pen a letter of her own.

It simply stated: *Out for a walk, will return shortly. K.*

She exited her bedroom and tacked the note to the doorway in case her grandparents came to check on her, then promptly descended the three flights of stairs to the ground floor.

Flinging open the front door, she took a look around to make sure she wasn't being followed, and that that *creature* of a woman wasn't within her field of vision. Luck appeared to be on her side, so she quietly slipped out and made her way quickly to the House of Healing.

The House of Healing held no mystery in its name. This was, plainly put, the building in Gallanor that helped the sick, the injured, and the infirm. It was *also* the place where the majority of their limited supply of Mages resided. There was a special segment of the building in the back that housed live-in tenants so that they may be close at hand in case of emergency. These quarters were free for anyone who agreed to share their powers.

The building itself was much like any other in Gallanor: A large tree that surrendered itself to the whim of the people and allowed for rooms to be crafted from its insides. This was a harmonious transaction between nature and creature, as it provided shelter and homes for the people and, in turn, the people would take care of regular feedings and waterings of it, just as any other in the plant kingdom may need.

Kiara steeled her sudden nerves and opened the blown glass door.

"Good afternoon, Princess!" said Azel. "How may we be of service to you today?"

Kiara offered her best smile and said, "Good afternoon, Azel. I am looking for Druce. Is he here?"

"I'm afraid he's not. He's still with Evony and the little girl."

Frustration clouded Kiara's eyes for a moment as she recalled that fact. She pressed on.

"Might there be someone else here that is gifted in speaking with animals? I know Druce had a talent for crafting magicks like that."

Kiara could see the wheels in her head turning as Azel paused in thought. She knew the second she had an answer, as the woman's matronly face lit up like a beacon of hope in its frame of weathered grey.

"You know, I think I've spotted Janmo a time or two conversing with the local wildlife. Let me see if he's available. One moment." She went to go fetch him, leaving Kiara to pace nervously until she came back.

"Look who I found!" Azel said upon her return.

She stepped to the side and Kiara saw the familiar face of a rotund gentleman she'd seen here a time or two before.

He bowed awkwardly and asked, "How may I be of service, Princess?"

Kiara hid her smirk and tried to appear the royal that she was. "Hello, Janmo. I was looking for Druce to aid in a mission that requires communication with animals, but as he is not here, I was informed that *you* may have the means to make that happen."

Janmo looked relieved and eager, and said, "Of course, Your Highness! It will take but a moment to collect the proper stones but, if you don't mind waiting, I will be right back with what I need."

"Thank you, Janmo. I will wait outside."

Janmo excused himself to get the supplies and Kiara exited the building to wait for his return. Now, which animal would be best for this task, she wondered?

After only three minutes, Janmo met her in front of The House of Healing and presented her with a rucksack filled with many different types of gemstones, both loose and set in wand form.

"Now," he said, "from what Druce has shown me in our past lessons, we will need a mixture of flint, blue topaz, and moonstone. I believe I have those all right here." He rooted around in his bag for a moment until he was able to acquire all three stones. In an expert motion, he flicked spider silk threads around them and fashioned them all along a clear quartz rod. It looked clunky but held firm. "Did you have a particular animal in mind you'd like to speak to?"

"Does that matter?"

"Oh, yes, I'm afraid it does. Well, it matters only because I am still quite new to this field of magick, you see. I can hold the spell for an average of around five minutes, depending on the size of the animal. The bigger the animal, the harder it is for me to hold it. Experts like Druce are able to hold the spell far longer and far easier, but in the hands of a novice, it takes its toll. Not that I mind, of course! I just do not want to disappoint you, Princess."

Kiara rewarded him with a smile, and said, "Five minutes should be just fine, I think. I would like to share a message with an animal or two and send it to a friend in the Fae Realm. Do you think we could do that?"

Janmo looked puzzled, but said, "I don't see why not. Will there be someone there with the power to receive it?"

"Yes."

Seeing he wasn't getting any more information, Janmo decided not to pry any further.

"Right! Okay, now, we just need the right animal, then! I've found that if you need something small that can go long distances, birds, rabbits, and raccoons work best."

Kiara gave it some thought, and said, "Could we do one of each?"

Janmo looked chagrined. "Sadly, I do not think I could hold out for all three, Highness. I might be able to do two of those, though."

"That's fine. How about a bird and a raccoon? A bird would work, as it can fly far and fast, and a raccoon would be better than a rabbit, as rabbits tend to be the subject of many more dinners than our furry bandit friends, don't you think?"

"A wise decision!" Janmo said.

Luckily, they did not have to search for long. There was a bird on a branch nearby that seemed interested in this human conversation, and Janmo was able to convince it to stay. The bird was also able to tell Janmo that he could find a raccoon hidden in its tree hole nearby, slumbering away. When Janmo woke it up with a mission from the princess, it arched its back, stretched its tiny black paws, gave one big yawn, and came down from its home.

With both animals at attention now, and Janmo's magick starting to fade, Kiara gave her message to them both, though out of hearing range for the waning Mage-in-training. It was an instruction for Cyndol, asking for aid. She thanked the creatures and sent them on their way.

This was a test. Kiara was asking for reinforcements, yes, but she also wanted to see if Cyndol was indeed someone who could be counted on in the fight she was sure was coming. She could feel it in her bones. As an added bonus, since animal magick was considered rare in these parts, she felt much safer entrusting her message with them than she did with a normal human. This way, no message could be intercepted or modified, and only Cyndol and her power to speak to animals could receive it. Okay, Druce as well, but she trusted he would pass the message along to Cyndol if he got it first.

Kiara thanked Janmo for his assistance and promised to put in a good word with his superiors. She also asked him not to give any details about today to anyone who may ask without her express permission first, not even the king or queen themselves. When he agreed, she took her leave of him and walked a little more confidently back to her room. She had some more planning to do.

CHAPTER FORTY-ONE: CYNDOL'S TRAINING

WHACK!

"Oww!" Cyndol's arms flew up too late to block the branch. "I think you broke my nose!"

The offending missile now lay innocently on the ground at her feet.

"You're fine," Hælgah said. "Next time, try faster!" She jerked her hand eerily at the branch and it sailed through the air to her. She caught it in one hand and posed for another go.

Cyndol blew out an irritated huff, flaring exhausted nostrils and overworked eye rolls. They'd been at this for two hours already and Cyndol wanted nothing more than to take a break to stuff her face. Magick training was draining work.

WHACK!

Cyndol cursed and covered her nose with both hands. "OWW! I wasn't ready!"

Hælgah belly laughed. "Do you think an enemy will wait until you are ready? Child, this is their favorite time to strike."

"I know that! I'm not stupid, I'm just…"

"Just what, child?"

"I'm just— I'm—"

WHACK!

Hit directly in the nose now thricely, Cyndol's anger boiled over. Before Hælgah could call the branch back to herself, Cyndol's bubble burst outward, hurling the tree branch in a blast towards Hælgah! The branch ripped apart at lightning speed. Hælgah narrowly jumped out of the way, letting the remaining shrapnel hit the tree behind her.

Silence settled softly around them, save for Cyndol's stressed breaths. Hælgah slowly stood up, brushed herself off, and turned to face the shaking girl.

Raising one hand calmly, she said, "Stop."

Cyndol felt as though her air had been sucked away from her. The bubble popped in a flurry of echoing rainbows, and she fell to her knees in the duff, shining sparkles floating all around her.

Hælgah approached the girl and lightly laid her right hand over her face. She took in a deep breath, let it out, took one more, and Cyndol felt a warmth envelop her like she was being loved by the suns themselves. She could feel the skin on her nose knit back together, and any swelling that had started was ebbing away. Cyndol's entire body relaxed for the first time in a long while, and she was able to breathe clearly.

"How do you feel now?" Hælgah asked.

Cyndol blinked a few times and wiggled her nose a bit. "Fine. Thanks."

Hælgah offered her a hand and Cyndol took it, both of them on their feet again.

"I believe that will be all for now. Go get some rest."

Relieved, Cyndol left the Training Arena to make a beeline for food. Kit, who had been peeking in at her through the trees, fell in step easily beside her.

"Well, that went well," he said.

"Shut up," she half-chuckled, and reached to scratch his ears. To comfort him or comfort herself, it didn't matter which.

"I snuck over to see what they were doing with that woman, Amy, and her dragon king husband," Kit said. "It looked sort of interesting. Want to go check it out? See if they'll let us watch?"

"As long as I'm shoving something edible in my face while we do it, I don't care where we go."

Kit gave a bark of laughter, and they went to get some grub.

With the wedding festivities from the other day over, life seemed to go back to normal for the Fae. Some of them were guards, like the ones they'd already met, others had little shops in the village. These were a collection of clothing and nick knack shops, eateries, cleaning services and, to Cyndol's surprise, a quite extensive library. All the buildings resembled some type of mushroom, fruit, or plant life, and all looked very whimsical in nature. Farther back, behind the village square, lay the farmlands that grew giant vegetation that could feed the realm for many long months.

"I think you are *actually* drooling right now," Kit said. "What would you like? I'm fine with anything."

"Me, too," she said.

That's when her eyes noticed a cute little veggie stand on the corner up ahead. It was shaped like an acorn, with a window that held a long, beige sill underneath. A pleasant face greeted them from inside of it.

"Hallo, there!" the smiling man called. "May I interest you in our lunch special?"

Cyndol's antsy feet beat her brain in responding, so the gentlemen took her rapid approach as a "Yes".

He disappeared momentarily but returned with a large platter to display.

"Here we have a beautiful salad, bearing all the colors of the rainbow. It's got a mix of fruits and vegetables, both sweet and bitter, along with some walnuts, and a drizzle of my cheese and strawberry dressing."

Cyndol's eyes widened at the gorgeous plate of food.

"There is also a delectable soup of broccoli, carrots, and sharp cheese, with a side of bread, if you're looking for something hot and comforting?"

Cyndol realized they had no money and almost cried.

"What's wrong, dear?" the vendor asked.

"I can't pay you for this!" she replied.

Kit blushed, as much as a fox could, and tried to explain.

"We are both orphans on a mission from—"

"Oh! That! Don't worry about that, little dears! Sovereign Sai has already explained that you needn't worry about a thing. Here, on behalf of the Fae Realm, please enjoy."

Cyndol and Kit were taken aback by such generosity.

"Are you sure?" she asked.

"Quite!" he said.

"Thank you," she breathed, still shocked by the kindness as she took the proffered platter with enough food for four people.

They said their goodbyes and headed over to the clearing where Sovereign Sai, Amy, Ellera, and Ibraxus were. Hælgah was just arriving to help Ellera in breaking through to Amy's memories. Poor thing. For one, Cyndol couldn't imagine not having full access to your own memories. That must feel so lonely. For another, she did not envy training with Hælgah. It was hard enough to do physically; she couldn't imagine how it would feel *mentally*. She hoped Amy fared better than she had thus far.

CHAPTER FORTY-TWO: AMY'S ONSLAUGHT

I swear to God, if she tells me to focus one more time, I'm having Brax fly her up to the highest mountain top to drop her from it!

"I heard that," Hælgah said.

I clenched my teeth and tried to keep my thoughts better concealed.

"Keep in mind," she continued, "if you shutter your thoughts from me, we will be at this for far longer."

Chipping a tooth in three... two... one...

"Begin."

The onslaught of foreign brainwaves pummeled my memory bank as visions of my youth flashed before my eyes on sepia-toned shuffle.

Sixth grade camp at Navarro.

Disneyland with my family.

Concerts at The Phoenix Theater.

Getting the lead in a school play.

Pageants.

Camping.

Fright Fest.

My crystal shop.

"Enough!" Hælgah shouted at me. "We need to go deeper, farther back than your memories of that life. Concentrate!"

"I *am*!" I growled at her, headache starting to pound now.

Sai stepped forward to interject. "Maybe we try something else, yes? What if you and Ellera gave it a shot at the same time? One of you can hold the recent memories at bay while the other presses onward?"

The ladies exchanged questioning glances.

Ellera shrugged. "I'm game."

Sai clapped their hands together. "Wonderful!" Then, to Brax, "Your Majesty, might you stand behind your wife and lend her some comfort?"

He jubilantly jumped at the chance and bounded over to me to do as the sovereign suggested. Before he laid his hands on me, however, he paused to make sure it was alright. I nodded, though it was still weird that I had a husband. Does it even still count if I died? Once his warm hands cupped my small shoulders, though, I ceased to care. It felt like Heaven, and I relaxed immediately, despite the sudden dance of butterflies in my stomach.

"Now, is everyone ready?" Sai asked.

We nodded in unison.

"Fantastic! You may begin."

By now, I was able to tell who was rooting around in my brain. Ellera had a soft, snaking glide, whereas Hælgah had a much more demanding poking and prodding method. I braced myself with Brax's help, and waited to see whose power would overtake the other.

A few seconds of a tickling sensation, and then *BOOM!*

All four of us were blasted backwards off our feet, tumbling every which way, until landing against whatever solid thing we came into contact with. For Ellera and Hælgah, it was a copse of trees. For Brax and me, it was Sai. How they managed to stay on their feet in all of that was beyond me, but I was thankful they were there to catch us before we hit anything else!

"Amy!" Ellera shouted from across the grounds. "Are you alright?"

I shook my head to clear the odd ringing echo. "I think so."

Brax got to his feet quickly and hoisted me up beside him. The second I was in his arms, a memory flashed in my mind. It was very quick and fleeting, but I saw a glimpse of Brax and I, laughing in my bed back on the island!

"Amy," Brax said, "what just happened? Are you alright?"

The look of concern on his face was so genuine and loving that I couldn't help myself. I grabbed his face and kissed him! And it felt so right, so completely and utterly correct that I couldn't help the tears that fell from my eyes.

Sai smiled and informed the ladies that they were definitely making some headway.

When I pulled apart from Brax (after Ellera's dramatic coughing noises prompted me to), I saw that his eyes were wet with tears as well.

"I'm beginning to remember you," I said.

"I will happily take whatever I can get!" he replied and tried to pull me closer.

Ellera made an impatient sound while swiping dirt off of her thin flowery dress, and said, "If you two are quite finished, I've got to get back in there."

Brax took a step back, looking like a scolded puppy.

"Now?" I asked. "But—"

Sai put up a hand to still my protest, and asked Ellera, "Did you see something? That was quite a blast back there."

"It was," she said, "but, with Hælgah's help, I was able to see something hidden there that I missed before. I should've known, too, the wretch. I've seen his handiwork before. He just hid it better this time."

"Who?" Sai asked.

"My brother. Viego."

CHAPTER FORTY-THREE: COLT'S MERRY CHASE

"What did I miss?" Colt whispered from over Cyndol's shoulder.

She squeaked, jumping a foot off the ground from her hiding spot in the bushes, and landed on what was left of her lunch.

Kit snickered as Cyndol swiped away green leaves from her bottom.

"Sorry," Colt said. "I didn't mean to scare you."

Cyndol's hunched shoulders relaxed a bit. "It's okay."

"So?" he asked. "What's all this about?"

Cyndol brought him up to speed on what had been going on that day, between her training session and Amy's attempted memory invasions.

Colt was loving the attention and trust he was getting from these people. It was always so quiet at home, nothing exciting ever happened. Well, look at him now! New friends, crazy magicks, the Fae— he was having the time of his life!

"You in?" Cyndol asked.

Colt froze for a second. What did she just ask him?

"Ummm…" he stalled.

She sighed and Kit took over.

"We're going to try to sneak in to get a closer look. Are you coming? Or would you rather wait here?"

Before he had a chance to answer, one of the sovereign's guards came running up to the group in front of them.

"Your Majesty!" He hurried up to them and bowed. "I bring news! Ruskin's men are closing in on the entrance. None of us can get in or out without being spotted. I'm afraid we are stuck here for the time being."

"Have you been able to find out what they want?"

"Somewhat, Majesty," he said. "Micah, the stable hand, was seeing to the horses, and heard some of them sneaking by the entryway. They were whispering about a boy they were after."

"Did they say who they were looking for in particular?"

"No, but they said he must be pretty important for King Ruskin to send so many troops after him."

Sai let out a deep breath. "Thank you, Draymon. You may return to your post."

The man bowed and left. The kids continued to watch on in silence.

"Can they get in?" Brax asked Sai after a moment.

Sai nodded with a stern look on their face. "They can. It might take a little while, and a bit of effort on their part but, ultimately, there is a chance."

"What can we do?" Amy asked.

Colt, his heart and his bravery louder than his restraint, stepped out of the bushes, and said, "I think I can help!"

All eyes turned to him, and Kit bonked his head on Cyndol's shoulder in disgust at Colt's inability to stay hidden.

Colt continued toward the group, no longer caring about getting caught. He just wanted to stay useful to these wonderful people.

Sai cocked an interested brow at the child. "Go on. How can you help, Colt?"

He swallowed his sudden nerves at the realization he would have to leave this place. He took one deep breath, exhaled, and said, "I can lure them away."

This caught the adults off guard. There were protests immediately. "He's too young!" and "There's no chance in Hell we're sending a child out there!" and "Over my dead body!"

Colt chuckled to himself. He really needed to know what that word "Hell" meant. Every time Amy used it, he laughed.

Amy leapt forward to get in Sai's face. "We can't send a child out there! They tried to kill us last time!" She flung her furious face at Colt. "Or have you forgotten?"

Colt paled a little, remembering how scared he was when he discovered Amy had been shot and was slipping off of him. Seeing all those arrows being fired their way startled him more now than it did in those fleeing moments. He knew he would be risking the same thing this time. But he also knew somebody had to do it, and his part of this journey was over the minute Amy reunited with King Brax.

Colt lightly laid his hands on Amy's wrists, pausing her anxiety. "No, I haven't forgotten. How could I? But I also know I can do this, I can help. Besides," he continued, dropping his hands, "I have this amazing new unicorn power.

Gotta show it off sometime, right? I might even get to skewer a guy!"

She took a breath to protest, but Colt gave her his best pitiful expression. "This isn't my home. As beautiful as it is, I belong home. My family needs me."

Amy deflated at the mention of his family, as he knew she would. She'd mentioned it a number of times already, so he figured that stood the most convincing chance of her letting him leave, much as he didn't want to.

Sai said, "We accept your idea, Colt. It is a wise and brave idea, and we will do what we can to help you."

Colt let out the deep breath he didn't know he'd been holding and smiled up at the royalty before him.

"Thank you, Sovereign Sai," he said, using manners his mother had taught him, "you have been a gracious host."

Everyone snickered at his very mature politeness and said their goodbyes.

"And what about you two?" Sai called to the girl and her fox, still in the bushes. "Will you come say goodbye to your new friend as well?"

A grumbling was heard from the shrubbery, followed by, "Yes. We're coming."

Cyndol and Kit got up from their hiding spot and wished Colt luck on his way.

"Are you sure about this?" Cyndol asked.

"It's not too late to change your mind," Kit said.

Colt smiled at them both. "You know, it's okay. I can do this. It was so nice to meet you both. I hope our paths cross again someday. Especially you, Kit!"

Kit nuzzled Colt's hand and chittered.

"If any of you are ever back in Gallanor, come find me!"

"If you're ready, Colt, we can show you a map of what we think might be the best route for you to take," Sai said.

Colt gave his attention to the sovereign.

"We will also be covering you with a highly effective, yet time challenging spell, to aid you in the start of this mission."

Colt nodded his understanding and remained silent for further instruction.

"Now, Colt," Sai said, "this spell will last for twenty minutes. In that time, you will need to get from our entrance, up the stream, until you pass the last large boulder on the bank. Then, you will go to the opposite bank on the other side of the army, before it expands you back to your proper size, otherwise you will be resized too close to us, and this will all be for naught. Do you understand? You must get to that spot before the spell ends, or you will be caught."

When Colt stated his understanding of the rules, Sai readied the spellcasting. They paused and said, "Should you ever wish to return, you will always be welcome here, you dear, brave boy."

Colt beamed and waved goodbye to everyone. "Thanks for letting me be a part of the team. I'll miss you. You can come visit me anytime! Really!"

He was answered by a round of claps on the back, shaking hands, and a tearful hug from Amy.

"You be careful out there, do you hear me, young man?" she said like his mother would have. He nodded his head seriously and she seemed satisfied.

With that, Sai resumed their stance and hit Colt fast with a practiced swish of their elegant hand, aiming the spell directly at his center. It enveloped him like a well-worn glove and washed him with a feeling of protection.

Sai whispered, "Go."

Colt sprang into action! He was led by a sparkling magick trail Sai had sent with him, leading him through the realm, up the stairs, and past the doors that opened into the Big Tree, out the other side, and across the correct steps on the water. When he reached the end, the sparks disappeared, leaving Colt alone to flee through the front gate.

Colt paused only long enough to make sure he wouldn't be crushed underfoot by anyone, then made a mad dash for the river, swatting giant fern fronds from his face before he leapt for the water. His dive sounded like a soft *splink*. He came up for a quick gulp of air under a thatch of long grass, then shoved off for the opposite bank. Hiding behind each steppingstone sized rock he came across, he checked his progress along the way. Luck was on his side. He didn't even feel cold! He continued onward, the running water making it a bit difficult, but not impossible. Almost there now!

Colt grabbed a handful of grass in an attempt to pull himself out of the water, but the grass snapped, and he fell back in. This time, his soft *splink* was more of a noticeable *plunk*! He kicked off from the bed of the shallow stream and aimed for the small area behind the grasses, carefully peeking out from behind a few fronds to see if anyone had taken notice. Rats! Someone had! He held his breath and tried to calm his racing heart, until the noticer finally passed him by. Letting his breath out quietly, he resumed his grappling of the grasses, trying to beat the spell. He could feel his body start to shake it off, the prickling of stretching skin and growing bones.

No, no, no, no! Not yet! He was almost there! With one final tug, he was on the bank, running as fast as his wet clothes would take him, air-drying as he went. The large world was shrinking before his eyes, and he knew the spell was breaking. In a last-ditch effort, he hurled himself face over feet to land in the spot Sai had instructed him to get to, right as his body reached its usual mass.

He took one deep breath as a few men turned to see a sudden strange boy pop up behind them, then said, "Hey, guys! Looking for me?"

Silence greeted him at first, but after a confused moment, a cry went up from the front of the pack to the rest. "It's the boy!"

"It sure as Hell is!" Colt shouted.

"Get him!" cried the crowd.

Colt bolted. He ran as fast as his young legs could carry him, until he was satisfied that enough of the army had taken the bait. When he reached the clearing up ahead, he knew it was time.

He could hear the sounds of drumbeats thumping in rapid succession. He knew it was a tactic meant to scare him, but it just filled him with renewed vigor. He ran faster and faster, wild with abandon, and felt the familiar sprouting of hooves and wings. His body elongated even as he ran, switching flawlessly into a gallop, gaining ground from his would-be captors. The arrows were flying by in earnest now. Colt could hear the evil tipped wooden sticks whizzing by his fuzzy ears, but onward he pressed, feeling the wind lift him easily under wing and propel him into the sky. He laughed, free like never before, stirring the rage in his pursuers! But still, they came, as Colt knew they would. Just a bit farther now! He had to be sure the Fae Realm would be safe before he cut ties with the army.

Colt led them a merry chase, all the while getting farther and farther from The Fae. He could see his target up ahead: A vast chasm with an unforgiving landing. If he could get them to somehow focus on him and not the chasm, perhaps they would just fall right into it? He flapped his wings harder and aimed for the chasm with all his might.

"I'm getting away!" he called over his shoulder. "Better catch me before I'm gone!"

He turned his head fully, just in time to see the men slowing to a halt when they reached the edge. However, as the army was running fast enough, not all of them were able to stop in time, and some in the back knocked some in the front off the ledge to fall screaming into the abyss.

Colt shuddered at the loss, hating that any harm was actually coming to people. He knew it was necessary, but he regretted that part all the same.

Now, to focus on where he was headed. Home. Time to go home. He wondered if that nice place by the water still had that great chowder and bread he'd gotten there before? Maybe he'd pay a visit to Tripp's Tavern on the way. He'd be plenty hungry after this flight!

He gave one final glance at the men gathered at the edge, turned around in the sky to give them a mocking wing wave, then sped off toward Tripp's without a care in the world.

CHAPTER FORTY-FOUR: CYNDOL'S MESSAGE

Cyndol couldn't believe Colt left. He'd seemed so happy to be a part of their ever-growing group that she thought he'd be with them indefinitely. She'd only just met him, but she was already sad the boisterous boy was gone.

"Maybe we'll see him again," Kit said, as if reading her thoughts.

"Maybe," Cyndol repeated. "Amy sure seemed to be upset he left."

"Yeah, well, he *did* save her life, brave kid."

"True." Another moment of internal pondering went by, then she said, "You know, I haven't been to see Ethan yet today. Should we go say hi and see how he's doing?"

"Sure."

The pair had started along the path that led back to the Healer's Hut when a great crashing was heard through the brush behind them!

"Cyndol? *Cyyynnndooollll...?*" called an unfamiliar male voice.

Cyndol saw a few passing Fae cover their ears against the noise.

"What's that horrid squeaking?" one of them asked.

"Oww! My ears!" said another.

Cyndol looked around to try to find who was calling her and saw that Kit's own ears were pinned to his head.

"What's wrong with *you*?" she asked him.

"That chittering! It's so loud! It hurts my ears!"

"What chittering? All I hear is someone calling my name. You don't hear that?"

Kit shook his head and peered into the woods to see what was heading their way.

"Cyndol, quick! Hide in the bushes! I think it's a raccoon, and it hasn't been shrunk down! It's going to squish us! Hurry!"

Kit sprang off from the ground as hard as he could and did a nose-dive into a shrub on the side of the path. Cyndol's curiosity kept her in place, and she faced the animal head-on as it came fully into view.

"I'm looking for Cyndol," the raccoon said. "Do you know where I can find her?"

Cyndol was astonished that one, she could understand him, and two, he was looking for her specifically.

"Umm, I'm Cyndol," she said.

The raccoon huffed a sigh of relief and sat on his haunches right there in the dirt. The release of breath blew Cyndol's hair back, pulling several strands from the braids she kept them in.

"Thank goodness! I've traveled for two days from Gallanor to find you!"

"You're from Gallanor?"

"I am!" he said. "I was sent by Princess Kiara to ask for your aid."

Kit peeked his head out of his shrubby hiding place and hissed, "Cyndol! What are you *doing*?!"

Cyndol waved him off with a hand flick, but kept her gaze fixed on the rather large animal towering over her.

"What does she need my help with?"

"A stranger has come to the village and is casting a dark shadow. The princess fears she means ill will to the people of Gallanor, and the queen seems to agree. The king is withholding opinion until she actually does anything wrong, but the queen and princess are afraid. The princess asks for you to come lend your powers, as well as bring any backup you can to help. She fears there may be a battle looming."

A chill went up Cyndol's spine. She remembered how Kiara wanted so badly to know what she could do, and of her willingness to help. The royal family had shown her so much hospitality and helped her rescue her brother, so she knew she would do anything she could to help them in return.

"When does she need me to leave?"

"As soon as you are able," he replied.

"What's going on?" Kit called, poking his nose out from under spiky green leaves.

"Just a second," Cyndol told the raccoon before turning to face her friend. She knelt down to his level, and said, "This raccoon was sent by Princess Kiara. Someone has come to Gallanor with some issues, and Kiara and Queen Miawae are afraid of her. She's asking me to come back to help, and to bring reinforcements, if possible."

Kit came all the way out and ventured over to the raccoon, still sitting on his bottom in the path, waiting for a reply. He looked up at the gargantuan animal and gave him a few cursory sniffs. Kit wandered around the rest of him, adding sniffs and snorts as he went, before going back to Cyndol's side.

"He does carry the scent of the princess," Kit confirmed. "I can't hear his words, but if you believe him, that's good enough for me."

"I do," she said. "And I think I should bring this to Sai's attention right away." She turned back to the raccoon and asked, "Would you mind waiting until I have spoken with Sovereign Sai about this? I'm sure they can help."

The raccoon said, "That is fine. I will come back here at nightfall. I need to eat and rest before I head back with your answer."

Cyndol agreed, and the raccoon bounded back into the woods, making quite the racket as he went.

"So, off to see Sai?" Kit asked.

"Yes," she said. "Ethan will have to wait. We can see him after."

***

Cyndol looked around at a sea of mismatched faces. She had just finished explaining what had happened with the messenger raccoon to Sai and her travel companions, and it seemed as though not all of them were convinced.

"Of course, we're going," said Evony. "Our home may be in trouble, and our princess requires our assistance. What is left to discuss?"

"Hey," said Ellera. "I'm not saying you shouldn't return home to help safeguard it, I'm just wondering why the rest of us are being asked to go? I have no stake in this game. I only came along in the first place to help out Amy and Ifyrus."

Evony sneered at her. "Well, I guess you're all done, then."

Amy put a placating hand up and turned to Ellera. "Look, I'm not saying you have to go. I'm just saying, if it weren't for Queen Miawae, who knows what kind of reception we would've had here? Her friendship with these good people helped us in our time of need, and now they need our help in return. How *can* we say no?"

Ellera chewed her right ring fingernail, then spit the debris in the bin beside her. She was quiet for a moment, then, "What about Ruskin's men? Are any of them still outside the gate?"

"Not that our guard was able to find," said Sai. "It seems Colt's plan to lead them away was successful. That's not to say they won't come back, but the way is clear for the moment."

Brax, who until now had appeared lost in thought, said, "I have some supplies that I'd like to fetch back in my kingdom. It wouldn't take very long, especially if I took Ifyrus with me. I think it would be good for him to get back up in the air. We could be back by nightfall if we left within the hour."

"What kind of supplies?" asked Sai. "We have plenty of weapons here, if that's what you need? Plenty of food we could send with you, as well."

Brax shook his head. "Thank you, Majesty, but that's not entirely what I meant. Those things would be helpful, of course, and we may take you up on it, but if there is going to be a battle, especially if Ruskin is involved, I need to fetch my royal ring. Ruskin apparently stole my crown, but the ring should still be in my castle. Hopefully, that will suffice as proof. I need to show leadership, not just strength. I need them to see I still have power."

"Power does go a long way in matters such as these," Sai said.

"What about my brother?" Cyndol asked. "Do we just leave him here? I can't do that, not again! I won't!"

Sai put a reassuring hand on her small shoulder. "It is our understanding that he is to be released today. But although your brother has healed physically for the most part, minus some scarring that will remain on his forehead, he might need more healing than we are capable of here. Perhaps Gallanor could provide some insight on how to assist him going forward?"

Druce spoke up then. "I am more than happy to keep him comfortable on the way back in whatever way I can. Having worked in our own Healer's Hut for more than half my life, I can assure you there are some wonderful and highly skilled folk that will do everything they can to help."

Cyndol sighed and turned to face Evony. "So, should I tell the raccoon we're in?"

Evony stood a bit taller and addressed the group as a whole. "By a show of hands, who is in to help the princess?"

One by one, hands went into the air. Bella's shot up so fast you'd have thought it was her idea in the first place. Fenix and Felix both went up as one, and Brax, Amy, and eventually an eye-rolling Ellera, joined in as well. Even Kit yipped and jutted his front paw out like he was going to shake someone's hand. Cyndol smiled a bit bigger and raised her hand with the others.

Kit's tail curled contentedly around Cyndol's ankles, so she knew he was pleased with the outcome. So was she, truth be told. She was hoping they would all return together. She knew Kiara would be pleased as well. This was her chance to show the allegiance Kiara so desperately craved. She *would* answer her call, and she would help in any way she could. Now, to tell Ethan.

CHAPTER FORTY-FIVE: RUSKIN RECEIVES AN UPDATE

Ruskin was pacing the battlements, claws scratching along the rock wall, sending sparks shooting this way and that as he went. He would never admit it to anyone, but he rather enjoyed the sparks. A blip of beauty caused by destruction.

"Message for you, Sire!" said a young guard behind him. "Just came in!"

Ruskin faced the young man and showcased his razored talons. "Be a dove and bring it here for me."

The guard was visibly shaking but, to Ruskin's mild surprise, he held himself together and delivered the letter without vomiting on himself. Ruskin chuckled at the boy's restraint and decided to let him live another day.

Curiosity piqued, he unfurled the rolled paper and began to read:

Boy child that escaped from The King's Guard was seen fleeing the deep woods from your army. Several dead in pursuit. Last known whereabouts was Tripp's Tavern in Seaport. He was spotted leaving shortly after, presumably headed towards Gallanor. He travels alone. —General Ironstone

"Well, well, well..." Ruskin said. "It appears we have a mission."

The young guard held his ground, waiting for his master's orders.

"Inform Davina to ready herself for travel. We are taking a trip to Tripp's."

"Yes, Your Majesty!"

"And have my guardsmen readied as well. We leave as soon as possible."

CHAPTER FORTY-SIX: TRIPP'S UNINVITED GUESTS

A sharp cry from a blackbird outside startled Tripp from his morning ablutions. He turned off the tap water and scrubbed a towel across his bushy beard to dry his face. Pausing to listen, he heard nothing but the jovial bustling of Moff as he got the tavern ready for opening, something he did for Tripp after nights spent sleeping in his rented rooms. It was nearing lunch time, and he knew the rush from the men spending their day out on the water should be starting any minute now.

A chill went up Tripp's spine when he realized there absolutely *should* be more noise from the men by now. By his accounts, the tavern should've opened fifteen minutes ago. He tried to listen again but couldn't even hear Moff.

Tripp left his bathroom and crept quietly down the hall, having lived here long enough to know which steps to avoid in order to silence any possible squeaking. He got to the curtain that led to the bar and stopped to listen. He could hear a voice, one that was dark, low, and melodious. It made the hair on Tripp's arms stand on end. It was a voice he hadn't heard in several lifetimes, but one he would've known anywhere.

"So, you do *not* know where your benefactor is?" Ruskin said.

Tripp could smell the fear radiating off his friend, giving the already salty air an extra pungency.

"N—n—n—n—no, Your Maj— Your Maj— Your Majesty," tried Moff. "He was supp-supposed to— supposed to be here half— a half hour ago."

Tripp peeked around the curtain to get a better view and caught the quick movement of Ruskin's right arm darting out to capture poor Moff by the throat!

"I think you're lying," Ruskin said.

Tripp's panic rose sky high, and he snuck quietly back down the hall to his bedroom. He closed and locked the door behind him with a practiced spell, promising himself he would be back to help his friend or, if the worst happened, his poor wife. When he was satisfied the door would hold, he shoved his meaty hand under his bed and yanked out his Go Bag. He knew this day would come; he was just hoping it never would. Most of what he would need to flee was already in there: Clothes, blankets, some rope and canvas for shelter, some food that had been spelled not to spoil by a witch he'd let stay for free one night. There were a few weapons varying in both physical damage and the crystals to invoke psychic damage, but... where was the egg basket? No! Where was the *EGG BASKET?!* He reached deeper under the bed, waving his hand frantically back and forth, hoping it would strike the basket and bring it to him.

His bedroom door blew off the hinges in one shot.

BLAM!

It crashed against the opposing wall and splintered into kindling.

Tripp tried to dive bodily under the bed, but he was snatched around the ankles by a loop of magickal energy rope. Ruskin let out a delighted laugh as his young Mage yanked him backward, straight into her clutches. For a woman of such small stature, she far outweighed Tripp's own strength. She had a hold of his neck and squeezed until he lost the ability to breathe or stay conscious. The world around him went dark.

***

Tripp awoke to the sound of water lapping the shore. He could hear birds cawing in the distance, but the seaside was much quieter than it usually was. When he managed to open one eye, then the other, he saw what was likely the culprit: Ruskin and his guard were standing along the shore, though Ruskin was a bit farther back than his cronies.

"Ah," Ruskin began, "he wakes! Welcome back, dear Caspaar! It has been far too long, old friend."

"Old friend, my ass," Tripp muttered, or tried to anyway, but found there was something shoved in his mouth that prevented any sound from escaping. In fact, his entire body was immobilized! Sweating now, Tripp took stock of his current situation: Gagged, bound to a wooden post/contraption of sorts, hovering above the water with no platform to jump to. Grim, very grim.

"So, a little bird told me that you recently had a young visitor at your very fine establishment. Is that correct?" Ruskin asked.

Tripp grunted behind his gag and tried to tell him what he thought about this whole situation.

Ruskin *tsked* and nodded to his Mage. This shadow of a woman twisted her outstretched right hand just a titch, and Tripp felt himself jerk to his left side, slightly off-kilter.

"Oh, did I forget to explain the rules? My, my, my, where *are* my manners these days? You see, dear Caspaar, for every answer you give that I do not like, or that my consort Davina here does not like, you will become better acquainted with the water you adore so much. *If* you happen to be able to withstand that particular punishment, rest assured, she is also fully capable of sending fireballs to alight upon your bottom half as your top half slowly drowns. Which will get you first, I wonder? The fire or the water?" Ruskin smiled mockingly and thrust both hands outwards in a weighing gesture. "Dragons or Mermaids? You seem to love them both, after all. Answer my questions poorly and I guess we shall see. Nod if you understand me."

Tripp glared as hard as his face would accommodate, but was allowed just enough give to let Ruskin know he understood the consequences.

"Marvelous!" The evil king clapped his clawed hands together and began to saunter along the shoreline. Again, not too close, but close enough to be heard. "Let's try this again, shall we? Who was that adorable little boy you hosted, and where was he going when he left?"

Tripp felt his magickal gag loosen enough for him to speak.

"What little boy?"

Ruskin sighed. Davina twisted her hand, and Tripp was turned a skosh to the side.

"Host children that often, do you?"

Tripp cleared his throat, but didn't comment further.

Another twist, even more off balance now. Tripp knew where this was headed.

"Alright, how about another one?" Ruskin dropped all joviality. "Where is my bride?"

Tripp laughed mirthlessly. "Ain't you already got one?"

Twist!

Tripp grunted. His head was getting closer to the water. It wouldn't take much more for his face to meet the surface and inhale the last few breaths of life.

"Amaryah. Where. Is. Amaryah?"

Tripp couldn't help himself. "Oh! Well, didn't you hear? She died! Yeah! Lon' time ago. In fact, weren't you there?"

He could feel the currents of rage boiling over in his enemy and he knew he was about out of time. A swift wrenching from Davina sent him a few clicks farther, and his face was about a knuckle's length away from being fully submerged.

"Last chance, Caspaar. The stone lit up."

Tripp's eyebrows raised in surprise. He didn't know anyone knew about the amethyst stones.

Ruskin's wolfy half grin appeared in mocking triumph. "Yes, I know what you did. And I know she's returned."

"How?"

Ruskin pressed on. "You do not get to be my age without the best magickal help in the world, you know. And in that time, don't you think I exhausted every resource I had? I know more than you think, old man."

"Ah! So that must be why you're sittin' here askin' me stupid questions when I got plenty o' work to get back to?"

Ruskin laughed.

Tripp laughed.

SPLASH!

Tripp went head-first in the water and was held there for several eternal seconds. When he thought he was about to run out of air, he was yanked back up just in time to catch one quick breath before being slammed back under. He could see stars forming in front of his eyes, knowing he was close to blacking out and leaving this miserable life behind him. But, as he was about to give up and succumb to his inevitable fate, a glimmer from underneath the small outcropping of the bank caught his eye, and he saw, to his immense relief, a basket of eggs. Dragon eggs, to be precise. There were five of them in total, all much smaller than you'd expect, and beautifully scaled and colored in iridescent colors of the rainbow.

Of *course*! Tripp mentally smacked his forehead. He had completely forgotten! One night, about a month ago, he had awoken from a frightful dream that left him in such a blind panic that he knew he just *had* to hide those eggs! Someone was coming looking for them, but he had sworn to protect them with his life. He intended to keep that promise. He'd hidden them in a place that no one would ever think to search for dragon eggs: The water. With all his time out here, he was more familiar with the water than his own village. He knew this tiny alcove under the shore's ledge would be the perfect hiding spot, so that's exactly what he did.

But now that he knew where they were, the tricky part would be getting to them and escaping from Ruskin. Rats. He might have to get set on fire after all. It might be exactly what he needed to free himself from this contraption. It looked as though he was attached to the post with spelled rope and, if it could burn, that would be all he needed to loosen his bonds and snatch the eggs! It would be a great gamble, but likely his only shot. *Time to push some kingly buttons.*

Tripp was once again relocated to the topside of the water, gulping greedily now, filling his screaming lungs with beautiful air. Three lungfuls this time, and his racing heart started to calm.

"Where is she, Caspaar?"

"The name's Tripp, *Your Majesty*. Caspaar died that day as well. Say, you got any of those fire bolts you promised me? Gettin' a bit chilly in all this seawater."

Ruskin growled loudly enough to make everyone's skin crawl, and Tripp just smiled and waited. He did not have to wait long.

"What are you waiting for, Davina? The man is cold. Heat him up!"

Davina raised her other arm, dancing it slowly upwards until she had looped a flame large enough to do some damage, then hurled it directly at Tripp's feet.

Tripp could feel the beginnings of his shoes melting. He knew this would not be pleasant. He steeled his resolve and said, "That all you got? That ain't gonna do squat, youn' lady! I said I'm *freezin'* out here!"

"Hit him again!" commanded the king.

Davina hurled another bolt of fire at the upside-down man, and it licked along his pants now. Tripp bit back a scream, but only just. Those flames were just as angry as the man instructing their mission.

"*Where?! Is?! SHE?!*"

"Not on your life!" Tripp shouted back.

Flames were raining down on him now. Tripp could feel his skin singeing through what fiery clothing was still attached to his body. The pain was so intense that he almost lost his nerve. But right as he thought he would lose this gamble, the bonds around him broke, and he fell bodily into the water, free of the post and the Mage's hold.

"Get him back here!" he heard shouted above him.

But Tripp acted fast and swam with all his might towards the eggs, snatching the basket as quickly as he could. Prize in hand, he felt along the underside of the embankment until he found what he was looking for: A discreet passageway that led to a secret Crannie, placed there centuries ago by the

Mermaids. It was to be used only in case of emergency, and Tripp couldn't think of anything more deserving than this! Without further thought (other than mourning his Go Bag and Moff, both sadly left behind), he pushed off the side and dove straight into the Crannie, out of the literal line of fire.

CHAPTER FORTY-SEVEN: DARRIAN'S DISGUISE

A great clamoring of horse hooves and weaponry came ringing down the quiet street. Darrian surmised from his stakeouts over the last few days that this was a strange sight to behold, as this time of day typically saw a large gathering of folk for food, drinks, and fish storage for the day's catch. Perhaps the villagers had seen the king's parade from their boats and wisely kept to themselves today? He wouldn't blame them one bit. If he didn't need information so badly, he'd avoid it, too.

As it was, he'd managed to pick up stray bits of info here and there about a boy who'd been arrested but had escaped the prison he was being held at with a young girl in tow. He would bet anything those were *his* kids, and he would do everything in his power to find and bring them home. Well, maybe not *home* as it was, but somewhere safe, safer than this, by far! This could very well end up being exactly the opportunity he needed.

He hid behind a rotting barrel in front of a building marked "The Farm Stand" in scrawled black lettering and watched the procession with pointed interest. From what he could see, these were definitely Ruskin's men, and, to his surprise, that was King Ruskin himself in the middle of it. *All the better to shield himself*, he thought. Ruskin seldom left his kingdom, and when he did, he was surrounded by guards at all times. Who was that woman with him? He could hazard a guess. He'd heard tell of a Gallanorian woman the king had promoted to King's Mage. He was shocked when he'd heard about that a while back, especially as Ruskin was the one that killed her parents. What an awful tragedy. Darrian wondered if she was under a spell of some kind, or if she was despicable enough to join forces with her family's flayer?

When the last of the men lined up to enter Tripp's Tavern, Darrian saw his chance. He bolted from his position behind the barrel and ran low towards the bar, managing to swiftly snag the last man in line, knocking him out with one forceful blow to the vagus nerve. The man dropped like a stone and Darrian hauled him around the side, stripping him of his uniform and changing into his clothes as quickly as possible. Darrian used his old clothes to gag and bind him to the post on the side of the tavern. When he was satisfied the man wouldn't pose a threat, and that no one had seen his transgression, he grabbed the man's weaponry and slipped into Tripp's like he was one of the gang.

The men were blocking a lot of his view, but he saw a familiar face behind the bar. It was a man he'd met his first day here, who was currently being interrogated by the king's company.

"N—n—n—n—no, Your Maj— Your Maj— Your Majesty," tried Moff. "He was supp-supposed to— supposed to be here half— a half hour ago."

"I think you're lying," he heard the king say.

"N—n—n—n—no," Moff repeated. "I p—p—p—promise!"

Ruskin nodded at the Mage, and she slammed Moff's head into the bar. The sound reverberated with a sickening crunch. The poor man screamed and hit the floor. Darrian could still hear him sniffling and crying out, but he held his position and waited to see what would come next.

Ruskin approached the bar casually and flipped up his elongated black and scarlet royal coat so that he could seat himself on the well-worn barstool. When he was settled, he said in a much calmer voice than Darrian would have suspected, "How about now? Did that help jostle your memory?"

The only sound Darrian could hear was the panicked sniveling of the man on the floor. After an eternal moment, Moff said in a barely audible voice, "He was gettin' ready. He might be in his room. Just back there, behind the curtain."

"Thank you. That is most helpful."

Ruskin gestured at Davina, and she spelled the glass shelves behind him to come crashing down, ending any noise the man was making. Whether he was alive or dead, Darrian could not tell from his vantage point.

The king and his Mage disappeared behind the curtain, and an explosion of wood drowned out all sound. Many of the men had to throw their hands over their ears to protect themselves.

There was a grand showing of hauling Tripp outside and rigging him to a torturous apparatus in the water. All Darrian could do was wait. Wait, and watch, and fuel his anger at this vile, evil, wretched excuse for a king. A king that had taken his son, burned down his village, hurt his family, left him for dead, and was continuing his pursuit of his children even now! He could feel his blood boiling over and had to remind himself, very loudly within his own head, to continue to do nothing and wait for opportunity. Now was not the time.

Darrian found his opportunity when Tripp encouraged the king and his Mage to set him on fire and made a miraculous escape! Nobody saw it coming, so the fallout was purely chaotic. Ruskin shouted orders left and right, Davina threw curses and magick at anything in the water that moved, and men all around him dove fully clothed into the sea to try to capture their prisoner.

Failure. Total and utter failure to recover him. Ruskin snarled and shifted, ripping men and landscape apart in equal measure. His fury was enough to make one's blood run cold. But Darrian had too much at stake and held his fear in check. His children. He needed to find his children! *Keep your head clear and focused!* He had no idea what had happened to his wife, Enid, but he could at least do what he could for the children. And, right now, that required joining the enemy.

With resolve set, Darrian hurled himself into the water, taking the obsidian sword he'd stolen from its previous owner from the scabbard at his side, and poked it sharply into the water alongside the other men.

It was at this moment that the skies opened up and a deluge of water poured down from above. Ruskin let out a hair-razing cry and called off the search.

"Men! Back inside! Now!"

Ruskin and Davina hied themselves back inside the tavern, presumably to wait out the rain, leaving Darrian puzzled in the water as to this strange aversion the king seemed to have to it. Knowing he wouldn't get any answers standing out here by himself, he followed the rest of the contingent of men inside to wait out the storm.

CHAPTER FORTY-EIGHT: KIARA'S CONFRONTATION

Her grandfather, kind though he was, was being a stubborn fool! He'd invited Ikah to dine with them again today in the hopes of getting to know her better. Supper the other night had gone well enough, but not much was said outside of casual formalities. The closest thing they'd learned about why she was here was that "The Grand King Ruskin wishes to learn more about his neighboring kingdoms".

Matthias wasn't so blind he couldn't see that her presence caused unease in his people, but he was confident he could get to the bottom of the issue with directness and a full belly. Kiara snorted at the thought that it could be so easy.

Her grandmother, however, shared Kiara's sentiments that this woman would cause more trouble than the king realized and, though she couldn't quite See it with her powers, her intuition was there to back her up. Without proof of wrongdoing, though, the king was determined to try his way first.

Kiara bit the inside of her cheek to keep from speaking these thoughts.

So, here they were, the four of them, seated at her grandparents' dining table, chock full of teas and treats, pretending like all was well and this was just a dinner party.

Ikah's sinister confidence in her all-black attire was the highest contrast this room had ever seen. Her presence alone was enough to raise anyone's hackles.

"So, Ikah," her grandfather said, buttering a thick chunk of bread, "what exactly brings you to my kingdom?"

Ikah drizzled a golden spool of honey over buttered bread of her own and took her time enjoying the first bite before answering in her own sweet time.

"Well, Matthias," she began, then licked a smear of butter from her thumb, "like I said the other day, King Ruskin is just curious about his neighboring kingdoms and might be interested in doing business in the future. He sent me ahead to get a feel for how Gallanor runs these days."

Matthias's face darkened, but he hid it with a practiced smile. "You mean, how it runs after he killed my daughter and her husband? Or how he then kidnapped and tortured my eldest granddaughter?"

Ikah returned the fake grin and raised him a chuckle. "Dear, sweet king. You know how hazardous leadership can be. It's nothing personal. Why not let bygones be bygones? You could start fresh and put the past behind you! Come on, what do you say?"

Kiara's short-cropped nails bit stinging half-moons into her palms. She was glad, though, as that was the only thing reminding her *not* to jump across the table to throttle this woman! How dare she gloss over the worst tragedy of their lives like that?!

Her grandfather's face clouded over and Ikah saw she was approaching his limit. When he took a breath to respond, she interrupted him. "May I use your facilities? I'm afraid I've had too much tea."

Miawae laid a calming hand on her husband's arm and instructed Avery, waiting just outside their door, to escort her there.

Ikah got up and exited the room, stopping Avery from joining her. She said she could find it just fine on her own. Before anyone could protest, she snaked her way down the hall and disappeared.

"Now do you see what we've been talking about?" Miawae asked Matthias.

He scowled and swiped a tear from his eye.

Kiara stood up.

"I'm going after her. I don't have a good feeling about her wandering around here on her own."

Her grandparents agreed, so Kiara slipped down the hallway after her. When she couldn't find her in the bathroom, she knew she was right to follow. She just wished she'd done it a few seconds sooner so she could see which way she went.

Kiara surreptitiously checked every room on that floor, finding nothing out of place, and no signs of the awful woman. She was about to descend to the next floor down when she heard a soft breaking of glass. Immediately, Kiara rushed to her grandfather's business chambers and saw a frightful sight: Ikah was gleefully standing over a demolished glass box that housed the fragment of the necklace that young boy Colt brought them. Her grandparents had called it "something special". Though they didn't give Kiara any additional information, she knew that this could not be good. If Ikah was here to steal it from them, she must do everything she could to make sure that didn't happen.

"Drop it," Kiara said, stepping into the room.

Ikah's wide grin elongated even more, and her pitch-black eyes seemed to swallow the light in the room. She cocked her head in a snap.

"Come and get it."

"Oh, good." Kiara cracked her knuckles. "I was hoping I'd get to punch you."

With that, the princess flung herself at the creature in full attack mode, flying through the air, arms poised to snag her around the waist and flip her upside-down in one smooth motion. The move was executed flawlessly, but the woman was able to right herself immediately to return the favor.

From her position on the floor, Kiara kicked her leg out, sweeping Ikah's legs out from under her. She landed flat on her back in a grunt of pain.

Kiara smiled briefly and hauled herself up to pin the woman while she was still down. She almost managed it, but Ikah's mouth opened up and razor-sharp teeth extended to bite down on the arm Kiara was using to hold her. Luckily, Kiara had her own brand of Seer power, like her grandmother, but hers was attuned to just a few seconds into the future, and usually only during battle. Kiara was able to avoid Ikah's teeth in the nick of time, but, as she had moved her arm out of the way, Ikah's attack worked anyway, setting the princess off balance enough for Ikah to throw her off.

"Alright, *Princesssss*," Ikah hissed, "you want to play? Let's play!"

Ikah leapt easily back to her feet, then crouched in a ready stance. Kiara focused her mind to engage her Seer power.

Ikah let out a battle cry and lunged at Kiara, arms elongating into actual snakes, both hissing, fangs dripping with what Kiara could only assume was venom. She made a hasty mental note to avoid those appendages at all costs! Kiara snatched the ancient golden battle sword her grandfather kept on the wall behind his desk and held it above her head.

"Not one step closer!" Kiara said.

Ikah laughed, a pure, evil, guttural laugh that held actual amusement, though she did pause.

"You can't hurt me with that stick, child."

But a button on the wall next to Kiara begged to differ.

"Oh, no?" Kiara asked. "Why don't you just ignore me, then, and come closer? Prove me wrong."

"With pleasure," Ikah said, and took one step toward the princess.

Kiara swung the sword hilt and smashed the button on the wall. Ikah dropped through the trap door in the floor that her grandfather had set up in case of emergency. Thank goodness for preventative measures! Her scream echoed throughout the shaft she fell through, and Kiara breathed a sigh of relief when she heard the inevitable *thud* when she hit the ground. Now, to inform her grandparents she'd caught a thief.

***

"I was hoping you would never have to see this place," Matthias said to Kiara. "The world is full of darkness, sometimes even in our own home."

He led his wife and the princess to the cell that Ikah had dropped into. She was screeching like a banshee, swiping her snake-tooth hands at the magicked bars of her cell, trying to free herself. When she caught sight of the approaching royals, she cackled maniacally and focused all of her attention on them.

"You're too late," she said. "He already knows."

"Knows what?" Matthias asked.

"You have the treasure he seeks. The moment I saw it, I sent him a psychic message. He will be coming for it."

"The necklace?" Miawae asked.

Ikah grinned. "Yes, Queen, the necklace."

Kiara could feel real fear tickling up her spine. "We should hide it. Yes! I can take it somewhere safe, somewhere far from here. Ruskin will never get his hands on it!"

"Absolutely not!" Matthias said. "I will *not* let the only granddaughter I have left leave this kingdom while that *murderer* is about!"

"He's right on this one, dear," Miawae said when Kiara made a move to protest. "I have Seen it. The necklace stays here, and so do we. Trust me. We stay and we fight. It will be worse if we do not."

All the air deflated from Kiara in one smooth motion, ceasing her argument in its tracks. She had seen more than her fair share of her grandmother's predictions and she knew better than to doubt them when they came. The queen never lied about what she had Seen. She wasn't always forthcoming about the details, either. She claimed that it's not always helpful to know those bits, otherwise we could get in our own way trying to change them. So, Kiara shut her mouth and glared daggers at the captive, who was busy smirking like a shark with its prey.

Ikah couldn't help but add one more dig. "I'm sure the Great King will be thrilled to add another princess to his pile."

That did it. Kiara hurled a punch through the iron grate bars and connected with that eerily beautiful face, knocking her out. Kiara left her grandparents to deal with that garbage as they saw fit. She had some preparing to do.

CHAPTER FORTY-NINE: IBRAXUS FINDS A CRY FOR HELP

With so much planning to be done, Brax was eager to be on his way back home. The sooner he got going, the sooner he'd be back and able to assist the others.

"Ifyrus!" he called. "Are you ready?"

Ifyrus's head poked from around the corner of the Healer's Hut doorway, infectious grin spread from ear to ear, and said, "Just waiting on you, mate!"

Brax beamed in relief to see him once again in good spirits.

"Good to have you back, brother." He clapped him on the shoulder and motioned for Ifyrus to follow him out.

A sincere thanks was left with the Fae at the entryway for all of their help, then they were on their way.

To their surprise, Sovereign Sai was waiting for them at the bottom of the steps.

"Your Majesty," Brax said, "are you here to escort us to the front gate?"

The monarch's mouth twitched in a funny sort of way, and they replied, "That's not *entirely* what we had in mind."

Brax's eyebrow cocked as he waited for what could possibly be coming next.

"You are both dragons, are you not? You know, we do still have our Dragon Door, after all. It hasn't been used in centuries, but it's there."

"You have a Dragon Door?" Ifyrus asked. "Well, then, point me at it!"

Sai laughed. "Of course. But we will have to be extra cautious and give you the same spell that we gave to Colt. It will be a time release, and you will resume full size after twenty minutes."

"That works for me!" Ifyrus said.

Brax was pleased to see him back to his jovial self. He had been so worried about him! It would've killed him to see anything strike him down for long. The Fae certainly did an excellent job setting him back to rights. He made a mental note to strengthen his alliance with this kind nation once he was fully righted back to his throne.

Sai explained that their kingdom was set in a dome-like shape. All they had to do was fly to the highest middle point and soar through a hole at the top. The magick had been set to recognize dragon blood and allow access to the other side— back when there were still dragons that came calling. Once they were through the door, they were to fly as far away as they could, as *fast* as they could, just in case any of Ruskin's men were still skulking about.

Amy came over to say goodbye. Brax's heart was already breaking. He hated the idea of leaving her, especially now, but he knew he had to do this.

"Sick of me already, huh?" she said.

Brax smiled down at her beautiful face. "Never." He held her soft cheek in the palm of his hand and laid his forehead against hers, his other large hand cupping the back of her head, twining his fingers in her dark locks. "I will be back before you know it, and then I am never leaving you again."

"I'm gonna hold you to that, *Your Majesty*," she said.

Brax could hear Ellera and Ifyrus making over-the-top retching noises behind him, but he ignored them. Silly children. He was going to say a proper goodbye to his wife, and he didn't care who made fun of him for it! Once he made good on that by kissing her softly on the lips, he scooped her up in his massive arms and held her there a moment before placing her gently back on solid ground.

"I won't be long," he promised.

With that, the boys readied themselves for Sai's spell, and they were off to Dragon Moon Castle.

***

It was *incredible* to be flying again! It felt like it had been ages since he'd done so, which, now that he thought about it, was astoundingly accurate. He had been frozen in a spell for 200 years and, right before that happened, he was cursed by Ruskin's then-lackey, Mage Bannon, to never fly again.

Bannon. Just the name alone made Brax shiver in disgust. Bannon had once been Mage to Ruskin's father, Lord Rousard. This was before the land had any high kings, just lords that ruled over sections of land sprinkled as far and wide as could be. Lord Rousard cast Bannon out after finding that he was stealing from him. Ruskin seized the opportunity to ask Bannon to be Mage to him instead, and the man agreed to do so. Neighboring kingdoms were already not thrilled with Lord Rousard's lazy way of ruling, so when they saw his son step up to help them with their various problems, they began to see Ruskin was a much more sufficient ruler than Rousard. Ruskin began to use his Mage to deliver gifts and promises to the neighboring kingdoms, winning him favor with the people in the process. He grew in popularity, thanks to his magickal friend Bannon.

According to Evony, after the events that led to Amaryah's death and Brax and Ifyrus's punishments, the love died down as people started to see how cruel Ruskin was becoming and turned on him. Ruskin blamed all the hatred on Bannon and sentenced him to death, delivering his first public execution via werewolf claws across the middle. The people now feared him where they once loved him. Ruskin had grown addicted to magick and had been picking up Mages ever since, gleaning what he could, then tossing them aside when he was through with them. Evony said this pattern continued for the entirety of the era he was missing. He wished he'd been there to stop him.

Ruskin and his jealous rage! If he could accept defeat and just let him be happy with Amaryah, none of this would have ever happened!

Brax shook off his dark thoughts when he felt the tingles start in his body, alerting him to the spell-change taking effect.

Not ten seconds later, he and Ifyrus were back to their normal dragon sizes. He hoped they were high enough now to appear as birds to any watching eyes below.

Luckily, they met with no foes in the sky today, nor any nearby threats that he could tell. How very fortunate.

The two finally arrived back home, landing with practiced elegance, and swiftly returned to human form. Brax could feel how lifeless this place was, and it brought him an overwhelming sense of sadness and defeat. The skin on the back of his neck crinkled, and a shudder wracked through his body.

As if Ifyrus could hear his thoughts, he turned to his king and said, "Now, I know what you're thinking, mate, and I get it, I do, but we are here for a different mission right now. This is something we can address once we dethrone the bastard and get life back to normal. First things first: Let's go get your ring, Your Majesty."

Brax chuckled at his best friend's use of his royal title but agreed with the sentiment. This was meant to be a quick mission, in and out, then back to the others.

He still couldn't believe how fortunate he was to have his wife back! After what happened in the past, he wasn't sure he'd ever see her again.

He held the thought of her in his mind to keep him on task as he clambered throughout his castle, bursting through this door and that, trying to find *where in all of creation he could have left his family ring?!* He could have sworn it was in the throne room, but not much there but chair and dust. He checked his bedroom, but it had fallen into disuse. Only a few trinkets left that he could see. On a whim, he checked his den.

Brax loved the den. Outside of his own bedroom, it was his favorite room in the castle. The den hosted the Ever-Flame that burned without tending, as long as a dragon lived in this world. Brax was relieved to see it still going, though he was concerned with how small it had become. This was the source of Dragon Magick, after all.

The Mer Kingdom had one as well, but their element was water. Amy had described it to him once, but he had yet to lay eyes on it himself.

Brax walked closer to the Ever-Flame, and noticed there was something on the floor... Why, it looked like a carpet of parchment! Letters— hundreds, maybe thousands of them— littered the entire ring around the freestanding fire.

"What's that?" came Ifyrus's voice over his shoulder.

Brax jumped a foot in the air, wings coming part way out from his back!

"Whoa, whoa! Take it easy, mate! It's just me!"

Brax puffed startled smoke from his nostrils and put his wings away.

Ifyrus pointed back to the sea of scrolls and repeated, "So, what's that, eh?"

The king shrugged and took a step closer to figure it out. As he approached the giant pile, he hesitantly took one and opened it.

Dear King Ibraxus,

Why won't you help me? I am begging you! Please! I need your help! I do not feel safe here!

~Orelle

Brax's blood drained from his face. Oh, no...

He tore into another one.

Dear King Ibraxus,

He has left us again, but I have no idea when or if he will return. He is never specific. I have been cursed to never see the water again, so I cannot go fish and keep food on the table. My daughter is too young to go out on her own. We need help, we need provisions! Please! I don't know who else to ask! My sister would help if she were here! Please!

~Orelle

Another one. And another one. And another one.

All the letters went on like this. Every single one of them some new cry for help from Orelle. At some point, Ifyrus had taken up a few to read on his own, and when Brax looked up at him, he saw a line of fiery tear tracks trickling down his face. He was sure his own face reflected the same.

Ifyrus growled low. "Where is she?"

Brax opened several more letters, none giving the exact location.

"I don't know! She never says!"

Both men were digging through paper now, frantically trying to find the one that may hold the key to her whereabouts.

Brax let out a howl of frustration when they both came up empty. Then he found a letter that simply said:

I'm sorry. I was wrong.

"Grandmother?" he shouted. "Grandmother!"

After a moment, the ghostly outline of Queen Helena floated in. "You're home! Thank goodness!"

"There's no time!" he said. "Two things: One, where is the family ring?"

"It's behind you, along the wall, dear, in the case near the window."

Brax jerked his eyes to the location and confirmed it was there.

"And the other?"

He faced her, eyes ablaze, and asked, "Why didn't you tell me about Orelle when I was here?"

The ghostly queen adjusted her wrinkle-free attire out of habit. "Well, I just... didn't think you needed the distraction, what with the search for your wife and all."

Brax's mouth gaped. "What? Why would I not want to know that?"

"Because! You had more important things to do!"

"But grandmother—!"

"She's a *mermaid*!" she screamed.

"She's her *SISTER*!" Brax screamed louder.

Silence filled the room as the two glowered at each other.

Finally, Brax said softly, "Where is she?"

The queen paused, but relented, "King Ruskin's Snowlands Castle."

Brax's heart skipped a beat. "Why would she be there?"

"She married him. Had a child, too."

Brax felt as if he had been punched in the gut. Ifyrus was having a similar reaction, knowing the history they all had together. He put a hand on his king's shoulder in a show of support.

Brax crammed a few of the letters into his pocket and made a beeline for his ring. Grabbing it roughly, he jammed the obsidian-gold jewelry with its black and red gemstones on his third finger and winced when he pinched the skin.

"Ibraxus—"

"I can't leave her with him," he told her. "He's hurting her, or he's abandoned her. But either way, from what I can see, he always comes back, and it's getting worse for her. She needs our help. I'm going."

"Don't! Please don't go!" Helena said. "I've been waiting 200 years to get you back! Do not let him take you away from me again! If you get in the way of his wife, he won't stop at simply spelling you. This time, he'll *kill* you!"

Brax sighed. He knew this would open old wounds and demand war with his enemy. But from what he understood of recent events, war was headed this way anyway. At least if they got Orelle somewhere safe, maybe back to the Mer Kingdom, he could rest easy knowing Ruskin was out of her life for good.

"He will not win this time," he promised his grandmother. "I'm not alone." He turned to Ifyrus and said, "Come. Let us be on our way."

"Be safe, and come home to me," Helena called after them.

The men went directly to the courtyard and shifted quickly, taking to the dark skies high above the planet, zooming straight back to the ground through the Gemstone Belts.

Ifyrus snagged a small geode from one of the belts on the way down, crunching through it with his massive jaws, sending the smaller shards he *didn't* eat to the planet below. That should make someone happy. As there haven't been any dragons in the skies for years to replenish the magick in this manner, Brax could only assume that the magick available in the world had been slowly diminishing. If he had his way, he would fill the skies with his kind once again and go back to the ways of old, with the dragon race munching on the geodes and releasing the magickal properties to the waiting world below. That is how it had been for Callembria for as long as anyone could remember, but if things didn't change, their world was in for a harsh reality. He figured that might have been why Ruskin had hunted his kin for so long— he wanted to be in control of the magick.

Brax's eyes scanned the approaching terrain for any sight of Ruskin's men or any other potential predators, happily finding none. Satisfied, he was about to make a turn to head back to the Fae Realm to let them know about the newest development with Orelle, when he saw a familiar shock of red curls bouncing through the brush below. He gave a quick screech to Ifyrus and nodded his head at his intended landing spot so his friend could follow suit.

As he came in for a landing, he could see Kavea's eager face and excitedly waving arms and wondered what could have possibly brought this young girl out here so far on her own?

"Ibraxus!" Kavea called as he changed into human form. "It *is* you! I've been looking for you! I was so worried!"

Brax was thoroughly confused. "Why? Why have you been searching for me?"

She stopped short, then said, "Because I'm supposed to help you."

The dragon king scoffed. "How could you help me? Do you even know what I need help with?"

She placed a hand on her hip and said, "Well, firstly, I am not a little girl, I'm fifteen. Secondly, no, I don't know what you need help with exactly, I just know I'm supposed to help you do it!"

"Because you've been watching over me in that ice cave for so many years?"

"Well, partly, but there was another reason, too."

"Oh, do enlighten me."

"Well, you see, there was a prophecy, from Queen Miawae herself! Most people know the gist of it, but not a lot of them know there was more to it. I have the original book, you see, my mother gave it to me. Well, it's back at home right now, but I'm supposed to help your daughter."

"I don't have a daughter," he said, thoroughly confused now.

"Oh. Are you sure?"

"Of *course,* I'm sure! I think I'd know if my wife had a daughter!"

Kavea's face fell. Brax instantly felt terrible, but this girl was so infuriating! He did not have time for this.

"Go home. I'm sorry, but I don't have time to help you. I have a friend in trouble."

Kavea's reaction to his continued rejections made her explode, and she yelled at him, full volume. "FINE! *Be* a jerk!"

As she stomped off in a huff, a scroll of parchment fell from her pocket and landed at Ifyrus's feet. He bent down to pick it up and noticed it was another one of Orelle's letters.

"Ah, Your Majesty?" he said. "Look at this. It's from Orelle."

He showed the letter to his king and the two of them read it together. It was much like the ones they'd read already.

Kavea turned around at the mention of her mother's name.

"How do you know Orelle?" she asked.

"I married her sister," Brax said. "How do *you* know Orelle?"

Kavea's face twisted in consternation. "She's my mother."

Brax's face went sheet white, and he clenched his overworked jaw. He balled up his fists and punched a nearby tree, instantly regretting it as pain shot through his fingers.

Kavea's eyes grew wide in understanding. "Are you my uncle, then?"

A moment of silence went by as the group processed this new information. Then Ifyrus burst into a fit of laughter, holding his right hand to his chest and his left across his stomach.

Brax growled. "What exactly is amusing about this?"

Ifyrus wiped a tear from his eye and said, "Your enemy's daughter is your niece, and she appears to have taken your side, mate! Your wee, fierce protector!" His massive guffaws continued.

"Your father... is Ruskin?"

Kavea blanched, suddenly nervous. "Yes. Is that bad?"

Brax looked at her incredulously and said, "Yes! That's *bad*! Do you not know who your father is, child?"

"Kavea."

"Grr! Fine! Kavea! Do you not know who your father is, *Kavea*?" he asked.

"He is a mighty king, and often leaves us alone in the castle to go about his kingly duties."

"And?"

"And... My mother is sad and has lost her mind? Because she misses him?"

Brax and Ifyrus exchanged glances. This young girl seemed to have so much knowledge about *him*, but not nearly enough about her own father. Brax roughly pulled a few of Orelle's letters from his pocket and held them out to her. As Kavea began to read, her brows furrowed in confusion.

"*King* Ibraxus, so… no longer just a lord?"

"Correct, for starters," he replied.

"My mother is asking you for help. How long has this been going on for?"

"From what I can see, decades, possibly centuries. It's hard to say. I've been locked in a spell in an ice cave for 200 years."

"*We've* been locked in an ice cave for 200 years," Ifyrus said.

"Yes, *we've*," he agreed. Then, turning to Kavea, he made a decision. "Hop on my back, niece, I'm taking you to the Fae Realm where we will gather reinforcements and go save your mother. We have much to catch you up on along the way."

Kavea, eager to ride dragon back and join her uncle on an adventure, happily obliged with no hesitation once he shifted again, though her mind was racing with questions.

CHAPTER FIFTY: AMY GAINS A NIECE

Brax should be back by now. He said he wouldn't be gone long and, while it's still the same day that he left, I was getting uneasy. Something happened, I just know it. Maybe if I keep pacing up and down this path like a lunatic, he will magickally appear out of thin—

"Dragons approaching!" someone said.

I *knew* I was onto something with my pacing! I ran full speed to the spot Brax took off from and tried my best to look as if I wasn't frazzled by his absence.

Ellera met me there and hit me with that suspicious side-eye/ smirk combination of hers and I knew I was busted. Damn! This chick could not only read my mind, but apparently my face as well, which was currently boasting a luscious shade of embarrassment-red. Oh, well, who cares, right? Why *shouldn't* I be concerned about my... *gulp*... "husband"? God, that's still so *weird*! Why is it so weird?

"Because you don't remember saying 'I do'?" Ellera guessed.

"Stop reading my mind!"

She laughed, because of course she did. She's lucky she's charming.

"Here they come!" shouted the same voice as before. From what I could tell, there appeared to be something on Brax's back. Was that a person?

"I wonder who that is?" Ellera asked without taking her eyes off the descending dragons.

"I have no idea," I said. "I thought they were just getting his ring?"

"Guess we'll find out soon enough."

As they landed, a small crowd gathered around to greet them.

"Where's my wife?" came Brax's booming timbre.

A thrill of excitement raced up my spine, and I felt a delicious shiver course through me. *His wife.* I have to admit, I didn't hate it.

"I'm here!" I said, making my way past the Fae and Gallanorians to reach his side. I pulled up short of him, though, when I noticed a teenager hopping off his back, looking happier than a kid at Christmas. Now, just who the hell was this?

Brax ignored everyone and made a beeline straight for me, pulling me into his warm embrace, smelling of the wind and heated leather, like a new car on a summer day. It was intoxicating.

I was perfectly content to stay tucked away in his arms for the rest of the day until I felt him trembling. He pulled me tighter to him, and a shock of sudden fear hit my stomach. Was he... *crying*? *What the hell happened up there?!*

"I'm sorry, Amaryah, I'm so sorry."

I was too scared to correct him, so I just held him for another moment before my curiosity got the best of me. I dropped my hug to lightly push his chest so I could see his face. I was right. The gentle giant *was* weeping!

"What happened? What's wrong? Are you hurt, or—?"

"Who's the girl?" Ellera asked behind me.

"Hi! I'm Kavea!" the bubbly girl said. "I'm Ibraxus's niece! Can you believe it?"

"You're—" I said, "who?"

"I'm so sorry, Amy, I didn't know. I didn't know she needed help. How could I?" Brax was spiraling and I still had no idea what was happening.

"Can someone just explain what's going on? Please? I don't have all my memories, remember? And I'm not a mind reader like some people I know!"

Ellera let out a single, "Ha!" I shot her a look to let her know how I felt about her contributions.

Finally, Ifyrus stepped in to explain.

"It's like this, love," he started in a soothing manner. "We just found out that your sister, Orelle, married Ruskin after you died, and he's held her captive in his Snowlands Castle ever since. She wrote to Brax asking for help, not knowing he had been frozen in her front garden this entire time, so he couldn't come to save her. This is Kavea, her daughter, your niece. There. You're caught up." He sent me a smile and an easy wink as if that explained it all.

"Hi, Auntie Amy! It's nice to meet you!" Kavea beamed at me, and flung her arms around me and Brax in as big a bear hug as she could muster. I gave her an autopilot hug back, but my mind was swimming with questions and confusion. I had a niece? And a sister? Who married the psycho that killed me?!

"Are you alright, Amy?" asked Sovereign Sai. They put a gentle hand on my shoulder, and I turned to face them, tears springing to my eyes. "Would you like to sit down? Perhaps a cup of water would help?" They motioned for someone I wasn't paying the slightest bit of attention to to hand me some water that I dutifully gulped and handed right back to whoever was standing next to me. Everything was becoming a blur.

"Sit down, sweetie," Ellera said. She pulled me from the arms that held me and plunked me down on a soft cushioned wooden chair. I couldn't even tell you where it came from.

"Any time I think I'm starting to understand things, I find out *nope*! Wrong again!"

"And now we have to go save your sister," Ellera said.

"And now we have to go save my sister," I repeated.

A voice from behind me piped up, hesitant, but concerned enough to speak. "What about Gallanor? I can't ignore the message Princess Kiara sent me."

I took a deep breath and turned to face Cyndol. "You're absolutely right. Yes, we will still go to Gallanor. Of course." I turned to Brax and asked, "How long does it take to get to Snowlands Castle from here?"

"Flying or walking?"

I rolled my eyes. "Walking. Only you and Ifyrus can fly, the rest of us aren't as fortunate."

"About two days, if we don't stop too much."

"Cyndol, would that be alright with you? We can go save my sister and then head to Gallanor from there?"

Cyndol looked at Kit and they exchanged a few quiet words before turning back to me and nodding.

"You're going to need some warmer clothing than that," Sai said. "Let's see what we can find for you to wear."

I turned my gaze to the radiant ruler and said, "How can we ever repay the kindnesses you've shown us?"

"You are our friends, and also our neighboring rulers, once everything is set back to rights. We do this to help, and because it is the right thing to do. We know you would show us the same level of hospitality and kindness if the situation were reversed."

I couldn't help it. I started to cry and pulled the sovereign into a hug. Screw it, everyone was getting hugs today.

"Thank you. We won't forget this."

"We suspect you won't." They chuckled and returned the hug before letting me go, then sent people off to help us pack a few last-minute things for our journey.

I returned to Brax and heaved a big sigh. "So I've got more family, huh? Tell me all about her, *and* this bouncy redhead you've returned with."

He laughed and wiped his eyes. "Gladly."

THE END

See you soon for The Callembria Chronicles
Book Two: Awakening

www.ingramcontent.com/pod-product-compliance
Lightning Source LLC
LaVergne TN
LVHW091614070526
838199LV00044B/795